MW01131309

A
Divine
Fury

By D. V. Bishop

City of Vengeance
The Darkest Sin
Ritual of Fire
A Divine Fury

A Divine Fury

D. V. BISHOP

MACMILLAN

First published 2024 by Macmillan
an imprint of Pan Macmillan
The Smithson, 6 Briset Street, London EC1M 5NR
EU representative: Macmillan Publishers Ireland Ltd, 1st Floor,
The Liffey Trust Centre, 117-126 Sheriff Street Upper,
Dublin 1, D01 YC43
Associated companies throughout the world
www.panmacmillan.com

ISBN 978-1-5290-9653-8 HB
ISBN 978-1-5290-9654-5 TPB

1 3 5 7 9 8 6 4 2

A CIP catalogue record for this book is available from the British Library.

Map artwork by Neil Gower

Typeset in Adobe Caslon Pro by Palimpsest Book Production Ltd, Falkirk, Stirlingshire
Printed and bound by CPI Group (UK) Ltd, Croydon, CR0 4YY

Visit **www.panmacmillan.com** to read more about all our books
and to buy them. You will also find features, author interviews and
news of any author events, and you can sign up for e-newsletters
so that you're always first to hear about our new releases.

For Annaliese Katrina Szöcs,

9 July 1977–24 July 2023

Everyone sees what you appear to be,
few really know what you are.

Niccolò Machiavelli, *The Prince*
Translated by W. K. Marriott (1908)

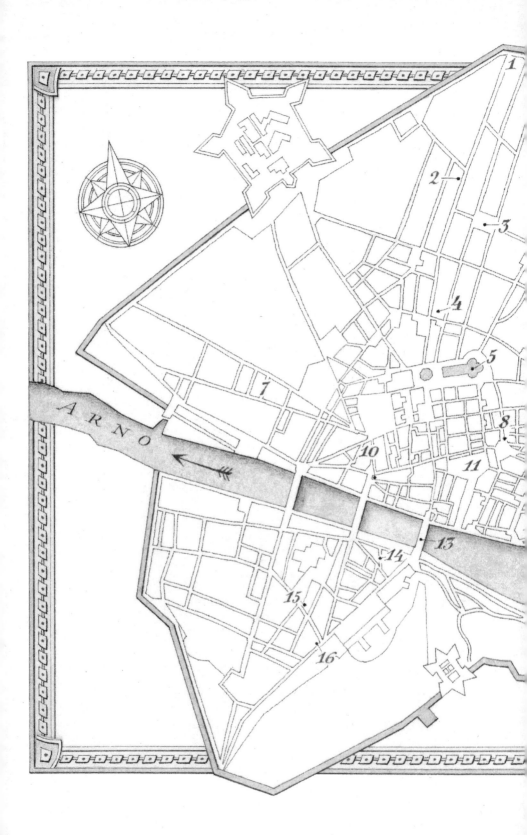

FLORENCE
(FIRENZE)

1. Porta San Gallo
2. Church of Santa Maria Magdalena
3. Piazza San Marco
4. Palazzo Medici
5. Duomo
6. Ospedale Santa Maria Nuova
7. Strocchi's home
8. Palazzo del Podestà
9. Letta's Tavern
10. Palazzo Coltello
11. Piazza della Signoria
12. Tannery
13. Ponte Vecchio
14. via dei Giudei
15. Palazzo Zamora
16. Church of San Felice

ARNO

Chapter One

Wednesday, October 29th 1539

In Cesare Aldo's experience the citizens most likely to break curfew in Florence were the drunken, the deceitful and the dangerous. The challenge was knowing which was which while following one of them through the city in the hours before dawn.

Only a select few were permitted to use the streets after night-fall: Duke Cosimo de' Medici, the city's ruler, and his guards; anyone carrying a letter of permission signed by the duke; and the unfortunate men of the night patrol, enforcing the curfew for the city's most feared criminal court, the Otto di Guardia e Balia. Aldo was one of the unfortunates on night patrol, a purgatory he had endured since returning to Florence almost a year and a half earlier. His experience of those who broke curfew was now there-fore extensive.

The drunken usually blamed wine for still being outside long after the bells had tolled for all good citizens to return home. Some drunks were friendly, others belligerent and a few even violent, but most were no match for the night patrol. The deceitful were those citizens using the darkness as a mask to hide their illicit behaviour, generally theft or fornication. Aldo had little sympathy for anyone arrested while succumbing to lust or avarice.

Yes, he had been guilty of both, but was not fool enough to get caught.

The dangerous, they came in many guises. There were those who had lost all reason, ready to harm themselves or others without warning. Some were looking for a fight, seeking somebody to hurt. And there were those with darkness in their hearts or murder in their heads. Once a person chose to kill, a fear of breaking curfew was unlikely to stop them.

The lone figure ahead was neither lurching nor staggering. That suggested they were more deceitful or dangerous than drunk. A heavy cloak and cap hid their face and build. But the care with which they used the shadows of alleyways and narrow streets to shroud their journey made Aldo crouch to pull the trusty stiletto from his left boot.

'What are you doing?' Benedetto asked. Like Aldo he was stuck on night patrol, but the young constable made no effort to conceal his disdain for it. Benedetto had been an eager, even enthusiastic recruit to the Otto three years ago. However, serving the court had soured him so much that every task now seemed a chore, and every question a cause for argument.

'When trouble arises,' Aldo whispered, 'a blade is better in the hand than the boot.' He rose to his feet. They were close to Piazza Santa Croce, the largest square in Florence's eastern quarter, having followed the curfew breaker from near the convent of Le Murate. Now their quarry must cross the piazza or make a much longer journey to avoid the wide, open space. Either choice would reveal something about them.

'What trouble? It's just someone creeping home in the dark.'

'Lower your voice,' Aldo hissed.

'Why should I? We've been following them since—'

Aldo put a hand over Benedetto's mouth to silence him, but it was too late. The curfew breaker twisted round to stare at them – and then sprinted into the piazza.

'Palle!' Aldo raced after the suspect, leaving Benedetto to swear and splutter. By the time Aldo reached the piazza his quarry was halfway across, getting further away with each moment. Cursing Benedetto for not doing as he was told, Aldo pressed on.

The suspect disappeared into a nearby alley as Aldo reached the far side of the piazza. He stopped to catch his breath, spots dancing in front of his eyes. Running was for children and dogs, not grown men who had seen more than forty summers. Benedetto soon caught up to him. 'Where did they go?' he panted. Aldo pointed to the alley. The passageway was dark and narrow, allowing only one of them to enter at a time – the perfect place for an ambush.

'Where's your knife?' Aldo asked.

'I didn't bring one. Didn't know I'd need it.' No wonder Benedetto was stuck on night patrol. He lacked the imagination for anything better.

A fat drop of water hit Aldo in the face, making him look up. The moon had been visible earlier, but now it was mostly hidden behind ominous clouds. Another drop fell on Aldo, and another and another. In moments it was a downpour, soaking into his cap and tunic.

'We should go back to the Podestà,' Benedetto shouted through the sudden, torrential rain. 'Anyone who wants to be out in this is welcome to it!'

'We have a curfew breaker to catch,' Aldo replied. He stamped through the puddles forming on the ground leading to the alley. 'If they get past me, it's your job to stop them.' Gripping the stiletto in his right hand, Aldo entered the inky darkness. Once inside the alley he paused, letting his eyes adjust. The walls on either side were solid stone, two sturdy palazzi with no shutters at ground level. No means of escape there. Aldo edged forward, shoulders brushing against either wall as he advanced.

Up ahead the alley opened into a small courtyard, the dead space between buildings. Again, no shutters, and no apparent way out. It was dark and gloomy, difficult to make anything out in the pouring rain. Piles of rubble and broken stones seemed to fill much of the courtyard, providing several places to hide. Aldo peered round, searching for any sign of the fugitive . . . Nothing.

Had he been mistaken? Or was there another way out, some hidden door or—

A movement to one side caught Aldo's eye. Then he was shoved backwards into a stone wall, all the breath knocked out of him. Fierce eyes glared at Aldo, a fist rising up—

He jabbed his stiletto forward, the blade finding his attacker. They howled, stumbling backwards. Male, definitely male. The fugitive lifted a hand to stare at his own blood before lurching back into the alley. Aldo wanted to pursue, but his legs crumpled beneath him. The blood on his stiletto was reassuring. The fugitive was wounded, they wouldn't get far.

A voice cried out – Benedetto, shouting at the fugitive to stop. A knife would have been more use. Aldo was getting to his feet when Benedetto rushed into the courtyard.

'Aldo? You in here?'

'Yes.'

Benedetto came closer, eyes widening when he saw the blade. 'Are you hurt?'

Aldo shook his head. 'It's the fugitive's blood, not mine.'

'He knocked me flying,' Benedetto confessed.

'Where did he go?'

'Towards Piazza della Signoria.'

'Then let's get after him.' Aldo pushed Benedetto back along the alley, turning west when they reached the other end. If not for the rain they might have tracked their quarry by the drops of blood his wound left behind. Instead, they had to rely on the likelihood that his injury would force the fugitive to take the most direct path, wherever he was going.

Piazza della Signoria was the most important square in Florence. It was there that its citizens gathered to praise and protest, and it was where condemned men were publicly executed. Tall stone buildings surrounded the piazza, Palazzo della Signoria the tallest of them all. The city's laws were debated there by the Senate, though true power was held by Duke Cosimo de' Medici. The likelihood of the fugitive being foolish enough to linger here was low.

Yet when Aldo and Benedetto reached the piazza, a figure was lying prone beneath the statue of David in front of the grand palazzo. 'There,' Aldo said. 'Must have cut him deeper than I realized.'

They moved closer, Aldo keeping his blade ready in case of another ruse. The rain was passing, making the way easier to see. The statue of David towered over the prone body, its bold white marble a stark contrast to the silhouettes of surrounding buildings. Aldo had been a young boy when the David was first brought into the piazza. Forty men had taken four days to move the statue there, such was the colossal size and weight. Seeing it that first time was the moment Aldo knew to whom he was drawn. It was the statue's shapely buttocks that caught his eye; the modest cazzo proved far less impressive, and was now hidden behind a cluster of copper leaves to spare anyone embarrassment.

The nearer Aldo got to the figure on the ground, the less certain he became that it was their quarry. He had not seen much of the fugitive, but the man beneath the statue wore no cloak or cap. He looked heavier, too. There was an angry red line round his neck. Lifeless eyes stared at the thin moon as it reappeared from behind parting clouds.

'This is someone else,' Aldo said.

'You think the fugitive killed him?' Benedetto asked.

'Unlikely. The fugitive was trying to move through the city unseen. Why would they flee this way after killing someone here earlier?' He put a knee down on the wet stones by the body to look closer. It was a corpse, there was no doubt about that. The clothes were soaked through, meaning the body had probably been left here before the rain came. Aldo searched the face but did not recognize the dead man. There was something curious about the way the body was positioned on the ground. Both arms were stretched out sideways, while the legs were close together, one crossed over the other at the feet. Almost as if he was—

'There!' Benedetto pointed across the piazza. Someone was limping away in the shadows on the far side: their fugitive. 'Should I go after him?'

'No.'

'But before you were—'

'That was before,' Aldo said. 'We can catch them another time. A man has been murdered. That matters far more now.'

Contessa Valentine Coltello politely stifled a yawn behind one hand. Her gesture was not caused by the lateness of the hour, nor indeed by its earliness since dawn must be close by now. Her weariness could not be blamed on a lack of sleep, despite having been kept awake all evening, as she had taken the precaution of resting through much of the previous day. Besides, the hours before sunrise were her domain, a world where she was at her finest.

No, the reason for her yawning was all too predictable.

The cause, inevitably, was a man.

She had invited Signor Federico Dandolo to dine with her alongside several other, far more interesting guests artfully chosen to avoid arousing suspicion or encouraging unwanted gossip. As curfew approached and the other guests rose to depart, the contessa contrived a reason for Dandolo to stay longer, claiming a need for his wisdom. She had led him to this richly decorated salone to assess the worth of certain tapestries left by her late husband. Dandolo knew nothing of art and even less about tapestries, but flattery and his own arrogance persuaded him to profess an expertise he did not possess. More than an hour passed while he blustered and bluffed. Once that was done, the contessa had patted the chair beside her own and invited Dandolo to share the story of how he came to be so significant, so important, and so admired.

Few men were immune to flattery and Dandolo was no exception, despite his receding hair, dull features and a belly running to fat beneath his gaudy silk tunic. But the contessa had not expected him to be quite so in love with the sound of his own voice. Hour after hour he droned on, regaling her in quite excruciating detail with the dreary, unimpressive events of his life. Most men possessed enough wit to realize they were being flirted with, courted, even lured. Somehow Dandolo had remained unaware or unable to grasp this simple fact.

Of course, there was no question of taking Dandolo to her bedchamber; the very thought was both repulsive and hilarious. No, she simply wished to learn whatever he might know about Duke Cosimo de' Medici and those around the leader of Florence. That mixture of secrets and gossip would be thoroughly sifted before the most useful morsels were duly reported to her paymasters at the Council of Ten in Venice.

In other circumstances – had Dandolo been more attractive or more intriguing – the contessa would have taken matters into her own hands. Alas, Dandolo possessed an opinion of his own magnificence that far outweighed whatever merits he might have below the waist. But to get what she wanted, it was sometimes necessary to tease and tempt the ugliest of wits.

'Please, tell me more,' the contessa murmured when Dandolo took a rare pause for breath while explaining his importance within the ducal court. She stroked one finger down the back of his left hand as a test. The fool's nostrils flared, and his eyes widened. It seemed what she was apparently offering had, finally, become obvious to him.

'Well, Juan de Luna is as tactless as he is haughty,' Dandolo said, licking his thin, unsightly lips. 'Typical Spaniard. Since being appointed to lead the garrison at Fortezza da Basso, this idiota has managed to offend almost everyone he encounters. The duke is so frustrated that he wrote to his father-in-law for advice after de Luna insulted one of Cosimo's segretarie and his mother, Maria Salviati, both in the same afternoon.'

This confirmed what the contessa had heard from others within the ducal palazzo. Cosimo had been married to Eleonora de Toledo but a few months, yet the young Medici was already making deft use of this connection with her father, Pedro de Toledo. The Viceroy of Naples was close to Charles V, the Spanish king and Holy Roman Emperor, without whose approval Cosimo would never have been appointed ruler of Florence. Seeking counsel from de Toledo demonstrated what the contessa had concluded about the young duke: Cosimo had the guile of a much older man, despite being no more than twenty.

'And what of the duke's new bride?' the contessa whispered, letting her gaze wander to Dandolo's groin before looking into his muddy eyes once more. 'I have heard whispers she is pregnant already. Can this be true?' The contessa knew it for a fact, but the question was a snare to see how much Dandolo was willing to divulge, how compliant he might be.

'I . . . I am not supposed to speak of such things,' he stammered before licking his lips once more. It was an irritating habit. The contessa doubted his lovemaking was any better.

'Of course not,' she said, resting a hand on Dandolo's thigh. 'I have no wish to do anything that might make you . . . uncomfortable.' Her fingernails slid along the hose, edging closer to the growing bulge that lurked between his legs.

Dandolo swallowed hard. 'No, I'm sure it would be . . . fine.' The fool's voice rose higher with each word. Soon it would be the equal of a soprano. 'I've heard tell that she—'

A sharp knock at the door interrupted them, stopping whatever tedious utterance had been about to spill from Dandolo's mouth. He half rose from the chair before sinking down again, face flushing crimson, both hands clasped between his legs.

'Come!' the contessa called, suppressing a smirk.

Her maggiordomo Pozzo entered, bowing low, hands behind his back. 'Forgive my interruption, Contessa, but a message of utmost urgency has arrived.'

'A message? So late after curfew?' Dandolo asked.

Truly, the man had less wit than the chair on which he sat, and none of its charm.

'Forgive me,' the contessa said, rising to her feet. 'I must discover what this matter concerns. Please, remain here. I shall return as soon as I am able.'

Dandolo rose in a half-crouch, still struggling to hide the

excitement in his hose. 'Of course, Contessa. It will be my pleasure to—'

'Good,' she interjected, sparing herself any more of his words by marching to the door. Pozzo held it open so she could depart, following her out into the hallway before closing the door behind him. 'Diavolo, where have you been?' she demanded. 'We were supposed to be interrupted long ago.'

'Forgive me, but I was actually busy with a messenger.' Pozzo produced a letter from inside his tunic, the folded page sealed with black wax. The contessa noted his nails on both hands had crimson beneath them. 'A night patrol pursued him through the city in the rain,' Pozzo continued, 'and one of the constables wounded the messenger.'

The contessa snorted her disbelief. 'I've watched better tales at the teatro. Night patrols are all fools and dullards, everyone knows that. It's why I send letters after dark.'

'It seems at least one of these constables was no fool and also handy with a blade,' Pozzo said. 'I've spent the past hour sewing the wound he made in the messenger.'

'That explains the stains beneath your fingernails, at least. Tell me, if this night patrol is so adept, how was it the messenger escaped while wounded?'

'It seems the constables were distracted by a corpse in Piazza della Signoria.' Pozzo hesitated before clarifying. 'The corpse was not of the messenger's making.'

'I take it back,' the contessa said. 'That story is better than anything I've seen at the teatro this year.' She snatched the letter from Pozzo, tearing it open to read the words within. The fact that it was written without any ciphers was surprising, but the content of the letter was shocking. If this was true . . . 'Is the messenger still here in the palazzo?'

'Yes, Contessa.'

'Are they capable of taking a letter back to who sent them?'

Pozzo nodded.

'Good. Fetch me ink and paper. This can't wait.'

A few minutes later she swept back into the salone, her face a mask of wistful regret. 'My dearest Dandolo, I am so dreadfully sorry, but you must leave at once.'

'I must?' he asked, rising to his feet.

'Yes.'

'But I thought we . . .'

The contessa waited, letting the fool stumble over the folly of his imaginings.

'I thought that perhaps you and I might . . .'

He might still be useful one day, she supposed. Better to let him down gently now, in case that day came sooner rather than later. Besides, if the letter brought by the messenger heralded what she thought, Dandolo could serve another purpose. The contessa glided across the salone to him, cupping the left side of his face with a delicate hand. 'And perhaps we might, perhaps . . . but not tonight. Not now.' She used the same hand to gesture at the door. 'My maggiordomo will see you out and advise on the best way to avoid the night patrols.'

'Oh. I see.' Dandolo appeared quite crestfallen, as if there had actually been some hope that she would allow a minor functionary from the duke's court to visit her bedchamber. He really was quite the fool.

She watched him dawdle to the door. 'My dear Federico?'

'Yes?' he replied, twisting round, fresh hope obvious in his face.

'I wonder . . . But no, it is too much to ask.' She looked aside. 'Forgive me.'

Dandolo hastened back to her, eager as an animal for the lure, unaware of a trap closing around him. 'Contessa, whatever you wish, please ask me for it.'

She suppressed a smirk of triumph. It was almost too easy. 'Perhaps you could write me a letter . . . if time allows. Once a day should be sufficient.'

'A letter, once a day?'

The contessa fixed her gaze on his eyes. 'I want to know more about you, Federico. I want to learn everything about you. What interests, what intrigues, what excites . . .' She glanced down at his groin so he would have no doubt what that meant. Dandolo had already proven himself insufferably dim in such matters. 'Tell me all the gossip from your day and I am certain I shall find some way to . . . reward you.'

Dandolo was quite crimson now. Yes, even he had understood her. 'And will you write to me in return?' he asked, perhaps hoping to read about her lusts and desires.

'Alas, no.' The contessa smiled at him. 'I am still a widow, and it would not be seemly for me to maintain any kind of correspondence with a gentleman, no matter how important and significant he might be. You understand how it is.'

'Yes, of course.' Again, a crestfallen expression haunted his face. Most unappealing.

'Then, it is settled. I look forward to reading your first letter later today.'

'Today?'

'It will be dawn soon, my dear Dandolo. You really should be getting home.' She ushered him to the salone door, a gentle but firm hand in the small of his back propelling the fool out. 'By the way, my maggiordomo tells me it has been raining quite heavily tonight,' she said once Dandolo was in the hallway. 'Do try not to catch your death out there.'

Aldo knocked at the door, hands cold and knuckles white. His clothes were still soaked from the downpour, making him shiver as a brisk wind whistled along via dei Giudei. Autumn was often cold and wet in Florence, the sweltering heat of summer no more than a distant memory. The first hints of dawn were lightening the sky at last, but the thin alley remained gloomy and dark. Aldo was familiar enough with it to have no need of a lantern here.

He knocked again, louder this time, knuckles rapping the sturdy wood by a Hebrew inscription, the name Orvieto carved below it. Aldo was more than familiar with the man who lived inside. A window opened above, and a bearded face peered out. 'Cesare?'

'Doctor Orvieto,' Aldo replied, making his voice as formal as possible. 'I am here on behalf of the Otto di Guardia e Balia. The court has urgent need of your expertise.' A light came on behind the shutters of the house on Aldo's left. Soon others would do the same, residents eager to know why anyone was at the doctor's door so early.

'Now?' Saul asked, rubbing his eyes.

'Yes,' Aldo said before mouthing an apology.

'Very well,' the doctor agreed. 'Will I need my satchel?'

'It would be wise. And bring a good cloak, in case the rain returns.'

Saul retreated inside, shutting the window. Aldo stamped both boots on the muddy ground to revive his numb toes, without success. Rain had seeped through the well-worn leather into his hose. He would not be warm again until both boots and hose were removed, and there was no prospect of that before sunrise.

The door opened and Saul emerged, a long cloak over his shoulders. He had a satchel in one hand, and a second cloak in his other. 'Where are we going?'

'North, over the Arno.' Aldo led the way, waiting until they had left via dei Giudei before saying more. The narrow alley was home to most of the Jews in Florence, and Saul was the physician for many of them. Word of the doctor being summoned away during curfew would spread around the commune faster than syphilis through a travelling army of mercenaries. Aldo had no wish to provide Saul's neighbours with further gossip.

'You look wet through,' Saul said, handing him the spare cloak. 'Put this on.'

'Grazie.' Aldo paused to slip the thick woollen garment over his shoulders.

'I've been wondering when you might visit next,' the doctor said. His warm hazel eyes twinkled with mischief, even in this murky light.

'Night patrol is a demanding mistress.'

'Ahh, so that's who you've been seeing . . .'

Aldo pulled Saul into the shadow of a doorway, silencing him with a kiss. The doctor dropped his satchel, their hands moving inside each other's cloaks, bodies pressing together. Aldo inhaled Saul's scent, savouring the aromas of sleep and sweat. He slid an urgent hand down between their legs, reaching for Saul, wanting him –

A sudden cough made them stop, both becoming still as statues.

Aldo closed his eyes, waiting for the shouted voices, the inevitable accusation. Men who sought the company of other men in Florence risked prison, even execution. He could face whatever punishment he must, but Saul should not – could not – endure such a fate.

The cough returned, wet and heavy, the sound of someone suffering an autumn cold. It came from above them in a room that must overlook the street. In a few moments the coughing ceased, silence claiming Borgo San Jacopo once more. There was no shout of accusation, nobody had seen them. They were safe.

'Palle,' Aldo muttered, breathing once more.

'Indeed,' Saul whispered, a rueful smile on his lips. 'We'd better move on before . . .'

Aldo nodded as Saul retrieved his satchel. They strode towards Ponte Vecchio, the nearest bridge for crossing the Arno. Aldo described finding the corpse in Piazza della Signoria.

'The Otto doesn't often call on my help with dead bodies,' Saul said.

'Most murders are simple matters,' Aldo replied as they marched up the bridge to its crest. 'Violent men and angry moments, with no puzzle to be solved. But this one . . .' The stench of blood and meat and spoiled fish assaulted Aldo's nostrils. During the day Ponte Vecchio was home to butchers and fish sellers. The bridge was washed clean by apprentices late every afternoon, but the stench always lingered.

'Before,' Saul said, 'when we were—'

'Shhh,' Aldo whispered, pointing at the small homes built above the butcher shops and stalls on the bridge. Light from lanterns was visible through several shutters. Aldo had nearly been undone by the keen ears of someone living over Ponte Vecchio. He had no wish to relive that.

Saul waited until they were off the bridge to speak. 'Before, when we were . . .'

'Enjoying each other?'

Saul sighed. 'We need to be careful, Cesare. I know it's hard—'

'Certainly felt so.'

Saul slapped at Aldo's arm, but that twinkle was back in the doctor's eye. 'We meet so infrequently, it is . . . difficult not to get carried away. But we both know the price to be paid should someone discover us.'

He was right, of course, yet it did not make the long gaps between their meetings easier, not when the hours of curfew offered the best chance to be together.

'Agreed,' Aldo said, leading Saul north.

'Is the body still in the piazza?' the doctor asked.

'No,' Aldo replied. 'It will be dawn soon, so Benedetto and I moved the corpse somewhere you can work in private. I wanted it out of sight before all of Florence wakes.'

Carlo Strocchi winced as Tomasia retched and retched again, emptying herself of the little food and water she had taken last night. He wanted to help his wife but there was nothing to be done except keep little Bianca busy in the other room. At least they had a proper home now, not just a space divided in half by a curtain. True, they had only moved across the street, but the middle level of this building was both larger and warmer than their previous home. That was important with winter coming, not to mention another baby. A year and a half as an officer of the Otto had brought more pay than he'd ever seen as a constable, and the chance to earn further coin from rewards and bounties. The famiglia Strocchi was prospering.

But it made little difference when Tomasia was ill.

She retched again, the sound of her distress a dagger at Strocchi's heart. 'Are you all right?' he called, cursing himself for asking such a stupid domanda.

'I'll be fine,' Tomasia insisted. He heard her spitting to clear bile before she shuffled into their front room, wiping a hand across her mouth. 'See?' She forced a smile. 'All better.' But Tomasia's washed-out features and the sweat staining her pale shift said otherwise.

Strocchi had never known her to be sick for so long. Yes, pregnancy had made her ill last time, but that was mostly in the mornings during her first few months carrying Bianca. This illness had gone on and on, morning and night, until Tomasia was close to collapse.

Bianca ran across to hug her mama round the legs. Tomasia sank on the bed before lifting the two-year-old up. 'You're getting so big, bambina. When did you get so big?'

'Mama!' Bianca shouted back. 'Mama, Mama, Mama!' It was her favourite word, one she could bellow for what seemed like hours on end.

'Shush,' Tomasia said, resting a finger on their daughter's lips. 'You don't want to wake Signora Bolzoni downstairs again, do you?' Bianca shook her head.

'I should stay here,' Strocchi said. 'I can play with Bianca, let you get some rest.'

'We'll be fine,' Tomasia replied.

'But you got no sleep—'

'I'll be fine,' she insisted, steel in her voice. 'Women have been carrying babies and giving birth since the Garden of Eden, Carlo. A few nights of being sick—'

'It's been months—'

'And it will pass.' Leaving Bianca on the bed, Tomasia came to rest a hand on his shoulder. 'Bianca and I can cope by ourselves. You need to work, so go.'

Strocchi couldn't keep the concern from his face. 'But—'

'You haven't shaved today.' Tomasia frowned. 'It doesn't suit you.'

'No? I was thinking of growing a beard. Make me look more like an officer.'

She laughed. 'I love your bambino face, Carlo. And it is an asset. People share things with you they wouldn't with others from the Otto.'

'You think so?'

'I know so.' She stood up to kiss him. 'But I don't enjoy a man whose face has the texture of a scrubbing brush. Now, go. Go! Bianca and I have a lot to do today. We can't get started until you leave. Isn't that right, bambina?'

Their daughter nodded.

'Very well,' Strocchi agreed. 'But if the sickness comes back, send a messenger to the Podestà and I'll come home straight away.'

'Yes, yes,' Tomasia sighed, ushering him to the door. He stepped onto the landing, pausing to straighten his tunic and hose. Strocchi took one last glance inside before closing the door behind him. Tomasia slumped on the bed by Bianca, exhaustion claiming her.

It took all his will to leave.

Aldo led Saul east towards Piazza della Signoria but stopped in an alley before the square. Benedetto was lurking outside a stable doorway on the right, his face sour as ever. 'Where have you been?'

he whined. 'The wind whistles down here, I've been freezing my palle off.'

'Go back to the Podestà,' Aldo urged Benedetto. 'You can get warm by the guards' fire.' He glanced at the sky, now mottled with the blues and blacks of a bruise. 'It'll be dawn soon. When Bindi arrives, tell him what has happened – the fugitive, us finding the corpse, everything. Understand?'

'I'm not a fool,' Benedetto muttered.

'It's important the segretario knows all the details before leaving to make his morning report to the duke,' Aldo continued. 'Otherwise, he'll be in a foul mood for days. Do you want another month on night patrol?' Benedetto shook his head, but Aldo wasn't satisfied. 'Repeat back to me what you need to tell Bindi.' Benedetto did so with even less grace than usual. 'Good. Now, go and get dry,' Aldo said. 'You've earned it.'

Benedetto stamped away, the words of praise making no apparent difference. Saul waited until he and Aldo were alone before speaking. 'Friend of yours?'

'Night patrol is where the segretario banishes idioti and those he hates. Benedetto is in danger of becoming both.' Aldo opened the stable door, gesturing for Saul to go first. Inside was a low-ceiling space that stank of horse, though no animal would enjoy any time spent in such a dank, dingy chamber. The floor was loose dirt, the walls rough stone. There was no well for drawing water, and no fodder to eat. A lantern, hung from the ceiling, provided the only illumination, the dead man's corpse lying beneath it.

'This belongs to the Otto?' Saul asked, putting down his satchel.

'Not exactly. It's owned by a grasping landlord called Pietro Martegli. The summer before last he rented it to the killer who burned people alive. After learning what happened in here, nobody has wanted to come near the place.'

'I wonder how people heard about that?'

Aldo shrugged. 'Gossip gets around.'

'Meaning you can use this place whenever you wish?'

'The wind that blows foul for one man sometimes favours another.'

Saul crouched on one knee by the corpse. He turned its head towards him – and jolted backwards into Aldo's legs. 'Diavolo!'

'What is it? What's wrong?'

'I . . . I know this man. His name is Niccolò Zamora.'

That was not what Aldo expected. 'How do you know him?'

'I . . . I was once the physician to his famiglia, in the days when I still treated people from outside the Jewish commune.' Crimson coloured Saul's cheeks above his beard of russet and silver. 'He is . . . was . . . a wool merchant. I . . . We . . . we had a brief . . .'

'When?' Aldo asked, hoping the answer would be long ago, before he and Saul met. The doctor being under suspicion for what had happened to Zamora could create all kinds of problems, but the possibility that Saul had strayed was equally troubling. He and Aldo had been apart more than together for three years, so Aldo could not blame Saul if he sought companionship elsewhere in that time. But still . . .

'Eight, nine years ago,' Saul replied. 'Long before you and I met.'

Aldo fought to keep the relief from his face. 'Where was Zamora living then?'

'Across the river, in Oltrarno. He shared a palazzo with his sister Tullia, and her children, close to Santo Spirito. She was a widow, if I remember correctly.'

Aldo nodded. Being able to quickly find the dead man's famiglia would make the next stage of his investigation easier. Saul knowing the victim was quite a coincidence, but not unlikely. Florence was a city of some sixty thousand souls, yet those who could afford to employ a Jewish physician of his skill were far fewer.

Saul got to his feet. 'Cesare, about Niccolò and I—'

'It's nothing,' Aldo said, smiling to reassure him. 'We both had lives before we met each other. What is in our pasts can stay there, yes?' It was a lie, of course, but Saul didn't need to know that. Aldo had known his share of men before meeting the doctor, there was no justifiable reason to be jealous of Saul's history. But still . . .

Saul returned his smile. 'Yes. The past is the past. Good.' Vigour restored, he returned to the corpse. 'Now then, let's see what we can find here.'

While Saul was examining the body, Aldo pondered what the doctor had mentioned about the dead man. 'Zamora was not married?'

'Not when I knew him.'

That suggested the victim might have taken his pleasure with others besides Saul. Marriage was expected of men in Florence, it was the way of things. Men who did not wed were suspect, unless they had a plausible explanation. That was why Aldo lived in a bordello. So long as he slept in Signora Robustelli's house, most men believed Aldo had no reason to take a bride – his needs were obviously being met in other ways – while most women pitied him. That served its own purpose.

Zamora preferring the company of men might be why he was killed. There were often attacks on such men, usually by those with hate or fear in their hearts. The hate came of being taught that such sinners must be punished for their transgressions against God's law. The fear seemed to come from attackers believing they might be the same as those they hurt.

Had there been more of these incidents lately? Aldo scowled. In the past he would already know the answer to that question.

One of the many problems presented by being on night patrol was knowing less about what was happening in the city. Nights spent enforcing curfew gave Aldo little chance to grasp the mood of Florence, let alone who was doing what to others during daylight. It also meant seeing a lot less of Saul. They could only meet after dark when Aldo could come and go unseen from the doctor's home. Night patrols put an unwanted, unhappy distance between them. That was part of the reason Aldo had summoned the doctor from bed to examine Zamora's corpse. It was good to see Saul again, even if they needed a murder to be together. That had been selfish, especially this early in the day.

'Are you sure you wish to continue with this? I can see if another physician is willing to look at Zamora's body for me . . .'

Saul shook his head. 'I have brought many lives into this world and been with more as they departed it. Death holds few fears for me. All that remains is the body, not the person they were. I'm happy to examine him.'

'Grazie mille.'

Saul leaned over the dead man, peering at the neck. 'He was garrotted, most likely from behind. The killer is probably a man, or a woman with considerable strength in her hands.'

'Why do you think he was garrotted from behind?' Aldo asked.

Saul pointed at the front of Zamora's throat. 'I would expect a gap at the site that the two ends of the garrotte were brought together.' He lifted the dead man's head to look at the back of the neck. 'Yes, there's a gap here.' Saul rested the head on the dirt again, before reaching for one of Zamora's hands and then the other. 'The knuckles are smooth,' he said, 'no bruises or breaks to the skin.' Saul turned the hands over to study the palms and fingers. 'No marks here, either. He did not fight back. So, either the killer surprised him—'

'Easier to do if you come from behind,' Aldo agreed.

'—or Zamora did not have his senses when the attack came.'

Meaning he was drunk or had been drugged to make the killing easier. Another possibility occurred to Aldo. He knew men who claimed that their pleasure was increased by being strangled at the time of sexual release. Signora Robustelli warned her women to turn away anyone requesting that service at the bordello. It was all too easy for such endeavours to go awry, and then they'd have to deal with a corpse.

The way Zamora's body had been left posed beneath the statue of David in Piazza della Signoria made that unlikely, unless it was an elaborate ruse to send the Otto looking elsewhere. No, the simplest explanation was usually the correct one. 'Can you give the body a complete examination?' Aldo asked, before explaining the alternative reason why there might be such a mark around the neck of the corpse.

Saul's eyebrows shot up. 'The more time I spend with you, the more I realize what a cloistered life mine has been.'

'Consider yourself fortunate,' Aldo replied. Bells began chiming outside, their tolling audible in the dank stable. 'That's the end of curfew. I had best go to the Podestà, make sure Benedetto has told Bindi everything. Are you happy to stay and finish what you are doing?'

'I can examine the body fully,' Saul said, getting back to his feet, 'but not here. This stable is too dark for me to see properly, even with a lantern. I need somewhere more suitable for finishing what you have asked me to do.'

He was right, of course. The single lantern hanging over Zamora's corpse was doing little to lift the gloom. Opening the door would bring further light but also invite those passing to peer inside. Aldo chewed his bottom lip, considering alternatives.

'What if the body was moved to Santa Maria Nuova?' he suggested. 'The nuns at the ospedale are usually willing to look after remains until a famiglia can collect them for burial.'

'Yes, that would be better,' Saul agreed. 'I can arrange that, and then examine Zamora there. Come to the ospedale in the middle of the day and I'll show you what I've found.'

'Grazie.' Aldo gave Saul a last kiss before striding from the stable. Better to go before temptation proved too difficult to resist.

ather Edoardo Visconti opened the doors of Santa Maria
Magdalena as he did each morning, uncertain who would
be waiting in front of the church. Some days parishioners came
seeking reassurance or absolution; other days brought beggars along
via San Gallo, desperate for a hot meal or shelter from an autumn
wind and rain that chilled a soul to the bone.

But it was not often Visconti found another priest waiting
outside his church.

He recognized Father Pagolo Zati at once, though the cleric
was much changed from their first meeting in spring two years
earlier. Zati had come to the parish with a diocesan visitation
to the Convent of Santa Maria Magdalena, which stood behind
the church. He was then no more than twenty-five, his back
was straight and his kindly face tanned by the sun. Zati had
brought an enthusiasm for God's work that made Visconti
smile.

But the visitation did not go well. Accusations were made
against the convent; a naked man's bloody corpse was found inside
the scriptorium and one of the visiting men was attacked by a
nun with a blade. The convent was dissolved soon after and when
Visconti saw Zati next, the young priest had changed. His eyes
were wide, his movements agitated. That was no surprise; what
Zati had seen would trouble anyone, priest or parishioner. Visconti

urged him to seek counsel from others, not to fear following his heart.

A few months later, Zati appeared far happier. Visconti chanced on him at a conclave of priests in the cathedral and was relieved to see the younger man close to being his carefree self once more. Yes, he was a little more guarded, a little less open with his words, but that was only to be expected. Zati admitted being deeply disturbed by the attack he'd witnessed at the convent, but daily prayers and good works in a new parish had brought him peace.

But the Zati who stood outside the church doors this morning . . .

This was a different man.

His shoulders were hunched forward where once they had been upright and strong. His skin was pallid and his face gaunt, the eyes rimmed with shadows from lack of sleep. He seemed to be carrying a great burden, one that was hidden from gaze but that weighed heavy on his heart, on his soul. What, in the name of God, had befallen this young priest?

'Father, may I ask you a question?' Zati said, a tremble in his voice.

'Of course,' Visconti replied, smiling at him. 'I have parishioners to visit, members of my flock too weak or unwell come here for Mass. If you care to accompany, you may ask your question as we walk.'

'Grazie,' Zati said.

Visconti headed north from the church and the other priest fell in step beside him, taking care to avoid the channel of human and animal waste in the centre of the street. It was still early, the air not yet ripe with the day's aromas. The road towards the city's north gate was empty aside from a few weary-faced farmers carrying baskets of produce to the mercato.

'Well, Pagolo,' Visconti said. 'What did you wish to ask?'

'I need your guidance. You were so kind to me after – what happened.'

'Of course.'

'It is . . .' Zati stumbled over his words. 'I don't know how to say this—'

Visconti was used to parishioners struggling to explain themselves, not knowing the right way to admit what was upsetting them. 'Start at the beginning and tell me what you can. Often it is enough to speak of our woes. The ears of another can help us to find solace.'

'How did you know something is troubling me?'

'Some things are obvious, even to an old man like me. You have not come to Santa Maria Magdalena in months, and your parish is across the city. Yet you sought me out today.'

'I don't have a parish,' Zati said. 'Not anymore. The diocese gave me other duties.'

Ahh. That went some way to explaining his unhappiness. But there was more to be said, Visconti believed. 'You miss being among the people you came to know well.'

'Yes, I do.'

'Do you know why the diocese made this decision?'

Zati cleared his throat with an angry sound. 'We both know why, Father.'

Visconti stopped. 'You mean what happened at the convent.'

'Yes.'

'But the diocese gave you a parish after that happened.'

'And took it away when Signor Cortese succumbed to his wounds,' Zati replied.

Visconti had not known that. Cortese was the visitation member who'd been attacked by the nun with a blade. He'd been badly wounded at the time, but had been recovering slowly, the last Visconti had heard. 'I'm sorry, that must have been upsetting.' Visconti rested a hand on Zati's shoulder. 'Tell me, do you still believe in the Church?'

'Of course.'

'And that your place belongs within it?'

Zati nodded. 'But I am not so certain the Church believes in me anymore. No, that is unfair. I'm not certain the diocese believes in me. That is closer to the truth.'

'Has the archbishop or one of his clerics told you so?'

'Not in so many words, but Monsignor Testardo made no effort to hide his disdain.'

That sounded like the monsignor. Visconti had known Testardo for many years. He was as much a political creature as he was a man of faith. Testardo had led the visitation at the convent which ended so ill. He would ensure the blame for that would fall elsewhere.

'You fear you have been set aside,' Visconti concluded.

Zati nodded.

'I don't wish to sound dismissive, but does this matter? You are still serving Our Lord, are you not, whatever the diocese asks of you?'

'That's the problem, Father. I'm not sure that I am.'

'Why? What do they have you doing?'

'Exorcisms. I am assisting with exorcisms.'

That made Visconti step back. 'And who are you assisting, my son?'

'Father Camillo Negri.'

'Ahh.' The situation was worse than Visconti had feared. He strolled on, Zati hurrying after him.'

'You know Father Negri?'

'Only by reputation.' Visconti tried to keep fear from his face, but did not succeed.

'You look like all the others when I told them. Once I started working with Negri, none of the priests I studied alongside were willing to speak with me anymore.'

'None of them?'

'Not one.'

'I'm sorry to hear that. Tell me, how long have you been assisting him?'

'It will be a year this Sunday, on All Souls' Day.'

'I'm surprised you have lasted so long,' Visconti admitted. 'From what I've heard it is rare for an assistant to stay in Negri's service more than a few months. But it explains why you came to me. I am an elderly priest, far enough removed from the archbishop and his clerics to offer advice unbiased by diocesan politics, yes?'

Zati nodded.

'How old are you, Pagolo?'

'Twenty-seven.'

Visconti could not help sighing. 'Still so young, less than half my age. I had many dreams of what I might become when I was your age. A monsignor, an archbishop perhaps – even a cardinal. But that was not the path Our Lord chose for me. I learned to be content doing his work, no matter where it led. You must do the same. The calling that brought you to the priesthood is for life, my son. This uncertainty you feel, it shall pass in time.'

Zati did not seem convinced. 'So, what should I do now?'

'Whatever you can. Listen to Our Lord and he will guide you. Be of help to those who need it. Keep hold of your faith and be true to yourself. Belief should be your fortress against whatever you may witness while at Negri's side. Remember, all of us work in service to the Almighty, each in our own way.' Visconti stopped, taking hold of Zati's hands. 'I shall pray for you every day. You have a good heart, Pagolo. Hold on to that, no matter what.'

He gave the younger priest a last, quick smile before striding away.

But when Visconti glanced back, the young priest looked as burdened as before.

Aldo strolled towards the Palazzo del Podestà. It had been some time since the sight of that glowering stone building had brought him any joy. The Podestà loomed over all the nearby buildings, a brutal fortress with little ornamentation, its bell tower stabbing at the sky like an accusing finger. Up to eight magistrates, each drawn from a respectable famiglia, met inside to judge those brought before the court. Each man served four-month terms before stepping aside, as was the Florentine way. The court's permanence came from its laws and those who enforced them: the segretario and his staff of administrators, along with investigating officers, constables and guards.

For years Aldo had served the Otto as an officer, reporting to Segretario Massimo Bindi. A petty and vindictive man, Bindi made no effort to mask his pleasure in tormenting those beneath him in rank. Bloated with self-importance, Bindi squatted in his ufficio like a malevolent spider, eager to inflict misery while boasting it was all in the best interests of the city and the court. When the chance came to demote Aldo to constable for exceeding his authority Bindi had grasped the opportunity eagerly, banishing him to the Tuscan countryside as a further insult.

But Aldo had found a way home, thanks to his investigative skills and an intercession by Carlo Strocchi, whom the segretario had promoted to officer. Bindi welcomed Aldo back with bad grace, putting him on night patrol as punishment for daring to return to the Otto. This unwelcome duty was habitually rotated among the constables, but Aldo had been on night patrol for seventeen months.

That would break the spirit of most men, yet he refused to give Bindi the satisfaction. Yes, it meant nights spent with Saul were infrequent. Yes, night patrol was exhausting and thankless work, especially with autumn closing a cold, damp fist around the city. And yes, it brought few opportunities for Aldo to do what he enjoyed: untangling mysteries that defied the wit of others. But he had vowed to become an officer again, no matter what it took. The murder of Zamora offered a chance to reclaim the lost rank.

Nodding to the guards standing sentry by the imposing Podestà gates, Aldo marched through the stone corridor to the large internal courtyard. He spied Benedetto muttering to two other constables near the well in the centre of the courtyard. 'Did you report what happened?' Aldo asked as he approached. 'Have you informed Bindi of what we found?'

'Yes,' Benedetto said. 'He wanted to know why you weren't telling him yourself.'

Of course. No matter what the night patrols did, the segretario always found cause to complain. Aldo glared at the middle level of the Podestà, home to the court's administrative staff. 'Has Bindi left to make his morning report to Duke Cosimo?'

Benedetto shrugged. 'I stopped being paid when curfew ended.'

Aldo left the young constable to his apathy, hurrying up the wide stone staircase that dominated the east wall of the courtyard. After a long wait outside Bindi's ufficio – the segretario made everyone wait as a way to show his authority – a haughty voice commanded Aldo to enter.

It was still early yet the sharp, sour stench of body odour assaulted Aldo's senses as he went inside. Bindi was a man heavy of belly with multiple chins. He sweated even when doing very little and seemed to mistrust bathing. A minute in his domain was eye-watering. Being careful to breathe through his mouth, Aldo approached the segretario. Bindi hunched in a sturdy wooden chair behind an imposing table. He shuffled court documents for a while before deigning to acknowledge Aldo.

'Yes?'

'I'm told Benedetto has reported what we found in Piazza della Signoria.'

Bindi grunted an acknowledgement. Saying as few words as possible was another of his stratagemmi, no doubt intended to make him appear more powerful.

'There are unusual aspects to this murder,' Aldo went on, 'so I've asked Doctor Orvieto of the Jewish commune to examine the body. He has been helpful in past matters.'

A second grunt. More rustling of papers.

'I now have reason to believe the dead man is Niccolò Zamora, a merchant who lived with his widowed sister and her children in a palazzo near Santo Spirito.' Aldo paused, letting the segretario take all the time he wished before replying, but no words came. 'I plan to question Zamora's sister first, and see what she can tell me—'

'I'm sorry?' Bindi cut in.

'I plan to question the victim's sister first—'

'Yes, yes,' the segretario snapped. 'I heard what you said. What I wish to know is why you believe you will have any further involvement with this matter?'

Aldo bit back an immediate response, keeping his face calm. Better to meet Bindi's question with silence, force the segretario to explain himself. Two could play at his games.

'Well?' Bindi demanded. 'Do you have an answer for me?'

'I found the body,' Aldo replied.

'Yes.'

'I have already uncovered the victim's identity, and a potential reason for his murder.'

'So?'

Aldo remained still, refusing to respond with anger. The bastardo was trying to make him beg for this investigation. Well, a little humility was a small price to pay. 'I have considerable experience in resolving such matters. I believe it would be—'

'What you believe is of no consequence,' Bindi sneered, waving a pudgy, dismissive hand. 'The Otto has officers for such tasks.' There was a knock at the door. 'And here is one now, if I am not mistaken.' He waited three rasping breaths before calling out. 'Come!'

Aldo could not help looking over his shoulder to see who entered.

Strocchi.

Of course. Bindi must be planning to rub their faces in the situation by giving the investigation to the younger man who had joined the court as a constable when Aldo was an officer. The segretario wanted to make them both suffer for Aldo's return.

So much for the value of humility.

'Ahh, Strocchi! Come in.' Bindi smirked, clearly enjoying himself.

'Sir,' Strocchi replied, bowing his head a little as he stopped beside Aldo.

The segretario's beam spread even wider. 'I do so appreciate an officer who is able to show the proper respect for the court and its humble functionaries.'

Aldo decided 'bastardo' didn't quite capture the self-satisfied smugness oozing from Bindi. Evil and malicious bastardo? Yes, that was more accurate.

'Have you heard all the relevant details of this matter?' Bindi asked.

'Most of them,' Strocchi replied. 'I've not yet spoken with Aldo—'

'Once you have,' the segretario interrupted, 'you will find whoever killed Kamora—'

'Zamora,' Aldo said. 'The victim's name was Niccolò Zamora.'

'I need you to find whoever killed this man,' Bindi went on, ignoring Aldo, 'and bring them before the Otto. Duke Cosimo will expect a swift resolution. See that there is one.'

'Yes, sir,' Strocchi replied.

'Very good.' Bindi sank back in his chair, arching an eyebrow at Aldo. 'Notice how simple that is? I give an order, and my officers obey – without question or query.'

Aldo smiled back at the segretario, knowing that would irritate him. 'Indeed. Most commendable. Perhaps I could suggest . . . But – no.'

Bindi's face soured. 'No what?'

'I'm sure an officer of Strocchi's . . . enthusiasm has no need of my assistance,' Aldo replied. 'I'm certain the matter will be resolved long before His Grace has reason to question the wisdom of the court giving such an important matter to an inexperienced officer.' Aldo noted Strocchi's right hand clenched into a fist by his side. Carlo had learned many things in three years with the Otto, but masking his anger was not yet one of them.

Bindi sniffed with disdain. 'Well, Strocchi, what do you think?'

'It could be . . . helpful . . . to have Aldo assist with this matter,' Strocchi replied.

'Then that's settled.' The segretario nodded towards his ufficio door. 'I shall expect a full report before curfew each evening. That's all.'

Aldo let Strocchi lead the way out, knowing Bindi could not resist making a final barb before they departed. Sure enough, the segretario cleared his throat as they reached the door.

'One last thing,' he called. 'It occurs to me that Strocchi used to assist you, Aldo, when he was a constable, and you were an officer. I trust your reversed ranks will not make things awkward for either of you?'

Aldo shook his head, keeping his true response hidden. Assisting Strocchi would be uncomfortable, but Aldo had little intention of only doing that. He had a murder to solve.

Strocchi stalked down the wide stone staircase, struggling to keep a grasp on his anger. When he glanced back, Aldo was sauntering down to the Podestà courtyard, a wide grin spread across his face. 'What have you got to be so happy about?' Strocchi demanded. 'A man is dead – murdered – and you look as if nothing could be more pleasing.'

Aldo frowned as if taken aback by the accusation. 'Forgive me, Carlo. I did not mean to diminish what has happened to Signor Zamora. It is a tragedy, of course, for him and his famiglia. I was simply savouring the fact that I no longer need to be on night patrol.'

That made sense, but Strocchi knew better than to accept the first words that came from Aldo's mouth. He was skilled at hiding his true intentions, after all, and his true self. 'What about the things you said in Bindi's ufficio? How I wouldn't be able to solve this without you to show me the way? I've been an officer more than a year. I've brought four different killers to justice while you've been on night patrols.'

'I know, I know. You're a good investigator, well on your way to becoming a great one.' Aldo smiled as if nothing was wrong. 'I have every confidence in you.'

'Then why say those things?'

'Because I need to be part of this investigation. If I help you catch this killer, Bindi will have to consider moving me from night patrols for good. And I knew he wouldn't let me help unless the segretario feared for his own future. I'm sorry, but it was necessary.'

Strocchi wanted to stay angry. But he knew there was a seed of truth in Aldo's words. Having the more experienced investigator assisting should be an asset. So why did it feel like buying a two-day-old piece of fish from the mercato while being assured it was still fresh?

'Tell me about this body,' Strocchi said, pushing his doubts aside.

Aldo gave a brisk summary as they strolled to the Podestà entrance, the curious positioning of the body with the arms reaching outwards and the legs crossed at the feet.

'Like Christ on the cross?' Strocchi asked.

'Exactly,' Aldo said. 'Doctor Orvieto is examining Zamora at Santa Maria Nuova. I was to meet him in the ospedale at noon to hear his findings, but since you are leading the case . . .'

'We can both be there,' Strocchi replied as they reached the street. 'Better to share what he uncovers. It'll help us find the killer faster. Is there anything else I need to know?'

'Yes.' Aldo explained his theory that the wool merchant was garrotted because Zamora preferred the company of men in his bed. This suggested the murderer could be one of the dead man's lovers, or someone with a deadly hatred for such men.

'Do you have any evidence of that?' Strocchi asked.

'No, not yet—'

'Then I don't think we can assume it is correct.'

'I'm not assuming anything,' Aldo insisted.

'You are leaping from one rock to the next without knowing if they cross the river,' Strocchi replied. 'When I was a constable, an officer warned me against deciding too much too soon, otherwise you can be guilty of only seeking evidence that matches your suspicion.'

'Are you quoting my own words back to me?'

Strocchi took a breath. 'I know you want to escape the night patrol. But we need proof before making any accusations or claims about the victim.' He glanced at the men standing sentry by the Podestà gates. Strocchi moved Aldo further away so only he could hear. 'We both know how dangerous it is to accuse a man of sodomy, yes?'

Aldo grimaced before giving a curt nod.

'Good. I will go to Zamora's palazzo and inform the famiglia of his murder,' Strocchi said. 'How they respond will help determine whether any of them need investigation. Zamora was a wool merchant, so he must have ties to the Arte della Lana. Go to the guild and find out if he shared his business with any partners. If so, talk to them. If not, talk to his rivals.'

'See if any of them stand to benefit from his murder?'

Strocchi let himself smile. 'Cui bono, as you once told me.'

'Very well. And what about those the victim took to his bed, or who hated him for it?'

'Please, just do as I ask. We meet again at Santa Maria Nuova at noon, yes?'

Aldo hesitated before nodding.

Strocchi watched him stride away from the Podestà. What Aldo said and what he did were often at odds, but perhaps Aldo would do as he was asked this time.

Perhaps.

Chapter Four

ather Zati struggled south through those crowding Ponte Vecchio in search of a bargain from the butcher shops and fish stalls. Once clear of the bridge the priest could stride faster, taking him past the unfinished Palazzo Pitti. But as he approached San Felice, his steps faltered once more. A woman was pacing in front of the church, the same woman who had been outside San Felice each morning for weeks without end: Signora Vanni. She had confronted Zati again and again. Finally, he had given in, promising to do as she asked. But now she was expecting answers and Zati had none to give . . .

She was a burly figure, wide of hip and strong of arm. When not accusing Zati outside the church, Vanni had mentioned working in a tannery by the river Arno's northern bank, helping scrub and move heavy animal hides. Good work, she called it, honest work. But the stench of that place clung to her, piercing and pungent, the urine and dyes used on the skins staining her meaty hands and simple peasant clothes. A black headscarf held back her unruly brown curls. She seemed to care little about how she looked or what others thought of her.

Vanni had made it clear she put other concerns first.

Zati hesitated, glancing to one side, to the long way round to the back door of the church. But while he hesitated, the opportunity to elude Vanni was lost. She had seen him.

'Father Zati!' she shouted, hurrying towards him. 'Father Zati, have you prayed on what I asked you yesterday, and the days before? Have you asked Our Lord for his answer?'

'Signora,' he said, bowing his head a little, 'I have done as you asked. I prayed to Our Lord. And, this very morning, I sought counsel from a wise priest I have known for years.'

Joy filled Vanni's face as she loomed over Zati. 'And? What did he say?'

'I'm sorry, signora. There is nothing I can do for you.'

'Nothing?'

'Yes.'

'Nothing?' she repeated, her voice growing louder. Servants and other workers passing by stared as Vanni pulled herself up to her full height. 'But you have already done nothing. Nothing at all is all that you have done.'

Zati reached out a hand to her. 'Please, signora—'

She slapped him away. 'Don't you dare touch me! You, the one person who I thought might understand how I have suffered. You were there when my little brother Cecco was overcome by spirits. I believed in you, Father Zati. I believed you could help me, that you might make the monster in there –' she pointed an accusing finger at San Felice – 'admit what he did to my own famiglia.'

A crowd was gathering around them, people stopping to watch this barrel of a woman shouting at a priest in the middle of the street, his face flushing crimson. 'I understand how difficult this must be for you—'

Vanni jabbed a finger into his chest. 'You understand nothing. Nothing!'

Zati staggered back, almost tumbling over his own feet. 'Signora Vanni,' he pleaded, his voice thin and weak, 'I am only a parish priest. I do not possess the power to undo what happened to your brother. If I could bring him back, I would. If I could persuade Cecco—'

'Don't you dare say his name,' she hissed, her spittle flecking Zati's face.

'I'm sorry . . .'

'That's all you ever say – "I'm sorry" – as if that makes a difference. But it's not enough. Not anymore.' She stepped back from him, her jaw clenched, a vein standing out on her forehead. 'I warned you what might happen if the Church did not listen. I did all I could to get you and the diocese to stop Negri hurting others as he's hurt my famiglia. But you're too scared of him, too fearful of what might happen if you speak out. You're a coward, Father Zati, too afraid to stand up for those who cannot. I pity you.'

The young priest shook his head, but no words came from his lips.

Vanni wiped a hand across her mouth. 'This is your fault. You could have stopped this. But I have suffered alone for almost a year. Now you will share in that.' She stalked past Zati, heading north towards the Arno. The crowd around Zati broke apart, going on their way to work, to the mercato or their homes. Soon the young priest was alone.

But not for long.

'I warned you not to speak with her,' a commanding voice said, deep and stern.

Zati nodded.

'I warned what would happen if you went near someone so lost in their grief.'

Zati closed his eyes.

'Come,' Father Negri called from the entrance of San Felice. 'We have much to do.'

* * *

Aldo should have been at one of the grand palazzi belonging to the leaders of the Arte della Lana, seeking answers about Zamora, his enemies and allies. The wool merchants' guild was one of the most powerful in the city; notorious for the cut-throat business practices of its members, but Aldo could not recall that ever leading to murder. And the way Zamora was killed, how his body was put on display . . . This was about something more than a broken contract or the price of wool. Garrotting a man was a close, often personal act. It took a resolve firmer than the grip needed to end his life, even if the victim was unable to fight back.

No, this was nothing to do with wool merchants.

Instead of visiting the guild's leaders, Aldo was halfway between Piazza Santa Croce and the river, knocking at the door of a small workshop. It stood on a squalid street so thin two men could not pass one another side by side. The tall, crumbling buildings lining the road meant the sun rarely touched the mud that squelched beneath Aldo's boots, nor would it dry the stinking channel of piss that ran down the gentle slope towards the Arno.

Aldo knocked again, eager to get inside.

The door opened at last, revealing a friendly if careworn face. 'Cesare! What are you doing here? I haven't seen you since – well . . .'

'May I come in?'

Renato Patricio stepped aside, gesturing with a grand sweep of one hand, his silk robe of gold and cerulean blue wafting through the air. 'Please!'

Inside, the intense aroma of camphor filled the air, making Aldo cough. Bolts of fabric lined three walls of the workshop, their vibrant colours bringing life to the cramped space. A sewing table dominated the centre of the room, several lanterns atop it lighting the work area. Tucked in one corner was a single cot, partially hidden behind a screen. The workshop was a relief from the fetid street outside, but it was still a long way from the grand salone where Renato had once welcomed the wives of Florence's wealthiest merchants who came to him for the finest gowns and dresses.

'I know what you're thinking,' Renato announced, returning to work on the camicia atop his sewing table. 'But it's a start. Here I can sleep and sew, create new pieces for those who still value my skills. Here I can do what I do best, yes?'

Aldo nodded. It was his fault Renato was living in such a place, after he'd forced the dressmaker to leave Florence several years earlier after a betrayal that had proved dangerous for them both, and fatal for a common enemy. But eventually Aldo had sent a letter inviting Renato home once it was safe for him to return. 'How long have you been back?'

'Almost six months,' Renato replied, licking the end of a thread before passing it through the eye of a needle. 'This might not look much, but it's better than the two tiresome years I spent in the north. Honestly, the poor people in Milan would not notice good sewing or gorgeous gowns if they tripped over such delights in the street. I doubt anyone in that city will ever appreciate what someone like me can do for them. Oh well, it's their loss.'

'Indeed.' Aldo smiled. As ever, Renato was making a fine gown out of a sow's hide.

'Would you like a drink?' the dressmaker asked. 'I have wine here somewhere.' He paused to glance round before gesturing towards his bed. 'Probably behind that screen.'

'No, grazie.'

Renato squinted at Aldo. 'So, why have you come to see me? Not for a fresh tunic, I suppose, although that . . . thing . . . you're in desperately needs replacing. However, the cloak is another matter – good fabric, and well cut. I'm guessing that belongs to someone else.'

Aldo had forgotten he was still wearing the cloak loaned to him by Saul. 'Yes, it does.'

'I thought as much.' Renato put down his sewing. 'I appreciated you sending me that letter, Cesare. After what happened, I'd have understood if you'd left me to wither in Milan.'

'That's all in the past. But perhaps you could help me, in return?'

'Of course.'

'What can you tell me about Niccolò Zamora?'

'The wool merchant?'

Aldo nodded.

'Can't say I had any dealings with him, before I left or since my return. Silks and damasks are more my fabrics of choice; wool can be so coarse. But, from what others have told me, Zamora is a rarity in his guild – honest, decent, even forgiving when things go awry. Shares his business with Bontura Empoli. The two of them are kind souls, apparently.'

Aldo noted the partner's name, knowing he would need to seek Empoli out later. 'I was more interested in Zamora as a man. I'm told he is not married.'

'Ahh.' Renato smiled. 'I try not to gossip about others . . .'

'But?'

'Let us say Zamora is careful, and very discreet. I doubt anyone but his past lovers know what sort of man he truly is, what his . . . preferences are.' A playful glint in Renato's eyes left his face. 'Why are you asking? Has something happened to him?'

Aldo gave a brief description of Zamora's murder. Renato gasped before making the sign of the cross while muttering a prayer. Word of the killing had clearly not got as far as the dressmaker. After letting him recover, Aldo pressed for more answers. 'What about attacks on the likes of Zamora? Have you heard of such men being targeted by others?'

'No more than usual,' Renato said, 'but I don't get as many invitations to dine with the wives and lovers of wealthy merchants these days. That's where I got my best gossip.'

'If you do hear anything, send me a message at Signora Robustelli's bordello.'

'Not the Podestà?'

'No.' Aldo frowned. 'I'd prefer to keep the private details of Zamora's life quiet, where possible. His famiglia will suffer enough from his loss. If Zamora was killed because of his choice of lovers, it will be easier to find those responsible while his secrets stay secret.' That was all true, but there was another reason for the request. Strocchi was less liable to learn about this additional investigation if Aldo kept it away from the Podestà.

Strocchi had little trouble finding Palazzo Zamora. The dead man's home was one of the most majestic buildings on Piazza Santo Spirito in the southern quarter of Florence. It stood smaller in stature only to the church that gave the square its name. While other palazzi nearby had the usual three levels, this one rose to four with a loggia at the top that no doubt provided stunning views of Oltrarno and north across the river. Rusticated stone encased the ground floor, while the levels above were far grander, with elegant brickwork framing the windows and sgraffito artwork scratched into black plaster walls around them.

Admiring the palazzo, impressive as it might be, was a way of delaying the task that Strocchi hated most about being an officer. He should be inside, informing the famiglia that Zamora was dead, and studying their responses to see if any of them was involved. The distinctive way the corpse had been laid out beneath the statue of David suggested something more than a famiglia dispute gone horribly awry. But it was too soon to decide such things, especially after he had berated Aldo for leaping to deductions without evidence to support them.

Unable to delay what must be done any longer, Strocchi strode into the palazzo. Once inside he announced himself to a servant, asking to speak with Signor Zamora's famiglia. The servant ushered Strocchi to the internal courtyard, a quiet rectangle bounded by stone pillars and porticos. Other servants moved back and forth, paying Strocchi little attention while he waited. It seemed Zamora, like most merchants, ran his business from the ground floor of the palazzo. The dead man's famiglia would likely reside on the level above, while servants slept nearer the top of the building, in rooms that roasted during the sweltering summer months.

Looking up, Strocchi could see open shutters on each level. The sounds of children laughing and playing echoed around the stone walls of the courtyard. Their joy reminded him of Bianca's infectious giggles, the happiness that filled her face most days. The news he had brought would put an end to such happiness here. Strocchi bowed his head, offering a silent prayer for the strength to do what he must, though duty brought no joy at times like this.

A polite cough got Strocchi's attention. 'Please,' the servant said, 'follow me.'

Strocchi was led up a grand marble staircase and shown into a vibrant salone. The walls were decorated with frescoes of a lush green forest, while elaborate tapestries showing scenes of the Tuscan countryside hung between the paintings. There were none of the flattering portraits or golden statues Strocchi often saw in such rooms. Two simple walnut chairs waited in the middle of the salone, facing each other. Where most merchants seemed to delight in displays of wealth to show their significance, this salone was quite different. It had no portrait of Zamora, nothing to announce his ownership of the palazzo.

A kind-faced woman swept in through a side door. 'Forgive me, I was busy with my younger daughter Olympia when you arrived. Please, sit.' She gestured to one of the chairs as she perched in the other, smoothing out her pale green dress. 'I'm afraid my brother Niccolò is not here, but he will no doubt return soon.'

'It is about him that I wished to speak with you, Signora . . . ?'

'Where are my manners? I have not introduced myself. I am Tullia Juvara.' She pushed a wisp of dark hair behind one ear. The rest was plaited and fixed atop her head. Fine lines at the corners of her eyes and mouth suggested she was close to forty.

'And you live with Signor Zamora?'

'Yes, as do my children. I am a widow. Niccolò invited us here when my husband died after a long illness. My brother always says that we bring life to his palazzo.' There was a loud squeal from beyond the side door. Tullia laughed. 'My children certainly bring plenty of noise to the place, if nothing else.'

'I have a daughter of my own,' Strocchi volunteered. 'She is almost two and has more life in her than I ever thought possible. May I ask, how old are your children?' He doubted any of them were responsible for the murder, but it was easier to obtain this information now before revealing what had happened to Zamora.

'My eldest daughter is fifteen, my son is twelve and my younger daughter is nine. Now, what was it you wished to say?'

Unable to delay the moment any longer, Strocchi brought his chair closer to Tullia. 'I'm sorry, but your brother was found dead this morning, not long before dawn.'

She shook her head. 'Dead? No, that can't be correct.'

'I am afraid it is. His body was examined by Doctor Orvieto, a Jewish physician who treated your famiglia some years ago. He recognized the dead man as Signor Zamora.'

'He must be mistaken . . . Yes, Orvieto helped us for a short while but that was . . . He can't have recalled Niccolò's face, not after . . . No . . .'

Strocchi had seen this before, people unable to accept a terrible truth when it was brought to them. They denied the possibility of it until the evidence was before their own eyes, and some kept denying it even then. 'There is no error, signora. The good doctor was quite certain, and I have never known him to be wrong. He is a most careful and diligent man.'

'Yes, I remember him well. It was a shame when he could no longer . . .' Tullia's face crumpled, her hands grasping each other in her lap. 'But when did this happen? How?'

Strocchi had prepared for such questions before entering the palazzo. The full details need not be shared with the famiglia, not while it was possible one of them was the killer. 'His body was discovered in a piazza north of the Arno. Someone ended his life.'

Tullia put a hand to her mouth. 'You mean he was . . . murdered?'

'I am afraid so, yes.'

That was too much for her. Tullia rose from the chair, shaking her head while staring at Strocchi as if he was a monster. She staggered backwards, knocking the chair over behind her. 'No . . . It can't be . . . Not again . . .' Strocchi reached to steady her, but she lurched beyond his grasp. 'Why, Lord? Why do you torment us like this?' Tullia's eyes rolled back into her head and she slumped to the wooden floor, great sobs convulsing her body.

'Help!' Strocchi called out, making his voice as loud as he could. 'Come, quickly! The signora has collapsed, she needs help! Come, come!' He knelt by Tullia, clasping her hands in his own. 'Signora, I'm sorry. Forgive me for bringing word of this to you.'

She stared but her eyes did not seem to see him, nor her ears hear his words.

Where in God's name were those servants? Strocchi dared not leave Tullia but—

Then servants were rushing into the salone, men and women all hurrying to help. Strocchi got out of their way, explaining how she had fainted but not why. Four servants carried Tullia from the salone, most of the others following.

The servant who had ushered Strocchi up from the courtyard remained behind. He had sharp features and a piercing gaze, his hair more silver than grey. 'My name is Querini, I am maggiordomo for Signor Zamora and his famiglia. What made Signora Tullia collapse?'

Strocchi repeated what he had told Zamora's sister. The maggiordomo made the sign of the cross. 'No wonder she—' A wail of grief cried out in a nearby room.

'I do not wish to disturb her or the famiglia further,' Strocchi said. 'May I ask you some questions that might help me find whoever did this to Signor Zamora?'

'Of course.'

In a few minutes Strocchi had the essential information he needed. The dead man had shared his business with a partner, Bontura Empoli. According to the maggiordomo, Zamora had made few enemies, if any. He seemed to have little interest in acquiring power within the wool merchants' guild. He had been a quiet man, a careful man, and quite discreet.

'He never married?' Strocchi asked.

'No,' Querini said. Strocchi remained silent, letting his question's implication linger. It was a trick he had learned from Aldo. Most people would answer a question immediately, but leave enough of a gap after that reply and they'd feel obliged to add more. Querini held his tongue for six breaths before succumbing to the silence, lowering his voice to a whisper. 'Signor Zamora may have taken an occasional lover, but never here in the palazzo. He did not offer any details about that part of his life to me, and I did not ask.'

'I understand. Was he here in the palazzo last night?'

'No. Not long before curfew I received a message that he would be staying the night at Palazzo Empoli, not far from San Marco.'

That meant Zamora's business partner might have been among the last to see him alive. It also made Empoli a suspect for the murder.

Chapter Five

The longer Strocchi remained at Palazzo Zamora, the more certain he became the famiglia had nothing to do with the murder. Tullia's initial surprise and then her overwhelming grief were compelling, while the children were too young to be credible suspects. Servants had nothing but praise for Zamora, speaking unprompted of his kindness and consideration.

Their one misgiving was how infrequently Zamora attended Mass. It seemed he had lost faith with the Church after the death of Tullia's first-born, Marsilio, but none of the servants was willing to discuss that any further. Strocchi sought out the maggiordomo, pressing him for answers. Querini was reluctant but eventually revealed Marsilio had ended his own life. The youth had been unwell for months, not in body but in spirit. A priest at San Felice persuaded Signora Tullia that he could drive out Marsilio's illness.

'What do you mean, drive out?' Strocchi asked.

Querini refused to reply inside the palazzo. He escorted Strocchi downstairs and out onto Piazza Santo Spirito before answering. 'While Signor Zamora was away on business it was decided Marsilio should be . . .' The maggiordomo shook his head.

'Should be what?'

'Exorcized.'

Strocchi knew the Church helped those possessed by the

diavolo – demoniacs, they were called – but had never encountered such an event. 'That happens in Florence?'

Querini's reaction suggested he thought Strocchi a fool. 'Of course.'

'And Marsilio underwent an exorcism?'

'Yes, in August last year at San Felice, not far from here. But it did not seem to help. He took his own life a month later. We still don't know where he got the poison.'

No wonder Querini had not wanted to speak of such things inside the palazzo. It also explained the violence of Tullia's response on hearing her brother had been murdered. Losing her husband and son was more than pain enough, but now her brother too . . .

'The famiglia was devastated,' Querini continued, 'but there was worse to come. The priest who exorcized Marsilio then refused to perform a funeral or let him be buried in the famiglia crypt. Signora Tullia was bereft, but Signor Zamora was furious.'

Strocchi was not surprised by the decision, no matter how hurtful it must have been. Taking one's own life was a mortal sin in the eyes of the Church. Many priests would have been equally adamant in refusing the grieving famiglia. 'What happened?'

'Signor Zamora persuaded another parish, one that did not know the circumstances of how Marsilio had died, to bury the young man.'

It was not uncommon for the richest merchants to have burial crypts beneath several churches in the city. Where Strocchi grew up everyone was laid to rest in the same graveyard, so this Florentine practice surprised him when he first heard of it. But, as with most things, the wealthiest pursued any advantage they could – even in death. Why the Lord might favour one crypt over another eluded Strocchi.

'Signor Zamora was not the same afterwards,' Querini said. 'He blamed God for Marsilio's death. No, that is unfair. He blamed the Church for what happened to Marsilio. Signor Zamora has been to Mass only twice since then, and solely for his sister's sake.'

A gaunt man strode towards the palazzo, fine woollen robes announcing his wealth and likely trade. Querini nodded to the man as he entered the palazzo.

'Who was that?' Strocchi asked.

'Signor Zamora's business partner.'

'Excuse me,' Strocchi said, hurrying after the gaunt man. He caught up to Empoli as the merchant was crossing the palazzo courtyard. Strocchi introduced himself without specifying why he was there. 'I'm told you work with Signor Zamora?'

'Yes,' Empoli said, still walking. He was a similar age to the dead man, with brown hair swept back from his thin face. 'We've been partners for twenty years. Niccolò and I built our business together. But why does an officer of the Otto want to know this? Unless . . .' Empoli stopped, his brow furrowing. 'On my way here, I heard talk of a dead body found at the Piazza della Signoria. Please, don't tell me . . .'

Strocchi wished he could have spoken to Empoli before word reached the merchant, but it was too late for that now. 'I'm sorry to say Signor Zamora was killed during curfew.'

'Killed? But that makes no sense.' Empoli appeared bewildered. 'The man doesn't have an enemy in the city. He's one of the few merchants in Florence who makes friends out of his rivals. Why would anyone want to see Niccolò dead, let alone kill him?'

'That's what I wished to ask you.' Gentle drizzle was falling into the courtyard, so Strocchi led Empoli to a stone bench under the cover of a portico. Zamora's partner seemed as shocked and dismayed by the murder as Tullia had been. One thing was clear: Empoli had not spoken with anyone from the Otto. What had Aldo been doing all morning?

Aldo strode north over Ponte alla Carraia, one of the lesser used bridges for crossing the Arno. After leaving Renato's workshop Aldo had spent the rest of the morning searching back streets and alleys in Oltrarno without finding his quarry. In the past he would have visited the disreputable tavern run by Zoppo. The pox-faced cripple was the best source of illicit information in the city, but since the murder of his brother in a Podestà cell, Zoppo refused to speak with Aldo. The killing had been Aldo's fault – indirectly, yet still his fault – which gave Zoppo good reason to withhold what he heard and knew. Being denied reliable intelligence was frustrating, so Aldo had gone searching for another source: a scruffy, brown-haired youth known as Freccia. But the thief was missing from his usual stomping grounds south of the river, leaving one obvious place where he might be.

The emptiness in Aldo's belly and occasional glimpses of the sun between drizzle and showers meant the middle of the day must be close. By now Aldo was usually slumping into bed at the bordello after sharing a morning meal with Signora Robustelli and her women. The chance to help find Zamora's killer meant staying awake all day, despite having been on patrol since dusk the previous night. But seeing the city in daylight did offer some joy. Aldo had missed the sight and sound of noisy traders hawking their wares in the street, shouting for customers even when the threat of more rain was keeping most people inside.

Aldo spied Freccia lingering at a corner at via tra' Pellicciai, a street unremarkable in appearance yet notorious in reputation. This was where foolish men came as dusk neared to find others like them, ready to abandon sense and safety for the promise of pleasure with another man. Those with more restraint wisely sought a partner elsewhere, but visiting via tra' Pellicciai added danger to the excitement of a furtive coupling.

Of course, most of the fumblings and fornications happened as curfew approached when the tall buildings on either side cast the narrow street into shadow. For now, via tra' Pellicciai was empty aside from the workers and servants hurrying along it. Freccia was so intent on watching them he didn't notice Aldo until it was too late to run.

An arm pressed against Freccia's throat made sure of that. The thief's jaw jutted out as he struggled to breathe, a distinctive cleft in his chin.

'Didn't I tell you to stay south of the Arno?' Aldo asked. Unable to breathe or speak, Freccia shook his head. 'I'm certain that's what I said, the last time I arrested you. Stay south of the river and you'll live longer. But you're back to your old ways, it seems.'

Freccia's face was turning crimson, his eyes widening.

Aldo used his spare hand to search the youth, finding two pouches of coin stuffed inside his hose. 'Are these meant to make what you've got down there more impressive? Or were you just in need of somewhere to hide what you've stolen?'

Freccia gasped out a word. 'Please . . .'

'Yes?'

The youth pointed at his throat.

Aldo pulled his arm away and Freccia collapsed, gasping and choking. While the thief recovered, Aldo emptied both pouches of coin on the ground beside them. 'Not bad for a quiet, rainy morning. I'm almost impressed. Almost.'

'What do you want?' Freccia asked, rubbing a hand against his throat.

'Tell me about Niccolò Zamora.'

'Who?'

The answer came straight away, fast enough to be credible. If Freccia had hesitated, that would have been a sign of deceit. But there was no furtiveness in his face. Not about this, at least. 'Thought you might have met him. He likes the company of men, I'm told.'

'I don't do that anymore,' Freccia replied with a sneer.

'Not for money,' Aldo agreed. 'You steal instead.'

'Why are you asking me about him?'

'Zamora? He took a beating from someone who didn't like his choices.' Freccia had no need of the whole truth to be useful as an informant.

'I don't hit anyone,' the youth said, getting to his feet. He had narrow, suspicious eyes and was quick of limb too. Aldo took hold of Freccia's tunic to stop him fleeing.

'No, but you probably know who targets men like him.'

Freccia shrugged. 'Drunken bullies in need of an easy target,' he said, 'or trying to prove something.'

'Has it been happening more than usual?'

'Not that I've seen or heard.' Again, the answer came without hesitation. 'Can I go now? Having you here isn't making my job easier, you know.'

'Yes, you can go.' Freccia reached down to gather the coin. 'But leave those.'

'That's not fair—'

'It's stolen. I'm taking the coin in case someone comes to claim it.'

Freccia glared a moment before stomping away, spitting on the ground as he left. Once the youth was gone Aldo shoved all the coin into one of the stolen pouches. On night patrol there was no call for it, but he would need coin for bribes and other informants. Aldo tucked the pouch inside his tunic while pondering Freccia's words. The thief had confirmed what Renato said earlier: attacks on men like Zamora were no more frequent than usual. That suggested there must be another motive for the murder. If so, the morning had been wasted. Aldo rubbed a hand across the stubble beneath his chin, cursing himself for being too stubborn to accept that Strocchi had been right.

It was past time to be at Santa Maria Nuova to hear what Saul had found from examining the victim's corpse. Being late wasn't going to please Strocchi. Nor would the lack of progress investigating Zamora's business allies and enemies. Finding the name of his partner, Bontura Empoli, was not nearly enough.

Strocchi was uncomfortable waiting outside Santa Maria Nuova. Not with the ospedale itself, the nuns there were doing good work, the Lord's work, in tending the sick and the dying. Nor was it the building's exterior which troubled him, despite those clustered by the main entrance seeking alms from anyone entering or leaving. In a city filled with rich bankers and wealthy merchants, it was shameful that people had to beg for scraps to stay alive. Strocchi had already given all his coin to them when he arrived, but it would never be enough.

No, his unease came from the many times he had been here before. It was always to witness someone's pain, or to watch them die. People who hurt themselves to escape their lives or those they feared. The good citizens attacked by robbers or wounded by those who were meant to care for them, love them. Men, women and children all close to the grave, brought to their last days by broken laws or broken promises. For Strocchi, Santa Maria Nuova had become the place where hope perished, where nothing good ever happened.

Waiting outside the ospedale was the same as lying atop a

mattress teeming with fleas and lice: it made Strocchi itch. The longer he stood there, the worse it got. Eventually he could no longer remain still, pacing back and forth in front of the main entrance to stop from clawing at his own skin. Finally – finally! – Aldo arrived at the ospedale.

'Where have you been?' Strocchi demanded, not bothering to hide his frustration. 'We agreed to meet here at noon. What have you been doing all this time?'

'What you told me to do,' Aldo replied, 'investigating Zamora's murder.'

'I told you to talk to any partners he had, and to his rivals in the guild.'

Aldo smiled. 'I did learn the name of his business partner—'

'Bontura Empoli,' Strocchi cut in. 'I've been questioning him at Palazzo Zamora. Strange, he never mentioned talking to anyone else from the Otto.' Aldo didn't speak. He couldn't hold Strocchi's gaze either. 'So where have you been all morning? No, let me guess. You've been following your own path, despite what I asked you to do. Well, have you had any success proving your suggestion about why Zamora was killed?'

More silence. That meant no.

Strocchi exhaled. 'If we are going to resolve this, if we are going to find the murderer, we need to work together – not against one another. Yes?' Aldo nodded. 'Then let's go inside and hear what Doctor Orvieto has found.' Strocchi stood aside so Aldo could enter the ospedale, before following him in.

Aldo asked a nun where Zamora's body had been taken inside the ospedale. She guided Aldo and Strocchi through the building, past rooms where the sick and dying were being tended. At times the smell of human waste and rotting flesh were overwhelming, but the nun seemed not to notice. Aldo supposed she must be used to the stench, or at least inured to it.

He was aware of Strocchi one step behind him, the young officer's boots stamping on the stone floor. Aldo wished Strocchi had shouted at him outside, got rid of all the anger that was still between them. Easier to let it out, unleash his recriminations and be done with them. Strocchi withholding his frustrations would not help anyone. But Aldo knew better than to say so out loud. Strocchi had a stubborn resolve when it came to such things.

Saul was waiting as they approached a room at the rear of the ospedale. 'My student Rebecca will be wondering where I am,' he said. 'I sent a message that I'd be back by now.'

'That's my fault,' Aldo volunteered. 'I got . . . distracted with other things.'

'Well, you're here now. Do you wish to hear what I've found?'

'Yes,' Aldo replied, 'that would be—'

Strocchi cleared his throat.

Aldo forced a smile. 'Probably best you tell Carlo. He's in charge of the investigation. I'm simply here to help. If I can.'

'Of course.' Saul ushered them into a small, empty room. In the centre of it, Zamora's corpse was lying atop a stone table. Early-afternoon sun streamed in through a single opening high in the back wall, warming a bundle of mulberry twigs that hung in front of it.

A shiver ran up Aldo's back. 'I've been here before,' he murmured.

'We both have,' Saul replied. 'It's where I examined the body of that poor soul Galeri who was killed at the convent.'

Aldo nodded. He'd spent a year away from Florence after that case, and even longer since on night patrol. Yet being back with

Saul in the same room, standing over another corpse . . . it was as if no time had passed, and yet so much had happened since.

'As I said earlier,' Saul continued, 'Zamora was garrotted from behind by a man, or a woman with considerable strength in her hands. There is no evidence he resisted the attacker, which suggests he did not have his senses when it happened. But I discovered several other things when examining the corpse more closely.' The doctor pointed to Zamora's forehead. 'Someone smeared ash here, above the eyebrows. Unfortunately, rain washed most of the ash away, but you can still see the last remnants.'

Strocchi stepped in front of Aldo for a closer look. 'Was the ash in the shape of a cross?'

Saul frowned. 'Perhaps, but it is difficult to be sure.'

'You're thinking there's a religious motive?' Aldo asked Strocchi.

He did not glance back, keeping his focus on Saul and the corpse. 'I was told Zamora was posed like Christ on the cross. If the killer also put ash on the victim's forehead . . .'

'This is your faith,' the doctor said, 'not mine.'

'And we're closer to Advent than Lent,' Aldo noted. Having been blocked by Strocchi from seeing the body, Aldo went round the table to stand beside Saul. 'You mentioned several things?'

'Yes,' Saul replied. 'The ash was one. The second is inside Zamora's tunic. I left that where I found it.' He peeled back the fabric to reveal a sodden piece of paper, stained with ink. 'Unfortunately, whatever was written on this has bled away, destroyed by the rain.'

'Is that Latin?' Strocchi leaned over the corpse to peer at what was still legible on the paper. '*Mando . . . vobis . . .*' He shook his head. 'I can't read anything else.'

'*Mando vobis* means "I command you",' Aldo said.

Saul smiled at him. 'You know Latin?'

'My papa wanted all his children educated, legitimate and bastardo.'

'Can we dry this out?' Strocchi asked, taking hold of the sodden document.

'I wouldn't move that,' Saul warned, 'the paper is very—'

The document came apart in Strocchi's hands, falling in shreds from his fingertips. 'Santo spirito!' He dropped what was left beside the corpse before wiping both hands on his hose. 'The rain has not been kind to us. What else did you find, doctor?'

'This.' Saul took hold of the victim's head. 'If you look here, at the mark round the victim's neck. What do you notice?'

Aldo and Strocchi leaned closer to the corpse from either side. 'The red line . . . it's not all the way round,' Strocchi said. 'There are small gaps in it.'

'You're right,' Aldo agreed. 'But it was unbroken before, except behind the neck.'

'Correct,' Saul said. 'Like a bruise that changes colour over time, so it can be with injuries. I believe this poor soul was garrotted with a beaded cord or rope of some kind. And there was one more thing . . .' He rested a hand on Aldo's shoulder. 'May I?'

Aldo stepped aside so Saul could be closer to the body. It took the doctor several attempts to force the mouth. 'Someone cut this man's tongue in two, from the tip down to its base.' Saul leaned back so Aldo and Strocchi could both see into Zamora's mouth. The two halves of the dead man's tongue were split apart, like a short flap of meat sliced lengthways.

'Diavolo,' Aldo whispered.

Strocchi stumbled backwards, staggering to a corner of the room before retching on the floor. He vomited again, his body spasming long after anything had come out of his mouth. Saul moved to help the young officer, but Aldo grabbed the doctor's arm to stop him. Better to let Strocchi recover his dignity first. Eventually the spasms passed.

'Are you . . . ?' Saul asked.

Strocchi held up a hand. 'I'll be fine.' He wiped his mouth. 'When did this happen?'

'When did he die? Or when was his tongue cut in two?'

Strocchi started to answer but swallowed hard instead, his face sweaty and ashen.

Aldo had witnessed enough horrors not to be unmanned by the obscenity of what had been done to Zamora. 'Perhaps give us answers for both questions, if you can.'

'Of course. Well, the body is stiffening now,' Saul said. 'You saw how difficult it was for me to open his mouth. That suggests Zamora died in the hours before dawn. I believe his tongue was probably split in two after death. It would be easier to achieve when he could not resist. Certainly, there are no signs in Zamora's mouth of him struggling against what was done. I should think the body would fight back against such a barbaric act, even if Zamora was without his senses. But it is the first time I have seen such a thing done to a body, human or otherwise. I am no expert here.'

A memory Aldo had done all he could to forget returned. 'When I was riding with Giovanni dalle Bande Nere as a man at arms, we entered a small village where brigands had stayed the night. They cut the tongues out of everyone there – men, women, even children – to make sure nobody could ever say where they went. It didn't occur to them that the villagers could still point.' Aldo found it difficult to swallow, the recollection of that place all too vivid. 'Saul is right. If someone puts a knife in your mouth and starts cutting, you fight back. You can't help yourself.'

The three of them stood silent, hushed sounds from the ospedale seeping in through the doorway. Eventually Strocchi cleared his throat. 'Doctor, was there anything else?'

'No,' Saul replied. 'If the killer left any other evidence, the rain took it. Now, unless you have any other questions, I need to get back to my student and our patients.'

Strocchi nodded. 'The famiglia have been told of Zamora's death. I'm sure they will send someone to claim him for burial soon.'

'Good.'

Aldo handed the borrowed cloak back to Saul. 'Grazie for lending me this.' Saul folded it over his arm before retrieving his satchel from the floor. On his way out the doctor paused to rest a hand on Strocchi's shoulder.

'I hope you find whoever did this and stop them hurting anyone else.'

When Saul had gone Aldo studied the corpse, picturing how Zamora was killed, what was done to his body. Garrotting was not an uncommon method of murder, though in most cases the victim fought back, injuring their fingers and hands. If the killer had taken Zamora's senses with drink, a sleeping draught or by some other means, why garrotte him? And then there were the other things Saul had found. 'What do you think is the significance of cutting the tongue in two?' Aldo asked. 'I've never seen a wound like that, but it must mean something.'

'Not here,' Strocchi said. 'I can't talk about this here.' His face was still pale, hands trembling at his sides. He seemed ready to collapse if they stayed any longer.

'Then let's go outside.' Aldo ushered Strocchi from the room. The last thing he needed was to spend any more time near the body. After pausing to thank the nuns and give them coin for cleaning the room, Aldo led Strocchi from the ospedale. Once they were in the open air, Strocchi's spirits seemed to return; the colour came back to his face, at least.

'I thought my belly stronger,' he said, 'but seeing what they did . . .'

'Consider yourself fortunate to still be shocked by such things,' Aldo replied. 'Come with me. I know a tavern nearby where we can get a drink and some decent food.'

Strocchi pressed a hand to his belly. 'I don't think I could eat. Not after that.'

'Then you drink, and I'll eat. I haven't had anything since before curfew last night.'

Chapter Six

The contessa was far from impressed. She had been expecting an imminent arrival ever since Zilio's letter had arrived. The fact that it was brought by a messenger while the city was under curfew offered proof enough of the urgency involved, never mind the messenger being wounded by the night patrol. Zilio's words made it seem that he could reach the palazzo at any moment. Instead, she had wasted far too much of the day waiting for him, like some witless girl expecting her beloved.

It would not do.

Finally, her maggiordomo entered the salone.

'He's here?'

A nod.

'About time. Tell him . . .' She paused, letting a smirk play across her lips. 'Please tell our guest that I am busy changing. Naturally, I wish to look my best for him.'

'Naturally,' Pozzo agreed. 'Should I send in one of your maids?'

'Whatever for? No, our guest has forced me to forego all other pleasures while awaiting his arrival. Now he may do the same a while for me.'

The maggiordomo smiled. 'Very good, Contessa.'

Those were not words often used in the same sentence when others discussed her, but that was of little consequence. 'I'll ring when I'm ready,' she said.

Pozzo withdrew.

It was quite some time before she summoned him back, but nowhere near as long as Signor Gonzalo Zilio of Venice had kept her waiting. The contessa rose as Pozzo announced her guest, letting a regretful sadness settle on her face.

Zilio strode into the salone, bowing low enough for the contessa to see how thin the hair had become on his scalp. Directing those who spied for Venice in the regions south of the city was clearly taking a toll on Zilio. His face was haggard, his tunic and hose dusty. He must have ridden to Florence rather than come in a carriage. That spoke of haste and hurry, as did the letter Zilio had sent ahead of himself. The Council of Ten did not usually permit any such communications without the use of elaborate ciphers composed from signs, geometric symbols and Greek letters. Whatever Zilio needed to say, it was urgent.

'My dear Gonzalo,' the contessa gushed, hurrying over to clasp him by the hands. They were sweaty and unpleasant, much like his face, and he stank of horse. 'I must apologize for keeping you waiting. Please, please, tell me you are willing to forgive me.'

'I . . .' Zilio frowned, undone by her sudden closeness. 'Of course, Contessa.'

'Grazie,' she cooed, all gratitude and grovelling, 'grazie mille. Please, come have a seat with me. You must be exhausted if you rode from Venice. That's two days on a horse.'

'If not more,' he replied, letting himself be guided to one of the chairs in the centre of the salone. The contessa sank into the seat beside him, saying nothing so he would continue. 'But I came by way of Bologna, where I had a matter requiring my presence.'

Bologna. Ugh. The contessa had little time for that city or its tiresome boasts about having the world's oldest accademia. The people there were so proud of the Due Torri, those twin towers of ugly stone that stabbed at the sky. Hardly a match for the Duomo. But Zilio going there first told her more about his mission. Venice's representative in Bologna, a self-important oaf called Tito Grossolano, had long expressed an interest in succeeding the contessa's late husband as spymaster in Florence.

'That matter also concerns you, Contessa,' Zilio went on, shifting uncomfortably in his seat. She let the Venetian squirm. There was no value in making this any easier for him. 'It is some time since your husband . . . since the count died. Naturally, the Council did not wish to impose upon your grief, so I suggested to them that the question of how best to find a successor for his work be set aside. Not long after that you stepped into the count's place, supplying reports which were almost the equal of those he had sent. At my behest it was agreed that you be allowed to continue this work for a while.'

Allowed! The arrogance of Zilio and men like him, believing that a woman needed their permission to do anything. Allowed! The notion that her reports were almost the equal of those made by her late husband almost made the contessa laugh. She was the one who had been gathering intelligence here in Florence all along, sending it to Venice in her husband's name. Any reports written by him would have been empty pages without her knowledge, her sources, or her insights into the city. Allowed! What nonsense, what folly.

Suppressing her fury, the contessa dabbed at the corners of her eyes with a cloth, as if close to tears. 'Yes . . . you have been very kind to me . . . so very kind and understanding . . .'

Zilio had the palle not to crumple at the sight of a woman near to crying, which was more than could be said for many of his sex. 'Were it up to me,' he said, 'that arrangement would have continued. But there have been changes within the Council, and these have now brought a shift in determining who should supply it with regular intelligence reports.'

There it was. There was the knife, waiting to be plunged between her shoulder blades. The contessa feigned surprise, her mouth forming a small 'oh', but she had long suspected – indeed, had long expected – this day would come. Just as she had several sources within the court of Duke Cosimo de' Medici, so she maintained fruitful contacts close to the Council of Ten in Venice. Her late husband had been a true Venetian and taught her the tongue of that city when they lived by the lagoon after their wedding. That enabled the contessa to charm those who assisted the Council, giving her intimate access to its internal machinations.

She had heard the Council was establishing a special tribunal of three men – two ordinary Council members, and one drawn from among the Doge's six ducal councillors. The Inquisitorie di Stato was to take primary responsibility for the protection of Venice's secrets, gathering counterintelligence on its enemies and allies. In the past the Council had relied on three groups of sources for such matters: ambassadors, diplomats and other state officials; Venetian merchants working outside the city; and those it deemed to be amateur spies.

The count had moved to Florence in pursuit of business, while she was the one who had gathered secrets on behalf of Venice. His death meant the Council now considered her intelligence the work of an amateur, despite the fact that it was at least the equal of what had been sent before. It seemed this new tribunal no longer wished to rely on those it deemed insufficiently important or significant. People such as her.

'May I ask who is to represent the Council here in Florence?' she said, letting a flutter of idle curiosity cross her face. Best not to appear too eager.

'That is why I stopped at Bologna on my way here,' Zilio replied.

So, it was to be Grossolano. On the three occasions the contessa had received reports from people unfortunate enough to spend time with the man, Grossolano had proven himself to be arrogant, insulting to any women he mentioned or saw, and unable to stop preening at his own majesty.

Zilio confirmed her suspicions, adding that Grossolano would arrive in Florence the next day. 'I hope you will be so kind as to introduce him to your late husband's sources of intelligence?'

The contessa smiled. Where possible, it was always better to answer a question with another question. There was little value in proffering an answer when nothing was being given in return. 'Surely a spymaster with the skills of Signor Grossolano would wish to use his own wits and resources to gather information for this new tribunal?'

'Yes, but until he is able to do so . . .'

That could be a long wait.

'It would be helpful for him to call on the count's contacts within the ducal court.' Zilio smiled, reaching across to pat her hand. 'I'm sure you understand.'

She understood perfectly well. Grossolano was as inept and ineffective as she suspected, but he possessed an ally within the Council or its new tribunal who had decided he should be given her prized post of Venetian spymaster here in Florence. Bad enough that she was being overlooked for an oaf such as Grossolano, but they also expected her to hand him the names of those within the ducal court it had taken years to nurture and cultivate as sources.

No.

If Grossolano was dying of thirst, she would not spit in his mouth.

But there was no sport in admitting that to Zilio.

He would find out soon enough.

The contessa rested her other hand atop that of her visitor. 'Nothing would give me greater pleasure,' she whispered, letting her voice sound like a new bride on her wedding night discovering the joys of a hard cazzo well used. 'When may I expect him?'

Zilio's shoulders ceased their hunching, his body relaxing. 'Tomorrow, I believe. I suggested he come here first, so you might advise him on suitable accommodation, the best places to eat and to be seen. That sort of thing.'

'Of course,' she lied. 'I can hardly wait.'

The tavern was hidden in an alley halfway between Santa Maria Nuova and the Podestà. Strocchi feared it would be like Zoppo's hovel, which served good information and the worst wine in the city. But when Aldo led him inside, Strocchi saw the tavern was warm and clean, with people eating and drinking at every table.

There was a familiar, tangy aroma in the air that Strocchi recognized; it was the smell of his mama's cooking. But the buxom woman behind the bar was certainly not his mama. She bustled over to greet Aldo, embracing him as an old friend. 'We haven't seen you in months,' she said, a smile on her face. 'Where have you been hiding?'

'Night patrols,' Aldo replied. 'Is the private room free?'

'For you it is.' She studied Strocchi. 'Who's your friend?'

'This is Carlo. He's an officer with the Otto, so be careful what you say.'

The woman nodded to Strocchi. 'I'm Signora Sifanto. Call me Letta.' She led them to a door behind the bar. Opening it revealed a cosy room with a table, four chairs and several lanterns already lit. 'Nobody will disturb you here. I'll bring food and wine.'

'I'm not hungry—' Strocchi said.

'Nonsense,' Letta replied, pushing him in. 'You look as pale as the sky today; a strong wind could knock you over.' Aldo followed Strocchi into the private room while Letta scurried away to serve another customer.

'She's worse than my mama,' Strocchi said.

'Then her heart is in the right place,' Aldo replied, closing the door. They sank into chairs either side of the table. 'Carlo, I'm sorry for this morning, for not—'

Strocchi held up a hand. 'Forgive those who trespass against us, as Our Lord says.'

'Would Zamora's famiglia agree with that?'

'No, I'm sure they wouldn't. The grief his sister has already known . . .' Strocchi recounted what he had learned about the dead man. 'His business partner says Zamora made friends, not enemies. The victim was quiet and careful, with no interest in acquiring power. His only disagreement was with the Church after what happened to his nephew, Marsilio.'

Aldo sat back, rubbing a hand across the stubble on his jawline. 'What about the partner, Empoli? Does he benefit from this murder?'

'No. Zamora's half goes to Tullia, his sister. Empoli fears the business will suffer without Zamora as he was the one who dealt with customers. There is no obvious reason for Empoli to want his partner dead, and no advantage arising from the murder.'

The door opened and Letta brought a tray laden with steaming bowls, a jug of wine and two cups. 'My best stew. I'll be back with some bread,' she promised, closing the door on her way out. Aldo poured two cups of wine before putting a bowl in front of Strocchi.

'I'm not hungry,' Strocchi insisted, pushing the stew to one side.

'Your loss,' Aldo replied, lifting his bowl to sup from it. 'What about Empoli?' he asked between mouthfuls of stew. 'Could he and Zamora have been more than partners?'

'I don't think so. Empoli has three daughters.'

'Plenty of men stray from marriage, and not always to the bed of another woman.'

Strocchi knew that was right. Before coming to Florence, he'd had no experience of men who took their pleasures in such ways. It broke the city's laws and the law of God, yet this did not stop that happening, just as laws and commandments didn't prevent murder. 'Nonetheless, I do not believe Zamora was killed by or for his business partner. Empoli was home all last night, I stopped at his palazzo to confirm that with his servants.'

'So where did Zamora go to get himself killed?'

The aroma rising from the stew was making Strocchi's belly rumble. This was what he had smelled earlier. It was tempting but he didn't want to start retching again. He took a sip of wine instead. 'Zamora sent a messenger to his maggiordomo not long before curfew to say he was staying the night at Palazzo Empoli. But Empoli's servants denied that was true.'

'Meaning someone sent a message to ensure Zamora's staff and famiglia would not worry,' Aldo said, finishing his stew as Letta brought in half a loaf of bread.

'You're done with that already?' she said.

Aldo offered her the empty bowl. 'Got any more?'

'Not if you come so late in the day.' Letta raised her eyebrows at Strocchi. His bowl was still full. 'If you're not going to eat that . . .'

Strocchi hesitated. 'Actually, I might.' He broke off a piece of bread, dipping that in his bowl before tasting it. Aldo was right, the stew was very good. 'Yes, I will.'

Letta left, closing the door once more. Strocchi tore more

bread from the loaf, using it to soak up the stew, while Aldo poured more wine. 'I did learn a few things this morning,' he said, 'mostly confirming what you were told. Zamora was both honest and decent in his business, willing to forgive the failings of others.'

'Not something you often hear when discussing members of the wool merchants' guild,' Strocchi said between mouthfuls.

'Indeed. Zamora preferred the company of men, but he was not one of those fools who liked to go to via tra' Pellicciai in search of excitement and get themselves a beating instead.'

Strocchi had arrested some of those men when he was still a constable. Their regret had been as obvious as their bruises, but it didn't stop them returning to that notorious street.

'And attacks on such men have not been happening more often,' Aldo continued. 'You were right, Carlo. I was jumping from one stone to another without proof.'

Strocchi nodded. Aldo admitting his mistake was gratifying. 'The truth is we can't be certain of anything yet. We don't even know if Zamora was killed where you found him.'

'I suspect the murder happened elsewhere. Killing Zamora in the largest piazza in the city, even during curfew, would be very bold. If Saul is right about the tongue being cut in two after death, it would be easier to murder Zamora and do what they did elsewhere, somewhere private – and then leave the body in the piazza afterwards.'

That made sense. 'You found Zamora outside where the Senate meets. That might be significant . . . but his sister and business partner didn't mention him being active there. I'll ask Empoli about that, or Zamora's maggiordomo. Best to leave his sister to grieve.' Strocchi mopped up the last of his stew. 'So, who else could have a reason to kill Zamora?'

'I'm not sure,' Aldo said. 'We may have been looking at his murder the wrong way.'

Not wanting to speak with his mouth full, Strocchi arched an eyebrow at Aldo.

'Good and blameless men are killed as often as those who break the law,' he went on. 'Perhaps the reason for this murder comes not from Zamora, but his murderer.'

'I hope not; that will make finding whoever did this far harder.' The two of them fell silent, murmurs and laughter from the tavern seeping into the private room.

Aldo put a hand over his mouth but couldn't stifle a yawn. 'Sorry. Not used to working in the day anymore, not after being on patrol all night.'

'Do you need to rest?'

'No, not yet.'

'Good. Let's consider all we know about what the killer did to Zamora. You found his body posed like Christ on the cross.'

'Yes. Then there is the ash on Zamora's forehead, and what was done to his tongue.' Aldo sipped his wine. 'Cutting that in two . . . are they saying Zamora was a liar?'

'Only if the killing was about him. It could signify something else.' What that might be escaped Strocchi. The killer was showing them something, offering clues, but their meaning remained hidden. 'The Latin words on that page inside Zamora's tunic . . .'

'*Mando vobis*,' Aldo said. 'I command you.' He shuddered a little.

'What's wrong?'

'The Latin, it reminded me of the purgatorial sermons I had to endure as a boy. Every Sunday the famiglia Fioravanti crossed the street from its palazzo for Mass in Santa Croce. I was only the bastardo, but Papa insisted I stand alongside him in church.'

He stifled another yawn. 'Staying awake was a challenge then, too, but the droning voice of the priests made it far harder. I'm sure the phrase *mando vobis* comes from one of the services.'

Similar thoughts had occurred to Strocchi. The ash, the Latin phrase, Zamora's tongue being cut in two . . . Put them together and the intense aroma of incense wasn't far away. 'You believe that faith may be part of this?'

'Let's say I suspect it,' Aldo replied.

'If so, it might be worth talking to the priest who exorcized Zamora's nephew. The victim lost his faith due to what happened with Marsilio.'

Aldo yawned again. 'Do you know where the exorcism took place?'

'Last year in the Church of San Felice.'

'That's in Oltrarno, not far from where I sleep. I could go there on my way home—'

'Better if we both go,' Strocchi said. 'Tomorrow, in the morning.' Aldo appeared to be penitent for following his own path earlier, but that didn't mean he would always do as he was told. That trust would take some time to be rebuilt.

'Agreed.' Aldo's eyelids were drooping, his head nodding forward.

'Get some sleep,' Strocchi urged. 'I'll report what we've found to Bindi. We can start again first thing at the Podestà.' Nodding, Aldo pulled a bulging pouch from his tunic and left a generous handful of coin on the table. 'Where did you get all of that?' Strocchi asked.

Aldo recounted confiscating the coin from Freccia. 'I'll walk with you to the Podestà,' he said, pushing back his chair to stand. 'Be careful what you tell the segretario, especially if he asks how long it will take to find Zamora's killer. Whatever you say to Bindi will be reported word for word to the duke. Fail to catch the killer soon enough to satisfy Cosimo, and Bindi will blame us for making him look bad in front of the duke.'

Strocchi grimaced. Most of the murders he had investigated since becoming an officer were simple matters, of little interest to the city's ruler. But he knew what happened when the segretario lost his temper with officers of the Otto. That was how Aldo had been demoted to constable. 'I'll keep my report brief.'

'Good.' Aldo led Strocchi from the tavern, thanking Letta as they left.

Outside was cold after the warmth of the side room, the best of the day's light already gone. The nights were getting longer, and the days colder as winter approached. Strocchi shivered as they strode towards the Podestà, a chill breeze cutting through his tunic. The voice of a priest speaking Latin echoed from inside a church as they passed its open doors.

'Let's hope our suspicions about faith being part of this are incorrect,' Aldo said.

'Why?'

'Investigating a murder that involves the Church never ends well in Florence.'

Chapter Seven

Aldo did not know the man waiting by the Podestà gates, but the clothing of a ducal servant was unmistakeable. Short of stature and harassed of face, he carried all the officious anger of those used to getting their own way. One of the guards standing sentry pointed at Aldo and Strocchi as they approached the entrance. 'That's him.'

The servant strode towards them, his impatience evident. 'Are you Cesare Aldo?' he demanded of Strocchi in a voice brimming with accusation.

'No,' Aldo said. 'I am.'

'You are to accompany me to Palazzo Medici,' the servant announced.

Strocchi glanced at Aldo who shrugged back.

'Now,' the servant snapped.

'I'll see what this is about,' Aldo told Strocchi. 'Go inside and make your report. Don't tell Bindi I've been summoned to the ducal palazzo, otherwise he'll demand to know why and punish you for not having an answer. Say I've gone to the bordello to sleep. If I'm not here first thing tomorrow, you'll have to get someone else to help with the case.' Turning back the way he'd come, Aldo strolled north. 'Shall we go?' he called.

The servant stamped after him, muttering and cursing. 'You kept me waiting for more than an hour. Nobody knew where you were.'

Aldo ignored the accusation. 'Why am I being summoned?'

'You will be told that when you arrive.'

'Meaning you don't know.'

The servant went back to cursing and muttering.

The curve of the Duomo appeared between tall buildings lining the road north. This late in the day its cupola tiles normally became a vibrant orange in the afternoon sun, but today they were as dull as the sky overhead. Florence never looked its best in autumn.

'Who sent for me?' Aldo asked, hoping to unlock a more helpful answer.

'I'm not authorized to share that information,' the servant replied.

'Did someone forbid you from telling me?'

'I . . .' The servant stopped himself from saying any more.

Aldo suspected there was no great secret. Instead, a frustrated, petty little man was using the only power he had – withholding a simple truth – to exact revenge for being made to wait outside the Podestà. So be it. Let this impotent functionary savour his triumph. It would be all the satisfaction he knew, judging by the sour face and sourer attitude.

After skirting the Duomo they turned north once more, Palazzo Medici now within sight. Aldo slowed his stroll still further, forcing the servant to check his own pace. Two could play at being petty. When finally they reached the ducal residence, Aldo quickened his stride to march inside, the servant scurrying after him.

'Where now?' Aldo demanded.

'I will let them know you have arrived,' the servant said, keeping his secret as long as he could. But Aldo saw him hurry upstairs to the middle level where Duke Cosimo kept a private ufficio, his personal staff working close by. That suggested the summons came from someone of importance within the court, perhaps even the duke himself.

Aldo had met Cosimo de' Medici several times, almost all of them before he became ruler of Florence. The first was when Cosimo was a baby and Aldo a mercenary, riding under the command of the child's father, the celebrated condottiere Giovanni dalle Bande Nere. Giovanni had returned home to his Tuscan estate after a battle, bringing his men at arms. Years later, Aldo went to the Medici castello at Trebbio, seeking refuge for the night after being attacked by bandits on the road from Bologna. There he met Cosimo again, then a youth of seventeen raised by his implacable mother, Maria Salviati. Made a widow by war, she fought for her son to be recognized in Florence. Maria had Cosimo educated for the court and tutored in the ways of intrigue, yet mother and son were still stuck in their crumbling country home when Aldo arrived. Cosimo appeared strong of body and quick of mind, but the same was true of many others. Maria asked Aldo to use any influence he had to speak up for Cosimo, proof of how she feared for her son's prospects.

Nine days later, Cosimo was chosen to lead Florence after the murder of his cousin, Duke Alessandro de' Medici. It was startling how fast circumstances could change, for good or ill. One moment there seemed little hope for the young Medici, but fate or fortune or God had other plans. Aldo had lost his faith long ago and found it difficult to believe there was any reason or guiding force behind events. Better to accept the tide of history for whatever it brought, and endeavour not to be swept away when the deluge came.

Aldo rubbed his eyes, weary from lack of sleep and tired to the bone. Every part of him aching for bed. It must be a full night and day since he'd last slept, if not longer. The sky overhead was darkening, twilight sipping the dull grey clouds. A chill wind whipped through the courtyard, making him shiver. Or perhaps it was fear causing his skin to resemble that of a plucked bird? An unexpected summons to the ducal palazzo was liable to have such an effect.

The servant returned, scuttling down the stairs and across the courtyard. 'This way,' he hissed, gesturing for Aldo to follow.

'Not until you tell me who I'm meeting,' Aldo replied, folding his arms.

'I should have thought that was obvious,' another male voice interjected. Francesco Campana emerged from the shadows at the edge of the courtyard, dismissing the servant with a snap of his hand. Campana was private segretario to Cosimo, one of two men fulfilling that role. But Campana was reputed to have the young duke's ear. He had also been segretario to Alessandro; the fact that Cosimo kept Campana was proof of his effectiveness. Dressed in sober black robes, Campana cut a severe figure, but for once he bore a hint of a smile.

Aldo bowed, showing Campana the respect he deserved. 'In that case, may I ask why the duke has asked to see me? He must know I am merely a constable of the Otto now.'

'Of course. But Cosimo places little importance on such things. He prefers to judge men by their words and actions, not their rank or title.' Campana stalked towards the staircase. 'Come, the duke does not like to be kept waiting.'

Strocchi did not consider himself quick to anger. If anything, he was liable to keep such things inside longer than he should. Better to let it out, Tomasia always told him, otherwise the anger eats away at you. But holding his frustration in check was necessary when reporting to the Otto's segretario. Bindi was a difficult man to serve, quick to find fault and slow to praise. Antagonizing him in his ufficio would only make matters worse.

But the segretario did not make such restraint easy.

'So, you and Aldo have spent an entire day discovering nothing,' Bindi announced.

'I would not describe our investigation as—'

'Are you saying I'm a fool?' The segretario leaned forward in his high-back wooden chair, glaring at Strocchi. 'Are you?'

'Of course not, sir, I simply meant—'

'I will not be corrected,' Bindi snapped. 'Your own words confirm what I said. You have deemed it unlikely that either Zamora's famiglia or his business partner had any part in his murder. You have no suspects, no witnesses, and no clear motive for why this citizen was strangled and his body dumped in front of Palazzo della Signoria. Is any of that wrong?'

Strocchi resisted the urge to reply that the victim was garrotted, not strangled. Best to stay silent and let Bindi's tempest blow itself out. He would run out of words – eventually.

But the ranting went on for quite some time, the segretario slamming a pudgy hand down on the table in front of him. The blow was so heavy it almost overturned an inkwell.

'Where is Aldo?' Bindi demanded after a while. 'He begged for the chance to assist you with this investigation. Can't he bring himself to share the blame for your failings?'

Strocchi counted to five before answering, another strategia suggested by Tomasia. What he wouldn't give for her to be here, telling Bindi where to put his words. Hopefully she was feeling better . . . 'Aldo was exhausted after being on patrol last night and working with me through the day. I sent him home to rest.'

'Home? You mean that bordello where he sleeps?' Bindi's face soured. He made no effort to hide his feelings, or his anger. Perhaps it was a privilege that came with the post.

'Yes, sir.'

'Have you anything else to tell me? Anything I can report to the duke that does not make this court appear utterly unable to find a murderer?'

'No, sir.'

'Then get out of my sight.' Bindi waved a dismissive hand. Strocchi did as he was told, grateful to escape further scolding from the segretario. But, inevitably, Bindi had a final insult to hurl as Strocchi reached the ufficio door. 'One last thing—'

Strocchi stopped, turning to face his tormentor. 'Yes, sir?'

'I expect a far more successful report by this time tomorrow. If not, I shall have to give this investigation to someone more capable. Those officers who are unable to fulfil their duties cannot expect to remain officers for long. Do I make myself clear?'

Strocchi nodded. One. Two. Three. Four. Five. 'Yes, sir. Completely clear.'

Aldo was led into the ducal ufficio at the rear of Palazzo Medici. He had been here before, back when Cosimo's cousin was still ruler of Florence. But the imposing table and ornate throne favoured by Alessandro were gone, replaced by a simpler wooden table and chair. Cosimo was sitting to one side, sifting through papers. In the past this room had been a place for Alessandro to receive guests and enjoy his command over them. It was a true ufficio now, somewhere for the duke to work and make decisions about the city.

Cosimo had changed too.

Gone was the youth of seventeen whom Aldo had last met, a little callow and uncertain. The duke was now twenty, more muscular of build, his chestnut hair cut close to the scalp. There was no sign of the recent illness reputed to have been smallpox. He wore a black and crimson doublet, a short cloak trimmed with sable over his shoulders for warmth. Cosimo put down his papers, not bothering with a stratagemma as Bindi would do. The duke fixed Aldo with a shrewd gaze. 'Tell me, how long is it since you were last here?'

'Almost three years, Your Grace,' Aldo replied, bowing.

'January the eleventh, if I recall correctly. A few days after I was elected leader by the Senate.'

'Indeed.'

'You looked tired, Aldo.'

'Segretario Bindi has had me on night patrols. I found a murdered man's corpse in Piazza della Signoria not long before the end of curfew this morning. I've been helping investigate the matter ever since.'

'Niccolò Zamora?'

Aldo nodded. Was that why he'd been summoned? Did the duke want to know more about the killing than Bindi had revealed in his report? Or was there an aspect to the case that drew Cosimo's interest, something yet to emerge? It was said he had the finest web of spies in Florence and far beyond, informing him of potential threats long before such news reached him by official means. This made sense, considering how many of his predecessors had been attacked or murdered over the years. But if the duke took a strong interest in Zamora's murder, it would complicate the investigation considerably.

'The segretario will doubtless report all progress on that to me tomorrow,' Cosimo said. 'No, I summoned you here because there is another matter we need to discuss. Tell me, what do you know about the Contessa Valentine Coltello?'

'A little, Your Grace. I have not encountered her myself, but I have heard about the contessa from others.' He glanced at Campana; was this the reason for the summons? But the administrative segretario remained impassive, standing to one side of the duke.

'And what do they say?' Cosimo persisted.

'That she is a true Florentine, despite having first appeared in the city on the count's arm some three – no, four – years ago. Unlike her late husband, she has the voice of someone who was raised here. Her command of the Tuscan tongue is further proof of those origins.'

'Yet you say she only appeared in Florence four years ago . . .'

'The count moved here from Venice with his wife in 1535, supposedly to establish himself as a merchant.' Cosimo and Campana exchanged a glance, but its meaning was unclear. 'I say supposedly because he spent a fruitless few months attempting to recruit informants, leaving a trail of coin behind him. I believe Count Coltello was, in fact, a spy for the Council of Ten, the Venetian authority for the command, direction and deployment of spies.' Aldo smiled. 'However, the count was not very accomplished.'

'In what way?' Campana asked.

'A good spy passes unnoticed. A bad one draws the eye.'

'Fascinating,' Cosimo interjected, 'but I asked what you knew about the contessa.'

'I suspect she is the true source of Florentine intelligence for the Council,' Aldo said. 'Her husband was merely a distraction, sent out to draw the eye while his wife found and employed those who could be useful to her. The count died a year ago in unexplained circumstances – a fatal fall on a hunting trip outside the city walls, it was said at the time. I was on night patrol so heard no more about it.'

'If the contessa only came to Florence four years ago,' Campana said, 'how—'

'How can she be a true Florentine?' Aldo smiled again. 'I would guess that she was born and raised here but later went to Venice, either with her famiglia or by other means. There she caught the eye of the count or was betrothed to him.' He stopped himself saying that young women often had little choice in such decisions, especially when being wed to far older men. It was only a few months since the duke's own marriage. That had been a political union, not a bond of love, but at least Cosimo's wife Eleonora was only three years his junior. The gap in age between Count Coltello and the contessa had been closer to twenty years. 'May I ask why Your Grace wishes to hear what I know about her?'

Cosimo nodded to Campana, who left the room but returned moments later. Beside him was a red-faced man of at least forty wearing the clothes of a minor ducal official. 'Go on, Dandolo,' Campana urged. 'Tell us all what you told me.'

'Y-Your Grace,' Dandolo said, bowing to Cosimo. 'Yesterday I was invited to dine with the contessa at her palazzo. There were several other guests present, but as curfew approached the contessa asked me to stay a while longer and offer my thoughts on several tapestries that had belonged to her late husband.'

Aldo listened as Dandolo described what had happened, the contessa's request that he send her letters detailing events at Palazzo Medici. It sounded a crude approach, not worthy of the woman Aldo had heard about from his own informants. Why would she make so obvious an attempt, one so likely to be reported? Unless that was the reason behind it . . .

Dandolo went on, detailing his agonies after leaving Palazzo Coltello about whether to tell Campana what had occurred. Tiring of Dandolo's voice, Aldo took the chance to ask a question when the court official paused for breath. 'At what point during this long evening did the contessa request that you send her these letters?'

Dandolo frowned, unused to being interrupted, it seemed. Aldo pitied all those who had to work with him. The contessa must possess the patience of a mountain to have borne his company for most of a night. 'It was after her maggiordomo interrupted us.'

'You didn't mention that before,' Campana said.

'This was not long before dawn,' Dandolo replied. 'She left the salone. I crept to the door to hear what she and her maggiordomo discussed in case they were talking about me.'

Aldo suppressed the urge to roll his eyes at such arrogance. 'And?'

'I couldn't catch all that passed between them, but I heard talk of a messenger who had been injured by the night patrol. The rest was murmurs and whispers.'

That solved the question of what had happened to the curfew breaker Aldo had cut with his stiletto. They had been a messenger on their way to the contessa, hoping curfew would help conceal their passage. Whatever they carried must have been urgent to take such a risk.

'Is there anything else you forgot?' Campana demanded.

Dandolo shook his head. 'No, sir.'

The duke nodded to Campana who led Dandolo away. Cosimo waited until his segretario returned before speaking. 'And what do you make of that?'

Aldo described his bloody encounter with the messenger. 'The contessa only asked Dandolo to send her letters after reading whatever message was brought to her. We cannot be certain one event caused the next, but . . . Her attempt to recruit Dandolo was rushed. Either she was forced into it, or else this was a ruse designed to prompt his reporting of it.'

'She wanted us to know about the approach to Dandolo?' Campana asked.

'It's as Aldo said earlier,' the duke replied. 'A good spy passes unnoticed. By making us aware of Dandolo the contessa hopes we will not search for the other spies she has here.'

Aldo smiled. 'Is that why you summoned me, Your Grace? To uncover anyone else among your staff and servants who is supplying her with secrets?'

'Campana will be making those inquiries,' Cosimo said. 'No, I wish you to approach the contessa yourself, and offer her your services as an informant.'

'Ahh.' Aldo was going to say more but surprise seemed to have stolen his words.

'Tell her that you are aggrieved at having been demoted to constable and banished to the night patrol. This will explain why you are willing to betray the Otto and it has the virtue of being true. I need you to discover what she is doing, why this abrupt change in strategia.' The duke rose, strolling to open shutters overlooking the rear of Palazzo Medici. 'All city states spy on one another, that is to be expected. But my own spy who was close to the Council of Ten reported that the contessa was one of Venice's most effective resources.'

Aldo noted the duke's choice of words – 'was close'. That suggested whoever had sent reports from Venice was no longer doing so. Was the contessa responsible for that?

'You may tell nobody else about this task,' the duke added. 'It must remain secret. You shall continue your duties for the Otto but will also undertake whatever is necessary to win favour with Coltello. Report whatever you learn to Campana.'

'I understand,' Aldo replied.

'If you succeed, I will ensure you are restored to your rightful rank of officer and rewarded for the information you supply. But, if you are injured or taken, my segretario shall deny all knowledge of this discussion.'

Aldo nodded. His loss would be of no consequence or cost to the duke.

Campana cleared his throat. 'Any questions?'

'One. Why was I chosen for this?'

Cosimo glanced over a shoulder at Aldo. 'My mother suggested you. The contessa has quite a way with foolish men like Dandolo, whose heads are easily turned and whose cazzi are easily tempted. I'm told you are less likely to succumb to such a woman.'

Aldo kept his face empty. Maria Salviati had learned he preferred the company of men and sought to use that as both threat and tether, making him act at her command. But Aldo had discovered something of her own behaviour that could have proven almost as ruinous, and employed that to defend himself. Now, almost three years later, she was twisting the knife and there was nothing he could do about it.

Strocchi stalked west from the Podestà, fuming all the way home. It was infuriating enough that Bindi was correct in saying the investigation had uncovered little so far. But threatening a demotion if progress was not made by the end of the next day . . . that was too much.

The temptation to tell Bindi exactly what everyone thought of him was strong, yet it would do no good. A moment of pleasure perhaps, but that satisfaction would be replaced with a need to find another post at another court. The segretario was a vindictive creature, he would do everything possible to step in Strocchi's path. Without a job, without the coin it brought – not to mention the bounties and rewards for catching fugitives – there was no way he, Bianca, Tomasia and the little one she was carrying could afford their home.

More than once, Aldo had described being an officer of the Otto as a gilded cage; now Strocchi understood what it meant. While he remained in the service of the court his famiglia knew warmth and comfort. But if he lashed out at Bindi all that would be lost. They might still be together but with nowhere to sleep, no place to call their own, and little chance of knowing peace or safety. It was a trap.

He might not be able to escape immediately, but there must be a way out. Talking with Tomasia would help. She had a gift for making him see other possibilities, for helping to find another path. Strocchi offered up a prayer to the twilight sky, thanking the Lord for bringing her into his world. Without Tomasia he would not know all the happiness and joy she created in his life. Nor would he be a father, another thing that made him smile, however painful the day had been. Famiglia was hope in the face of darkness.

Strocchi stopped at the stairs that led up to his home, listening. From all around he could hear people – talking, laughing, some shouting, murmuring. These were the ordinary citizens of Florence, living their lives and praying for a better day tomorrow. They deserved to be safe, to be protected. That was what the Otto could do if it chose. That was what he could do for them and for his own famiglia – Bindi or no Bindi.

Leaving his worries outside, Strocchi hurried up the stairs to his front door. But when he went in, Tomasia and Bianca were not the only ones waiting.

'Mama? B-but . . .' Strocchi spluttered. 'What are you doing here?'

Chapter Eight

❧

Thursday, October 30th 1539

*A*ldo woke with no recollection of where he was. Weak light seeped through shutters above the bed, while gentle voices murmured beyond the door. There was no one by him in the bed, and only his clothes were strewn across the floor. Bells were chiming in the distance, but why? Those voices, he recognized those voices . . . Palle!

This was Saul's bed, and the bells were chiming for the end of curfew. Aldo cursed himself for not waking sooner. Normally he rose before dawn, a habit borne from his time as a mercenary. But after so long on night patrols and working through the previous day . . . He should have left by now, slipping out the back door before anyone was awake.

Aldo scrambled from the bed, snatching at his tunic and hose. They were ripe with body odour, no surprise after wearing and working in them for a night and a day. No time to wash, he had to leave now. After pulling on his hose Aldo crept to the door, listening to the voices beyond it. Saul, and a woman . . . Rebecca Levi, his student. Saul had taken her on about two years before, training Rebecca to replace him one day as physician to the Jewish commune. What would happen if she found out about him and Saul? A shiver ran through Aldo, and not just because it was cold in the bedchamber.

Someone was coming up the stairs. It sounded like Saul, but Aldo stepped behind the door in case he was wrong. It swung open and Saul peered in. 'Are you up yet?'

'Nearly,' Aldo said softly, emerging from behind the door.

Saul was fully dressed and ready for the day, yarmulke already on his head. 'When you are, come downstairs.' He sniffed the air. 'You might want to wash first.'

'What about Rebecca?' Aldo whispered. 'Does she . . . ?'

'I've already told her what happened. You came by as curfew was near, asking a question about that body I examined for the Otto. You were dozing at my table, so I sent you up here to rest. I slept downstairs last night.' Saul moved closer to whisper in Aldo's ear. 'Regrettably, that's all true. Our first night together in months and you spent it snoring.'

'I don't snore.'

'The rafters would not agree with you, my friend.'

Strocchi had never realized his mama was so loud. Back home in the village of Ponte a Signa she was known for having a big spirit, always being hopeful, always full of joy. It was said if Mama Strocchi couldn't put a smile on someone's face, they were not long for this world. But in a two-room residence when others were trying to sleep, she was creating enough noise to fill the Duomo. 'Mama, you don't have to do that,' Strocchi whispered, struggling to be heard over the sound of her cleaning. 'You're our guest here.'

'Nonsense, bambino!' she shouted while scrubbing the floor with a stiff brush. 'I'm not a guest, I'm famiglia.'

'Yes, of course you are,' he said, trying to ease the brush from her grasp, 'but there's no need to do this now. It can wait until later.'

'Start each day with a clean home and the Lord smiles upon you,' Mama insisted. She swapped the brush for a broom, ready to sweep the wooden floor. 'Besides, it's my way of helping Tomasia. You can't expect her to be doing all of this while she's so sick. The poor thing needs to look after herself!'

Strocchi stepped into her path. 'She does, Mama, that's true – but her getting some rest will be a little easier if we aren't making quite so much noise, yes?'

Mama stopped. 'Oh.' She looked down at the brush. 'Oh!'

It had been like this since her arrival the previous day. If Mama wasn't cleaning, she was washing. If she wasn't washing, she was cooking. If not one thing, then another. And she never stopped talking no matter what she was doing, according to Tomasia. Yes, Mama was wonderful with little Bianca, and the two rented rooms hadn't looked this immaculate since Tomasia's pregnancy became such a burden, but still . . .

'Perhaps you could go for a walk?' Strocchi suggested. 'See some of the city.'

'Of course,' Mama replied. 'Let me fetch a shawl.'

Much as Strocchi loved his mama, her unexpected visit was all his fault. He had written her a letter about the new baby coming, and mentioned in passing how Tomasia was having a harder pregnancy. Mama couldn't read and was usually too proud to ask for help from Father Coluccio, the parish priest in Ponte a Signa. But she had taken him the most recent letter and fretted about what it said. Coluccio was coming to Florence and had offered to escort Mama to the city. How long she was staying remained unclear, and Strocchi hesitated to ask.

In the other room his two-year-old daughter was now making almost as much noise as Mama had been. 'Why don't you take Bianca too?' he asked.

'Good idea, bambino,' Mama said, pinching his cheek between her thumb and fingers.

'Please, Mama, I'm a grown man,' Strocchi protested.

'But you'll always be my little boy!'

He nodded, not wanting to contradict her. While she was getting Bianca ready in one room, he went to the other where Tomasia was in bed, facing the wall. 'Are you asleep?'

'What do you think?' she replied before rolling over.

'I'm sorry about Mama, she's . . .' He shrugged.

'She wants to help, I know she does, Carlo, but we only have the two rooms.' Her meaning was obvious. Having Mama stay with them for long was too much.

'I'll talk to her tonight,' Strocchi said. 'Find out when she is going home. I promise.'

Tomasia gave him a kiss. 'Grazie. And you look better now you've had a shave.' She kissed him again, their lips lingering—

'We're ready to go!' Mama shouted from the next room.

'I'll be right there,' Strocchi called back, rolling his eyes at Tomasia.

That made her laugh, and her laughter always lifted his spirits.

Perhaps this day wouldn't be as bad as the one before.

Instead of going north towards the Podestà when he left Saul's home, Aldo turned south. He needed fresh clothes and a wash before starting the day, especially if he was presenting himself to Contessa Coltello for potential recruitment as one of her informants.

The task set by Cosimo brought many snares. If the contessa was as accomplished a spymaster as the duke believed, that made her a very dangerous individual. Men in such positions were ruthless, willing to sacrifice anyone and anything to protect themselves. For a woman to command such a role was remarkable. Not because women lacked the necessary skills or cut-throat nature for it – Aldo had known plenty of women far more adept and vicious than their male counterparts – but because city states such as Venice and Florence habitually denied women opportunities to prove their worth. For the contessa to have succeeded in such circumstances showed she was even more formidable than the duke realized.

Then there was the secretive nature of the task, the fact that Cosimo had forbidden it being discussed with anyone but him and Campana. That meant no help could be sought from others, unless they did so unwittingly, putting most of the Otto's resources out of reach. Yes, Aldo still had the limited authority of a constable for the court, but no more than that. And then there was the need to keep what he was doing hidden from Strocchi. The two of them had managed to overcome at least some of the differences and disagreements that had sundered their friendship before. The attempt to prove Zamora's murder was linked to his preferring the company of men had been foolish, yet Strocchi seemed willing to forgive that transgression. But another unexplained disappearance would not be so easily accepted.

Aldo shook his head. No, what he was doing for the duke should not be kept from Strocchi. He would understand the need for such secrecy, too. Strocchi's moral nature lacked the flexibility of a true Florentine, but it also made him far more trustworthy.

Crossing Piazza della Passera, Aldo let himself into the bordello run by Signora Tessa Robustelli. It was closed to visitors until the middle of the day, giving the women a chance to rest. Most would still be sleeping but the yaps of tiny Piccolo meant his mistress was already bustling about. Aldo crept upstairs to his room at the rear of the bordello, not wanting to wake anyone. Stripping naked, he washed with a bowl of cold water. Aldo considered scraping a blade across his greying stubble but chose to leave it. It gave him a grizzled look, the face of a man who had stopped caring about his appearance. That could be useful with the contessa, indicating his dissatisfaction with the Otto.

After pulling on a fresh tunic and hose, Aldo dragged his good boots from beneath the bed. He'd had them made with the last reward he received while still serving as an officer. Constables had few chances to earn more than the coin they were paid, so these boots would have to last a long time. But his old pair were worn through in places and coming apart in others thanks to seventeen months trudging the streets in all weathers on night patrol.

When Aldo returned downstairs, Robustelli was waiting. She was still in her shift from bed, a shawl draped across her considerable bosom and little Piccolo tucked in one arm.

'And where have you been?' she asked, arching an eyebrow. 'You don't look like a man recovering from yet another night patrol. Far too lively for this early in the morning.'

Aldo told her about being assigned to help Strocchi find whoever killed the corpse found in Piazza della Signoria. 'That still doesn't explain where you slept last night,' she noted.

'We all have our secrets,' Aldo replied on his way to the front door.

Robustelli persisted, following him to the entrance. 'True, but that doesn't explain the young man who came here not long before curfew last night, looking for you.'

That made Aldo stop. 'What was his name?'

'Didn't give one. Didn't seem interested in any of my women, either.'

'Not everybody thinks with what is between their legs.'

'Most men do.' Piccolo yawned, earning a squeeze from Robustelli.

Aldo couldn't argue with that. 'What did this young man look like?'

'Shifty. Couldn't stand still for more than a moment. Bruises on his knuckles.'

'Was he tall? Thin? What colour was his hair?'

Robustelli closed her eyes. 'Half a head shorter than you. Had a distinctive cleft in his chin. Fair hair, but dirty and in need of a wash.'

That sounded like Freccia, but why would the thief come looking for Aldo? Their meeting the previous morning had not been on good terms. Unless Freccia had recalled something about Zamora and hoped to claim a reward for that . . .

'Did he give a reason for needing to find me?'

'Claimed he was being followed.'

'Followed?'

Robustelli nodded. 'That's what I said. Why would anybody follow that scrap of a man? Doubt he owned much more than the clothes he had on, nothing worth stealing.' She patted her tiny dog on the head. 'Piccolo gave him a nip on the ankle. That sent him away.'

'I'm sure. Did this youth say anything else before Piccolo bit him?'

'Not that I can recall. We were busy, you know how it gets here before curfew. Too many men with a belly full of wine and palle in need of emptying before they go home to their poor wives.' Robustelli smirked. 'The women were all run off their feet.'

After thanking her Aldo stepped back out onto Piazza della Passera. He could look for Freccia later. There were far more urgent things that needed to be done first.

Strocchi had thought Aldo was jesting the previous day about getting someone else to help if he didn't return from Palazzo Medici. But there was no sign of Aldo when Strocchi finally reached the Podestà after leading Mama and Bianca on a stroll through the nicer streets of the western quarter. None of the guards had seen Aldo that morning, and nobody had heard from him. Santo Spirito! Bindi was already threatening demotion unless Zamora's killer was found soon; now it seemed Aldo was pursuing his own path. Again.

Strocchi offered up a silent prayer for patience in the face of such agitazione. If the Lord could send a sign that all would be well . . . At that moment Manuffi ambled into the Podestà courtyard. He was burlier than most constables but had a good heart and a gentle manner. 'Manuffi,' Strocchi called. 'Are you busy?'

The constable shrugged, a smile creasing his bearded face. 'Do you need my help?' Where Benedetto and others complained about being asked to do their jobs, Manuffi was always eager to assist in whatever way he could. He also lacked the insistent ambition some constables possessed, forever searching for a way to usurp those above them. Manuffi was simply happy to be useful. How he came to be working for the Otto remained a mystery.

'Come with me.' Strocchi led Manuffi out of the Podestà before turning south.

'Where are we going?' the constable asked.

'Oltrarno. There is something I need to confirm at Palazzo Zamora.'

Manuffi nodded. Where others might have demanded to know more, he accepted the answer to his question as honest and true. Manuffi would never be an officer, he lacked the suspicious nature required for such work, but he seemed happy with whatever task he was given. And he had a gift for asking obvious questions that evaded other minds. Strocchi led Manuffi west, crossing the wide expanse of Piazza della Signoria. The sky was a dismal grey, the clouds threatening rain later in the day.

'After that, we'll visit the Church of San Felice,' Strocchi said. 'I need to question the priest there, Father Negri. He exorcized a nephew of Niccolò Zamora, the man whose body was found in this piazza yesterday . . .' He stopped. Manuffi was no longer by his side, the constable standing still as a statue several steps back. 'Manuffi?'

'You're going to San Felice?'

Strocchi noticed Manuffi's hands were trembling. 'Yes.'

'That's where the priests drive out demons and evil spirits.'

Strocchi went to him, unused to seeing such fear. The constable was shivering like it was the coldest hour of winter, not a dull autumn day. 'What's wrong?'

Manuffi shook his head. 'I . . . I can't go there.'

His response bemused Strocchi. A day ago, he hadn't known there were exorcists in Florence; now gentle, kind Manuffi appeared terrified of going to a church where they took place. 'Come over here,' Strocchi said. He led Manuffi past the statue of David to Loggia dei Lanzi on the piazza's southern edge, the side closest to the Arno. Manuffi sank onto a stone bench under the loggia's impressive portici, his hands clasping at each other. Strocchi sat by him, giving Manuffi time to say whatever he wished to share.

'My brother, Ercole, he was always good to me,' the constable murmured after a while. 'Ercole was much older than the rest of us, but he looked out for me. Then something changed . . .' Manuffi sniffed, his nose running. 'Ercole was sneaking out during curfew. My sister said he must be visiting a girl, so why would he need to do that in the dark? I didn't ask. He was still my big brother.'

Strocchi stayed silent, listening to the constable's quiet words.

'Papa found something out about Ercole, I don't know what. There was shouting. They fought. Papa said our mama would be ashamed of Ercole if she was still alive . . . Papa gathered us all together to tell us Ercole had been given over to the priests at San Felice. They would drive out the demons tormenting our brother. Papa said it was to make my brother better, but when he came back . . .' Manuffi shook his head. 'Ercole was never the same.'

Strocchi watched self-important men and their servants marching into Palazzo della Signoria; senators, no doubt, going to debate what the city and its people needed. Everyone knew the true power in Florence lay with Duke Cosimo de' Medici.

The constable wiped a hand across his eyes. 'He still looked like my brother, spoke with his voice, but Ercole was different. He stopped being him. Stopped being my friend.'

Strocchi waited as Manuffi took a long, deep breath. 'Thank you for telling me that. It can't have been easy. You do not have to come into San Felice with me if you don't want to. There are many other ways you can help. I can talk to Father Negri on my own.'

'I should try,' Manuffi said. 'It is a church, a house of God. There should be nothing to fear in such a place . . .' He peered at Strocchi. 'Should there?'

'No,' Strocchi replied. 'We should have nothing to fear from Our Lord.'

* * *

99

Father Zati crossed Ponte Vecchio earlier than the previous day. The bridge was quiet as he strode up and over it, the butchers and fishmongers still setting out their wares. A cold wind whipped through the gap between buildings, bringing a first hint of winter on the air. Pulling his cloak closer, Zati blew warm air into his fists.

The city's southern quarter was stirring from its slumber when Zati stepped off Ponte Vecchio. Wives were leaning out between shutters on the palazzi, shouting across the street to their neighbours. Servants hurried by, most likely going to their masters' homes in the wealthier areas north of the river. A few women in widow's clothes gathered outside a church near the Arno, waiting for Mass. The aroma of baking bread hung in the air, a pleasant relief from the harsher smells that would drift through Oltrarno as the day wore on.

Unlike the previous day, Signora Vanni was not waiting outside San Felice as Zati approached the church. He slowed his pace, as if expecting her to appear from the shadows to accost him – But no. Vanni was not there. Zati lifted his rosary beads to his lips and kissed them.

Turning east onto via San Agostino, he strolled to the back door of San Felice and let himself inside. The church was dark, as usual. In the grey days of autumn, the pairs of arched windows high up in the walls gave the interior little light. Dozens of candles burned around the church walls, adding a sense of warmth if no actual heat. Zati shivered in the cold air.

A crack resounded, accompanied by a grunt of pain. The noises were repeated again and again, each crack louder than the last. It was weeks since Zati had arrived at San Felice this early. He stopped, head tilting to listen. A fresh grunt of pain filled the air.

It was Father Negri's hour to mortify his flesh.

The exorcist was kneeling in front of the great crucifix that dominated San Felice. The image of Christ painted on the wooden cross depicted all his pain and suffering. The crucifix was supposedly crafted by Giotto; the painting was a masterpiece of tenderness and horror. Below it, Negri was stripped to the waist and striking himself with a scourge made of plaited cords, whipping them over each shoulder in turn so they lashed his bare back. The skin was red raw, bruises of purple and black already mottling together. In places the skin had split open, Negri's blood soaking into a cloth tied round his waist.

Zati did not watch, but the steady whip of the scourge through the air before it hit Negri's back with a wet thud was inescapable. A grunt of pain followed each blow, while the murmur of prayers was audible between each swing of the scourge.

Eventually, finally, Negri stopped.

The older priest rose to his feet, staggering a little on the uneven stone floor. 'Look at me, Father Zati,' Negri called. 'Witness what I have done in the name of Our Lord.' Zati watched Negri remove the cloth from his waist, using it to wipe at the wounds on his back. 'Even those of the greatest piety and moral integrity can be consumed by unclean spirits,' Negri said. 'We must face our illusions, our self-deceits. We must confront our abuses and our shortcomings. We must recognize our failings and make penance for our trespasses.'

'Yes, Father,' Zati replied.

'Help me put my cassock back on.' Negri pointed to his black robe, cast aside on the floor. Zati retrieved it, handing the garment to the exorcist. Negri was broad-shouldered but narrow of waist. He insisted on fasting and abstinence as further means of overcoming his weaknesses. Negri shaved his scalp each day, insistent that the grooming of hair was a sin of vanity. 'You still doubt the value of mortification,' Negri said, wincing as the cassock settled across his back.

'I do not doubt the sincerity of this punishment . . .'

'But?'

'Is it truly necessary?'

'You might as well ask if our prayers are necessary.' Negri rested a hand on Zati's shoulder, staring at him with cold blue eyes. 'Is what we do in this church, purging malign spirits and demons from those who come to us for help, is that necessary?'

'I do believe in our mission here,' Zati insisted.

'Then you should join me in driving out the father of lies. Our greatest strength is a well-tested faith and a purity of heart. Let nobody doubt the godliness of what we do in this church. Otherwise, we can never save this city from itself, nor the sinners who live here.'

Chapter Nine

ontessa Coltello usually paid no attention to those who came and went on the ground floor of her palazzo. If the visitor was an expected arrival or a person of particular significance, her maggiordomo would soon come upstairs to announce the presence of this individual. Pozzo had worked in her employ long enough to judge well whether any newcomer deserved an audience, but the final say in all such matters was naturally hers and hers alone. However, there were occasions when the maggiordomo erred on the side of caution; visitors who might provide the contessa with some amusement or diversion yet still got sent away. Pozzo was a skilful judge of character but he was not always correct.

Today the contessa craved an entertainment or, at the very least, an amusing folly. Either would help to pass the hours while she awaited the unwanted presence of Signor Tito Grossolano, a man as boorish as he was ugly if gossip were to be believed. The contessa paid well to ensure the best gossip reached her exquisite ears. A rumour was invariably far more compelling than truth, even if it proved inaccurate.

She was passing the shutters that opened onto the palazzo's internal courtyard when the sound of Pozzo arguing with a visitor echoed around the stone walls below. The contessa paused, intrigued. Alas, whoever was with the maggiordomo was hidden from her view. The arrival was obviously male – no woman would ever cause Pozzo to raise his voice – and a true Florentine, judging by their choice of words. A particular phrase caught her ear: the Otto. Why would the city's most powerful criminal court send an officer to her palazzo? And, if so, why was Pozzo intent on refusing this newcomer an audience with her? Eager to discover more, the contessa swept along the hall to the staircase that descended to the main entrance. There she could see this visitor and judge his significance for herself.

The contessa was disappointed to find the newcomer standing with his back to the stairs, denying her a view of his face. So be it. She would judge him from what she could see and hear and infer. The clothes he wore were unremarkable: a simple tunic, plain hose and what appeared to be a rather good pair of boots. It was possible to learn a lot about a man by what he put on his feet. Most men's boots were as unremarkable as their wearers, poorly made and often poorly chosen. Few gave much consideration to boots beyond matters of function and fit. Wear a pair until they fall part, then buy another was the common approach.

But this pair of boots had the appearance of quality. That told her more about this man than his clothes. The way he held himself was also worthy of note: upright, but not stiff. He was lithe of limb, not guilty of surrendering to excess. An active man, it seemed. The hair was swept back from the face, greying above the ears, suggesting he was nearer forty than thirty. And there was a quiet authority about him. In the unlikely event the dis-agreement with Pozzo should become violent, this man would be ready.

Yes, he was intriguing.

The contessa watched her maggiordomo quarrel with the visitor, careful not to catch Pozzo's eye. She wanted – no, she needed – to know why this man was in her palazzo.

'You deny anyone came here during curfew the night before last?' the visitor asked.

'I have denied nothing,' Pozzo replied. 'I enquired about the source of this allegation.'

'The Otto has responsibility for numerous laws in the city. One of these is enforcing the curfew between the hours of sunset each night and sunrise the next morning.'

'I am quite aware that observing curfew is a legal requirement in this city,' Pozzo fumed. 'But you did not respond to my question.'

'And you have yet to answer mine. Did anyone come here during curfew the night before last? If so, what was their name and their business here at that hour?'

The contessa knew someone had come to the palazzo then: the wounded messenger who interrupted her tiresome encounter with Dandolo. Pozzo was never going to admit that, and certainly not to an officer of the Otto. But the longer she let him grapple with the visitor's questions, the more likely it was that her maggiordomo might incriminate himself.

Now she knew the reason for the newcomer's presence, it would not be difficult to satisfy his enquiry. Besides, it might be amusing to sport with him while waiting for Grossolano.

'Pozzo,' she called down the staircase, 'please bring our visitor up to the salone.'

'Contessa, that is not necessary. This—'

'Now,' she cut in.

Pozzo's face reddened. 'As you wish, Contessa.' He bowed his head.

Through all this the visitor did not move. He did not turn to look at her, did not even acknowledge her presence. Yes, it seemed he was going to provide her with some sport.

How delightful.

Strocchi was grateful to have Manuffi by him while crossing Ponte Vecchio. The constable's imposing size made those searching for bargains from the butcher shops and fish stalls step out of their way. Once over the bridge Strocchi led Manuffi west towards Santo Spirito.

It would be better not to bother the grieving famiglia further, but it was necessary to know for certain whether the dead man had been active in the Senate. Judging by what others had said, it seemed unlikely. If Zamora had had no appetite for power or politics within the Arte della Lana, Strocchi doubted the victim had sought such things elsewhere. But his body had been left in front of Palazzo della Signora where the Senate met, so the question had to be asked.

Strocchi and Manuffi were approaching Piazza Santo Spirito when a voice cried out.

'Murder! Murder!'

Everyone stopped to see from where the cry came, but Strocchi was already sprinting into the piazza. If a life had been taken, the killer could still be close. People were gathering outside the Church of Santo Spirito with more joining them, eager to see.

'Step aside!' Strocchi shoved a way through, not caring who complained. The sooner he got to the victim, the better. The cry of murder might be wrong, there might still be hope for whomever had been attacked. 'I'm an officer of the Otto. Step aside!'

But there was no hope for the body in front of the church.

The corpse was male, dressed in a shabby tunic and with his

hose torn at the knees. He was young, perhaps a summer or two less than Strocchi's twenty-three years. The face was not familiar, despite a distinctive cleft in the chin. Greasy hair covered the forehead, hiding any ash there. But Strocchi had seen that angry red line round the neck before; the victim had been garrotted. And the way the body was lying on the well-worn stones of the piazza . . . Arms stretched out sideways, legs overlapped at the feet. Like Christ on the cross.

Whoever murdered Zamora had killed again.

Strocchi swallowed hard. No, he couldn't be sure of that, not yet. But still . . .

Manuffi pushed through the circle of people to join him, huffing and puffing. Seeing the body, Manuffi made the sign of the cross. Strocchi did the same, chiding himself for not doing so sooner. There were at least twenty people around them, and Strocchi could hear more coming, voices calling out. He needed answers before it was too late.

'Does anyone know this man?' Strocchi asked.

'He's a buggerone,' someone called out.

'Used to be one,' another replied. 'Not anymore.'

'Sucked cazzo for coin,' a third voice said. 'Makes him as bad as them.'

That brought murmurs of agreement from some, but others protested. Strocchi didn't have time for a debate about how the victim had lived his life. 'What's his name?'

'Freccia. He's a thief.'

'He's a Jew, they're just as bad.'

'Living on via dei Giudei doesn't make him a Jew.'

'Well, he's still a thief. Merda stole my coin pouch last month.'

'Enough!' Strocchi shouted to silence the argument. 'Tell me, who found the body?'

An older woman in the black clothes of a widow stepped forward. She clutched a scrubbing brush in one hand, a wooden pail of water in the other. 'I came to clean the stones in front of the church before Mass. I do it every day. I thought this poor soul was drunk, or sleeping . . . Then I noticed his neck . . .'

The crowd surged forward, eager to see what she meant.

'Stop!' Strocchi commanded. 'Keep away from the body!' He glared at Manuffi, urging him to help. The constable put himself between the nearest people and the corpse.

'I need everybody to take a step back,' Manuffi said, waving his arms at the throng like a farmer herding cows in a field. 'Grazie. And another step.'

While Manuffi kept the grumbling crowd occupied, Strocchi crouched beside the body, putting a knee on the stones in front of the church. They had been worn smooth by the passing feet of the faithful, but cold still seeped through his woollen hose. Yes, that was why he was shivering. Nothing to do with the corpse in front of him.

Strocchi brushed hair from the victim's face. There was more confirmation it was the work of the same killer. Like Zamora, ash had been smeared on Freccia's forehead. Rain had washed most of the ash off Zamora, but here it remained in place. Six letters formed a single word: *Patris*. Strocchi had heard a Latin phrase his whole life in church: *In nomine Patris et Filii et Spiritus Sancti*. In the name of the Father and of the Son and of the Holy Spirit. But why would the killer write the Latin word for 'father' on Freccia's forehead? The victim did not look old enough to be a father to anyone, not unless they were a baby or infant.

It was tempting to open the mouth, to see if Freccia's tongue had also been cleft in two. But this desecration was known only to a few within the Otto, and anyone present when Bindi had briefed Duke Cosimo about Zamora's murder. Better to keep that truth a secret. Bad enough the killer was choosing to leave their victims in public places like this piazza.

How had they been able to bring a body here without anyone noticing, let alone pose the corpse to resemble Christ on the cross? Why did nobody challenge what the killer was doing? Strocchi got back to his feet, brushing down his hose. 'Did anyone see who brought this man's body here?' he asked. A few of those gathered shook their heads, and none of the others spoke. 'Does anyone know how long he has been here?' Still nothing.

'He was here when I arrived,' the old woman with the brush and water replied. 'I cried out when I realized he was . . . what had been done to him.'

Strocchi nodded. 'Anyone else?' He could see market stalls around the edge of the piazza, some ready to trade, others still being set up. 'Somebody must have seen something.'

A dark-skinned woman with a basket full of brassica cleared her throat. 'Not long after dawn there was a sound like a sack of vegetables being dropped. It was after the bells for the end of curfew finished chiming, otherwise I wouldn't have heard it.' She pointed at shutters on the top level of a building that overlooked the piazza. 'When I glanced out from up there, I saw the body in front of the church. But I thought he must be asleep, or drunk.'

'Was there anyone close by?'

She frowned. 'Somebody was pushing a cart away from the church, going south.'

'What did they look like?'

The woman shook her head. 'Could have been anyone. I didn't see their face. They were wearing a long cloak with the hood up over their head.'

Strocchi thanked her for speaking up. 'Did anyone see or hear anything earlier?' But nobody else seemed willing to reply. One stallholder did bring an old, coarse blanket to lay across the corpse, which Strocchi accepted. He took Manuffi to one side, asking him to find a cart they could borrow. He pushed coin into the constable's hand. 'I'll stay here. Buy a cart, if you must, but we need to move the body.'

Manuffi strode away, leaving Strocchi with the corpse. Once he'd laid the blanket over it, those who had gathered around drifted away. How soon they lost interest when there was nothing more to see, yet none had noticed a dead man lying in front of the church. Strocchi could not imagine such an indignity happening in his home village. But here in the city a man might die or be murdered, and it would be forgotten before the day's end.

Florence. So much beauty, yet so much barbarity.

Aldo had never been attracted to a woman. His eyes did not follow them when one passed on the street. His hands had not ached to touch a woman, no matter how beautiful she might be. His lips did not want to kiss or taste a woman, no matter how handsome her face. His hips had not longed to press against those of a woman, and his cazzo did not rise when he encountered a woman most other men considered alluring.

He'd had no lack of offers from women while riding as a mercenary, and more still while an officer of the Otto. An endless parade of semi-clad and naked woman surrounded him every day at the bordello. Yet in all that time and on all those occasions, no woman had ever stirred lust within him, no urge arose in need of satisfaction.

But, in the unlikely event he was ever to be tempted by a

woman, Aldo suspected the Contessa Valentine Coltello would be the one to make that happen.

When Aldo was shown into her richly decorated salone, the contessa was wearing a gown of the finest silk embroidered with golden thread, its bodice created to draw attention to and enhance the swell of her breasts. The contessa most obligingly sank into a chair as he approached, ensuring he could admire even more of her bosom if he wished.

This was not what caught his eye.

She had a heart-shaped face, her fine hair drawn back into a golden net studded with tiny emeralds. Her skin was pale and flawless, giving little hint to her age; she might be closer to forty than twenty. But it was her gleaming green eyes that arrested Aldo's gaze. The contessa regarded him with amusement, a hint of mischief making itself apparent in the slight arching of one eyebrow and the tiniest pursing of her lips. She was assessing him as he was assessing her. Aldo could not help wondering what the contessa saw and found himself wanting to impress her.

He bowed his head. 'Grazie for seeing me.'

'I hear you have questions,' she replied.

'Yes.'

'About a messenger who came to my palazzo the night before last?'

'Indeed.'

'Well, since you apparently have a witness to this visitation . . .' She rolled her eyes, letting him know the lie had not been believed but it was being tolerated. 'I shall spare you any denials that this happened. I would not wish to insult your intelligence, Officer . . . ?'

'My name is Cesare Aldo,' he said, 'but I am merely a constable of the Otto, not an officer.' Aldo had introduced himself as such to the maggiordomo, who, no doubt, had passed that on to the contessa. 'I've no wish to insult your intelligence by pretending to be otherwise.'

She nodded in acknowledgement, while her eyes said: Go on, tell me more.

'In truth, I have little interest in the messenger,' Aldo continued, 'beyond wondering if they ever recovered from the wound that I gave them.'

The contessa laughed. 'So, you're the night patrol member who's quick with a blade. Yes, my maggiordomo was able to sew the messenger back together.'

'My apologies. If I may be so bold as to ask an impertinent question . . .'

'You may.'

'What was so urgent it required your messenger to risk meeting the night patrol?'

The contessa frowned a little. 'The messenger was not actually mine. He was sent by an acquaintance of mine. It was a risk, and a foolhardy one, as your blade proved. Now, will you answer a question for me?'

'Of course.'

'Was there actually a witness who saw the messenger arrive here?'

Aldo considered lying, but the contessa was too shrewd to be easily deceived. Better to speak as much truth as he could. It would make any later deceptions more credible. 'No, I lied to your maggiordomo about that. It was necessary to get an audience with you. Besides, he thinks far too much of himself. I wanted to irritate him, make him raise his voice.'

'Well, it certainly worked. I haven't seen Pozzo so vexed in years.'

'Grazie.'

'Tell me, how did you know about the messenger?'

Aldo had had an answer ready should this question arise. If the contessa was as adept a spymaster as Cosimo believed, only a fool would come without having prepared for all the questions she might ask. 'Dandolo, the ducal functionary you sought to tempt into your service. He heard you and Pozzo discussing what happened to the messenger.'

A smile spread across the contessa's face. 'Dandolo scuttled back to Palazzo Medici and reported my attempt to win his favour, yes?'

'As you wished him to do,' Aldo agreed. 'Doubtless you already have better sources within Cosimo's court. You sought Dandolo out to distract attention from them.'

The contessa laughed again. 'My dear Aldo, it is quite some time since I had a caller so willing to speak the truth. I was right to think you would provide an interesting diversion.' She patted the seat next to her own. 'Come, sit beside me. I wish to know more about you.'

He did as she suggested, positioning himself in the chair so he and the contessa were close enough to touch. The aroma of her scent enveloped him, a heady mix of jasmine and musk. If her gaze had been piercing at a distance, this close it was inescapable. Now he knew how an insect felt as it settled on a spider's web, believing it could still fly away if danger approached. But the danger was already there.

'If your question about the messenger was simply a stratagemma to secure a meeting with me,' the contessa said, 'perhaps you would share the real reason you came here.'

'With pleasure,' Aldo replied. 'I want you to seduce me.'

Chapter Ten

*G*etting the corpse to Doctor Orvieto's home was easy enough. Strocchi and Manuffi pushed it to via dei Giudei on a borrowed cart, the body hidden beneath a blanket. But persuading the physician to examine Freccia proved less simple. 'This isn't a good time,' Orvieto said. 'I have patients waiting inside. I've a student to teach, and fresh remedies to make.'

'I understand, and I apologize,' Strocchi replied before lifting the blanket to expose Freccia's head and neck. 'But you can see why I brought him to you.' The red line encircling the throat was more vivid now, appearing even angrier than before.

Orvieto murmured something in Hebrew. Strocchi did not understand the words but dismay was apparent in the doctor's face, and in the way his shoulders sagged. Orvieto pulled at his russet and brown beard. 'Very well. Give me a few moments.'

Strocchi and Manuffi waited outside, listening as Orvieto explained to his patients why they would have to come back later. Jewish men and women came out into the narrow street, glancing at the blanket-covered corpse atop the cart before hurrying on. Were those accusations in their eyes? Strocchi resisted the urge to explain what he and Manuffi were doing, that they were not responsible for killing the corpse. Even if he could find the words, it would not make the waiting any less awkward or uncomfortable.

Orvieto thanked each patient as they left. When the last was gone, he sighed. 'I suppose you'd better bring this poor soul in.'

Strocchi and Manuffi carried the corpse inside, the blanket still draped across it as a shroud. They followed the doctor through to the back room where he treated patients. The walls were lined with shelves, each crammed with jars of remedies and ingredients. Orvieto pointed at the long wooden table in the middle of the room. 'On there, please.'

Once Freccia's corpse was in place, Strocchi gave the borrowed blanket to Manuffi. 'Give this back to its owner and return the cart as well. After that, go to the Podestà and report what we found. Bindi should be back from his morning meeting with the duke, and the sooner the segretario knows about this the better.' Keeping Bindi fully informed would deny him one reason to complain, not that he was ever short of grievances.

Orvieto was already leaning over the body as Manuffi left, while Rebecca was ready with ink and paper to take notes. She had not flinched when the corpse was revealed. Strocchi knew she was familiar with violent death, having seen her own father's murdered body. She must encounter many things while studying with Orvieto. Physicians must be as familiar with death as they were with the living.

'This man was garrotted,' the doctor announced. He lifted Freccia's head to peer at the back of the neck. 'Attacked from behind, most likely by a man or a woman with a strong grasp.' Orvieto pointed to the red mark around the neck. 'You can see small gaps here, suggesting a beaded cord was used to garrotte him.' The doctor looked at the dead man's hands, examining them in turn. 'There are cuts and blood on the knuckles, and inside the fingers. He fought back against his attacker – without success.'

'What about the ash on his forehead?' Strocchi asked.

'I was getting to that,' Orvieto replied, his voice a little testy. 'The Latin word *Patris*, meaning father, has been smeared on the forehead.' The doctor reached for the mouth, easing it open to look inside. 'And the dead man's tongue has been cleft in two, cut from the tip down to the base.' He glanced at Strocchi. 'Do you wish to see for yourself?'

Recalling what happened during the examination of Zamora, Strocchi shook his head. He had no wish to empty his belly on the doctor's floor as well.

'May I?' Rebecca asked, setting her ink and paper aside.

'Of course.' Orvieto held the mouth open while Rebecca bent over the corpse. She used one hand to keep her long brown hair out of the way.

'It's not a clean cut,' Rebecca said. 'They needed several attempts.'

'What does that tell you?' Orvieto asked.

'It suggests several possibilities,' she replied. 'Whoever did this may have been nervous or hesitant. It can't be easy cutting a man's tongue in two while it is still inside his mouth. The edge of their blade might have been dull – a sharp knife would have cut cleaner. Or they could have been forced to cut in haste.'

Strocchi willed his belly not to rebel, struggling to keep what Rebecca was describing out of his thoughts. 'Was the victim still alive when . . .' Strocchi searched for the right words.

'When this happened?' Orvieto said. 'No. Rebecca's last suggestion is the most probable answer – this was done in haste.' He smiled at her. 'The previous victim's tongue was also cleft in two but with a single cut. This was the work of someone rushing.'

'But you still think it was the same hand?' she asked.

The doctor nodded. 'The differences are minor, most likely the result of changed circumstances. The first victim had their senses taken before being garrotted, so the killer could be careful while

A DIVINE FURY

dividing the tongue. This poor soul fought back. After that
everything was done quickly. Either there was less time to do what
the killer wanted—'

'Or their excitement got the better of them,' Strocchi interjected.
Twice, while still a constable, he had witnessed one man attacking
another, intending to kill. Madness seemed to take hold of them,
as if a demon had claimed the man and he could not stop. It was
terrifying. To see such madness in someone approaching with a
blade . . . That would be far worse.

'Indeed,' Orvieto agreed. 'To know what drove the killer, you
must ask them.'

'We have to find them first.' Strocchi's shoulders were heavy,
the burden of solving a second murder settling on him. He had
been responding by instinct until now, doing what was necessary
in the moment. But the significance of what was on the doctor's
table could no longer be denied. A lone killing with no obvious
motive was challenging enough; if that same hand had claimed
another soul before its time . . . This was beyond his limited
experience as an officer of the Otto. Vendetta killings were
uncommon in Florence, but not unknown. These murders . . . they
were something else, something that did not have a name. Not
yet.

Strocchi set his worrying aside. Gather the facts first, deduce
what they meant later. 'Can you tell me when this man was killed?'

The doctor gestured to his student, but Rebecca shook her head.
'This is the first murder victim I have helped examine.'

'Think back to the patients who died while we were tending
them,' Orvieto said. 'What did you observe? Compare that with
those you have seen who have been dead longer.'

Rebecca stepped back, her gaze still on Freccia's corpse. 'The
body lets go when life ends. The spirit departs and the flesh becomes

pliant, heavy but otherwise easy to move. Later, the remains become stiff and rigid, almost frozen in place.'

'Correct.' The doctor smiled. 'The body's temperature also changes as its natural warmth diminishes.' Orvieto pressed his fingertips to Freccia's skin. 'This man still has some warmth, so he has been dead a few hours at most. That suggests he was killed around the time that curfew ended.' Orvieto turned to Strocchi. 'Do you wish us to make a full examination? There may be more to discover that is not immediately evident.'

'If you could . . .'

'It will take time. I imagine there are other things you need to do?'

Strocchi recognized the hint. On his way out he paused by the door. 'I was told this man lived here on via dei Giudei. Do you know where?'

'He has – had – a room upstairs in the house next door where Moise Bassano lived,' Rebecca replied. 'It's on the right as you leave here. Signor Bassano's nephew Bonfantino owns the property now, though he doesn't spend much time there.'

'Is that correct?' Orvieto asked. 'I don't recall seeing this poor soul before.'

She smiled. 'You know most of our neighbours because they are your patients. This man never came to you for help, so he is a stranger to your eyes.'

'Do you know if Freccia had any famiglia?' Strocchi asked. The sooner any relatives knew about the death, the sooner he could ask them the difficult questions he must.

'Yes, a wife,' Rebecca replied.

Strocchi hadn't expected that. The way people in the piazza had described Freccia, the possibility of him being married had not even occurred to him. 'Can you tell me her name?'

'Fiora. She works in a tannery, I think, so might not be home now. I've seen her leaving for work as curfew ends most mornings.'

'Grazie.' Strocchi nodded to Orvieto before departing. Even if Fiora was elsewhere, there might be an answer to be found in their room that explained why Freccia had been murdered. Indeed, searching for those answers might be easier while she was absent.

The contessa was accustomed to making men uncomfortable, having them respond to her presence even when they had no wish to do so. Most were simple creatures, unused to a woman being quite so direct or disarming in her approaches. A few flirtatious glances, the touch of a hand on their skin and a coy comment or two were often enough to make their breath quicken and their hose bulge. It was useful, but also rather dreary and predictable.

Cesare Aldo was, it seemed, a different kind of man.

Her earlier assessment of him when viewed from above and behind had proven accurate. He was lean and brisk yet able to remain still, showing a quiet confidence. Aldo had no need to strut around as some men did, no desire to display himself or fill the room with his presence. He favoured one leg a little when standing, suggesting an old injury that was still troubling him as autumn made the city cold and wet. Having taken in the salone when he was first shown in, Aldo kept all his attention on her thereafter, listening to whatever she had to say without interruption. This, too, was the mark of a man who knew his own mind and possessed no need to impose it on others.

But sitting close to Aldo revealed more about him.

Most men who visited her palazzo were as plain as their clothes, but this constable of the Otto had a watchful quality. He measured his words before speaking, while his gaze was direct, even penetrating. The greying bristles across his chin suggested he was perhaps forty, though the firmness of that jawline meant he avoided indulgence. Why, then, at his age was he merely a constable? He should be an officer by now at least, or holding a post of far higher significance if all of this was true.

Aldo must have made someone very angry indeed.

Of course, there was another thing that doubtless prevented him from rising to a rank befitting such a careful and intriguing individual: he seemed to have no interest in women. The contessa had given him ample opportunity to admire her bosom, while a lick of her lips when admiring what was below his waist did not bring the usual response. If anything, he appeared a little bored by such attention. Either this man was a monk (and the contessa had known plenty of religious men unable to contain their lusts), a eunuch, or he preferred the company of other men in his bed. So, why was he asking her to seduce him?

'I was summoned by Duke Cosimo de' Medici to his palazzo,' Aldo replied when she asked for clarification. 'His Grace told me to offer you my services as an informant.'

The contessa smiled, despite herself. 'I don't imagine the duke suggested you persuade me by being quite so . . . candid about your intentions here.'

Aldo shrugged. 'He left the method to me.'

'And how did he propose that you win my favour?'

'By mentioning how aggrieved I was at being demoted to constable and enduring more than a year on night patrol.' Aldo leaned closer to her. 'All of that happens to be true, as I'm sure you will discover when your maggiordomo or one of his men investigates my history.'

The contessa mirrored his movement so the two of them were

within whispering distance. 'Tell me, what does His Grace hope you will discover about me?'

'He's concerned by your strategia with Dandolo, how blunt and obvious that approach was. The duke suspects it is a heavy-handed thrust intended to draw his attention while you bury a blade in him elsewhere.' Aldo stared into her eyes. 'Cosimo sees you as a most effective adversary and wants to know why you were so clumsy with Dandolo.'

The contessa supposed she should be flattered. Assuming anything that came from her visitor's mouth could be believed, it seemed the duke of Florence held her in higher regard than Venice's new Inquisitorie di Stato. 'And what do you hope to gain by sharing all of this with me? You don't expect to see the inside of my bedchamber, I hope?'

A different man might have stiffened at that question.

Aldo simply smiled. 'I'm sure you have your choice of companions there. No, my hopes are quite simple. To convince both you and the duke of my usefulness. You may tell me whatever you wish Cosimo to know, and I shall bring back whatever morsels or lies he wants Venice to hear. I am at your service, Contessa.' Aldo spread his legs wider, arching an eyebrow at her. 'Look on me as a tool to be used however you see fit.'

Perhaps she had been wrong about his choice of bedfellow? Not that it mattered. Aldo was quite correct about her needs being fully met already, and she only allowed herself to take lovers who were no threat to her. Young men, quick to recover and easily dismissed were usually the best choices when she desired a cazzo. And when she did not . . . The contessa recalled her visitor the previous night, their look of wonder and ecstasy at discovering what two women could do together. She suppressed a smirk of satisfaction.

'Very well. Tell me something I don't already know about matters before the Otto, and I shall share with you a truth that might intrigue the duke.'

Aldo tapped a finger to his lips, as if pondering how to reply. The contessa was sure a man this nimble of mind would have decided what to say, the limit of what he might reveal, long before coming to her palazzo. After a few moments, he smiled at her. 'There was a murder in Florence yesterday and it is baffling the Otto's investigators. The victim was garrotted, his corpse left by the statue of David in Piazza della Signoria.'

'Most of this is common knowledge,' the contessa replied, stifling a yawn.

'True, but there are aspects of the case that have been kept quiet. Ash was smeared on the victim's forehead, and his body posed to resemble Christ on the cross.'

That was more intriguing. 'Why keep back that information?' To his credit Aldo did not rush to provide the answer. Most men could not stop themselves, too eager to preen by demonstrating their cleverness. But this one kept his silence, letting her deduce the truth. 'Ahh,' the contessa said. 'You suspect there may be an element of faith or zealotry to the murder and wish to keep it hidden. I'm not surprised after those merchants were burned alive last year, and their killer claimed Savonarola was returning. The last thing Duke Cosimo needs is another religious uprising.'

Aldo gave a small nod of appreciation. 'Indeed. The body in the piazza is why that messenger made it to your door. Finding a murdered corpse did rather distract us.'

A man was shouting on the street below, loud enough to be heard through the shutters of the salone. His voice was not familiar, but that bullying manner and his lapses into the Venetian tongue left little doubt as to who he was.

The contessa pushed back her chair to stand. 'Now I shall share my intriguing piece of news for you to take back to His Grace.' She strolled to the shutters, opening them to look down at Piazza di Santa Trinita outside her palazzo. The triangular space was dominated by a tall column erected long before by the Romans, a statue of Justice atop it. A carriage had stopped between the column and her home. 'I am being replaced. The Council of Ten has a new tribunal in charge of intelligence gathering. It believes the man shouting outside is better suited to representing Venetian interests here in Florence. Come, have a look at him.'

Aldo joined her, standing close enough that their shoulders touched.

'His name is Tito Grossolano,' the contessa went on, gesturing at the buffoon below. The heavyset Venetian had stepped from the carriage straight into a pile of horse merda. He was shouting abuse at the driver, blaming him for the mess now coating Grossolano's boots. That the carriage had come to a halt in precisely that place could be accidental, but the driver's glare of hatred said otherwise. He had deliberately chosen to stop there, hoping Grossolano would not look first.

The contessa made a note to have Pozzo reward the driver handsomely.

'From this day onward,' she said, 'Signor Grossolano will be spymaster here in Florence, gathering intelligence about the duke and sending it back to Venice. If you go downstairs now you should encounter him at the main entrance. That will help you get a measure of the man sent to take my place, and you will be better able to describe him to the duke.'

'Grazie,' Aldo replied. 'May I ask, will Grossolano be staying here at the palazzo until he has a residence of his own?'

'I fear so.'

'In that case, I shall return tomorrow and formally introduce myself to him as your informant within the Otto di Guardia e Balìa. That should give you ample opportunity to tell me anything more I need to know about this . . . newcomer.'

The contessa nodded, welcoming an opportunity to joust with Aldo again. He had a playful quality she enjoyed and an awareness that they were mere pawns in a much larger game. He was certainly a far more interesting visitor than Tito Grossolano was likely to be.

Strocchi got no reply when he knocked at the door of Bonfantino Bassano, but the Jewish landlord appeared a few moments later, hurrying along via dei Giudei grasping an empty basket. He was round of belly and face, a man used to living well without having to work hard. 'Did you want something?' Bassano asked, accusation in his eyes.

'You've been at the mercato?'

'For all the good it did,' the landlord replied. 'Seen fresher fish floating on the Arno.' When Strocchi announced himself as an officer of the Otto, Bassano squared his shoulders. 'I know what is said about my tenants, how people gossip. But Freccia and his wife are good tenants. Never late with the rent. Because they are not Jews, is that enough reason to refuse them a home? What they do outside these walls is not my concern.'

'That's not why I'm here,' Strocchi replied. As he described Freccia's murder, the landlord paled. Bassano pushed open the front door, fussing with his basket before letting Strocchi inside. The house was dark and stank of damp, plaster crumbling from the walls. 'Fiora will be at the tannery by now,' Bassano said. 'She works from dawn to dusk, poor thing. You can always smell when she gets home. But you're welcome to look around upstairs. They have the first room on the left. The other two rooms are unoccupied at present.'

'You're not coming with me?'

'I don't like to intrude.'

Strocchi climbed a dozen wooden steps to the upper level. The two doors directly ahead were both closed and locked, but the door on his left was ajar. 'Do your tenants usually leave their room open during the day?' he called down the stairs. Bassano had the manner of a man who protested too much about his innocence and his ignorance.

'I don't think so,' he replied.

That meant no. They locked their room to keep the landlord out.

Strocchi pushed at the door. It swung back, creaking on neglected hinges. The room was in disarray. A few pieces of simple furniture were turned over or broken. The couple's mattress had been pushed to the floor, and clothes were strewn everywhere. Had someone been here before him, scouring the room?

'You'd better come up,' Strocchi called. Bassano was at his side within moments. The landlord must have been lurking and listening by the staircase. But Bassano gasped when he saw the room, and his surprise seemed true.

'What happened?' he asked.

'You tell me. You must have heard this.'

Bassano shook his head. 'I swear that I didn't.'

Strocchi realized what this meant. 'Where were you last night?'

'I . . .' The landlord's face reddened. 'I was with a friend.'

'And that empty basket you were carrying?'

'In case my neighbours see me and ask where I've been.'

His comment about the lack of fresh fish had seemed well

prepared. Sending Bassano back downstairs, Strocchi studied the room. All this mess and damage was too random for thieves. If Fiora left early for work at the tannery, that suggested an obvious explanation.

Freccia had been murdered here.

Chapter Eleven

When Aldo emerged from Palazzo Coltello the contessa's supposed replacement was still shouting at his driver. Tito Grossolano was a heavyset man with a permanent scowl. Judging by his behaviour, Grossolano believed humiliating those in his service demonstrated his significance. His gruff voice bounced around the small piazza, bringing curious faces to the shutters of nearby palazzi. Grossolano kept lapsing into Venetian words and phrases. Not the behaviour of a new spymaster seeking to enter Florence unnoticed; more that of a man used to announcing his presence with authority.

Noticing Aldo by the palazzo entrance, Grossolano stamped across to him. 'Are you the maggiordomo here?' Grossolano demanded, scraping one boot against the stone step. This close, the pox scars across his face became apparent, despite his attempt to hide them behind a thin, scratchy beard. The contrast between him and the contessa could not have been starker. She possessed sufficient charm and guile to slip a blade between her target's ribs while still smiling to their face. Grossolano would use a hammer to strike a blow upon a bruise and yet still believe this would win his favour.

Stupid and cruel, it seemed.

'No, signor,' Aldo replied. 'I was simply—'

'I don't care,' Grossolano snapped, dismissing him with the flick of a hand. 'Where is the maggiordomo?' he shouted past Aldo. 'I need to see him. Now!'

Pozzo strolled out of the palazzo, hands clasped behind his back. 'May I help you, signor?' he asked, voice dripping with disdain.

'Yes!' Grossolano roared. 'What kind of welcome is this? I've travelled all the way from Bologna and the first time I set foot in your city my boots get covered in merda!'

'Most regrettable,' the maggiordomo replied with all the sincerity of a politician. 'Do you wish to wait while the streets of Florence are cleaned, or would you rather come inside?'

Aldo's appreciation of the maggiordomo increased. He truly was the contessa's man.

'Don't you mock me,' Grossolano roared, jabbing a finger at Pozzo. 'I will not be made a fool of, mark my words!'

'Indeed, signor. Nobody in this palazzo could make a fool of you.' The maggiordomo stepped aside, gesturing for Grossolano to go in. The newcomer stamped through the entrance, leaving a trail of merda behind him. Pozzo shook his head before following.

Aldo noted a Latin inscription above the door: *Carpere promptius quam imitari* – it is easier to criticize than to imitate. Judging by Grossolano's initial behaviour, he would pay no heed to such advice. Aldo stepped into the street to look up at the shutters where the contessa had been. She was still there, her face as sour as an unripe limone. Aldo bowed his head to her, getting a nod in return. Grossolano's voice boomed out as she turned away, a shudder of disgust on her fine features. One thing seemed quite certain to Aldo: the contessa and her replacement would be the best of enemies.

Strocchi persisted with his search of Freccia's rented room, but the hope of finding anything useful was as weak as the daylight spilling in between the shutters. If the killer had garrotted Freccia here, they had left no clues to their identity. An obvious reason for the murder was also absent. Yes, the room was littered with stolen items Strocchi recognized from complaints that had been lodged at the Otto: sentimental keepsakes, small pieces of ugly jewellery, a crude painting of a big-nosed man. Freccia had already sold anything of value. The rest would be dumped in an alley or end up in the Arno where most of the city's waste went.

It was possible the killer had attacked Freccia for stealing from them . . . but so simple an answer seemed unlikely. This murder was a twin to that of Zamora, meaning the victims were linked in some way – but how? One was an honest merchant who, everyone said, made friends of his rivals, while the other was a thief who apparently used to suck cazzi for coin. Perhaps Aldo had been right, and it was the victim's behaviour that had got him murdered. Yet Freccia was married, the presence of his wife Fiora evident in the rented room. Her clothes were among those strewn about, her personal things amid the debris of a dozen thefts.

If there was a link between Zamora and Freccia, it remained unclear.

The notion that Freccia was killed in this room also raised more questions than it answered. The absence of Fiora and the landlord explained how a murder could take place in the house unnoticed, but getting the corpse on a cart and taking it to the piazza without being seen . . . That needed good fortune, or a reckless disregard.

Voices arguing on the level below demanded Strocchi's attention. Going downstairs he found Bassano stopping Rebecca from coming in. 'Signorina Levi?'

She pushed past the protesting Bassano. 'We've found something you need to see.'

Strocchi followed her next door to the doctor's home. A long cloth covered the body of Freccia on the table. Orvieto was washing his hands in a bowl of water. 'There was a piece of paper inside the dead man's clothing,' he said, 'just like the first victim. But this one is far more intact.' Orvieto nodded his head to the left. 'It's over there.'

Strocchi went to a bench by the back door. A single page lay there, numerous creases in the paper where it had been folded several times. The edges were singed as if the paper had been held to a flame for a moment, and there was a familiar odour rising from the page. He leaned closer, inhaling with both nostrils. Yes, he knew that smell very well.

'I noticed an aroma,' the doctor said, drying his hands, 'but couldn't place it.'

'You wouldn't,' Strocchi replied. 'It's incense, from a church.'

'There is writing on the other side,' Rebecca said.

Strocchi turned the page over and read aloud what was written on the reverse in ink: '*Exorcizo vos, Pater Mendacii . . .*' The words went on, but the Latin text was beyond him. 'Can either of you translate this?' Strocchi asked Orvieto and Rebecca.

Father Zati was sweeping the floor of San Felice when two newcomers entered. Negri insisted the church be cleaned twice a day. Exorcism was a sacrament, he often said, and where it was performed must be pure as the hearts of those helping those plagued by demonic possession. Zati did not argue with Negri. The exorcist's mind was not for changing.

The newcomers were a couple, the woman clutching her husband's arm for support, rosary beads dangling from one hand. The couple was at least forty, though the fear and worry in their faces made both look older. They appeared beaten down, as were most visiting San Felice for the first time. Only those in need of an exorcist came to the church unasked.

Setting the broom aside, Zati went to the couple. He approached them with a kind face and open arms. A more urgent or demanding manner sent visitors fleeing without the answers they sought. That was why Negri no longer greeted new arrivals. His abrasive, accusing manner was too much for most newcomers.

'My name is Father Pagolo Zati, how may I help you?'

The husband exchanged a fearful look with his wife. 'Is this the church where . . . ?'

Zati nodded. 'Why don't you come inside, and tell me what has brought you here today?' The woman shook her head, worry in her eyes. 'You have nothing to fear,' Zati went on. 'Anything you say here, it is as if the words were spoken in confession. I shall tell nobody what you share, not unless you grant me permission.'

Again, a look passed between the couple. The husband had an oval-shaped face, framed by his greying beard and hair. There was flour on his hands and in the folds of his tunic, typical of a baker. His wife was careworn, a once handsome face now haggard with worry, yet her clothes were clean and well kept. She had taken time to look her best, despite the fears that brought the couple to San Felice. The woman nodded to her husband.

'Our name is Gheradini,' he said. 'I am Andrea, and this is my wife, Maria. We have come about our daughter, Cara. She is . . .' He shook his head, unable to go on. It was Maria who said what her husband could not.

'Cara is lost to us. She was our little girl, our only child. We had others but the Lord chose to take them to his side only a few days after they were born.' Maria made the sign of the cross, kissing her rosary beads.

'How old is Cara?' Zati asked.

'Sixteen,' Maria replied. She glanced over her shoulder as people passed by the church outside.

'Please, come in,' Zati said, stepping to one side. 'Then we can talk in private, yes?' The Gheradinis let Zati guide them to a wooden bench at one side of the church. Once all three were settled, Zati asked the couple to tell their story.

Cara had been a good girl, Maria said, a dutiful daughter for twelve years. But as she changed from a child to a young woman, so had her behaviour. Cara became obstinate and wilful, questioning her parents' beliefs, their rules and choices.

'We thought in time she would learn to love us again,' Maria explained. 'My older sister, Ghella, her girls fought with her as they grew, but now the famiglia knows nothing but love. It is the way of mothers and daughters sometimes.'

'I have no sisters myself,' Zati replied, 'yet I have heard tell of such things.'

'Cara became worse,' Andrea said. 'She would not listen to Maria or myself, would not help us in the bakery. She even started refusing to attend Mass with us. Tears were brimming in his eyes. 'It was as if our own daughter, our only child, was ashamed of us.'

Maria clasped her husband's hands. 'We told ourselves it would pass, that Cara would find her way back to us, back to the Church. But then . . .' She shook her head. 'We discovered our daughter performing ungodly acts.'

'Ungodly acts?' Zati asked.

'Yes. With . . . another woman.'

Zati fell silent.

'We came home and found her doing these things,' Maria said. 'They were—'

'You don't need to tell me more,' Zati cut in.

Maria nodded. 'Grazie.' In the distance a deep voice began offering up prayers to the glory of God, the resonant words echoing inside San Felice. 'Is that . . . ?'

'Father Negri? Yes. He is the exorcist here, and I assist him.' Zati hesitated before speaking again. 'What makes you believe that Cara needs an exorcism?'

The Gheradinis stared at him. 'Is it not obvious, Father?' Andrea asked.

'Our daughter, our little girl, she would never do such things,' Maria said. 'She is – was – a good soul, with a good heart. We raised her to believe in the Lord as we do. For her to become such a wanton creature, to disgrace herself and her famiglia like this . . . it can only be that a demon has taken hold of her. That diavolo rules Cara from within. But we believe you and Father Negri can bring our daughter back to us. You can save her.'

Andrea grabbed Zati by the hands. 'Please, you must do this for us. For her. Please.'

'Let me speak with Father Negri,' Zati replied. 'If you permit, I will share with him all you have told me about your daughter. Is that what you wish me to do?'

The Gheradinis nodded without hesitation.

Zati followed the sound of Negri's voice to his private ufficio where the exorcist was pacing and praying. Zati recounted what the Gheradinis had told him while Negri listened. 'They seem certain their daughter is a demoniac, possessed by some creature of Satan. But couldn't her behaviour have another explanation?' Zati asked. 'The true demoniac might be this other woman who tricked their daughter into her disgrace.'

'Perhaps,' Negri agreed. 'Satan has an eternity of tricks to deceive and dull the wits, while his spawn can use all kinds of hidden persuasions on their victims. Demons will adopt human form, appearing in the guise of a saint or even as Christ himself to dupe the unwary. Their daughter could have fallen prey to such a diavolo . . .'

'They could send Cara to stay with relatives, away from the temptations of the city. Or she could be cloistered at a convent to reflect on her sins while praying for guidance—'

'We give the sacrament of exorcism here to those who are truly worthy of God's forgiveness. The Lord's work cannot be done by wringing your hands. I shall judge if the Gheradinis are worthy of my help, not you.' Negri slammed the heavy bible on his desk shut before stalking from the ufficio. 'Come, Father! We have a soul in need of our attention.'

After leaving Palazzo Coltello, Aldo had gone to the Podestà, where he found Manuffi sharing news of a fresh corpse in Piazza Santo Spirito. Cursing himself for being distracted by the contessa, Aldo had hurried to Saul's home. As he strode south, Aldo mulled the name Manuffi had given for the second victim: Freccia. A day ago, the thief had denied knowing anything about Zamora. Yet now both men had been killed, apparently by the same hand. That could be happenstance, but it was doubtful. Then there was Freccia coming to the bordello the previous evening, claiming he was being followed and demanding to see Aldo. Would pursing that matter as soon as Robustelli mentioned it this morning have made any difference? Or was Freccia already dead by then?

As Aldo approached Saul's back room, he heard Strocchi reading out the Latin words *Exorcizo vos, Pater Mendacii*, asking Saul and Rebecca for a translation.

'It says, "I exorcize you, Father of Lies",' Aldo interjected, announcing his arrival. 'I suspect that's a page taken from an exorcist's handbook.'

'Where have you—' Strocchi began before stopping himself. 'We can talk about that later. You said that exorcists have handbooks?'

'Many of them, yes. There is no approved text for what they do, so most exorcists have a book in which they gather different prayers and exhortations.' Aldo nodded to Saul and his student Rebecca. 'I encountered an exorcist while riding as a mercenary,' he added as an explanation for this knowledge.

'The variety of your life before we met never ceases to surprise,' Saul said.

Aldo joined Strocchi by the bench to examine the torn page. It was heavily creased, the edges burnt on three sides, with a strong odour rising from the paper. 'Incense?'

Strocchi nodded. 'What else do you make of it?'

A close study of the page confirmed Aldo's suspicions. He read out more of the Latin text, translating as he did. '"*Mando vobis, Filius Perditionis, constringo vos . . .*" I command you, Son of Perdition, I bind you . . . Yes, this is from an exorcist's handbook.'

'Could it be a copy?'

'Perhaps, but if so then someone has gone to a lot of effort to make it appear true.' Aldo picked up the paper for a better look at the burnt edges. 'The exorcist I met boasted about his handbook. He said it had been aspersed with holy water, signed by the fire of a baptismal candle, clouded with the smoke of incense, and spat upon by seething demoniacs.'

'Demoniacs?' Rebecca asked.

'It's the name given to those possessed by Satan or his demons,' Aldo replied. 'We should show this page to the priests at San Felice.'

'I will show it to them,' Strocchi said, folding the paper and tucking it inside his tunic. 'I was on my way there when Freccia's body was discovered in Piazza Santo Spirito.'

'Manuffi told me what happened,' Aldo replied. 'If you're going to San Felice, what do you need me to do?'

Strocchi ignored his question, addressing Saul instead. 'Doctor Orvieto, did you discover anything further during your examination?'

'No more than I told you earlier,' Saul said.

'Then Aldo can fetch a cart and have the body removed from here. You have given up enough of your time for us already.' Strocchi went to the doorway, pausing to smile at Saul and Rebecca. 'Again, grazie for your assistance.' He stalked out, leaving Aldo behind.

Saul arched an eyebrow. 'I see you two are on the best of terms.'

Aldo hurried after Strocchi. This had to be resolved.

For good or ill.

Chapter Twelve

 y the time Aldo was outside on via dei Giudei, Strocchi had reached the bottom end of the street and was turning east. 'Carlo, wait!' But Strocchi ignored him. Aldo ran in pursuit, determined to make the young officer see sense. They could be a formidable pair working together, but fighting against each other would do neither of them any good. Aldo caught up to Strocchi as he approached the unfinished Palazzo Pitti. 'You must let me explain. Even the condemned man is given that chance, yes?'

Strocchi stopped, folding his arms. 'Where were you? Why did you leave me waiting at the Podestà like a fool? What have you been doing all morning?'

'Not here,' Aldo said, conscious of people brushing by on their way to Ponte Vecchio. 'I'll tell you everything, but not out here on the street.' When Strocchi nodded his agreement, Aldo led him down a narrow alley and round a corner to a door that bore no name, offered no hint of what was beyond it. When Aldo opened the door the room inside was dark and warm, the aromas of woodsmoke and red wine reaching out as a welcome. This was where Signora Robustelli's women and others like them came to drink when they were not working. There was not a man in the place. 'Can we come in?' Aldo asked the sturdy figure at the bar.

'For now. But you know the rules.'

'Grazie, Luca.'

Aldo ushered Strocchi in and closed the door. They took a table by the hearth, sitting opposite each other. Luca brought two cups of wine, for which Aldo give them a generous handful of coin. The tavern owner towered over them, short-cropped hair brushing against the low ceiling. Strocchi stared as Luca returned to the bar. 'Is Luca a man or a woman?'

'Does it matter?'

'I . . .' Strocchi shrugged. 'I suppose not. Tell me, what is this place?'

'A refuge for those whom the Otto does not protect. Drink your wine.' While Strocchi did so, Aldo explained his secret task for the duke. 'That's where I was earlier, ingratiating myself with the contessa. I didn't realize it would take quite so long.'

'Did you succeed?'

'The contessa is an elusive creature. What she says or does is little guide to her thinking.'

Strocchi grimaced. 'The contessa sounds a lot like you.'

Aldo ignored that comment. 'Why were you so angry with me earlier? When I was summoned to Palazzo Medici, I warned you that you might need someone else's help today.'

'I thought you were jesting.'

'I was, but when the duke involves you in his plans, they take priority.' Aldo studied Strocchi. He had dark smudges of exhaustion under both eyes, and could not keep his hands still. This was about more than the day's events. 'Carlo, I've known you long enough to recognize when you are troubled. Is something wrong with Tomasia or the baby?'

'No, praise God.' Strocchi made the sign of the cross. 'Tomasia has been sick, worse than she was with Bianca, but that isn't— Besides, my mama has come to stay with us. She's at home now, looking after Tomasia and the little one.'

Aldo doubted Tomasia was enjoying that. 'Then what?'

'It's the segretario.'

'Ahh. And what has the bastardo been doing now?'

'You shouldn't call him that,' Strocchi said. 'As segretario he deserves our respect.'

'When Bindi does something worthy of my respect, he will have it. Until that day I'll call him whatever I wish. So, how has that bloated piece of—'

'Aldo . . .'

'How has he been tormenting you?'

Strocchi slumped back in his seat. 'He promised to demote me and have someone else investigate Zamora's murder unless I found the killer soon.'

That was typical of Bindi. The self-important merda seemed to believe that threats and abuse were the best ways to motivate those at his command. 'Ignore him,' Aldo said.

'I can't. He's expecting my report in a few hours.'

'Yes, you will make your report, but you should ignore his threats. They're as hollow and empty as his belly is full. Ignore him. Your life will be much easier if you do.'

'But how can I?'

'You're the best officer Bindi has for this investigation, and he knows it. I suspect the duke has been demanding quick progress from the segretario, so Bindi demands the impossible from you. It is the way of things in this city.'

'Merda always travels down,' Strocchi said.

'Sorry?'

'It's something Cerchi once told me.'

'He was right about that,' Aldo agreed. But not much else. Fortunately, that bastardo had been dead several years. Even the worms would be finding Cerchi a bitter meal. 'Do your job to the best of your abilities. Nobody can expect more than that. Not even the segretario.'

'Perhaps you're right,' Strocchi said, but he didn't sound convinced.

'Then let's talk about what we can do to find this killer. You should know that I have a link to Freccia. He has been an occasional informant for me. In fact, I questioned him about Zamora yesterday, but he had nothing useful to tell me.'

'Is it true that Freccia . . .' Strocchi's face reddened.

'That he sucked cazzi for coin? Yes. People do desperate things to stay alive.'

'But he was married. He and his wife, Fiora, they rent a room from Bonfantino Bassano, upstairs in the house next to Doctor Orvieto.'

'I've told you before, Carlo: don't judge others until you know them better. Each of us makes our own choices about how we live, and some of those choices are not always what is permitted by the word of God, or the laws of this city.'

Strocchi sipped at his wine. 'Life was simpler when I lived in a village.'

'Perhaps it seemed simpler because you had fewer choices or responsibilities.'

'Perhaps.'

Aldo finished his wine. Luca kept a fine cellar, better than most merchants, but also kept their prices cheap. 'Tell me what Saul found when he examined Freccia's corpse.'

Strocchi shared the morning's discoveries. It seemed Freccia was murdered by the same hand that took Zamora's life, but the killer was rushed this time. Strocchi described the disarray in Freccia's rented room, suggested he was attacked there. Quite how the killer got the body to Piazza Santo Spirito without anyone noticing was unclear, as was the reason for taking Freccia's life. 'He was a thief, so he may have stolen something from the killer.'

'Maybe. But to use the same method as they did for Zamora . . . There must be a link between them. Something that we cannot yet see. But what is it?'

Strocchi rubbed his tired eyes. 'It would be better if you led this investigation, not me. You would have found who killed Zamora by now.'

'No, I wouldn't. We are dealing with something beyond both our experience.' Aldo lifted his cup, gesturing for Luca to refill it. 'Do you want another?' he asked, but the young officer shook his head. Aldo waited until Luca had been and gone before continuing. 'Let's ask the obvious question: what connects Freccia and Zamora?'

'They both lived in Oltrarno,' Strocchi said. 'Their homes were within a few minutes' walk of each other. Both spent time in the company of men.'

'But for different reasons. Zamora preferred them, Freccia did so for coin.'

'And they were killed the same way.'

'That says more about the murderer than it does about the victims.'

'They both had ash smeared on their foreheads, their tongues cut in two, and similar pieces of paper placed inside their tunics,' Strocchi observed.

'I suspect the rain-soaked page that Saul found on Zamora's body was also torn from an exorcist's handbook,' Aldo said. 'Remember what was written on it.'

'*Mando vobis* . . .'

'"I command you." That's an exhortation by someone driving

out a demon. And I wouldn't be surprised if the ash on Zamora's forehead also spelled a Latin word before the downpour washed most of it away. But what word?'

'All we have is pieces of a puzzle,' Strocchi said.

'We need to find out more to know who is behind these killings. We should—' But Aldo's words were interrupted by the tavern door bursting open and two giggling young women tumbling in. The newcomers stopped, surprised to see Aldo and Strocchi. Then they dissolved into giggles again before demanding Luca bring them wine.

The tavern keeper emerged from behind the bar, bringing cups and a fresh bottle. 'You and your friend have to leave now,' Luca told Aldo. 'Rules are rules.'

'Grazie for bending them on my behalf,' he replied. 'Come, Carlo, time to go.' He ushered Strocchi from the tavern, more giggles following them to the door.

A fine drizzle was falling outside, but glowering clouds overhead showed that worse was on its way. Aldo cursed himself for not wearing a cloak to keep out the rain. The cold autumn air made his head spin a little. Drinking so much without food had been a mistake. 'I'm at your service until the end of the day when I must report to the duke. What do you need me to do?'

'Find Freccia's wife and tell her that he has been murdered,' Strocchi said. 'She works in a tannery, but that's all I know. Doctor Orvieto's student may be able to help with that, she seemed to be familiar with Fiora.'

'I'll go to Saul's first. That will give me a chance to have the corpse removed, too.'

'Grazie,' Strocchi said. 'When you speak with Fiora, see what she knows about her husband's enemies. Someone chose to kill Freccia, we need to know why.'

'He was being followed,' Aldo remembered.

'Who, Freccia?'

'Yes. He came looking for me at the bordello not long before curfew last night, claimed he was being followed. Robustelli told me about it this morning.'

'But where were you last—' Strocchi shook his head. 'No, it doesn't matter. Where you sleep is your choice. So, if Freccia was being followed . . .'

'It could well have been his killer,' Aldo said.

'Agreed. Ask Freccia's wife if he mentioned it, or if she had noticed anyone.'

'I will. Where are you going next?'

'To San Felice. We know Zamora blamed the priests there for his nephew's death. I was on my way to talk with them when Freccia's body was found.'

'You can ask the priests about the page that was inside his tunic,' Aldo said, 'get them to confirm it is from an exorcist's handbook.'

Strocchi smiled. 'Yes.'

'You were already going to do that, weren't you?'

'Yes.'

Aldo patted him on the arm. 'You're a good investigator, Carlo. Don't let Bindi make you believe otherwise. But be careful how you question the priests. The diocese is adamant that anything which happens on Church property falls under its jurisdiction. If you accuse the priests at San Felice or they think you suspect them of a crime . . .'

'Why would I suspect a priest of a crime?'

For someone with such a keen mind, the young officer still had a childlike innocence about some things. 'Just . . . be careful,' Aldo said. 'Bindi is already looking over our shoulders. We don't need or want the Archbishop of Florence getting involved too. Agreed?'

Strocchi nodded 'We'll meet at the Podestà before curfew to share our findings.'

The contessa's initial impression of Tito Grossolano was not promising. He appeared to be an oaf of a man, with a voice that bruised the ear and a face quite liable to close the legs of every woman in Florence – even if they worked in a bordello. The man stank of horse merda yet seemed not to notice the odour and certainly did not apologize for it. His clothes were equally repulsive, as if Grossolano had been dressed by servants who hated him.

Nonetheless, experience had taught her it was dangerous to judge a person at once; better to spend time in their company and discover what secrets or depths lurked behind the mask they presented to the world. And, as time went on, it became apparent that her initial impression of Grossolano as unpromising was, indeed, incorrect.

In fact, he was far worse than that.

Grossolano swaggered around her salone examining the contents of the room as if it were a comely pig he planned to purchase. He talked at great length about his time in Bologna representing the Council of Ten, regaling the contessa with tiresome details about several minor triumphs. 'I do not consider myself a great spymaster,' Grossolano announced, 'but there are those who say I may be Venice's most effective weapon against its enemies.'

'Is that so?' the contessa replied, between sips of wine.

'Oh, yes. My time in Bologna was quite remarkable for the successes it brought and the secrets it unearthed. Just before I was summoned to your city, I had secured a reliable source of information within the lower administration of Bologna's accademia.'

'How remarkable.' It was more remarkable that Grossolano seemed to consider this worthy of a passing mention, let alone something about which he should boast. Even more remarkably, he was making her wistful for that dull evening she had spent in this very room with Dandolo. In some ways the two men were alike. Both were equally fond of their own voices, and both failed to notice how bored she was of them. But Dandolo was a submissive, grateful to be invited to her home, let alone hope she might listen to what he might say.

Grossolano was a different creature, one who clearly believed himself to be the master of all he encountered, the most powerful and potent presence in any salone. That made him far more dangerous than Dandolo, and therefore required careful handling. 'The Council was truly fortunate to have you working there,' the contessa said. 'What a shame you had to leave it all behind.' She feigned a thin smile, but he did not notice. He was too busy preening.

'Yes, it is. But I'm sure my efforts here in Florence shall be even more successful!'

Not if he didn't learn to stop using the Venetian tongue for every second word or phrase. Florentines were accustomed to visitors and foreign merchants being less able in the Tuscan dialect, but nobody would divulge secrets to a man unable to speak as they did.

Blessedly, Pozzo came in to announce a meal was ready. The contessa had her servants set a table in the salone. Normally she ate in the sala, but having Grossolano stamp horse merda across its floor as well was unforgivable. She suspected his table manners would be as crass as his conversation, and so it proved.

Grossolano attacked the spiced veal and sweetmeats like an animal might a carcass. He tore and gnawed at the food yet continued talking. Shreds of meat got caught in his beard, but he did not seem to notice, so enthused was he by praising himself. Eventually he was sated and sank back in the sturdy wooden chair, belching and patting his belly. 'Not as good as the feasts in Bologna,' Grossolano announced, 'but not bad.'

'You're too kind,' the contessa replied.

'Now, tell me about the informants your husband secured before his death. Zilio said you had done quite well in managing those sources over the past year.'

'Did he?'

Grossolano lifted one hip and loudly broke wind, sighing with contentment as he settled back down again. 'Yes, yes. He seems quite impressed with you, though I'm not sure why. Any fool knows that a woman lacks the qualities needed for a good spymaster.'

'Indeed? And what qualities might those be?' The contessa simpered a smile at him. 'Please, tell me more. I have so much to learn from a man of your . . . unique abilities.'

'Very well.' He picked at a morsel of food caught between his yellowing teeth. 'A good spymaster must first be a man of strength. He knows his own talents and those of his enemies. He can break through any resistance. He does not step aside when threatened and he does not allow others to dominate him. He is always right, and he knows it well.'

'That is . . . quite remarkable.'

'You agree, my dear?' Grossolano bowed his head to her a little. 'I'm glad that you so readily understand and appreciate the wisdom I am bestowing upon you. In my experience most women lack the intelligence and the wit to grasp such things. They are better off devoting their time to raising children and serving the needs of their husband.'

The contessa did not reply. She had called his opinions remarkable because it was rare to encounter someone so entirely incorrect in their beliefs and yet so wholehearted in their certainty that those beliefs were indisputably true. The fool had not even noticed that she'd told him nothing of her informants, those sources deep within the ducal court and other institutions she had found and fostered. If Zilio ever thought she might surrender such hard-won eyes and ears to this blustering bastardo . . . No, it would not happen. Not while she drew breath.

Grossolano had kept talking, but now he seemed to have stopped and was looking at her expectantly. The dolt must have asked a question. 'Forgive me, signor,' the contessa whispered, fanning herself with the fluttering fingers of one hand. 'I was still pondering the wisdom you shared earlier about what a wife should do to help her husband.'

That seemed to satisfy Grossolano, but it prompted another question.

'I understand you are a widow, yes?'

She nodded, feigning a smile.

'No man is currently courting you?'

'Not at present, no.'

'That's a shame. You're not a bad-looking woman.'

'Grazie, signor. Grazie mille.'

Grossolano grinned at her. 'For your age.'

The contessa let a winter's frost settle on her face. 'My age?'

'Yes. But I'm sure with the right man between your legs there still might be a chance of you producing an heir. Probably still a little fire down there, I imagine!'

The contessa had long ago decided she would not have children. There were many reasons for that. The discomfort of carrying a baby those long months. The pain and indignity of giving birth. The prospect of having some mewling infant suckling at her breasts, draining the life away. The fear of being reduced to nothing more than a compliant womb required to produce heirs capable of taking all that she had earned when they reached their majority. But one reason stood above all others for ensuring she never had children: the thought that any such offspring could grow up to become a man like Grossolano.

'I'm sorry, what was that you said?' she asked, staring into his eyes.

'I imagine you still have a little fire there, between your thighs.'

'Do you now?'

Grossolano grabbed his cup of wine, spilling half of its contents. 'Yes, of course! I could show you a thing or two in the bedchamber myself.' He lurched up from the table, his chair tumbling over behind him, cup raised. 'Here's to working together, my dear.'

The contessa stood. 'Signor Grossolano, you must excuse me for a moment. I have a personal matter to which I must attend immediately.'

'Got you all hot and bothered, have I?' he called as she stalked from the salone. 'Can't say I blame you. Never had any complaints about the contents of my hose!'

Chapter Thirteen

*A*ldo was pleased to see Manuffi sheltering from the rain in Saul's doorway. The drizzle had become a steady shower as Aldo strolled to via dei Giudei. It was dampening his tunic but did clear his head a little after the wine. 'What are you doing here?'

'I'm supposed to be working with Strocchi,' Manuffi replied, 'but he isn't here now. Doctor Orvieto didn't know where Strocchi has gone or when he might return, so . . . I'm waiting.'

'Strocchi has gone to question the exorcist,' Aldo said. Manuffi made the sign of the cross in response. 'You could go to San Felice or help me here.'

'I'll help you,' Manuffi volunteered.

'Good. You used a cart to bring Freccia's body here?'

'Yes, I borrowed one from a stall in Piazza Santo Spirito.'

Aldo handed him several coins. 'Go back and hire their cart for the rest of the day. You'll need a blanket as well. Bring both back here and then load the body onto the cart.'

Manuffi nodded. 'Where is it going?'

'Santa Maria Nuova. The ospedale will care for Freccia's corpse until someone claims it.' He passed over more coin. 'Give this to the nuns as payment.' Once Manuffi had gone, Aldo went inside. Saul was busy with patients, a cloth draped over the body still lying on the table. Aldo gestured for Rebecca to join him in the

149

hallway. 'I'm sorry about earlier. Tell Saul we'll have the remains removed soon.'

She shrugged. 'It does not bother us having a corpse in the room perhaps so much as you. Jewish tradition requires that a body must be watched over until it is buried.'

'Strocchi tells me you are familiar with Freccia's wife?'

'Fiora, yes. She works at a tannery across the Arno.'

'There are several tanneries there, do you know which?'

'It's east of Ponte Vecchio, the one closest to the bridge.'

'Grazie.' Saul called for Rebecca, but Aldo needed one more piece of information. 'I knew Freccia but have never met his wife. Can you describe her for me?'

'She's . . .' Rebecca frowned. 'I would say Fiora has never known an easy life, nor a comfortable one. She and Freccia have both fought for the few things they have. Neither are Jewish, so most on this street did not welcome them.'

'But you did?'

'I follow Saul's example. He does not judge others by their faith or his own.'

'Could you tell me what she looks like, so I can find her at the tannery?'

'Of course. Fiora is about my height, with long brown hair. To say that she has a face older than her years would be a kind way to describe it.'

'Rebecca!' Saul called again.

'I shouldn't keep him waiting.' Rebecca paused in the doorway. 'There's one other thing to know.'

'What's that?'

'She is heavy with child. Be gentle with her, it hasn't been easy.'

Aldo thanked Rebecca, but inwardly he was cursing. Telling a woman her husband had been murdered was difficult enough. Now Fiora faced raising a new-born alone.

Questioning an exorcist would be easier.

Strocchi shook off the rain before entering San Felice. He dipped his fingers in the holy water near the main door, dropping one knee to the cold stone floor while making the sign of the cross. It gave a chance to study the church without drawing attention to himself. The interior was gloomy, pairs of stained-glass windows high in the walls letting in limited light. The familiar aroma of incense hung in the air, transporting him back to a thousand Sundays spent praying for forgiveness.

This church was grander than that in Ponte a Signa, but still humble by Florentine standards. Its most striking feature was a large painted crucifix depicting Christ on the cross, a circle of gold leaf behind his head. Other churches fostered faith, bringing hope to those who had lost it. Yet San Felice inspired only dread. Why was it so dark in here? Yes, the afternoon was fading outside, but most churches were illuminated with candles paid for by the faithful. There were few candles burning in this place of God and that number diminished further as a priest in a black cassock snuffed out another.

Strocchi got back to his feet. 'Excuse me, Father . . . ?'

The priest startled. 'Forgive me, I didn't hear you enter.' He approached Strocchi with caution. 'I'm Pagolo Zati. Welcome to San Felice.'

'Grazie.'

'Your face is not familiar. Have you moved to the parish?' A shadow seemed to pass across Zati's face. 'Or did another reason bring you here?' The priest was younger than most Strocchi had met, no more than thirty, yet he had a slump in his shoulders. Zati carried pain and wariness in his eyes, as if afraid of what the answer to his questions might be.

'I did not come seeking an exorcism,' Strocchi said, 'and my parish is across the river in Santa Maria Novella. No, I'm here for another reason.' He reached into his tunic while introducing himself as an officer of the Otto. 'We found this page while investigating a case before the court and thought you might be able to translate the words on it for us.' He handed the torn paper to Zati, leaning closer to the priest. 'Reading Latin is beyond me, I'm afraid.'

'There's no need to apologize,' Zati replied as he unfolded the page. His eyes widened on seeing the text, confusion evident in his face. 'Where did you find this?'

Strocchi fought back an instinct to answer the question. Withholding the truth was a sin of omission, as bad as lying, let alone keeping it from a priest. But working for the Otto meant that to discover what others knew it was often necessary to share as little as possible. 'Do you recognize it, Father?'

'Yes, I . . .' Zati read the page, frowning as he did. 'This is written by Father Negri, whom I assist here at San Felice. I believe it is a page from the handbook he uses to perform the sacrament of exorcism.' Zati turned the page over. 'These words – *Mando vobis, Filius Perditionis, constringo vos* – are how he commands the demon to leave its host.'

'I see.' Strocchi took the page back. 'When did you last perform an exorcism here?'

'Perhaps nine days ago? No, ten. The demoniac was a young man who believed himself a woman trapped in the wrong body. Father Negri needed all his faith and skill to drive out those unholy thoughts.'

Strocchi noted Zati's careful choice of words. 'I thought the sacrament of exorcism was intended to drive demons out of those that they possess?'

'It is,' the priest agreed. 'But Father Negri believes the sacrament can be used to save others. To help those who perform unholy acts or carry unholy beliefs in their heart.' Zati still spoke only of what the other priest believed. Before Strocchi could press him further, a deep voice boomed across the church, making Zati gasp. 'Father Zati? Is something wrong?'

A stern figure marched towards them, his black cassock snapping with each stride. Strocchi braced himself; this must be Negri. The priest was broad-shouldered but otherwise thin, showing none of the indulgences some men of God favoured. His head was shaved clean, making it difficult to be certain of a precise age – perhaps fifty? His stern face was gaunt, a cleft in his chin adding to his severity. Everything about Negri spoke of fierce belief – perfect for driving out demons.

'No, Father Negri,' Zati whispered as the exorcist came closer.

Strocchi introduced himself, holding out the torn page. 'I was showing this to—'

Negri snatched it away, glaring at the handwriting. 'Where did you find it?'

'I'm sorry?' Strocchi was not used to such curtness from a priest.

'I said, where did you find it? And where is the rest of it?'

'The rest of it?'

Negri brandished the paper. 'This is a page in my handbook which was stolen from this church four days ago. Now, are you going to tell me where it was found, or do I have to ask the archbishop himself to intercede on my behalf?'

Aldo's advice about being careful not to get entangled with diocesan politics was proving all too prescient. Strocchi smiled at the exorcist. 'There's no need for that, Father Negri. As I was about to tell your colleague, the page was found on the body of a man in Piazza Santo Spirito earlier today.'

'And who was this man?'

'We are still confirming his name—'

'Who was he?' Negri snapped.

Before replying, Strocchi glanced at Zati. The younger priest was squirming, eyes cast down at the cold floor. 'We believe his name was Freccia,' Strocchi said.

Did Negri flinch when he heard the dead man's name? If so, he recovered immediately. 'My parishioners have spoken of him. A thief, and worse. Was this all you found? Have you searched where this Freccia lives?'

'I scoured his room myself. There were no similar pages, and no handbook.' Strocchi kept his suspicion about the page found on Zamora quiet. He might have shared that with Zati but had no wish to offer Negri anything beyond simple courtesy.

'And you have nothing more to tell us?' the exorcist demanded.

'No, Father. I came here to ask questions. Was anything else stolen?'

Negri ignored the question. 'You have no jurisdiction here,' he insisted. 'San Felice is Church property. If you wish to question myself or Father Zati . . .' He gestured at the other priest dismissively – 'then you must put those questions to the diocese. In writing.'

'Father Negri, is that necessary?' Zati asked. 'This officer came here quite—'

'I have said all I am willing to in his presence,' Negri replied, glaring at him before pointing past Strocchi to the entrance of San Felice. 'You may leave now.'

But Strocchi refused to be dismissed so easily. 'I will when you return that page.'

'Why? This is my property.'

'It is evidence in a murder investigation.'

'Murder?' Zati took a step back. 'You never mentioned that.'

'I did not believe it was necessary,' Strocchi replied.

'What you believe is of no consequence,' Negri announced. He folded the torn page in half before slipping it into one of his cassock sleeves. 'If you wish to have this, you must ask the archbishop to agree. I answer only to him, the Pope and Our Lord. You have no authority here.' The exorcist stepped closer to Strocchi, so near their noses were almost touching, the intense aroma of incense surrounding them. 'Leave this church. Now.'

The contessa had retreated to her private ufficio, grateful to escape Grossolano's insufferable presence. Returning to the salone and listening to more of his boorish, belligerent blustering was too dreadful for words. Fortunately, her maggiordomo was available to intercede.

'Is he . . . ?' Pozzo asked.

'Yes. As bad as I feared,' the contessa replied. 'No, I do believe he is worse. I would be hard pressed to think of a man less suitable for the task Venice has entrusted to him. What he stepped in outside the palazzo would be a better choice.' She smiled at Pozzo. 'Grazie for the placement of that horse merda, by the way. Most artfully done.'

The maggiordomo bowed his head, acknowledging the praise. 'And what is to be done about Signor Grossolano? If his arrival is as calamitous as you believe . . .'

'He cannot be allowed to take my place. The man was studying the salone earlier as if he already owned the palazzo and couldn't wait to have a fresco of himself on each wall.'

'Can he be persuaded to return to Bologna?'

'Perhaps, but the order which sent him here came from the new Inquisitorie di Stato in Venice. That will demand answers if Grossolano does not fulfil its wishes.' The contessa tapped a finger to her lips. 'How did the tribunal select such an unsuitable man? What have you been able to uncover about Grossolano? How is he connected to the Council of Ten?'

'It seems, Contessa, that your guest is a nephew of the Doge's councillor appointed to this new tribunal. When the three men gathered to review Venetian intelligence gathering in rival city states, this uncle pressed for Grossolano to be given Florence.'

That explained the appointment. Venetians would always promote the interests of their own blood relatives over anyone they deemed an outsider, no matter how unsuitable the preferred choice. She had married into the famiglia Coltello which had a significant heritage in the history of Venetian merchants and intelligence gathering, yet becoming the Contessa would never absolve her of being born elsewhere. To the Council of Ten and its new tribunal, she was always going to be a Florentine and therefore a subject of suspicion.

She had promised her husband on his deathbed that she would act in the best interests of his beloved Venice. There were few vows to which she had remained faithful during their short, eventful marriage, but this was different. He gave her so much and asked for so little in return. This promise must be kept, she had sworn to it. Besides, she had an innate talent for spying. The only pity was in her having taken so long to discover her true calling.

But now the Inquisitorie di Stato wished to follow another path. If her replacement were more able, or at least more promising than Grossolano, she might have helped him. But the man was an idiota, liable to do more damage than good. All her work of the past few years would be undone in days if Grossolano became Venice's spymaster here in Florence.

No, it would not do. It would not do at all.

'Pozzo, I have three tasks for you.'

'Yes, Contessa?'

'First, I need you to offer my apologies to Signor Grossolano. Say I have taken ill and retired to my bedchamber.' She paused, letting a smile play about her lips. 'No, please tell him that I have womanly troubles and thus I need to be alone. That will reinforce what he thinks of me and embarrass a man like him far too much to question you any further.'

The maggiordomo nodded. 'Of course.'

'Second, have one of the prettier servant girls bring our guest more wine and food as he desires. She is to tempt and tease him as much as she can stand but warn her to always stay beyond his reach. Signor Grossolano has the mark of a man who does not keep his hands to himself. He's had so much to drink I doubt his cazzo could penetrate wet, uncooked polenta, but ensure the girl suffers nothing worse than Grossolano's company. I want him incapable of leaving this palazzo tonight. Best that we contain the damage he might do.'

'Very good, Contessa. And the third task?'

'That will require more planning. But, when it is done, I am certain the Inquisitorie di Stato shall see the wisdom of retaining my services as its spymaster here in Florence.'

Aldo smelled the tannery before he saw it; the rancid aroma of animal waste was unmistakeable. The rain had eased by the time he reached the dank building. Inside, Aldo noticed none of the workers seemed to share his revulsion; they must be used to the stench. Each wore a leather apron as they stirred foul liquids in the tannery vats. Steam rose from animal hides that hung in front of a roaring fire. The acrid aroma of stale piss filled the air, making Aldo's eyes water. He didn't believe in Hell but, if it did exist, damnation would resemble this place.

A burly woman stamped towards him, wide of hip and plain of face. Her brown curls were tied back beneath a black headscarf, and her muscular arms were stained from working the tannery vats. 'What do you want?' she demanded, wiping a hand across her brow.

Aldo introduced himself as a constable of the Otto before asking for Fiora.

'She's resting outside, by the river,' the woman replied. 'Baby coming soon means she can't work the same long shifts as the rest of us.' Her eyes narrowed. 'The Otto? That's a criminal court. Why do you need to see Fiora?'

'I'd rather tell her.'

'Fine. This way.' The woman led Aldo through the tannery, introducing herself as Signora Dea Vanni while they weaved between the other workers. 'Fiora and I usually scrape hides, removing the hair from one side and flesh off the other. Not an easy job.'

'Probably needs strong hands,' Aldo said.

'Do it long enough, you get strong.' Vanni opened a door, revealing the Arno beyond it. The river was flowing by fast, made high by recent downpours. A platform jutted out over the water. A small woman sat on the edge, legs dangling over. Her long brown hair was tied back under a black scarf. 'Fiora, this man from the Otto needs to talk with you,' Vanni said.

Aldo saw Fiora's shoulders slump. 'What's Freccia done now?'

'It's not what he has done,' Aldo replied, 'but what was done to him.'

She twisted round to face Aldo. Rebecca's description had been accurate. Fiora could not have been more than twenty-five, but she had the hard face of someone who had seen a lifetime's pain and worse. She clutched a hand to her belly, the pregnancy obvious behind her apron.

'Freccia was murdered early this morning, not long after curfew.'

'How?' Vanni asked. 'Where?'

Aldo decided she might as well know too. It would spare Fiora the need to retell others later, and Vanni's eagerness suggested she was happy to share. 'In your room on via dei Giudei,' he said, crouching down beside Fiora. 'I understand from Rebecca Levi that you leave for work soon as curfew lifts each morning.'

Fiora nodded. There was no grief in her face, not yet. 'Did he suffer?'

'His death was quick,' Aldo said.

'That's something, I suppose.' Fiora looked past him to Vanni. 'Dea, you go back to work. I'll be in soon, yes?'

The other woman nodded before returning to the tannery.

'I've known Freccia for several years,' Aldo said. 'Before he was a thief.'

'Then you know what he was.' Fiora grimaced. 'We both took coin to let men use us. That's how we met. But you can only do that for so long. I found work here, and Freccia took to thieving. He always did have quick hands.'

'I remember. He took my pouch once. I was lucky to catch him.'

'Is that why he was killed? Was it one of the people he stole from?'

'We aren't sure. Freccia sought me out last night, not long before curfew. I wasn't home but he told my landlady that someone had been following him.'

'He said the same to me. Called them his shadow.'

'How long had this been happening?'

'A few days, maybe.' Fiora winced, stroking her belly. 'The baby's kicking.'

Grief would find Fiora soon. When it did, Aldo doubted his questions would get many answers. 'Did he describe whoever was following him?'

'Not their face. They always wore a cloak with the hood pulled up.'

'Beside those Freccia stole from, was there anyone else who might have wanted him dead?'

Fiora hesitated. She knew the answer, but would she share it? Eventually she spoke.

'He was getting coin, but I don't know from who. Enough each month to pay for the rent of our room and put a little aside for when the baby comes.'

'And Freccia never said where he was getting it?'

She shook her head. 'I knew not to ask.'

Regular payments meant Freccia was getting paid – or paid off. Extorting coin was not his usual crime, but the prospect of father-hood might have compelled Freccia to try. It was a dangerous pathway. Sooner or later the person being extorted would run out of coin or patience. When they did, the response could be deadly.

That gave a reason for killing Freccia, but not Zamora, and it was clear the same hand was responsible for both murders. Unless one was a stratagemma to disguise the other . . .

'Where is he?' Fiora asked.

'His body is being taken to Santa Maria Nuova. The ospedale nuns will care for his body until you are ready.'

She nodded. 'And what will happen if I don't? If I leave him there.'

'The nuns will have him buried in a pauper's grave.'

'Then that's what they must do. All the coin I have is for our baby.' The tears came at last, Freccia's death seeping into her. Fiora had no more words. Aldo went to the tannery door and gestured for Vanni. He left her tending to Fiora beside the river.

Chapter Fourteen

The heavens opened as Strocchi approached the Podestà, making him run to escape the downpour. The sky had darkened to a glower while he strode back from San Felice, matching his mood after the encounter with Father Negri. Priests were friendly, welcoming souls in Strocchi's experience, men who sought out ways to help others whether familiar or a stranger. But the exorcist had protected his domain with fierce resolve, treating anyone who questioned his judgement as a threat.

Strocchi paused in the sheltered stone corridor between the Podestà entrance and its courtyard, waiting for the rain to ease. Negri's insistence that his handbook had been stolen seemed credible enough, but why did he not report this loss to the Otto? There had been no chance to ask him that question, nor whether he had informed the diocese. Negri made no mention of anything else being taken, which most citizens would. If that was the case, it suggested the thief wanted only the handbook.

Did they steal it so pages torn from inside could be hidden in their victims' clothing as a marker of some kind? If so, what did that signify? The fact Freccia was a thief was quite a coincidence. Had he stolen the handbook for somebody else, not realizing they intended to claim him as one of their victims? Strocchi shivered. A cold wind was blowing through the corridor, and the sleeves of his tunic were wet from the rain. But that was not the reason for his chill. How many pages were in the exorcist's handbook? How many more bodies might they find before the murderer was brought before the Otto to face justice?

Aldo ran in through the Podestà entrance, cursing loudly as he ran a hand through his dripping-wet hair. His tunic was soaked through, and his boots looked equally sodden. 'Diavolo! Knew I should have worn a cloak today.'

'Not even the best of cloaks would have kept you dry,' Strocchi said.

'True, but it might have helped.' Aldo shook his hands, letting out a long breath. 'How was your meeting with the exorcist?'

'I was getting some answers from his colleague, Father Zati, but then—'

'Zati? I met a priest called Zati when I was investigating the killing at Santa Maria Magdalena. That was two – no, two and a half years ago. What did he look like?' Strocchi described the priest. 'That's him. Seemed to have a good heart but he was out of his depth.'

'Zati was helpful enough until the exorcist saw us talking.' Strocchi recounted his meeting with Negri, how the older priest appeared to flinch when Freccia's name was mentioned and how the exorcist claimed his handbook had been stolen.

'We won't see that page again,' Aldo said when Strocchi was finished. 'The diocese will never let us question Negri without a monsignor observing, and probably not at all.'

'You were right to warn me. I should have been more careful.'

'Nonsense,' Aldo insisted. 'Our best chance of discovering whether Negri has any part in this will be via Zati. Sounds as though you were getting through to him. If you can approach him outside of San Felice, when Negri isn't around . . .'

Strocchi nodded, it could work. 'What did you learn from

Freccia's widow?' Aldo described his meeting with Fiora at the tannery, how Freccia had also told his wife that he was being followed, and her suspicion that he had been extorting coin from someone. 'It would explain why Freccia was killed,' Strocchi said, 'but not why Zamora's death was so similar.'

'Agreed,' Aldo said.

'What should we do next?'

'It's a good question. Wish I had a good answer.'

Strocchi frowned. 'I need to go and make my report to Bindi. Now we've got two murders to solve instead of one. He won't be happy.'

'The segretario rarely is. But he needs you on this case. Ignore all his threats, they're hollow words. He can't do what you can – remember that.'

'Grazie. Is the duke expecting a report from you before curfew?'

'Probably.' Aldo peered at the gloom outside the Podestà. The rain was easing a little. 'I had hoped to get dry first, but that is a fool's wish it seems.' He rested a hand on Strocchi's shoulder. 'Go home after your report. Be with Tomasia and your daughter.'

'And Mama, don't forget her.'

Aldo laughed. 'Oh, Carlo! You've quite the night ahead of you.'

Father Zati knelt in front of the painted crucifix at San Felice while Negri stalked back and forth behind him, muttering and snarling. 'I shall be reporting this outrage when I am next at the diocesan ufficio. How dare the Otto send an officer to accuse me, a man of God!' Negri stopped. 'No, it cannot wait. Father Zati, come with me.'

Zati was saying a rosary, fingers pulling the beads through his grasp. 'I'm sorry . . . ?'

'Come with me,' Negri repeated, stalking towards his private ufficio. 'Now!'

Zati got up, brushing dust from his cassock before following the exorcist. Once they were both in the ufficio, Negri pushed Zati to sit behind the desk. 'I am too angry to write, you must do it for me. What I have to say is too important to be made unreadable by rage.'

Zati found a fresh sheet of paper and ink, preparing to write.

'Make it for the attentions of Archbishop Buondelmonti and Monsignor Testardo,' Negri snapped, returning to his pacing. 'And then write this: I must report a grave injustice which has been perpetrated against the Church here in Florence. An upstart officer from the Otto di Guardia e Balia came to San Felice today, making wild accusations against myself. This criminal court has no jurisdiction over any representative of the Church, and yet this . . .' Negri paused, his brow furrowing. 'What was his name?'

'Carlo Strocchi, I believe,' Zati replied.

'And yet this Carlo Strocchi had the unmitigated temerity to suggest that I, a true and faithful servant of Our Lord, might have some involvement with mortal sins which have been committed within the walls of this city. He even sought to suggest that the theft of certain valuable items of mine from San Felice was part of these terrible transgressions, as if their loss – which has been a great cause of sorrow to me – was somehow my fault!'

Zati was struggling to keep up. 'I shall have to make a clean copy of your words—'

'Yes, of course,' Negri said. 'Begin a new paragraph. Write this: Satan lurks in most things. To be pure enough to perform the sacrament of exorcism I make great sacrifices each and every day. None can question the pains to which I have put my body as contrition for all sins. Cleanliness of heart and soul are indispensable for those who act as instruments of God's work, even if our flesh is as weak as that of any other.'

Zati nodded, his hand flying across the paper to keep up.

'I must ask the diocese to intervene and ensure that neither Strocchi nor any other representative from the Otto shall dare set foot within San Felice again, either in pursuit of answers to this matter or whatever else they may be investigating. Those within the walls of this church answer only to Our Lord, to you, Archbishop Buondelmonti, and to your representatives. You know what I have done on behalf of the Church, the burdens I have borne for it. I ask for no reward but to be left in peace to continue my good works. Praise be to God, Father Camillo Negri – and put today's date at the end of that.'

Zati kept writing, ink spattering the page.

'Have you got all of that?' Negri demanded. 'Well?'

The younger priest nodded.

'Very well.' The exorcist drew himself up to his full height. 'I shall have to mortify my flesh again. It is the only way to drive this anger out of my soul.' He paused at the door on his way out. 'When you've finished with that, go and deliver it to the diocesan ufficio. I refuse to have my work here disturbed any further. Never again.'

When Strocchi concluded his report in the segretario's ufficio, Bindi did not speak at first. Instead, he tapped a finger on the table in front of him, letting the silence widen until it seemed they had been there for hours. In the past Strocchi would have rushed to fill that emptiness, believing it would satisfy the segretario. But nothing could ever satisfy Bindi, and few things brought praise from his lips.

Remembering what Aldo had said, Strocchi remained silent.

Eventually, Bindi cleared his throat. 'Last time you came to my ufficio, there was one murder to solve, one killer to find. Now you tell me there has been a second murder, another body displayed on the streets for everyone to see – and you have no idea who is responsible.'

Strocchi did not reply. Do not reach for the lure, and the snare could be avoided.

'What am I to tell the duke in the morning? "Forgive me, Your Grace",' Bindi said, affecting the apologetic voice of an annoying child, '"but my men are too incompetent to keep your citizens safe and they are no closer to catching this killer".' The segretario laughed, but there was only bitterness in his voice. 'No, I don't think that will do.'

Still Strocchi kept his own counsel, ignoring the sneers and provocations.

'Well?' Bindi asked. 'Have you nothing to say to me?'

'I have given my report.'

'And?'

'I await your instructions on what should be done next,' Strocchi replied.

The segretario scowled, nostrils flaring, but his finger stopped tapping the table. 'Very well. I shall explain to the duke that this matter has proven more complicated than was evident at first, but the Otto remains confident the killer will be found.'

Strocchi nodded. Better not to interrupt Bindi when he was acknowledging the truth.

'Do you need more constables to help with the investigation?' the segretario asked.

'No, sir. Aldo is enough, and Manuffi has been assisting us at times.'

Bindi huffed his annoyance. 'You may go.' Strocchi strode to the door, waiting for a barbed comment. The segretario always had to have the final word. 'But I have noted your behaviour,' Bindi said. 'Clearly you are spending too much time in Aldo's company. You are becoming almost as annoying as him when he was an officer. Dismissed!'

Strocchi gave a respectful bow of his head before leaving the ufficio, holding back a smile until he was out on the loggia, over-looking the courtyard. Almost as annoying as Aldo? There were worse things to be called. Far worse.

Curfew was near by the time Aldo reached Palazzo Medici. The days were getting shorter as autumn tightened its grasp on the city, while all that rain earlier had masked the sun's descent. Most of the year it was easy to know how much daylight remained. A glance at the orange terracotta roof tiles on buildings ahead or behind gave the answer. But dull grey clouds were hiding the sun today, so it was stalls closing for business and workers hurrying home that told the time instead. The downpour had absolved the streets of their usual ripe aromas, but forced Aldo to step carefully to avoid the flowing channels of human waste. He would not be welcome in the ducal residence wearing damp boots stained with merda. At least the brisk walk had dried his clothes a little.

Entering Palazzo Medici by the rear door to avoid prying eyes, Aldo sent a servant to summon Campana. The private segretario soon brought Aldo before Cosimo. The duke seemed surprised to see him. 'I thought it would take several days to ingratiate yourself with the contessa, perhaps by finding an ally within her household.'

'I chose a more direct path,' Aldo replied. He gave a summary of his meeting with the contessa, and the stratagemma employed to win her favour: the truth.

'You offered to spy on me for her in return for spying on her for me?'

'She was too clever to believe I was anything but Your Grace's agent. Besides, the contessa may not be Venice's spymaster here in Florence much longer.' Aldo relayed her claim that the Council of Ten had a new tribunal in charge of intelligence gathering, and that it had appointed Grossolano to replace her. 'He is staying at Palazzo Coltello tonight.'

Cosimo and Campana exchanged a guarded look.

'You already knew about Grossolano's appointment,' Aldo said.

'We knew of his arrival,' Campana replied. 'All newcomers to the city are observed and noted, for obvious reasons. Grossolano came from Bologna but spoke as a Venetian; that was worthy of bringing to the duke's attention.'

'My former spy in Venice reported that some Council of Ten responsibilities might be taken by a new organization,' the duke added, 'so what the contessa told you confirms this. But we need to know more, either from her or this Grossolano. When are you returning to her palazzo?'

'Tomorrow.' Aldo smiled. 'I'm introducing myself to Grossolano as his new informant within the Otto. Both he and the contessa will be present for that.'

Cosimo nodded his agreement. 'If this Grossolano is usurping her as spymaster here in Florence, you have an opportunity to win his trust immediately. Campana will supply you with some secrets that can be shared without endangering the interests of Florence.'

'And if Grossolano is not replacing her, give them to the contessa instead,' Campana said.

'Understood.' Aldo bowed to the duke before withdrawing from the ufficio. Having met the contessa, he doubted she would surrender without a fight. Any apparent withdrawal would more likely be a ruse to tempt her new rival into an unwise advance.

Aldo suspected Signor Grossolano would not be Venice's spymaster in Florence for long.

Strocchi stood on the street in front of his home, listening to bells chime across the city for the start of curfew. The prospect of going up the stairs to two rooms full of his wife, his daughter and his mama was daunting. He loved all three of them, but they were equally headstrong in their own way. Mama expected him to set aside everything because she had invited herself to visit. Bianca was a child of only two but already bending and twisting him to her will, craving near constant attention. And as for Tomasia . . .

His wife was as stubborn as the other two. But she said far less, keeping her fears and pain hidden away. Tomasia spoke rarely of her life before meeting him, though he kept note of the few things she did reveal. Her famiglia home had been uncertain, and later lost. She and her brother had survived by their wits until illness claimed him, leaving Tomasia with all his debts. That led to her imprisonment in Le Stinche, the prison where she first met Aldo. She saved his life there and, in return, he had Strocchi pay for her release.

That was when Strocchi first met Tomasia, emerging from the prison. His heart had been lost in that moment, yet he still harboured doubts. Not about their love for each other – Bianca was proof of that – but more about what Tomasia saw in him. Had she married him for his stability, his certainty, his trustworthiness? He did not know and could not bring himself to ask in case the reply was something he did not wish to hear.

Gathering his resolve, Strocchi went up the stairs. He opened the door expecting a babble of voices and sounds, his mama talking faster than a horse could race while Bianca bounced up and down. Instead, there was the most unexpected thing: quiet. Mama was asleep in a chair, head lolled down on her chest, gentle snores slipping from her mouth. Even more miraculous, Bianca was dozing in his mama's lap, arms wrapped round her.

Tomasia appeared from the other room, saying nothing. She took Strocchi's hand, leading him to the back of their home. 'Don't wake them, whatever you do.'

Strocchi nodded. He was not going to spoil this moment of blessed calm. Only when they were in the other room did he speak, and then in a whisper. 'What happened?'

'They exhausted each other a while ago,' Tomasia replied. 'It's been wonderful.' She was looking better than she had for days, the exhaustion gone from beneath her eyes. 'Your mama kept Bianca busy so I could rest. And she made me a remedy with herbs she brought from the village. It tastes disgustoso, but I felt better after.'

Mama had always been good at making remedies, using recipes her mama had passed on. There was no doctor in Ponte a Signa, so the villagers relied on the balms and remedies she made. 'It's good to see you looking better. I've been so worried.'

Tomasia kissed him before patting the bed. 'Come here and tell me about your day, Carlo. But quietly, yes?'

Strocchi settled beside her and shared all he had seen and learned. Another murder, by the same hand as the first. The fact someone was following Freccia before his murder, and that nobody saw the killer. The word *Patris*, written in ash on Freccia's forehead, and the page from a stolen exorcism handbook tucked in his tunic. The strange taverns that Aldo knew. How curt and dismissive

171

Father Negri has been. Keeping calm with the segretario, despite his goading. It took a while, but Tomasia listened intently to everything.

'Well done for standing up to Bindi,' she said.

'That was Aldo's doing, he told me to value what I do.'

'And he's right, but you're the one who had to face the segretario alone.'

'Bindi was right when he said we're no closer to knowing who is behind this, and now there are two victims.' He rested his head on Tomasia's shoulder. 'Santo Spirito, what if another body is found in the morning?'

'Then you will do what you should. Find out who they are, tell their famiglia what has happened, and look for clues that will help you discover the killer.'

'Yes, but—'

'Shhh,' Tomasia said, putting a finger to his lips. 'Enough, Carlo. You need to rest too. You can do no more now.' She replaced the finger with her lips. 'Well, maybe there is something you can do . . .'

'But –' he said, between kisses – 'Mama is in – the next room . . .'

'Then you shall have to be quiet about it . . .'

Aldo lingered in the shadows of via dei Giudei as twilight claimed the sky. The bells for curfew had long since chimed but Rebecca was still standing on Saul's doorstep, talking with the doctor about their patients. Eventually she left, and Saul closed his door for the night. Aldo strolled to the narrow alleyway that gave access to the back of Saul's home. Better to look as if he belonged. People always saw those who were furtive or appeared out of place.

Was that how someone was able to go inside Freccia's room,

kill the thief and get his body out unnoticed? Was the person responsible so familiar on via dei Giudei that its Jewish residents did not see the killer? No, that was leaping too far ahead. Freccia's neighbours had yet to be properly questioned about what they saw or did not see. That would be a task for tomorrow.

Aldo tapped at the back door, waiting as darkness embraced the city. A flutter danced in his belly, as it always did in these moments before they were together. Then the door opened, and Saul was smiling at him, those warm hazel eyes inviting him in.

Tomorrow could wait for tomorrow.

Chapter Fifteen

❦

Friday, October 31st 1539

Aldo left Saul's bed before the bells chimed for the end of the curfew. He would rather stay pressed against Saul's back, enjoying the warmth of him. But neither of them could risk Aldo being seen leaving the house two mornings in succession. One day they might be able to live together without the constant fear of being accused, of being attacked, of being shamed for who they were and how they loved. Yet Aldo knew that day would probably not come, not for him and Saul. Perhaps it might be true for others in years ahead, or perhaps it would never be true. Not while people were taught to hate difference by those with closed minds and too much certainty in their hearts.

There was another reason to rise early. Aldo wanted to stand outside on via dei Giudei as curfew ended and watch those who passed the house of Bonfantino Bassano where Freccia had died. Most people were habitual, doing the same things day after day. They got up at a particular time, left their homes at a similar time, and usually followed a familiar journey to wherever they went. There were variations, of course, such as going to Mass on Sundays and the feast days that Florence observed as a city. But the patterns of most lives were as well worn as the dirt road that cut between the homes on this narrow street.

The first people appeared as bells rang out across the city, Jewish men hurrying away to their work as cloth makers and dyers; women emerging to pour waste into the channel that ran down the middle of via dei Giudei. Almost everyone here was Jewish, men wearing skull caps and sombre clothes, women in shawls and modest dresses, all of them wrapped up against the autumn chill. Aldo's questions were answered by many of them in Hebrew, suggesting they weren't willing to talk or simply didn't understand him. But some were eager to share opinions of Freccia and Fiora, calling them outsiders or strangers. Several women were sympathetic towards Fiora, now a widow carrying a dead man's child.

But none recalled seeing anything or anyone unusual the previous day at this time.

After the initial flurry of departures Aldo rubbed his hands together, blowing warmth into them and stamping his boots on the ground. The languid days of summer and its hot, humid nights had long since been replaced by the chill of autumn and the promise of worse to come. Colder air might help stifle the city's riper aromas, but it was a poor exchange for numb toes and cracked lips. He could not – would not – endure another winter on night patrols, freezing his palle off while smug Bindi slept in a comfortable bed.

Newcomers entered the street, using its narrow length to avoid the busier roads that led to and from the bridges across the Arno. A few of those passing were Jews, most were not, but all had the tired look of workers trudging towards another day of labour. Aldo could tell the administrators and servants by how clean their clothes were, while those bound for butcher shops and tanneries wore rougher tunics and hose stained by their work. Most were more concerned with getting to their jobs than talking about what they had or hadn't seen a day ago. Few could recall noticing anything unusual.

One female servant remembered a cart in front of Bassano's door because it blocked her way and there had been nobody to complain to. A fishmonger's assistant saw someone pushing the cart along the street but struggled to describe the person. 'They were well ahead of me,' he said. 'And they were wearing a cloak, with the hood over their head.'

'If they were ahead of you, what was their size, their shape?' Aldo asked.

'Big.'

'Big?'

The assistant nodded.

'Big as in tall, or big because they were heavy of body?' Aldo persisted, breathing through his mouth to avoid inhaling the stench of old fish that surrounded the assistant.

'Tall as you, but more powerful. Broad across the shoulders, too.'

'Anything else?'

The assistant shook their head, already hurrying on. 'Sorry, but I'm late.'

It was a Jewish woman called Tamar who proved most helpful. She came out of a house three doors along from Bassano, an infant on one hip and a basket in her spare hand. Aldo introduced himself and explained his purpose. 'Can't be easy getting people to talk to you,' Tamar observed. 'We Jews are often suspicious of outsiders, even if they are good friends with Doctor Orvieto.' Aldo smiled at her to conceal his discomfort at others knowing about his closeness to Saul. He would have to be more careful.

Tamar had seen the cloaked figure outside Bassano's house,

loading something heavy and cumbersome onto a cart. 'I don't know what it was,' she admitted, leaning closer. 'I was more interested in why they were bringing it out.' She had been hopeful Freccia and Fiora were leaving because she coveted their room. 'Then this one might sleep better,' Tamar said, bouncing the child on her hip. 'The pair in there were always arguing, we all heard them.'

Pressing her to describe the cloaked figure brought no more than the fishmonger's assistant had said: tall, strong, broad-shouldered. No, she hadn't seen anyone lurking in via dei Giudei, watching the room where Freccia and Fiora lived. Satisfied Tamar had nothing more to tell, Aldo let her go to the mercato before heading north himself. Yesterday he and Strocchi had wondered how Freccia's body had been moved from the Jewish commune without being seen, but they had been asking the wrong question. The killer had been seen but went unchallenged and largely unnoticed. There had been no reason to suspect them as they had not acted suspiciously.

Tamar's comment about Freccia and Fiora arguing might be gossip, but it did explain the limited grief Fiora showed after hearing her husband was dead. She was not a suspect for his killing, her small frame and heavy pregnancy precluded that, but Fiora might well know more than she had revealed at the tannery. Better to have Strocchi question her next time. His being a father with another baby on the way might help to win Fiora's trust.

When Strocchi woke, Tomasia was already sitting up in bed, one hand clasped to the swell of her belly, her eyes narrowed. He knew that expression well. It meant she was sifting what he had told her the previous night. 'There are two pathways that ought to lead you and Aldo to the killer,' she announced.

Strocchi put a finger to his lips while pointing at the wall that separated them from the front room. 'Mama and Bianca must still be asleep,' he whispered. 'We mustn't wake them.'

'Carlo, they were both up when the bells chimed,' Tomasia said. 'Your mama took Bianca for a walk so that you could rest.'

He rubbed the sleep from his eyes. 'That was kind of her.'

'It was my suggestion.'

'Ahh.' Strocchi sat up beside her. Tomasia had a gift for solving riddles. She was able to take what was known about something puzzling, twist and turn it around in her head until she found a key to unlock what was baffling everyone else. More than once Strocchi had wished the Otto employed women as officers. Tomasia would put him and Aldo to shame if she was ever given the chance. 'Tell me about these pathways,' he said.

'The first is obvious: the killer had a reason for choosing Zamora and Freccia as their victims. If so, that means both men were known to their murderer.' Tomasia smiled at him. 'You simply need to find the link between them.'

'Aldo and I have been trying, but there's nothing that the victims had in common. One was a merchant, the other a thief. Zamora had no children of his own, Freccia's wife is carrying a baby. Zamora was twice Freccia's age. They both lived in Oltrarno, but aside from that . . .'

'Well, if nothing links these men beyond their killer,' she said, 'then consider what is being done to the victims. Posing the bodies to look like Christ on the cross, putting ash on the foreheads, cutting their tongues in two . . . All of that must have a meaning, even if it is only known to the killer. You need to—'

'Shhh!' Strocchi held up a hand.

'Don't shush me, Carlo.'

'No, I didn't mean . . . it was something you said.' He got her to repeat what the killer had done to his victims. 'There is something which links Freccia and Zamora: the exorcist, Father Negri. When I said Freccia's name at San Felice, Negri flinched. The rest of the time he was so assured, so certain of himself. But when I mentioned Freccia—'

'Negri responded.' Tomasia nodded. 'And Zamora?'

'His nephew was exorcized at San Felice. Soon after Marsilio took his own life, and Negri refused to bury the young man in the famiglia crypt beneath the church. Zamora stopped attending Mass after that. He blamed Negri for what had happened to Marsilio.'

'You need to talk to that exorcist.'

'We can't. He refused to answer my questions, said I would have to seek permission from the archbishop, or at least from the diocese. Bindi will never approve that. If the case leads us to the Church, it becomes an argument over who has authority.'

'Then you need to find a way of investigating Negri without telling Bindi.'

Strocchi grimaced. 'If he learns what we're doing, Aldo goes back to night patrol, and I'll be demoted. We need the extra coin me being an officer brings – now more than ever.'

Tomasia stroked a hand down his face. 'We'll get by. We did before.'

'We didn't have a child then, or another on the way.'

'Carlo, you can't be afraid of what might happen. That's no way to live your life.'

'I know, but—'

'But nothing.' She smiled at him. 'Think of it another way: what would Aldo do?'

'Him?' Strocchi laughed. 'He'd probably arrest Negri.'

'Aldo takes risks, but not often that much of a risk.'

She was right, as usual. What would Aldo do? 'He would investigate Negri by talking to those around him, questioning them. He would watch San Felice, see who comes and goes. He would find a way to uncover the truth, even if it made others angry with him.'

'Then you have your answer. Aldo is helping you investigate, yes?'

'Yes.'

'Then let Aldo be Aldo. The two of you make a stronger team if you work together.'

Father Visconti stepped out of Santa Maria Magdalena, eager to feel the sun on his face. Much as he loved his church, inside the stone building was always cold and often dark. Stained-glass windows cheered the soul in summer when light blazed through them, throwing multi-coloured patterns across the floor. But in autumn and winter those same windows kept out more light than they admitted, making the church interior dark and gloomy.

Visconti nodded to passing parishioners, smiling at those who waved or called to him. But the approaching figure of Father Zati brought no smiles and less joy. The young priest glanced over his shoulder, as if expecting to see someone he knew there. Zati seemed even more harried than he'd been on his last visit. 'Back so soon?' Visconti asked, his voice warm and friendly. All deserved a welcome, no matter what troubles they brought with them.

'May we speak inside?' Zati asked, glancing behind himself again. 'It's Father Negri.'

Visconti ushered him into the church rich with its aroma of incense, away from the eyes and ears of others. 'We talked of him only two days ago, Pagolo. What has changed?'

Zati recounted events from the previous day: Negri's eagerness to intervene with the Gheradinis, though there was no evidence of demonic possession; the visit by an officer of the Otto asking questions about the murdered thief Freccia, and Negri's vehement response; the fact that the exorcist's handbook had been stolen from San Felice, yet Negri only mentioned the loss when Strocchi came to the church.

Visconti listened, nodding encouragement for Zati to continue but not interrupting. Better to let the young priest say what he needed, in his own time and way. When the words ran dry, there was little in them to explain Zati's agitation. 'You have told me many things, Pagolo, but what is it you truly came here to say? Something else is troubling you, yes?'

Zati stared at the carved wooden Christ on the cross that stood atop the altar. 'I fear . . . I fear that Father Negri may have had a hand in the killing of this thief.'

Visconti made the sign of the cross. 'Taking a life is a mortal sin. Have you proof?'

'None that I can show you.'

'Yet you still believe it.'

Zati took a deep breath. 'I do not have proof of Our Lord in Heaven above, yet I still believe in him. Can I not also believe in the worst of sins?'

'Of course, but . . .' Visconti did not know what to make of Zati's accusation. The words were brimming with sincerity, he seemed utterly certain of what he was saying. But to claim another priest – even one with a reputation as fearsome as that of Negri – could be capable of participating in the taking of a life . . . 'Why would Negri kill this Freccia?'

'There is something I did not tell you last time I was here,' Zati replied. 'Something I have not dared tell anyone. But you need to know the truth about Father Negri. When you do, you will understand why I believe him capable of this mortal sin.'

The contessa never enjoyed being woken before the middle of the day because little of note ever occurred during the dull, un-imaginative hours of morning. People only came alive when wine or stronger spirits had taken hold of them, when the urge to stray or betray quickened the blood and loosened their morality. Yet sometimes she found leaving her bedchamber before the sun had reached its highest point was regrettably necessary.

People expected a contessa to attend Mass, for example, despite it being quite the dreariest thing she'd ever had to suffer through (and that included the inept fumblings of her first and – to date – only husband). If the Lord was looking down on everyone and everything they did, it was no wonder he chose to rest on Sundays. Watching over tedious sermons and turgid church music would exhaust the patience of any saint, let alone the Almighty himself. Fortunately, her grief over the death of the count had proven a most effective explanation for why she had attended Mass less frequently this past year.

The sound of Pozzo tapping at her bedchamber door was not a welcome one, but she recognized it must be urgent for him to do so. Leaving her current lover strewn across the mattress, the contessa wrapped a silk robe around herself while strolling to the door. She opened it enough to see Pozzo's face.

He wore a studied regret while offering his apologies. 'Never mind all that,' she said. 'Why have you got me from bed at this ungodly hour?'

'I regret to inform you that Signor Grossolano is missing from his bedchamber.'

'Missing?'

'Yes, Contessa.'

'And he's not in another bedchamber? The fool hasn't wandered off in search of a latrina and got lost, or forced his affections upon one of my long-suffering servants?'

'No, Contessa. The maid I sent to serve him in the salone after your departure last night was prepared for any misbehaviour on the part of your guest and dealt with him in a suitable manner when his hands sought to wander beneath her skirts.'

'I should hope so. A swift blow to his palle, I trust?'

'Several, I am reliably informed.'

The contessa smiled. She must give that maid a reward for having to suffer the company of Grossolano. And for giving his groin the pain it so rightly deserved, of course. 'Very well. Are our guest's clothes and other possessions still in his bedchamber?'

'They are, but the signor himself is absent.' Pozzo sighed. 'He became increasingly drunk after you left and may have wandered out into the city without anyone to guide him.'

'I understand Signor Grossolano is not familiar with Florence,' she said. 'He is liable to have got lost. Well, if he does not return before day's end, we must report him missing.'

Pozzo bowed his head in agreement. 'Very good, Contessa.'

'Since I'm now awake, please have some food prepared. I had a most torrid night, full of tossing and turning. It has given me rather an appetite.' She beckoned him closer. 'Did all go as we discussed?' she murmured so her lover could not overhear.

Pozzo nodded.

The contessa smirked. That was excellent news. Perhaps there were some merits to rising this early in the day after all.

Father Visconti listened to what Zati had to say about Negri, what the younger priest had been too afraid to reveal during his previous visit to Santa Maria Magdalena. If this was true – and Visconti had no reason to doubt Zati's word – then Negri had every reason to want Freccia silenced. But making such an accusation without proof . . .

'I understand why you came back,' Visconti said. 'You have meaningful concerns.'

'Yes.'

'The evidence against Father Negri shows he has questions to answer . . .'

'And?' Zati asked.

'But it is not your vocation to ask those questions,' Visconti concluded. He knew that was not what Zati wanted to hear, but it was still the truth.

'Why not? Why shouldn't I take my concerns to the diocese?' Zati pulled a sealed letter from inside the sleeve of his cassock. 'I have these furious words Negri made me write on his behalf. I should be delivering them to the diocesan ufficio now, that's where he thinks I am. Why shouldn't I tell the archbishop or one of his clerics what I know about Negri?'

'Because they will not listen,' Visconti replied. 'I wish it were otherwise, yet I believe that is a fact. Buondelmonti and his disciples did not wish to hear accusations against one of their priests, let alone against a man with such close bonds to many of those around the archbishop. If you do this, your name will forever be

tarnished within the Church. You will be known as the man who
spoke out, the one who could not be trusted to keep the secrets
of those who possess power in this diocese.' He stopped, shaking
his head.

'But I would be doing the right thing,' Zati protested.

'This is not about doing right or wrong. It is about men in
positions of authority protecting themselves and those who support
them. You would not be punished directly, of course. Buondelmonti's
clerics are too subtle with their intrigues to be caught with a knife
in their hands. Instead, the diocese would ensure you never rise
beyond being a parish priest. Any ambitions you have to do more
will be thwarted whenever possible.'

'But I'm a humble priest, no threat to anyone . . .' Disgust
twisted the young priest's face. 'You're telling me not to share what
I know, to keep quiet. But that would make me as much a sinner
as Negri.'

'The decision about whether to speak up is for you alone, Pagolo.
I'm simply telling you the consequence if you do this.' Visconti
gestured at the church around them. 'Why do you think I have
been parish priest here at Santa Maria Magdalena for so long,
while far younger men have become monsignors and cardinals?'

Before Zati could reply, a sour-faced woman in shapeless clothes
and a widow's headscarf bustled into the church, raising a hand
to greet Visconti.

'That's Signora Gonzaga,' he whispered to Zati. 'She comes
every day to complain about her neighbours, her crumbling home,
or her aching joints. Mostly I think she needs someone to listen
to her. I doubt she has ever had that, not even while she was
married.' He waved to the widow before ushering Zati to the door.
The young priest paused in the entrance, glancing north and south
along via San Gallo before stepping outside.

'You did that as you arrived,' Visconti said. 'Who or what are you looking for?'

'It's . . .' Zati hesitated. 'You will think less of me if I tell you.'

'Never.'

'I – I believe someone may be following me.'

'Following you? Who would do that? Why?'

'I do not know.'

Visconti peered along the road but could see nobody watching them. 'Can you describe them, what they look like?'

'Not really. They wear a long cloak, with a hood up to hide their face,' Zati said. 'They are tall and broad of shoulder.'

Visconti looked again. 'Well, I see nobody in a cloak now.'

Zati nodded. 'If you were in my position, what would you do about Negri?'

'I would pray for guidance. When you believe you have prayed enough, search your soul and you will find the answer.' He shook Zati's hand. 'I still have a friend or two within the diocesan ufficio. I could talk to them, see if there is anything that can be done. Perhaps you could be moved to another parish?'

'Grazie, Father, but I am the only one who can change this.' Zati stumbled south towards the cathedral, shoulders hunched forward as if bearing the weight of the world.

'May God be with you, my son,' Visconti called after him.

Chapter Sixteen

When Strocchi arrived at the Podestà he found Aldo already there, talking with Manuffi by the wide stone staircase. Hopefully Aldo would not neglect the tasks asked of him, as he had the last two days. But Strocchi also recognized that Tomasia's suggestion – to let Aldo be Aldo – was more likely to succeed than giving him orders or getting frustrated. Aldo was going to do as he saw best. Better to make use of those talents than stifle them.

Strocchi beckoned Aldo and Manuffi to the well in the middle of the courtyard so they could discuss what to do next without easily being overheard. Bindi would be at Palazzo Medici by now, giving his morning report, but several guards at the Podestà were known to watch and listen on the segretario's behalf. Best to keep what needed to be said private, especially if it might involve trespassing on the jurisdiction of the diocese. Strocchi thanked Manuffi for helping with the investigation. The heavyset constable shrugged and smiled.

'It's better than trying to stop people having their coin stolen at the mercato,' Manuffi said. 'One of the new magistrates lost his pouch there last Friday so the segretario has had us patrolling the stalls to drive away thieves and pickpockets. Like that has ever worked.'

Strocchi did not miss being a constable, sent from one quarter of the city to another in pursuit of whatever was troubling Bindi or irritating the Otto's magistrates. The courtyard around them was quiet, guards and constables ambling about at the start of a new day. There was none of the urgency that gripped the court and its men when a murder was discovered. 'It seems our killer has not claimed another life,' he said. 'Not yet at least. I feared we might be dealing with a third corpse this morning, having had two in the last two days.'

Aldo nodded. 'Both those bodies were left in piazze to be found early. If there was another, we would have heard about it by now.'

'Agreed. This gives us time to pursue the leads we already have.' Strocchi gave a summary of what had been learned the previous day to Manuffi. The constable shuddered on hearing Negri was the clearest link between Zamora and Freccia, but Manuffi's face regained its usual happiness on hearing they could not approach the exorcist directly. 'We will need to find another way of investigating Negri,' Strocchi said.

Aldo revealed he had been at via dei Giudei as curfew ended to question those on the street the previous morning when Freccia was murdered. The description he had gathered for the killer was frustrating – a broad-shouldered figure pushing a cart, face and head hidden behind the hood of a cloak – but talk of Freccia and Fiora's arguments gave a reason to question her again. 'You should talk with Fiora,' Aldo urged. He described the tannery where she worked. 'She knows more than I heard from her yesterday. Mention the baby Tomasia is having, and what it was like when Bianca was first born. That might win Fiora's trust.'

Strocchi could see the sense of this, but the notion of using his famiglia to get secrets from a dead man's wife made him squirm. 'I'll go see her,' he agreed, but no more than that. 'Aldo, can you go back to via dei Giudei and question the landlord? If Freccia was extorting coin to pay his rent, Bassano may know more than he told me.'

'And I can search Freccia's room for evidence about the extortion,' Aldo volunteered. 'You didn't know about that when you were there yesterday.'

'It's worth looking,' Strocchi said. 'Manuffi, go with Aldo and knock at all the doors in the Jewish commune. Many of them only speak Hebrew, and others will refuse to talk with someone they don't know, but keep trying. Somebody there could have seen the killer or heard them without knowing it. I'll find you both once I've talked to Fiora.'

The contessa was about to take her first meal of the day when there was a knock at the salone door. The servants had been exemplary in cleaning away the slovenly mess left by Grossolano but the dining table was still in that room, so she chose to eat a few morsels there. Nothing too heavy, of course. A light insalata, some candied fruits to follow. To maintain a command over the men who hoped to share her bedchamber and eagerly brought secrets in return for an audience, it was a tiresome necessity that she maintain some command over her waistline. Perhaps one day a woman of wit and perceptiveness would be valued for those qualities, rather than for the swell of her bosom or the promise of what was waiting between her thighs. But that was not the way of things now.

'Come!' the contessa called, setting aside the colourful plate in front of her.

Pozzo entered, his face full of apologies. 'Forgive the interruption, but you have a visitor who insists on seeing you before he returns to Venice.'

Zilio was back, no doubt come to ensure she was treating Grossolano well so he could report the same to his new masters at the Inquisitorie di Stato. The contessa had hoped Zilio might be too busy to bother her again but was still prepared for such an intrusion. Those who relied on hope to ensure their success would not survive long in a world of lies and spies.

'How does he seem?' she asked, rising to her feet.

'A man in haste,' the maggiordomo replied.

'Then I must give him a worthy performance. Have one of my maids bring powder to make my face pale. If I am worried about poor Grossolano, I should look it.'

'Very good,' Pozzo said, retreating to the door.

'Keep Signor Zilio down in the courtyard a while before bringing him up.'

'Of course.'

Once the maid had finished her work, the contessa took a two-pronged serving fork from the table and forced its points hard into the palm of her left hand. They were too dull to break the skin yet succeeded in creating a pain so exquisite it made her eyes water. There would be bruises later, but sacrifices were always necessary to attain the desired result. She put the fork down as Pozzo knocked at the door before showing Zilio into the salone.

'My dear Zilio, thank goodness you have come!' the contessa exclaimed, rushing across to him. She grabbed both his hands, ensuring he could see how pale her skin seemed and the tears brimming in both eyes. 'I've been so worried about poor Signor Grossolano.'

'Worried about him?' Zilio's confusion was obvious. 'Why? What has happened?'

'I fear it's my fault,' she replied, leading the Venetian to the chairs by the table. 'We had a celebratory meal last night to mark his arrival here in Florence. Signor Grossolano indulged in rather a lot of my late husband's finest wines.' She sniffed and dabbed a cloth at her face, as if fighting back more tears. 'You never told me he was such a drinker . . .'

'I . . . I didn't know.'

'He drank and he drank, and then . . .' She sank onto the nearest chair.

Zilio took the seat beside her. 'And then?'

'And then Signor Grossolano announced he was going out into the city! He wanted to see Florence by night, or so he said.' She leaned closer. 'I fear he may have been looking for something else. Something less . . . reputable.'

'But Grossolano knows that Florence has a strict curfew—'

'Yes, I told him so myself. Yet he would not listen. Not to a widow, I fear.'

Zilio huffed out his cheeks. 'When did he depart the palazzo?'

The contessa twisted round to her maggiordomo, as if too overcome to recall. 'Pozzo, I can't recall. Do you know the answer?' She winked at him, a smirk on her lips.

'I believe it was several hours after curfew began,' he replied.

Rearranging her face to appear distressed, the contessa turned back to Zilio. 'I've been awake all night, waiting for Signor Grossolano to find his way here, praying for his safe return – but to no avail. I fear he may have stumbled and hurt himself in the darkness, or . . . or something even worse might have happened to him.' She sank forward onto Zilio's lap, weeping and wailing, one fist clenched against her mouth.

Zilio responded as if he had never known a woman, let alone how to comfort one. He patted an ineffectual hand on her back. 'There, there,' he said. 'I'm sure Signor Grossolano will be fine. He is sleeping off the wine somewhere in the city.'

She pulled herself back upright, letting hope fill her eyes. 'Do you think so?'

'I'm sure of it.'

'Yes?' she asked.

'Quite sure,' Zilio said, nodding for extra reassurance.

'Grazie, grazie,' the contessa gushed, clasping his hands in her own again. 'I have been so very worried. Then, when I heard you had come, I feared you were bringing news that something dreadful had befallen Signor Grossolano. I was contemplating whether I should report his disappearance to the Otto, or one of the other courts—'

'There's no need for that,' Zilio interjected. 'No need at all. We must remember why he came to Florence, what he is tasked with doing here.' The Venetian lowered his voice to a whisper so only she could hear. 'The authorities must not know about Grossolano's mission.'

The contessa nodded. 'Of course.' Letting go of Zilio's hands, she rose from her chair. 'Grazie for coming, signor. I appreciate your kindness in this matter.'

Zilio also got to his feet. 'I was planning to leave for Venice once I had met with Signor Grossolano, but now . . .'

'You must not delay your journey a moment longer,' she replied, ushering him towards the door. 'I'm sure you are quite correct, and that my guest will return to the palazzo any moment now. Perhaps sore of head, even a little embarrassed, but no more than that. You were quite right; I was foolish to worry and fret so about Signor Grossolano.'

Zilio's brow furrowed but he could not deny her words since she was repeating what he had already said. 'Very well. Please, have the signor send me a letter by the usual means when he does return. I will be comforted to know he is settling well here in

Florence. He is fortunate to have such a kind and understanding host as yourself.'

'Prego.' The contessa bowed her head to Zilio a little before the maggiordomo led him away. She went to the shutters to watch the Venetian depart, waving as he strode away from the palazzo. Pozzo returned, joining her by the shutters. 'Was I too much?' she asked. 'There are few things I dislike more at the teatro than someone who overplays their part.'

'No, Contessa. You were, as ever, perfezione.'

Light drizzle was falling when Strocchi approached the tannery, but it did nothing to cloak the stench that hung in the air. There had been a tanner who came to Ponte a Signa twice a year when Strocchi was a boy, collecting hides to turn into leather, but their work was done elsewhere. He ventured into the tannery, his stomach souring at the pungent aroma rising from the vats of animal waste. How anyone could work in such a place was beyond him.

The bulge of Fiora's belly against her apron made her easy to find. Men and women worked side by side in the tannery, but she was the only one heavy with child. He introduced himself and asked if she was willing to answer more questions.

'I told the other one everything I know,' Fiora complained. Her eyes were rimmed red, probably from crying, and her hair was trying to escape a black scarf tied round it. She let him guide her out onto the street, away from the fetid stench. 'Well?'

'We've heard you and your husband argued at lot,' Strocchi began.

'Which of the Jews said that? Was it our useless landlord?' She spat on the ground after saying the word Jews, her anger towards them all too plain.

Strocchi ignored the accusation. There were plenty of people in Florence eager to state their hatred of the Jews. He had learned that trying to persuade them there was no reason for such an attitude was the journey of a fool. 'Were you two fighting more than usual?'

'What if we were?'

That was a yes. 'What were you arguing about?'

Fiora sighed. 'It was always about coin. I'll have to stop working soon, and what Freccia made from thieving wasn't enough to pay our rent, let alone buy food as well.' She wrapped an arm under her belly to support it. 'Can I go back inside now?'

'You told my colleague Freccia was getting coin from someone. How?'

'How do you think?' Strocchi didn't reply, certain he could outlast her impatience. 'He knew a secret about someone,' Fiora soon went on. 'One they were willing to pay to stop him from telling others. Freccia wouldn't say what it was, just that it would ruin this man.'

'Which man? Was it Niccolò Zamora?' He described the dead man to her.

'I don't know, Freccia never told me who was paying him. He said it was safer if I didn't know.' She stepped back. 'Why, do you think that's who killed him? Am I in danger?'

'I don't believe so.' But he couldn't be sure. 'How long until the baby comes?'

'About two months. He's been kicking all morning.'

'It's a boy?'

'I think so.' Her smile was sad and wistful. 'I hope so.'

Strocchi remembered how Tomasia had been the last weeks

before Bianca was born but kept that to himself. He would not use his famiglia to get answers from Fiora. 'Do you have somewhere you can stay? Someone to help you?'

She shrugged. 'Maybe Dea Vanni. We work together. She's been good, listening to all my complaining about Freccia . . .' Fiora trailed off, tears brimming in her eyes. 'Sorry, I keep crying. Must be the baby. Having one seems to push all your feelings to the surface.'

Strocchi nodded. 'Where does Signora Vanni live? If we do find the person who killed Freccia, I'd like to tell you myself.'

'On via Maggio, not far from San Felice.' Fiora described the front door.

'Grazie.' He looked past her to the tannery entrance. 'Is she working today?'

'No. Dea often arrives late, but she's usually here by now.'

Drizzle had become rain by the time Aldo and Manuffi reached via dei Giudei. At the first few homes Aldo asked the questions when Manuffi's knocking got a response, but none in the Jewish commune seemed eager to speak. Leaving Manuffi to his task, Aldo strode to Bassano's house. When the landlord opened his door Aldo used the rain as an excuse to push his way inside, ignoring all protests. The cloying smell of mildew hung in the air. Bassano hurried after Aldo, puffing and panting as if hard work was unknown to him. 'You have no right to come in here without my agreement.'

'I'm told you regularly break curfew,' Aldo said, stepping closer to the landlord. He needed answers and had no wish to waste time on gentle persuasion.

'What? No, I never— Who told you that?'

'An officer of the Otto. You confessed it to him.'

'No. He must have misunderstood, what I said was—'

'I don't care what you think you said. I'm sure his testimony would be more than enough for the magistrates. A week in Le Stinche is the punishment for such crimes.'

'A week? In prison?' Bassano's eyes widened with fear. 'No, please, I didn't—'

'Perhaps you'd prefer two weeks? Le Stinche is a cold and dangerous place with winter coming. A very dangerous place.' Aldo loomed over the landlord, making him stumble backwards. Bassano sank into a chair, hands trembling in front of his face.

'Please, no, I can't—'

'Can't what?'

'I don't—'

'Then be quiet and listen,' Aldo hissed. He leaned forwards, resting both hands on the arms of the chair, until his face was within breathing distance of Bassano. 'I'm going upstairs to search Freccia's room. When I come back, you're going to answer my questions. If you lie to me, I will know. If you do, I will drag you before the Otto myself. Do you believe me?'

Bassano nodded.

'Then say it.'

'I-I believe you.'

'Good.' Aldo straightened up, happy to escape the sour aroma of Bassano's stale sweat. He marched upstairs and set to work scouring the rented room. It was far tidier than the scattered mess Strocchi had described from the previous morning, no doubt thanks to Fiora. That made searching a simpler task, but there was nothing to find. If Freccia had left evidence of his extortion strategia, it was gone now. Frustrated, Aldo stamped back down the stairs to confront Bassano. The landlord had not moved from his seat.

'We've been told your tenants argued,' Aldo said.

'Y-yes.'

'About what?'

'I-I'm sorry?'

'About what did they argue?'

'Money. Coin. The baby she had coming. If they were both home, they were probably arguing.' Bassano opened his mouth to add more but stopped himself.

'What else? You were going to say something, what is it?'

'Freccia argued with someone else – a man. It was during the day when she was working. You can tell when Fiora comes in, the stench she brings in with her.'

'Never mind that. Who else did Freccia argue with?'

'I told you, it was a man. His voice was gruffer. He sounded as if he was used to giving orders.'

Aldo paused before asking another question. He had come expecting gossip about a husband and wife arguing, but Bassano had something far more interesting to share. 'What were they arguing about, this man and Freccia?'

'I couldn't hear most of it, but Freccia kept calling him Father.'

To the best of Aldo's knowledge Freccia had no famiglia, certainly not in Florence. That suggested another possibility. 'Where did they argue?'

Bassano pointed at the rented room overhead.

'Did you see the visitor arriving?'

'No. I sleep after my midday meal. He must have come then. But I did see him go.'

Aldo fought to keep the eagerness from his face. He turned from Bassano, strolling over to the shutters to look out at via dei Giudei. It was still raining outside. Manuffi had reached the doorway opposite, his tunic soaked through, but the elderly woman who lived there was shaking her head. 'What did this man look like?'

'I was too slow, I didn't see much of his face,' the landlord replied. 'But his head was shaved close to the scalp, and he wore a long, black robe.'

'You mean a cassock?' Aldo glanced over his shoulder. 'He wore a priest's cassock?'

Bassano shrugged. 'I'm a Jew. How do I know what a priest wears?' But when he described the garment, it was the cassock of a priest.

'You said you didn't see much of this man's face. That suggests you did see some. Was there something unusual or memorable about him?'

'Yes, he had a cleft in his chin.' The landlord rubbed a finger up and down in the middle of his own chin. 'You don't see that much in Florence.'

'And which way did he turn on his way out?'

'I don't understand . . .'

Aldo jabbed a finger towards the front door. 'When this stranger went outside, which way did he go – north towards the Arno, or south from here?'

Bassano frowned, staring off to one side. 'South. I think he went south.'

'Grazie,' Aldo said, marching from the room.

'Where are you going?' The landlord came after Aldo, following him out into the rain. 'Am I still being brought before the Otto?'

'Not if you keep your silence,' Aldo said, glaring at him. 'If you value your life, tell nobody else what you told me. Do you understand?'

Bassano nodded.

Spying Manuffi further along via dei Giudei, Aldo strode towards him.

This new evidence was not proof, not yet. But it suggested Freccia had been extorting coin from the exorcist at San Felice. If so, that made Negri a leading suspect for the murders.

Chapter Seventeen

After dashing the length of Piazza Santo Spirito in the rain, Strocchi was grateful to reach the shelter of Palazzo Zamora. He found a servant and sent them to fetch Querini, the household maggiordomo. Strocchi had no wish to disturb the grieving famiglia, but he needed to know more about Zamora's dispute with Father Negri. When Querini came down the stairs he was not pleased to see Strocchi. 'We have answered all your questions,' he said, 'and Signora Tullia is still distraught from the loss of her brother. I cannot allow you to disturb her.'

Strocchi paused, letting Querini believe his objection was being considered. If the maggiordomo thought he'd won a concession, he might be more willing to answer questions in Tullia's stead. Querini did not need to know this was always the intention. It was a sin of omission, but an officer of the Otto needed to extract any advantage he could from such situations. Lying and withholding were the Florentine way. Doing so would never have occurred to Strocchi when he was a constable. Now it was simply another sin for him to confess the next time he was in church.

'Then perhaps I could talk with you instead?' Strocchi suggested, making it sound more a request than a negotiating tactic. A servant bustled past, peering at them.

'Very well,' Querini agreed. 'Come with me.' He took Strocchi to a staircase at the rear of the palazzo, leading him up to the top level and out onto the loggia that overlooked the piazza. Despite the rain Strocchi could still see much of Oltrarno and across the river to the northern quarters. On a late-summer evening this vista would be breathtaking.

'The signora and her children rarely come to the loggia in autumn,' the maggiordomo said, 'so we will not be disturbed here. Now, what is it you need to know?'

Strocchi began by asking if Zamora had any interest in Senate politics. Querini stated that Zamora neither sought nor craved political advancement. Yes, he had served in the Senate when required, but nothing more than that. 'He found it tedious and odious in equal measure. Politics were for those with nothing better to do, he once told me.'

'Grazie,' Strocchi said. 'There is one more thing I need to ask—'

'Have you not bothered us enough?' the maggiordomo demanded. 'I worked for Signor Zamora for more than twenty years. I am remaining steadfast for his sister and famiglia, but everyone within this household needs to grieve his loss—'

'I understand, I do. But I need to ask about his attitude to the exorcist at San Felice. You told me the priest there refused to bury Marsilio after he ended his own life.'

'You want to know what Signor Zamora thought of Father Negri?' Querini's face darkened. 'He hated him. The signor was willing to forgive and forget almost any slight. But something about the exorcist seemed to incense him. He wrote several letters to the diocese, demanding that it intercede against Negri, but received no reply. He sought an audience with Archbishop Buondelmonti to plead his case, yet the diocese refused to grant that comfort.' The maggiordomo shook his head, appearing saddened as he went to the loggia's stone balcony to stare out over the piazza. 'Not long after that Signor Zamora became entangled with a woman who blamed the exorcist for a death in her famiglia. She had heard of Signor Zamora's efforts and said she wished to help him, to work with him against Father Negri.'

'How did she hear of this?' Strocchi asked.

Querini shook his head. 'I do not know. Perhaps one of the servants was gossiping at the mercato. When Signor Zamora mentioned that this woman had approached him, I tried to dissuade him from meeting with her again, that he had already done all that was possible, but he would not listen. His grief and anger were too strong.'

'Why did you warn him to stay away from this woman?'

'I asked him what she looked like. When Signor Zamora described her, I recognized the woman from his words. She stood outside San Felice each morning, berating anyone who went inside, warning them about Father Negri. Her rage was all-consuming, and I feared Signor Zamora would be infected by it. Eventually he saw sense and withdrew from her. But she did not take that well. She kept coming here, demanding to see him. When he went out on business, she followed him. Finally, the signor asked me to . . . dissuade her.'

'You threatened her,' Strocchi said.

'Of course not. I made her understand the signor was not her enemy. If she wanted satisfaction, she would have to seek it from the diocese or from Negri himself.'

'And she accepted that?'

'She seemed to.' Querini straightened up. 'You don't think she's the one who . . . ?'

When he'd first joined the court as a constable, Strocchi had not believed a woman could be capable of murder, but the past three years had proven that was folly. Doctor Orvieto said the garrotting had probably been done by a man or a woman with very strong hands. 'What did she look like?'

'She was big, with broad shoulders. Wore a black scarf over her hair, and her clothes were always stained and stank to Heaven. I believe she worked in a tannery.'

'What was her name?'

'Vanni. Signora Dea Vanni.'

If what he said was true – and Querini had no apparent reason to lie – it sounded as if Vanni was obsessed with Negri. That had brought her and Zamora together as allies initially, but also had driven them apart. Did Vanni consider that a betrayal and, if so, was it reason enough for murder? Fiora seemed to consider Vanni her friend, but what had Vanni thought of Fiora's husband, Freccia? Did she carry anger towards him as well? If her true target was Negri, why would she not attack him directly? Strocchi set aside those questions for the moment. One thing was certain: the investigation had another potential suspect to investigate.

Rain fell steadily as Aldo huddled in the doorway of a palazzo opposite the Church of San Felice. As expected, questioning the residents along via dei Giudei was uncovering nothing new, so Aldo had left Manuffi to that thankless task. But he gave Manuffi a message so Strocchi could find him. After the misunderstandings of the previous two days, Aldo wanted to prove he could follow instructions. He would need Strocchi as an advocate when the case was done, otherwise he was likely to be cast back into the purgatory of night patrols by Bindi.

For a parish church there were not many people coming and going from San Felice. Most churches were a hub for the surrounding community, providing a place where the faithful could gather to help one another, or a refuge for those in need. But San Felice offered no such welcome. Being home to the exorcist marked it out as somewhere to be avoided, a church unlike any other. A couple did emerge from San Felice, a husband and his distraught wife. The man had grey in his hair and beard, with a dusting of flour on his tunic. The woman was weeping as they stumbled away, the rain mingling with her tears. Whatever they'd seen or heard inside the church seemed to have broken them.

Only those with business in the stark stone building went near its forbidding entrance. Everyone else crossed the road, passing in front of Aldo as they headed north towards Ponte Vecchio or south to the lower reaches of Oltrarno. A pair of elderly widows ambling by stopped to ask what Aldo was waiting for, and he almost missed Zati leaving San Felice. Making his excuses to the women, Aldo hurried after the priest.

'Father Zati,' Aldo called to his quarry. The priest kept walking, either not hearing Aldo through the rain or choosing to ignore him. Zati wore a cloak to protect his cassock, but a black biretta was doing little to keep his head dry. Aldo soon caught up with the priest. 'Father Zati?' he said again.

'Yes?' the priest replied, pausing to look round. Zati was still young of face, as he had been when Aldo first met him, but there was now a wariness in his eyes. No, not wariness – fear. Zati reminded Aldo of those who had suffered at the hands of others. He carried himself like a victim, as if afraid of when the next blow would come.

'I thought it was you.' Aldo smiled at him. 'My name is Cesare Aldo, we met during that tragic business at Santa Maria Magdalena. We were members of a visitation there with Monsignor Testardo, and the unfortunate Signor Cortese. What happened to him?'

Zati peered at Aldo through the rain. 'You were the officer from the Otto.'

'Yes.' He chose not to mention his demotion. 'Has Signor Cortese recovered?'

'He seemed to, but his health took a turn for the worse. I was with him at the end.'

'I'm sorry to hear that.'

'Grazie. Please excuse me, I have an urgent errand,' Zati said, before striding away.

Aldo was not letting the priest escape, not without getting some answers first. He followed Zati north. 'I understand you work with Father Negri now, at San Felice.'

'That is hardly a matter for your concern.'

'But I believe it is,' Aldo persisted, matching him stride for stride. 'My colleagues at the Otto and I are investigating two murders. We believe both are connected to Negri.'

Zati's steps stuttered, his pace wavering before it quickened again. 'You must be mistaken. Father Negri is a man of God. He could not have any involvement with such terrible crimes. It is beyond imagining.'

'You think so?'

'Of course.'

'Yet when you were part of the visitation, you were quite ready to accuse the sisters of being involved with a killing there. They were women of God. Were the nuns not worthy of the same belief that you profess to have for Father Negri?'

'You are twisting my meaning. Putting words in my mouth that I did not say.'

'Am I twisting your meaning or putting words in your mouth? I can't be doing both at the same time, surely?' Aldo stepped in front of Zati, forcing him to stop. 'Well, which is it?'

'I may have misspoken,' the priest replied. 'All women of God naturally deserve the same respect, the same faith in their goodness as priests and other clerics.'

'Or perhaps men of God can be equally guilty of committing a mortal sin?'

Zati's hands were trembling at his sides. 'I don't know what you mean.'

'But I think you do, Father.' Aldo wiped the rain out of his eyes. He needed to see Zati's response to the next question. 'I believe you have doubts about Negri, as I do. My colleague visited San Felice yesterday. When Strocchi sought answers to a few questions, Negri refused to help and threatened to involve Archbishop Buondelmonti. Did that seem like the actions of a man with nothing to hide, with no guilt in his heart?'

Zati did not reply, but nor could he hold Aldo's gaze.

'If Negri will not help us,' Aldo went on, 'we must talk with those who can. You, who knows what happens inside San Felice. You are the only one who can tell us the truth.'

'I . . . I have a responsibility to respect the wishes of Father Negri,' Zati stammered.

'Why? I saw the couple that came out of the church not long before you did.'

'The Gheradinis? You . . . You've been watching the church?'

'What did Negri do to them?' Aldo stepped closer. 'Or would you prefer I ask them myself? Signor Gheradini looked like a baker, judging by the flour on his clothes. It wouldn't be difficult finding him or his wife. I doubt either wishes to recount what they've just been through, but the Otto is very persuasive.' Aldo had no intention of troubling the Gheradinis, but Zati was not to know that. 'Well, Father? What's it to be?'

The priest shook his head before answering. 'Their daughter

Cara has been guilty of unholy acts – with another woman. Father Negri had promised he could cure her, persuade their daughter to turn away from the path of sin. Bring her back into God's grace.'

Aldo struggled to keep hold of his anger. So, Negri's sacrament was no more than an excuse to torture and torment those who sought love with others like themselves. Aldo could imagine what would have happened if he had been taken as a young man to Negri, how the exorcist would have used the power of the Church against him, all in the name of God.

'And did Negri do it?' Aldo demanded. 'Did he exorcise Cara?'

'He never got the chance. The Gheradinis came back to say they had changed their minds. They no longer wanted to bring their daughter to him.'

'Why?'

'Yesterday Father Negri told them that young women are one of the devil's snares. He said such creatures can convince an exorcist he is dealing with a natural illness, not the presence of a diavolo. When Signora Gheradini asked for a promise that the sacrament would save her daughter, Negri said that was impossible to know with a young woman.'

Aldo was grateful the Gheradinis had seen through Negri's bluster. Hopefully they would find another way to reconcile with Cara, who she was and who she loved. 'And how did Negri respond when the parents told him their decision?'

'He threatened to have them excommunicated,' Zati admitted. 'He vowed to seek out their parish priest, demand the famiglia be banished from all holy sacraments.'

No wonder the couple looked so distraught when they fled San Felice. Aldo fought the urge to stalk into the church and tell Negri where to put his threats. It would do no good. Besides, the exorcist's behaviour offered an opportunity to get the truth from Zati.

'That is why you must answer our questions, Father. You have seen for yourself the wrongs Negri is doing in God's name. Would you have the suffering of more famiglie like the Gheradinis on your conscience? You can put an end to this if you have the courage.'

The priest shook his head. 'Please, let me go by. I cannot do what you ask.' He pushed past Aldo, scuttling away in the rain.

'Then who will?' Aldo called after him. 'You are the only one who can change this.'

Strocchi asked more questions about Signora Vanni, but the maggiordomo had nothing else to add so Strocchi moved on to other matters. 'There was another murder yesterday, a man killed the same way as Signor Zamora. The victim's corpse was found out there,' he said, gesturing down at Piazza Santo Spirito, 'not long after curfew ended.'

Querini nodded. 'We heard about this, of course. Two of the servant girls were in the piazza when the body was discovered. But I didn't realize . . .' He peered at Strocchi. 'Killed the same way? You mean one person was responsible for both murders?'

'That's what the evidence suggests, yes.'

'Who was this second victim?'

'A young man called Freccia. Is that name familiar? Did Signor Zamora know him?'

The maggiordomo shook his head. 'No. I knew all those with whom he had business.'

'Freccia was a thief, not a wool merchant. It is unlikely they ever made a deal. Might Signor Zamora have known him another way?' Strocchi didn't want to accuse Zamora of paying to use another man, not if he could avoid it.

'I'm not sure I understand what you're asking . . .'

So much for trying to be discreet. 'Before he took to stealing, Freccia offered himself to men who prefer the company of other men, in return for coin. We know Signor Zamora was not married. Might he have encountered Freccia in ways other than the wool trade?'

Querini's face reddened. 'No.'

'You're quite certain?'

'Yes.'

Pursuing this further risked being asked to leave, but Strocchi needed an answer. 'How can you be so sure?'

A scowl settled on the maggiordomo's face. 'You said this Freccia was young?'

'No more than twenty-five, perhaps less.'

'On the rare occasions Signor Zamora sought . . . companion-ship . . . he spent his time with those his own age. He had no interest in anyone young enough to be his child.' Strocchi let the silence between him and Querini linger in the hope of prompting more. It did. 'Once, when Signor Zamora had drunk far too much wine, he complained about those who took lovers much younger than themselves. He said it was unseemly and vowed never to disgrace himself or his famiglia in such a way. He would rather be alone than desperate.'

Before Strocchi could form another question, he noticed the maggiordomo staring down at the piazza. 'What is it?'

'It can't be . . .' Querini whispered.

'Can't be what?' Strocchi followed his gaze. A single figure was hurrying north across the piazza, wearing a thick cloak with the hood covering their head. The rain was dying away, making it easier to see them.

'For a moment, I could have sworn I saw Marsilio . . .'

'The signore's nephew? You said he died.'

Querini nodded. 'Yes, more than a year ago. I saw the body myself.'

'The body – but not his face?'

'No, we couldn't.'

'Why not? You told me he took poison.'

'That was what Signor Zamora urged me to say if anyone asked. But poor Marsilio, he went to the famiglia estate in the countryside and set fire to himself. We knew the body was him by what was left of his clothes, and a ring he inherited from his father.' The maggiordomo put a hand to his mouth. 'You don't think Marsilio's still alive, do you?'

The figure was nearing the northern end of the piazza. 'Are you sure it was him?'

'No,' Querini said. 'He's been on my mind since we lost Signor Zamora. I glimpsed a face for a moment, no more than that. I must have been mistaken.'

Strocchi leaned out over the stone balcony. 'Marsilio! Marsilio!' The figure did not respond, disappearing round the corner. Cursing himself for not moving sooner, Strocchi dashed to the staircase. He hurried down to the ground level, racing out through the internal courtyard to the piazza. Turning north he sprinted away from Palazzo Zamora, his boots slipping and sliding on the rain-slick stones.

By the time Strocchi reached the corner where the hooded figure had disappeared, there was no sign of them on the street heading east towards Ponte Vecchio. But there was a burly woman with broad shoulders approaching, her hair tied back beneath a black scarf. 'Are you Strocchi, the officer from the Otto?' she asked.

'Yes,' he replied. 'How did you know my name?'

'Fiora told me when I arrived at the tannery. She described what you look like, said you talked about coming to the piazza.'

Strocchi had mentioned it in passing, but no more than that. The woman stopped in front of him, a damp cloak under one arm. 'My name is Dea Vanni,' she said. 'I want to make a denunzia against the exorcist at San Felice.'

'What kind of denunzia?' Strocchi asked.

'Father Negri killed my brother!'

Chapter Eighteen

*A*ldo was grateful the rain had passed as he returned to via dei Giudei, but he was still soaked to the skin. He considered going to the bordello for dry clothes before remembering his other tunic and hose were festering in a corner of his room. Years as an officer had accustomed Aldo to having coin when needed, thanks to the rewards and bounties that rank brought. But constables had far fewer opportunities to supplement their meagre pay, especially those on night patrol, and most of that went on wine and food. Buying a cloak, even well used, was beyond his means and he refused to ask Saul for coin. Pride had its price.

Manuffi was leaning against a wall in the Jewish commune, rubbing his nose. He straightened up as Aldo approached, face brightening. 'I was starting to wonder if you or Strocchi were coming back,' Manuffi said. 'I've finished knocking at all the doors. The last one got slammed in my face. Hit me on the nose.'

Aldo suppressed a smile. 'Anything new from those who answered?'

'Maybe, but I don't speak Hebrew, so . . .' He shrugged.

'Never mind. Investigating a murder means knocking at a lot of doors to find the one person who may be able to help.'

'Is Carlo Strocchi here?' A boy ran towards them from the northern end of via dei Giudei. 'Is one of you Carlo Strocchi?'

'He should be back soon,' Manuffi replied.

The boy pulled a letter from his tunic. 'Message for him from the Podestà.'

'I'll take it,' Aldo said. 'Manuffi, have you any coin?' Once the boy was paid, he handed over the letter to Aldo before sprinting away. The document was sealed with wax to prevent the messenger knowing what was inside, though Aldo doubted the boy could read.

'Should we open it?' Manuffi asked. 'Or wait for Carlo?'

It was rare for messengers to be sent to officers within the city, suggesting the letter was urgent, while the wax seal showed how important the contents were. There was no way of knowing when Strocchi would arrive, so Aldo broke the seal. 'If Carlo complains, this was my doing,' he said while unfolding the letter.

It was from one of the segretario's administrative assistants. Bindi rarely committed ink to paper himself, believing if he never wrote anything down it could not be used against him later. It was the stratagemma of a true Florentine. Only the foolish and those who believed themselves beyond attack risked creating evidence of their actions. The contents of the letter were brisk: another body had been discovered, this one in an alleyway opposite the Church of Santa Maria Magdalena, in the city's northern quarter.

Aldo stared at the address. Minutes ago, he had been reminding Father Zati of their previous meeting near Santa Maria Magdalena; now a fresh corpse had been found close to that same church. Palle! This could not be happenstance, there must be a connection. There was little other detail beyond the means of murder: garrotting. The letter ended in a strident request for Strocchi to investigate and report his findings to Bindi before curfew.

'What does it say?' Manuffi asked.

'Nothing good,' Aldo replied.

* * *

Strocchi had heard many denunzie in his time with the Otto. Tearful accusations by those who had witnessed terrible crimes, angry allegations made by those who believed they had been wronged, and sly claims from citizens hoping to cause trouble or torment for their rivals and enemies. Each was different, and each required care when deciding how best to respond. Not just to the accusation, but also to the person making it. The grieving, the furious and the duplicitous all needed a measured approach to ensure justice was done.

Signora Vanni claimed to have evidence of a killing yet she was also a potential suspect. If Vanni ever stood trial for murder, Strocchi would have to give evidence to the Otto's magistrates, with Bindi watching. The segretario took every opportunity to punish any officers found wanting by the court.

'You say Negri murdered your brother?' Strocchi asked.

'Yes!'

'When did this happen? How did he kill . . . ?'

'Cecco, my brother's name was Cecco,' Vanni replied. 'He was overcome by the spirits, had been most of his life, ever since he hit his head as a boy. When they came, he would fall down, his whole body would twitch and jerk, froth coming from his mouth. There was nothing I could do for him but wait for the spirits to leave him in peace. Poor Cecco, they came for him more and more towards the end.'

Strocchi nodded, letting her tell the story in her own way, her own words. Yet Vanni spoke like someone who had said this many times before, as if reciting more from memory than experience. How often had she shared her tale without finding the response she sought, the justice she needed? Often enough to drive her to take a life, perhaps two? She certainly appeared strong enough to garrotte a man.

'I blame myself for what happened next,' Vanni went on. 'One of the other workers at the tannery was gossiping about their neighbour taking a cousin to be exorcized at San Felice, how it cured them of their ills. I wondered if the sacrament might help Cecco, ease his burden. So, I took him to see Father Negri . . .'

Vanni described the initial meeting, how the spirits came for her brother in front of Negri. The exorcist vowed he would cure Cecco, urged Vanni to return with her brother once Cecco recovered his strength. She was not allowed to witness the sacrament, but her brother seemed well afterwards. 'It was a miracle, as if Cecco had never been afflicted. I gave thanks to God and to Father Negri for saving my brother. I did not know what was to come. If I had, I never would have gone to San Felice.'

Convinced he was cured, Cecco went out for a walk by himself when Vanni was asleep. He fell while climbing a stone staircase and hit his head, dying two days later. 'My brother would be alive if not for Father Negri,' she said, becoming more passionate as her testimony neared its end. 'The exorcist promised to cure Cecco, my only famiglia, to make him well. Instead, Father Negri killed him, murdered him. That priest is a monster, and he must face justice for what he did!'

Strocchi resisted the urge to nod his agreement as she finished, so compelling was her belief. Her whole body was trembling with anger. Vanni was utterly convinced what she had said was true . . . yet that didn't make her right. What she had described was unfortunate, her brother's death a terrible accident, but no more. Even if a priest could be brought before the Otto – something Bindi would not attempt, and the diocese would never allow – Vanni's denunzia against Father Negri was not enough to convict.

However, Strocchi knew he could not tell her that. Not now, not to her face. She needed to be listened to, and she certainly deserved to be heard. Her denunzia should be properly written down and presented to the segretario for his consideration. Yes, Bindi would reject it as far too troublesome to pursue further, but that was a problem for another day. And there was another reason to give Vanni the chance to make her denunzia official: it would bring her to the Podestà, giving a chance to question Vanni formally about the murders of Zamora and Freccia. Querini had described her as obsessed, filled by a craving for vengeance, and Strocchi could see why the maggiordomo had said so. She was an intense presence, always coming a step too close, the sickly scent of the tannery all around her.

'If what you say is a true account of your brother's death—'

'It is!' Vanni insisted.

'—then it should certainly be recorded,' Strocchi continued. 'I will present it to the segretario of the Otto di Guardia e Balia, Signor Massimo Bindi.'

Her whole face brightened, a smile replacing the anger. 'Grazie! Grazie mille!'

Strocchi considered taking her back to the Podestà now, but he needed to find Aldo and Manuffi, hear what they had uncovered. 'Can you come to the Palazzo del Podestà later today? We can write down your denunzia and ask you questions about Father Negri. We need to know more about him, yes?'

Vanni nodded. 'I know where the Podestà is. I was there once before, trying to get justice for my brother, but nobody would listen to me.'

'Who did you speak with?'

'A constable, I think his name was Benedetto.'

Strocchi nodded. It did not surprise him that Benedetto had dismissed Vanni. The constable was often a sullen and unhelpful presence at the Podestà. Vanni's tale of a troubled brother and the exorcist would have found little sympathy with him. 'Come to the Podestà before curfew tonight and we shall make sure you are heard.'

Vanni grabbed his hands. 'Grazie, signor!' She kissed Strocchi on both cheeks, embracing him so close it almost crushed the breath from his body. He was grateful when she eventually let go, stepping back to escape her while offering a smile of reassurance. 'Forgive me,' Vanni said. 'I've been searching so long for someone, anyone, who would listen.'

'You've no need to apologize,' he replied. 'Now, if you will excuse me.' Strocchi gave her a final nod before walking past Vanni, heading east towards via dei Giudei. But she hurried after him, still eager to say more.

'I've talked to so many people. I found another man, one who was willing to hear my story. But he betrayed me, betrayed the memory of my brother.'

'Indeed?' Strocchi suspected she was talking about Zamora but took care not to let that show in his face or voice.

'I thought the younger priest at San Felice was my ally too, yet Father Zati was no better than the others. He's too afraid of Negri. But he shall see the truth when I'm done.'

Strocchi glanced at Vanni. She appeared happy, at peace. If she had killed Zamora or Freccia, it might have been with that same smile on her face . . .

Reaching the northern end of via dei Giudei, Strocchi stopped. 'Signora, may I ask you a question?' Vanni nodded. 'I notice you are carrying a cloak.'

'It was raining, I didn't want to get wet while I was looking for you.'

'Before we met each other, had you been walking across Piazza Santo Spirito?' If so, it would mean Querini had not seen Zamora's dead nephew Marsilio. The maggiordomo had seemed so convinced at the time; Strocchi needed to know if Querini had been right.

Vanni frowned. 'I'm not sure. I walked around most of Oltrarno looking for you. Fiora wasn't very clear when she said where to find you. It might have been me.' That did not solve the mystery of what Querini had seen. Strocchi noticed Aldo talking with Manuffi outside Doctor Orvieto's home. The two constables seemed agitated.

'Forgive me, but my colleagues are waiting,' Strocchi said. 'I will see you later, yes?' Reassured by Vanni's nod, he strode towards Aldo and Manuffi. Strocchi offered up a silent prayer that Vanni would present herself at the Podestà. If she did not, it would be difficult explaining why he had walked away from a leading suspect in two murders.

Aldo saw Strocchi striding towards them from the north end of the street. Aldo held up the letter. 'There's been another killing.'

'Santo Spirito!' Strocchi said. 'Where?'

'Across the river.' Aldo handed him the letter. 'North of San Marco, not far from Porta San Gallo. We should get going. Bindi hasn't given us much time to find answers.'

Strocchi read the letter, his shoulders sinking. 'Lead the way.'

Aldo took Strocchi and Manuffi west to Ponte alla Carraia. The bridge was an easier place to cross than fighting through those seeking bargains from the butcher's shops and fish sellers on Ponte Vecchio. Once over the river, Aldo told the others what Bassano had revealed about Freccia's argument with Negri. 'I suspect the thief was extorting coin from the exorcist. Perhaps Freccia demanded too much and that's what drove the exorcist to kill him.'

'What could Freccia know that Negri would pay to keep secret?' Strocchi wondered.

'The priest might have been one of Freccia's visitors when he used to satisfy men.'

'You mean he . . . ?' Manuffi asked but was unable to finish his sentence. 'A priest, doing that? Sainted Madonna . . .'

Aldo had encountered priests who did far worse but kept it to himself. 'I haven't met Negri. What does he look like?'

Strocchi described the exorcist. 'He does not seem a man who finds pleasure or joy in anything but his work. Why do you want to know about his appearance?'

'Because it confirms a suspicion I've been carrying,' Aldo replied. 'Bassano heard Freccia call Negri "Father" several times. It seemed to infuriate the exorcist.'

'Everyone calls a priest Father,' Strocchi said.

'True, but I think it had another meaning. I suspect Freccia was Negri's son.'

'But . . . he's a priest,' Manuffi said. 'They don't . . . He can't have a child . . . can he?'

'Negri is still a man, despite his calling. He could have had a child before taking his vows. And there have been priests who strayed from their sacraments with a woman.'

'That's all true,' Strocchi agreed, 'but what makes you think he is Freccia's papa?'

Aldo tapped his chin. 'You mentioned Negri having a distinctive cleft here. Freccia had the same cleft in his chin. It's a trait that often passes from father to son.'

Manuffi nodded. 'I've seen that before. The Arigho famiglia lived next to us when I was growing up. Their papa had that cleft in his chin and so did all the Arigho boys.'

'It's possible,' Strocchi conceded. 'What else did you learn?'

As they marched north, Aldo gave a summary of his encounter with Father Zati. Strocchi and Manuffi did not need to know how hard he had pushed the priest, and it was better they didn't if the priest should make an official complaint to Bindi.

'I'm confident Zati will talk to us about Negri soon,' Aldo said. 'The question is when. He wants to share what he knows, but something or someone is holding him back.'

'Someone?' Strocchi frowned. 'You mean the exorcist.'

'Negri was right to tell you he is beyond our power to arrest. That makes the exorcist dangerous, especially to Zati, so it's no surprise the younger priest is reluctant to help us. We must hope his conscience proves too much for him to ignore, and soon.'

Manuffi cleared his throat. 'If the Otto cannot arrest the exorcist, why are we trying to prove whether he committed these murders?'

'We're not certain Negri did,' Aldo replied, 'not yet. But if he is innocent, we need to know so we can pursue other suspects. Even if Negri had no hand in these killings, his refusal to help still hampers our investigation.'

'And we need to know for the famiglia of each victim,' Strocchi added. 'They deserve the truth of what happened, even if we cannot bring the killer before the court.'

'Justice and the law are not the same thing in this city,' Aldo said. 'We want to discover who killed Zamora, Freccia and this new victim – and why. If the evidence leads us to Negri, you can be sure Bindi will not ask Archbishop Buondelmonti for permission to arrest the exorcist. But that doesn't mean we shouldn't keep looking. Uncovering the truth, wherever that leads, could help us prevent anyone else from being murdered.'

Manuffi nodded his understanding. 'If Negri isn't responsible, who else could it be?'

'There is another suspect worth investigating,' Strocchi replied as they passed Piazza Santa Maria Novella. He detailed his encounter with Signora Vanni, her obsession with Negri and her overbearing behaviour with Zamora. 'She talks as if she is an avenging angel.'

Aldo recalled how interested Vanni had been when he visited the tannery to tell Fiora about Freccia's murder. Perhaps she simply possessed a fondness for gossip. It was a vice shared by many Florentines, and no proof of being a murderer. Strocchi's belief she should be a suspect was compelling. Vanni was certainly strong enough to garrotte a man. Aldo was not yet convinced – her motivation for murdering Freccia was unclear – but it was possible.

The three men strode on in silence. When Santa Maria Magdalena came into view, a cluster of people was gathered outside the alley that stood opposite the church entrance on via San Gallo. 'There should be someone from the Otto keeping these people back,' Strocchi muttered.

Pushing through the throng took time. Even threats to make arrests had little effect. Eventually Manuffi cleared a path by grabbing those unwilling to move and pulling them out of the way. That soon had the rest stepping aside, letting Strocchi and Aldo into the alley.

It was little more than a narrow dirt pathway between two palazzi, the buildings on either side so close Aldo's shoulders were almost scraping against the stone. A broken barrel and discarded building materials blocked part of the alley. Little of the weak autumn light reached down between the palazzi, further disguising what was in the alley. A pair of legs was visible beyond the debris, one crossed over the other at the feet. A dirty blanket had been laid across the body, hiding the rest from view. Aldo stepped over the body, inhaling the acrid stench of stale piss and bad wine. He peered at where the alley met via San Gallo. No wonder the corpse had not been found sooner. From back there the body would have looked more like a sleeping drunkard than a murder victim.

Whose body would they find under the blanket? The first had been a noble merchant and the second a thief, both with connections to the exorcist Negri. Aldo looked beyond the crowd to the Church of Santa Maria Magdalena, its entrance standing opposite the alley. Might this victim be a priest? If so, the diocese would seize control of the investigation before the day's end, making matters a dozen times more difficult.

Strocchi asked Manuffi to move the crowd further back. The constable faced the throng, using his size to block their view. 'You've all had a good look. Time to go home or go to work and tell everyone what you've seen, yes?'

Aldo suppressed a smile. Manuffi might be trusting, but he was no fool.

Once the crowd was leaving, Strocchi crouched by the corpse, reaching to lift the blanket away. Aldo held his breath, preparing himself for what lay beneath it. He had no fear of seeing a dead body, there had been too many of those to recall in his time with the Otto, and more before that. Truth be told, the prospect of uncovering a fresh victim sharpened Aldo's thoughts. He would never admit it to Saul or anyone else, but moments like this were why he worked for the Otto. A new puzzle, or a new piece of a larger puzzle. Yes, he wanted to see justice done, far more than he cared about enforcing the laws of Florence. But he also enjoyed the challenge of solving a mystery that eluded others. If pride was a sin, it was also far from being his only such trespass.

'Ready?' Strocchi asked. Aldo nodded, watching as Strocchi took hold of the blanket. 'This is wet,' he said. 'That could mean it was laid over the body before the rain came. But why would the killer try to hide their work? They put the other victims on display.'

'That's if the killer brought the blanket,' Aldo replied. 'It could have been placed over the corpse by someone else after the body was dumped here.'

Strocchi lifted the blanket away, revealing a heavyset man with the red mark of a garrotte round his neck. Like the previous victims he had been posed to resemble Christ on the cross, both arms spread out sideways. A thin, scratchy beard could not hide the pox scars on his ugly, boorish face.

'Palle,' Aldo said. 'I know this man.'

'Who is he?' Strocchi asked.

'Signor Tito Grossolano. He is – or was – Venice's new spymaster here in Florence.'

Chapter Nineteen

Strocchi took a moment to consider what Aldo had said, the consequences that could come from the murder of a visitor to Florence, let alone the spymaster of another city. The first two killings had piled pressure on the court to find whoever was responsible, leading Bindi to demand answers and threaten demotion. But attacking the representative of another city was pushing the investigation into new, uncertain territory.

'Just like the others,' Strocchi said, 'posed as Christ on the cross.'

'True,' Aldo agreed, studying their surroundings. 'But why is the body here? The others were put on display in a piazza for everyone to see. Leaving Grossolano here . . . it's as if the killer was ashamed of what they did. There was no pride taken from this murder.'

Strocchi brushed the dead man's hair away from the forehead. There was a smear of ash above the eyebrows, but it formed no obvious symbol or shape, let alone a word. 'Grossolano does have ash on his forehead.'

Aldo put a knee to the dirt to study the ash. 'The killer wrote a word on Freccia.'

'There was only a cross on Zamora.'

'He was left out in a downpour; rain may have washed some ash from his forehead. Grossolano was hidden beneath a blanket when today's rain fell.'

Strocchi was becoming frustrated by these contrary comments. 'What are you saying? That this man was killed by somebody else?'

Aldo shrugged. 'I'm simply pointing to what's in front of us. Trying not to leap from one stone to the next without any proof. A wise man once told me that was the best way.'

'Then what do you suggest?'

Aldo searched inside the dead man's clothes, peering beneath the fabric. 'No torn page here that I can find. Do you want to look inside Grossolano's mouth, or should I?'

Strocchi turned away from the body. 'You do it.'

'Nothing,' Aldo soon said.

'Nothing? What, they've cut the tongue out this time?'

'No, I mean there was no cutting at all. See for yourself.'

Strocchi had no wish to look, but it was necessary. Bracing himself, he crouched forward over the corpse while Aldo held the mouth open. It reeked of stale garlic and wine, but there was no evidence the killer had taken a knife to the tongue. Strocchi sank back on his haunches. 'Perhaps you're right. Perhaps this is another murderer's work.'

'This could be happenstance,' Aldo said, releasing the mouth and wiping his hands dry. 'A thief attacked Grossolano and hid the body here to gain time for their escape. A garrotte is a common enough weapon. Nobody in the neighbouring buildings would have seen anything.' He gestured at the palazzi on either side. Neither had shutters overlooking the alley.

Strocchi could hear doubt in his voice. 'You don't sound convinced.'

'I might believe it if Grossolano had only been garrotted. It's an effective way to kill, stops the victim crying out for help. But posing the body, and putting ash on the forehead . . .'

Strocchi considered the implications of this. 'You're suggesting whoever murdered Grossolano tried to make it look like the work of whoever killed Zamora and Freccia.'

'It's a possibility. This killer knew a little, but not enough to be convincing.' Aldo got back to his feet. 'How many people at the Podestà have the details of these murders?'

'Most of them, probably. You know how constables and guards gossip. But they would know more than the person responsible for this killing did, it seems . . .' Strocchi studied Aldo's face. 'Could someone from the Podestà have murdered this man?'

'I doubt it. What reason would they have?' Aldo tapped a finger against his lips. 'There are others who had knowledge of what the killer does. Bindi will have reported the details to Duke Cosimo and his private segretario, Campana.'

'You think the duke had Grossolano killed?' Strocchi knew little about such things, but eliminating the new spymaster from a rival city state seemed a dangerous stratagemma. 'Would Cosimo make such a bold move?'

Aldo shook his head. 'Probably not. When the duke strikes against an enemy, he does not hide his hand afterwards. If Cosimo wanted to move against Venice, he would find another way. But one of his courtiers might have done this, believing it was in the duke's interests.'

Strocchi got up, brushing mud from the knees of his hose. He hoped Aldo was wrong. Searching for a killer among Cosimo's staff would be a dangerous and thankless task.

'There is another possibility,' Aldo ventured. 'But proving it will be difficult.'

Strocchi sighed. 'That doesn't help much.' Most of the people gathered outside the alley had gone, only a pair of wizen-faced widows still lingering. 'Manuffi, can you go back to via dei Giudei and ask Doctor Orvieto to come here? Tell him we have another body for examination.' The constable nodded and strode away south.

'Getting a second opinion?' Aldo asked.

'We need to be certain,' Strocchi replied. 'Bindi will want proof Grossolano was killed by a different hand.'

'Good thinking.' Aldo stepped over the dead man. 'You don't need me to stay here and watch over the body until Saul arrives, do you?'

'Well, I was . . .' Strocchi recalled Tomasia's advice: let Aldo be Aldo. 'Where are you going? In case I need to find you quickly.'

'Palazzo Coltello,' Aldo replied.

'Should I ask why?'

'To test a possibility.'

When Father Zati returned to San Felice, the front door was closed. He let himself in through the back door, but the church stood empty. Negri had left no note and nothing else to explain his absence. Zati stood before the large painted cross, studying the pained expression on Christ's face, the torment in his eyes. When Zati turned away, his gaze fell on the braided scourge Negri used to mortify his flesh each day. Each strand was stained a dark crimson with the exorcist's blood. Zati picked up the scourge, staring at it in his grasp.

'Do you use that during your barbaric sacrament?' a woman's voice demanded.

Zati whirled round. Signora Vanni was stalking towards him. 'How did you get in?'

'You left the back door ajar,' she replied before pointing at the flagellator in his hand. 'Well? Did you use that on my brother? Or is it for your own sins?'

Zati put the scourge back where it had been. 'That belongs to Father Negri.'

'Of course it does. A monster like him enjoys inflicting pain.'

'You don't know what you're talking about.'

'I know all about pain,' Vanni insisted.

'Why are you here? You swore never to set foot in this church until Father Negri was no longer an exorcist.'

'That day is close enough,' she said. 'So, I came to thank you.'

'Me? Why?'

'You helped me see things as they truly are. I realized you were too afraid, too much of a coward to do what was needed, just like others before you. But I have found someone willing to help me, and you will bear witness to the cost of your weakness soon enough.' Vanni strolled away from the priest, back the way she had come in.

'Help you? How?' Zati hurried after her. 'W-what are you talking about, signora?'

'Farewell, Father. I doubt we shall meet again.'

'What have you done? Tell me!'

Vanni kept walking. 'Make your peace with the Lord. I hope he has mercy on you.'

'Signora, tell me what you've done!' Zati shouted as she left through the back door of the church. It hung open behind her, people staring at the priest as he burst out into the street. 'Signora Vanni, come back here!' But she ignored him, leaving Zati behind.

Strocchi laid the damp blanket back over Grossolano. With Manuffi away fetching Doctor Orvieto and Aldo seeking answers elsewhere, there was nobody else to stand vigil over the murdered man. Only two elderly widows remained of the crowd that had gathered, both women dressed in black with headscarves round their silver hair. Strocchi asked if they'd seen anyone near the corpse, but each denied witnessing anything. There had been a crowd pointing and gossiping, so the women had come to see for themselves. Yes, if they heard anything, they would come to the Podestà with the information. A reward would be welcome, it was not easy surviving as a widow in Florence.

Eventually they tired of watching Strocchi do nothing and shuffled off, one looping an arm through that of her companion. When they had gone, the main door of Santa Maria Magdalena opened. A priest in his later years emerged from the church, hurrying across via San Gallo to join Strocchi. He introduced himself as Father Visconti with a friendly manner that reminded Strocchi of the parish priest in Ponte a Signa.

'Is it true?' Visconti asked. 'Has a man been killed close to my church?'

'We do not know for certain that he was killed here but his corpse was left in this alley,' Strocchi replied. 'How did you know?'

'One of my parishioners came in to tell me.'

'Did they give you any other details? We need to find anyone who witnessed the body being placed here.'

'I cannot tell you the sins that are shared with me in confession . . .'

'No, of course,' Strocchi said in haste. He would never ask a priest to betray such a trust. The thought had not even occurred to him, though he doubted Aldo would hesitate.

'. . . but none of my flock has spoken of being involved with this sin,' the priest confirmed.

'Grazie, Father.'

Visconti nodded. 'Do you know the name of this poor soul?'

'I will say it if you promise not to share the name with others.'

'Of course.'

'Signor Tito Grossolano. We believe he is a visitor from Venice.' The priest did not need to know more than that.

'May I offer him the last rites? His body may be dead, but perhaps we can still help the journey of his immortal soul.'

'Of course. A doctor is coming to examine the body, so I must ask you not to touch it. But I'm sure Signor Grossolano would have welcomed the last rites if he were still alive to receive them.' The priest returned to Santa Maria Magdalena to gather what he needed for the sacrament.

Strocchi was left alone with the corpse once more. In truth, he could not be certain of Grossolano's faith, but offering reassurance to the priest seemed worthwhile. From what Aldo had said about Grossolano, the Venetian was neither a charitable nor a kind soul. But everyone deserved the chance of God's forgiveness. Let the Lord judge whether they were worthy of that forgiveness when the day of judgement came.

The more urgent question was what Grossolano's murder signified. The evidence offered by his body suggested a different hand had been responsible for this killing, but that still needed proof. Bindi would demand answers, whether Grossolano was murdered by the same person who killed Zamora and Freccia or by someone else. Having two different murderers at work in the city would complicate matters still further.

Then there were the consequences of Grossolano's death for Florence. Aldo had said this victim was the new spymaster for Venice. Strocchi knew little about such matters and had no interest in learning more. But the killing of Grossolano so soon after his arrival in Florence could only be seen as an attack upon Venetian interests. That would not pass unpunished, Strocchi imagined. He had witnessed the way a vendetta between one famiglia and another could lead to bloody, brutal consequences. Should a city state declare a vendetta against one of its rivals . . .

Wars had begun with less reason.

The sooner Grossolano's killer was found and punished, the better.

The contessa had been expecting a visit from a representative of the Otto. The fact it was Aldo seeking another audience made that visit more welcome, but also more of a challenge. He was unlikely to be disarmed by feigned tears or an overwrought woman collapsing onto a chair. In fact, she was not sure any woman would be capable of turning his head, despite their flirtations of the previous day. Years of dealing with different men, knowing when to tease and when to keep clear of their grasp, had taught her to recognize lust in their eyes and hose. She had seen little of that in Aldo. He had been performing for her as much as she had for him. Whatever the truth of his desires, she was delighted to have him return.

Now their jousting could resume.

The contessa arranged herself by the shutters in her salone, looking down at Piazza di Santa Trinita while Pozzo ushered Aldo in. She did not speak until the maggiordomo had gone, closing the door after him. 'Welcome back. But if you are hoping to introduce yourself to my successor, I have grave news.'

'Indeed. How grave?'

She suppressed a smile at Aldo joining in with her wordplay. So, he already knew Grossolano was dead. Good, that spared them both time wasted on less interesting feints and parries. 'Most grave,' she replied, whirling round. 'I wish to report the disappearance of my guest, Signor Tito Grossolano.'

'Naturally.' Aldo was remarkably good at remaining still, masking whatever he was thinking and feeling. That slight arching of his left eyebrow was for her benefit, saying without words that he was quite aware of the stratagemma being played here. 'And when did he disappear?'

'It was well after curfew last night,' the contessa said, sweeping across the salone to sink into a chair. 'I cannot be certain when, as I had retired earlier. It pains me to say this but Signor Grossolano was not the most entertaining of men, especially after his third bottle of wine, so I made my excuses and went to my bedchamber.'

'Did your servants continue assisting him after that?'

'Sadly, yes. I should have left instructions to offer him no further wine but, alas, it slipped my mind. You know how it is, dealing with those you would rather not.'

Aldo gave a nod to acknowledge the frustrations of such matters, but said nothing more. A wise person knew when to let their enemy speak, and when to remain silent. Aldo was proving his wisdom again today. But this came as no surprise to the contessa.

Once Aldo had departed the previous day, she'd set her maggiordomo the task of determining whether her visitor's claims and promises were accurate. Pozzo had confirmed much of what Aldo had said on his previous visit, thanks to sources and the idle gossip of those who knew Aldo. He had indeed been demoted by segretario Bindi to constable despite being the most accomplished investigator at the Otto. Aldo had a reputation for following his own path, no matter the circumstances or the cost. As far as Pozzo could determine Aldo had never been married, nor sired any children. Yet he lived in an Oltrarno bordello, a detail that had made the contessa laugh. As a way of diverting questions about his preference of partners, it must be most effective. But one more detail stood out from the intelligence Pozzo had gathered. On occasion, Aldo was known to have the ear of Duke Cosimo de' Medici.

In short, he was an interesting and dangerous individual. Those were always her favourites. But how much should she tell him? Too little and it might not satisfy; too much and Aldo could use it against her. Whatever was said next would be critical.

Chapter Twenty

'There was an unfortunate incident with one of my maids,' the contessa said. 'It seems Signor Grossolano wished to take advantage of her, and she responded with several kicks to his palle after which his enthusiasm . . . lessened. He drank more of my best wine and then staggered from the palazzo, despite my maggiordomo reminding him that Florence has a strict curfew between sunset and sunrise.'

'Have you any further information that might help the Otto find him?' Aldo asked.

She recognized this snare for what it was, an invitation to say something that could not easily be denied later. Far better to leave a means of escape, in case it was ever required. The contessa arranged her face to appear as if she was carefully considering all that she knew. 'Not that I can recall at present.'

A smile appeared for a moment on Aldo's lips before vanishing as he became more serious. He gestured to the chair beside her. 'May I?'

'Of course.'

Aldo perched on the seat, leaning towards her. 'I regret to inform you that the body of Signor Grossolano was found earlier today.'

'No!' she gasped, letting her eyes widen in apparent surprise. 'Are you sure?'

'I am afraid so. I saw the corpse myself, there can be no doubt.'

The contessa sank back in her chair, putting a hand to her chest. 'But this is . . . dreadful news. May I ask, how did he die?'

Aldo also leaned back in his seat, mirroring her. 'He was garrotted. Posed to resemble Christ on the cross. And ash was smeared on his forehead.'

'You mean . . . He was killed the same way as that poor merchant?'

'The one I told you about on my previous visit here? Yes.' He smiled at her, but there was no warmth in Aldo's eyes. 'At least, that is what the killer wishes us to believe.'

He knew. He knew what had happened, or he strongly suspected it. But Aldo did not have proof, otherwise they would not be talking like this. They would be in an interrogation cell at the Podestà, not seated on these comfortable chairs in her salone.

'You see, there was another killing yesterday,' Aldo continued, his eyes still fixed on her. 'I did not know of that when I was here, otherwise I would have shared its details with you in good faith. But this second killing told us much more about the person responsible. The murder of Signor Grossolano, while similar, has some significant differences, enough to show it was the work of another hand. Someone who knew a little about the first victim, but none of the second.'

In normal circumstances she would have expected Pozzo to hear about the second killing and share any relevant details with her, but they had been too occupied dealing with Grossolano. It was unfortunate, but the contessa kept the realization from her face and her posture. Instead, she simply nodded, letting Aldo continue. Again, the hint of a smile played across his lips. He was enjoying this. And so was she. To have an opponent searching for weaknesses in your armour while you probed their defences for the same . . . it was exhilarating. After the doltish Dandolo and the boorish Grossolano, it was a delight to trade words with an individual worthy of her best.

'There are not many citizens who fulfil that description,' Aldo said, 'knowing a little of the first victim but none of the second. You are one of them, Contessa.'

'I am? How so?'

'I shared some of what I knew of the first victim with you yesterday, but that was before I saw or knew of the second. And you made it clear to me during that visit how unwelcome you considered the arrival of Signor Grossolano, how much you resented being usurped from your position. That gives you a clear motive for his killing.'

'This is all true,' she agreed, 'but I stayed in my bedchamber all night, as my servants will confirm. I could not have garrotted the unfortunate Grossolano, even if I'd wanted to. Alas, as a woman who spends all her days in saloni and her nights in bedchambers, I lack the strength for such endeavours.' She held out her hands, turning them over to show there were no marks on either side, no tell-tale sign of where clenched fists would have grasped a garrotte as it choked the life from a victim.

Aldo held up his own hands, as if asking for forgiveness. 'Contessa, I would not dream of accusing you of committing such a crime against the laws of Florence or the law of God. But there is another possibility.'

Strocchi was hungry, which told him it must be mid-afternoon, if not later. No more rain had fallen but the sky was a brooding canopy of cloud, hiding the sun and making it hard to be certain of the hour. He had expected Manuffi back sooner, bringing

Doctor Orvieto. But when the constable did return to the alley, the Jewish physician was not with him. Instead, Manuffi was escorting Orvieto's student, Rebecca Levi.

'The doctor gave me a message for you,' the constable said before Strocchi could question his lengthy absence. 'Much as Doctor Orvieto appreciates the opportunity to assist the Otto with its inquiries,' Manuffi recited, concentration etching furrows into his brow, 'he is unable to abandon his patients at such short notice. The doctor has sent Rebecca in his stead. She is an accomplished student and more than capable of assessing the cause of death for a murdered corpse.'

'Is that all?' Strocchi asked.

Manuffi shook his head. 'In future, if the court wishes to seek Doctor Orvieto's assistance, it should offer payment for his time and expertise.' The constable puffed out his cheeks. 'That's all of it, I think.' Rebecca nodded beside him.

'I'm sorry Saul couldn't come,' she said, 'but autumn and winter are the worst time of year for many of our older patients. I hope my help will be enough.'

Strocchi wanted to be annoyed by the doctor's message, and the demand for payment, but Orvieto made a valid point. The court had been exploiting his friendship with Aldo while offering nothing in return. Persuading Bindi to part with coin for such services would not be easy, even though Orvieto had proven a valuable resource for the Otto. But that was an argument for another time.

'I understand,' Strocchi replied, welcoming her with a brisk smile. He led Rebecca to the corpse. 'Are you sure you are comfortable with examining the body of a stranger?'

Rebecca dismissed his concerns with a wave of one hand. 'Working for Saul, I have seen bodies of all shapes and sizes, clothed and naked, women and men. This poor soul will need to be quite remarkable to surprise me.'

Strocchi lifted the blanket aside before leaving Rebecca to her task. He talked with Manuffi while she examined the corpse. 'How angry was Doctor Orvieto?'

'He was . . . not pleased, at first. But his student took him aside and they spoke for some time. I waited for them to agree, that's why I was away for so long. Doctor Orvieto made me repeat his message several times to be certain I told it to you correctly.'

'That can't have been easy. Well done.' Strocchi pulled a small pouch from inside his tunic and gave Manuffi several coins. 'Sorry to send you on another errand, but we will need a cart to take this body to Santa Maria Nuova. Can you . . . ?'

'Of course.' Manuffi ambled away, humming to himself. It would have been a different matter if Strocchi had asked Benedetto, but Manuffi remained amiable in almost any circumstance.

The contessa could see where Aldo was leading her but still asked him the question he wanted to hear. 'So, if I am not a suspect for the murder of Signor Grossolano, who is?'

'Perhaps one of your servants, knowing your dislike of him, chose to take matters into their own hands. They might have feared for their own future, knowing this newcomer was going to replace you as Venice's representative here in Florence. Or they may have sought retribution for Grossolano attempting to force himself on one of your maids. It would be understandable in the circumstances and might even be grounds for mitigation if offered alongside an admission of guilt.'

There it was. A way for her to escape any culpability for the murder in exchange for providing a servant as a suitable suspect.

The Otto could close its investigation, avoiding the need for any further questions or accusations against her household. But this assumed she was ruthless enough to sacrifice one of her own servants to avoid any further unpleasantness.

The contessa prided herself on being able and willing to do whatever was necessary to survive such a threat, and to prosper while doing so. But she would not cast a servant aside simply to save herself, not if it could be avoided. Besides, there was another suspect ready and waiting to be offered if the need arose.

'I do have a name for you,' she told Aldo, enjoying the gleam of triumph that brought to his eyes, 'but it may not be the one you expect.'

'Indeed? And who is this individual the Otto should be pursuing?'

'Signor Gonzalo Zilio.'

'Signor . . . Zilio?'

'Yes, that's right. The same man who serves the Council of Ten in Venice, travelling from city to city and port to port, gathering intelligence from its spies in rival territories and ensuring the safety of those spies.'

The triumph had left Aldo's eyes, replaced by a creasing of his brow while he doubtless grappled with the intricacies of her counter-offer. 'And what makes you think Signor Zilio had reason to want Grossolano dead?'

'The two men hated each other,' she whispered, as if providing the juiciest morsel of gossip. 'Zilio considered Grossolano an oaf and a buffone, incapable of mastering the courtly intrigues required to succeed as a spymaster in Florence. However, there was no choice about bringing Grossolano here as he has – forgive me, had – a famiglia connection to the new Inquisitorie di Stato in Venice.' It was a mixture of lies and fact. Always better to present a falsehood in the company of truth, that made it more difficult to discern one from the other. Besides, Aldo had no way of proving her wrong. That was more important than all the other considerations.

He was not convinced yet, but he would not be as formidable a man as she suspected if such a tale was swallowed whole at the first offering. 'That suggests Zilio had a reason to harm Grossolano,' Aldo said, 'albeit a slight one. There is no shortage of hatred between men here in Florence, but that does not often lead to murder.'

'Zilio also had a partial knowledge of the recent killings,' the contessa said. 'He came here yesterday, after you departed, to ensure Grossolano was comfortable. The two of them argued, that was how I first discovered their enmity.' She must tell Pozzo to share this lie with several servants so they could offer evidence in support of it, should that be required. 'Afterwards, I may have mentioned to Zilio what you told me about that poor soul's body found in Piazza Della Signoria, how they were garrotted and so forth. Zilio seemed quite interested, and even asked me to repeat some details more than once. Had I known what he might do with that information . . .' She shook her head, as if saddened to have played some small part in these tragic events.

Aldo would see past that, of course, and suspect she had used Zilio's alleged antipathy to manipulate him into murdering Grossolano. But, again, there was no proof. 'And where is Signor Zilio now?'

'On his way back to Venice, I believe. He came to the palazzo this morning. I must say, he appeared most agitated.' She paused, letting realization seep into her face. 'You don't think that's because he . . . ?'

Aldo gave no sign of what he was thinking. It was a quality that Pozzo said infuriated the Otto's segretario, if reports from within the Podestà were accurate. The contessa found it intriguing.

She wanted to know what was happening behind those flinty eyes. Much of it she could surmise, but Aldo held part of himself back. Perhaps even his lover, if he took lovers, did not know the whole truth of Aldo's capabilities, what he was willing to do if forced into a trap with no apparent escape.

'I told Zilio that Signor Grossolano was missing, how he had left the palazzo during curfew while drunk and not returned. I wanted to send a messenger to you at the Podestà to ask for help finding Signor Grossolano, but Zilio forbade it.'

Aldo frowned. 'Forgive me for saying so, Contessa, but you do not seem the sort of woman whom men are able to control, let alone forbid.'

She bowed her head a little, accepting that as a compliment. 'Nonetheless, Zilio forbade me from seeking your help and I foolishly agreed to his urgings. He said he was leaving for Venice immediately. By now he must be halfway to Bologna.'

'And thus, beyond the reach of the Otto.'

'Is that so? How unfortunate. But I'm sure you could persuade the court to issue a standing order for Zilio's arrest, should he ever be foolish enough to return.'

'Perhaps,' Aldo agreed.

The contessa rose from her seat. 'Well, if there's nothing else . . .'

He got to his feet and strode to the door. But, as he opened it, Aldo smiled at her. 'Grazie for granting me this audience, Contessa. It has been most illuminating and, if I may say so, equally entertaining.'

She returned his smile. 'I must agree with you. Most entertaining.'

'I hope we have a chance to talk again. In less . . . fatal . . . circumstances.'

* * *

When Rebecca completed her examination of Grossolano, she laid the blanket back over the corpse. 'I'm ready for you,' she called to Strocchi as she stood up. He moved closer so her findings would not be heard by anyone passing the alley.

'At first appearance, this killing looks very similar to the first two. The victim was garrotted, and his body posed in the way you described the others were. There is ash on the forehead as well – a smear, not a written word.' She glanced down at the corpse. 'But there are significant differences from the previous victims. No attempt has been made to cut or divide the tongue. And the cord used to kill this man is different.'

Most of what Rebecca had said confirmed what Strocchi and Aldo had deduced from their own study of Grossolano's body. But her last statement was unexpected.

'Different? How?' Strocchi asked.

'The victim I saw yesterday had a pattern in the red line around their neck, as if whatever was used to garrotte them was a rope or cord threaded with thick beads. This man was garrotted with a length of cord, so the red line is unbroken.' She bent down, lifting the blanket to show Strocchi. Rebecca was right, the angry mark around Grossolano's throat was different from what had been around the necks of Zamora and Freccia.

'There's something else,' Rebecca added. 'Saul said the others were garrotted from behind, leaving a small absence in the red mark above the back. But you can see this man was garrotted from the left, creating an absence in the line below their ear.'

Strocchi could see she was correct about that, as well. Why had he and Aldo not noticed this earlier? It did not matter now, but was further proof that having a good physician – or their student – assisting the Otto was helpful in such matters. 'Grazie,' he said. 'That had escaped both Aldo and myself.'

'A doctor looks for different things,' she replied. 'Saul often tells me we should help others find the solution they need, not impose our judgement on them.'

It was a noble approach and, in Strocchi's view, the opposite of what the Otto did. 'Do you have a conclusion for me?'

She nodded. 'Saul briefed me thoroughly on Niccolò Zamora, as I did not examine that body myself. Nonetheless, the differences between the second victim and this corpse are significant, which suggests two possibilities. Either the killer has changed their method . . . or this man was killed by someone trying to make the murder seem the same as the first.'

'Grazie,' Strocchi said. 'Grazie mille.'

The low rumble of a cart approaching on via San Gallo announced the return of Manuffi. Rebecca held the blanket while they moved Grossolano's body onto the cart before laying it back over the corpse. Strocchi thanked her again, and asked Rebecca to make his apologies to Doctor Orvieto. 'Tell him I will seek permission to pay for such expertise in future.'

'How likely is it that the court will agree?' she asked.

Strocchi didn't have a good answer for her question.

Chapter Twenty-one

Aldo marched north-east from Piazza di Santa Trinita, intent on questioning the guards at Porta San Gallo. They were expected to note the names of all those coming and going through the city's northern gate as it was the most direct road to Bologna, Venice and beyond. But few if any of those standing guard could read or write, so it was essential to question them while memories were fresh. The contessa's maggiordomo had helpfully provided a description of Zilio and what he had been wearing earlier that day.

Aldo could not help wondering how the contessa had come to be the self-confessed spymaster of a rival city state. She seemed able to say or do whatever best served her own interests, but that did not make her the obvious choice for such a post. He knew little beyond what the duke and Campana had shared about her past, and that did not explain why a woman born in Florence was providing intelligence about that city to the Council of Ten. Where did the contessa's true loyalties lie? If put under duress, would she act in favour of Venice or Florence? Aldo suspected neither city mattered more to the contessa than her own prospects. That made her a true Florentine, despite the contradiction.

Thinking about her caused a stirring in his hose that Aldo could not understand. He had no lust for the bodies of women, yet something about the contessa attracted him. She had a playfulness that was intriguing, and a knowing quality in her gaze which spoke of her talent and skills in the bedchamber. If she had possessed a cazzo, Aldo would find her almost impossible to resist. But there was another quality the contessa possessed which enticed Aldo: she reminded him of himself.

To Aldo's eye the contessa was a collection of masks, worn one atop another as protection. Like him, she had learned – had needed to learn – how to guard against the betrayals and lies of others. He doubted the contessa would ever willingly or easily let down her guard. Trust would be the hardest gift of all for her to bestow, but it was the one most valuable when a threat or danger appeared. Loyalty would be rewarded with the same, yet lies and deflection were her daily weapons. It was unlikely anyone could ever truly know what the contessa was thinking. Perhaps that was for the best.

Setting the contessa herself to one side, Aldo considered what she had told him. It was a mixture of truth and deception, of course, but he expected no less and certainly no more. Her responses had confirmed his suspicion that the killing of Grossolano did not stem from the duke or his staff, but instead came from within Palazzo Coltello. There was no way of proving the contessa was complicit in the murder of her rival, not without a witness or a confession. Neither of those seemed likely to emerge. She was far too formidable and ruthless a woman to leave any loose threads dangling from the fabric of her stratagemma.

For a moment during their meeting, Aldo had believed the contessa might be about to name one of her servants as Grossolano's killer, a pawn sacrificed to preserve the queen. But she anticipated his attack and offered another, pre-prepared suspect: Zilio. It was quite brilliant, Aldo had to admit. Not all that the contessa had said about the Council of Ten's representative was true, but there had been enough in her words to present Zilio as an ideal target for the investigation. She provided a motive for him wanting to kill Grossolano. The fact Zilio had almost certainly left Florence only enhanced his value as a suspect. The Otto could and would convict Zilio in his absence, effectively banishing him from the city.

That also explained why the contessa had named Zilio. Having eliminated her replacement – Aldo did not doubt for a moment she was responsible, though it was the hands of another that had pulled the garrotte taut around Grossolano's neck – the contessa had now struck a blow against the man who tried to replace her. Zilio could never return to Florence, not if a warrant for his arrest and imprisonment remained outstanding. In two simple moves she had both secured her position and ensured that it would continue.

The contessa had played well, and she had won.

Aldo was grateful not to be her enemy.

The end of the day was approaching as Strocchi returned to the Podestà. Stallholders were closing for business, and workers stumbled home after their day's labour. He still had much to do before curfew, including making his report to the segretario. Facing Bindi's anger after a third murder in as many days was not a welcome prospect. But the figure pacing in front of the Podestà pushed that worry to one side.

'Signora Vanni,' Strocchi said to the woman. Grossolano's corpse had consumed most of the afternoon, so much so that Strocchi had forgotten the tannery worker was coming to make her denunzia.

'Why have you kept me out here?' she demanded, confronting him as he neared the guards by the main entrance. Despite the cool autumn air there were large sweat stains visible under her arms, body odour and the stench of the tannery surrounding Strocchi as she loomed over him. 'These men would not let me inside till you arrived. I have lost hours of work waiting for you.'

Strocchi resisted saying that Vanni had chosen to search Oltrarno for him and had willingly agreed to come to the Podestà. Before asking any questions about the murders of Zamora and Freccia, it was important to win back her favour first. Meeting accusations with more accusations would only make her angrier. 'Forgive me, signora, but an urgent matter arose north of San Marco that required my presence.'

He ushered her into the Podestà, adding further apologies in a low, reassuring voice as they went through the stone tunnel to the large, open courtyard. Vanni looked around, eyes wide as she took in the high internal walls, open shutters on the upper levels overlooking the courtyard, and sentries guarding doors on three sides of the courtyard. 'This is what the Otto looks like?' she asked, a shiver in her voice. The anger she had carried was lost amid the forbidding interior of the Podestà.

Strocchi nodded. He had become used to this cold, unwelcoming place. To see her response reminded him of the power the court held over ordinary Florentines. 'Yes, signora. May I ask you to wait here? I need the help of an administrator to note down your denunzia. My writing is not good enough for such an important task. You may sit over here.' He escorted her to a stone bench at the courtyard's edge.

Once Vanni was settled, Strocchi hurried up the wide staircase that led to the administrative level. Unfortunately, the door to Bindi's ufficio was open as Strocchi passed by, a clerk emerging ashen-faced. The segretario bellowed from within. 'Is that Strocchi waiting outside? Tell him to come in. Now!'

Having no choice, Strocchi went to the doorway but remained there. 'Forgive me, segretario, but I am not yet ready to offer my report.'

'Why not?'

There was no point lying; Bindi probably knew Vanni had been seeking admittance to the Podestà. If she had been enough of a nuisance, the guards would have sent someone inside to see whether Vanni could be admitted, and that would have reached Bindi. 'I am about to question a suspect for the murders of Signor Niccolò Zamora and the thief Freccia.' Strocchi described the victims that way to soothe the segretario. To Bindi, a merchant from one of the guilds was worthy of respect; common workers and those found guilty of crimes deserved no such honour when being mentioned. 'Once that is complete, I shall—'

'There has been a third killing,' Bindi scowled, 'or did the messengers I sent fail to find you?'

'A messenger did come to me,' Strocchi said, 'and I have been investigating that as well. I can tell you more once I have questioned my suspect?' He phrased that as a question to make Bindi believe it was his choice. The segretario pondered a moment before dismissing Strocchi with the wave of a flabby hand.

'Very well. But be swift. I've no wish to be here until curfew waiting for your report.'

'Yes, segretario. Of course.' Strocchi closed the ufficio door before going in search of someone to assist with Vanni's denunzia. He had not lied about the quality of his own writing, despite efforts to improve such skills. But having it put to paper by another's hand served a further purpose: delay. Strocchi wanted Aldo present for the questioning of Vanni once her denunzia was finished. Aldo had far more experience interrogating suspects. Despite his demotion, he would be a useful asset in the room. But first Aldo had to return to the Podestà, and there was no sign of him yet.

After visiting Porta San Gallo, Aldo strode south to Palazzo Medici. The duke would already know about the latest murder, thanks to his spies and informants within the city, but the victim's name might not have reached Cosimo yet. Considering the significance of Grossolano's killing, it was important that Aldo shared what he had uncovered with the duke. Campana agreed, taking him directly to see Cosimo in his private ufficio.

'Tito Grossolano is dead,' Aldo announced. 'He was garrotted, his body posed to look like Christ on the cross, and ash was smeared on his forehead.'

'This killer the Otto is hunting has struck again?' the duke asked.

'I do not believe so.' Aldo explained the suspicions he and Strocchi shared, how the murder was made to appear like the same killer's work. 'Grossolano was in the city only a day before being attacked. He had no meetings with the suspects we are investigating for the other murders and was known to none in Florence except the Contessa Valentine Coltello.'

Campana shared a glance with the duke. 'You think she had Grossolano killed?'

'After talking to her, I believe so – not that she admitted it, of course.'

'I'm surprised you didn't come to ask if one of my men was responsible,' Cosimo said. 'Florence's recent relationship with Venice has been . . . strained. The new Inquisitorie di Stato may be responsible for the death of one of my men there.'

'I did consider that possibility,' Aldo said. 'But I suspected the contessa was more likely to be responsible for this killing. I questioned her about it, and am now certain she was behind the death of Grossolano. Her maggiordomo Pozzo probably commissioned the murder, but that is supposition. Whoever garrotted Grossolano has almost certainly left Florence with a handsome pouch of coin, most likely with orders never to return.'

Cosimo rose from his chair to stroll around the ufficio. Aldo had noted before that the duke tended to pace while considering how to respond to unexpected events. 'You suspect the contessa had her replacement killed to preserve her position as spymaster in Florence?'

'Yes, Your Grace,' Aldo replied.

'Won't Venice simply appoint a new replacement?'

'They could, but the contessa has offered another Venetian as a potential suspect to ensure she cannot be easily usurped again: Signor Gonzalo Zilio.'

'He works for the Council of Ten,' Campana told the duke.

'I know who Zilio is,' Cosimo snapped. 'Unlike my predecessor, I read every briefing document. A man who does not grasp such details does not deserve to lead this city.'

'Forgive me, Your Grace—'

The duke silenced Campana with a glare before facing Aldo. 'The contessa suggested it was Zilio who murdered her replacement?'

'Or had him murdered, yes.' Aldo let a small smile cross his face. 'I've just come from the northern gate. Guards there confirmed Zilio left the city earlier today. He appeared anxious and in haste to return to Venice.'

'Then Zilio did kill Grossolano?' Campana asked.

'No, it was the contessa,' Cosimo said. 'She said or did something that drove Zilio from the city, knowing it would make him a clearer suspect for the murder.'

The ufficio fell silent but for the duke's pacing.

'Your Grace, may I make a suggestion?' Aldo asked. A gesture told him to continue. 'Order the Otto to convict Zilio for this murder and issue a warrant for his arrest, should he ever return to Florence. That will prevent him coming back into the city or easily meddling here. It should also ensure the contessa remains as Venice's spymaster in Florence, proving my value to her. This will encourage the contessa to believe she has the measure of you.'

'Better the diavolo you know,' Cosimo said.

Aldo nodded. 'If I might have the order in writing, it would make matters easier with my segretario.' Even the obstinate Bindi could not refuse such an edict.

Having secured a clerk with ink and paper, Strocchi found an empty room near the Podestà entrance where Vanni could make her denunzia. It was a simple chamber with a wooden table and chairs, but two lanterns added a honeyed light that warmed the cold stone walls. He wanted Vanni comfortable and confident, believing she was being listened to, her words given importance. She had been ignored until now, this was her chance to speak. That should help lower her guard.

Vanni was hesitant as Strocchi brought her into the room, so he kept the door ajar as a reassurance. She could leave whenever she wished, he told her. It also meant Strocchi could watch for Aldo returning to the Podestà. The tannery worker's fears seemed to recede as she retold the story of her brother and the exorcist Negri. Having heard it a few hours earlier, Strocchi listened for any changes, but the words were the same as before. Mostly he watched Vanni, the way she spoke, how the anger in her face matched the clenching and unclenching of those powerful hands.

She had the strength to garrotte a man, and the rage. There were angry red lines and scars across her palms. Some were probably from working in the tannery, but others could be proof she was responsible for the murders of both Zamora and Freccia. Her anger towards Negri was absolute. But if Vanni wished to see him dead, why not attack the exorcist directly? Why murder Zamora and Freccia instead? Those were questions that must be resolved before Vanni could either be arrested for the killings or dismissed as a suspect. Strocchi glanced through the gap in the doorway. Several guards and constables had been by, Manuffi among them, but not Aldo. And Vanni was reaching the end of her story.

When the denunzia was completed, the clerk gave it to Vanni to read. Strocchi peered through the gap again, but there was still no sign of Aldo. Vanni made her mark at the bottom of the page to affirm that it was her sworn testimony. Strocchi asked her to stay behind while he ushered the clerk from the room. 'There are a few other questions you might be able to help me answer,' Strocchi said, smiling at her. 'You have been so patient with all of this. I hoped you might indulge me a while longer . . . ?'

'Of course,' Vanni replied. Her relief at having given evidence against Negri was evident. She sat back in the chair, a smile across her face.

'Grazie.' Strocchi bowed his head to her, a mark of respect. The longer he could keep her trust, the more honest her answers would be.

Outside the room Strocchi thanked the clerk for his help, all the while preparing fresh questions to ask Vanni. As the clerk returned to the administrative level, Strocchi offered up a silent prayer for help. No sooner had the words left him than Aldo strolled into the Podestà clutching a coil of paper secured with the ducal seal. 'What's that?' Strocchi asked.

'Something to show Bindi that you are doing a good job.' Aldo gave a brisk summary of his findings about the murder of Grossolano before tucking the document inside his tunic. He gestured through the doorway to Vanni. 'Has she made her denunzia?'

'Yes. But I need your help questioning her about the murders.'

'You can do this without me, Carlo.'

Strocchi acknowledged the praise. 'Nonetheless, you have more experience in such matters. And I would value your judgement on how she responds.'

'Very well. Let me go in first.'

Strocchi followed Aldo into the room. Aldo introduced himself as Strocchi closed the door, reminding Vanni that they had met at the tannery. She thanked Aldo for the way he'd told Fiora of Freccia's death.

'How is she?' Aldo asked. 'I understand Fiora is staying with you now.'

'Yes, for a few days,' Vanni replied. 'She cries a lot. Fiora loved Freccia, despite everything, and she is carrying his child. Raising a baby alone will not be easy for her.'

'Why despite everything?' Strocchi asked, taking the chair opposite her.

Vanni grimaced. 'I should not speak ill of the dead . . . but he was a thief, and a cruel one at that. People often said Freccia would steal the crutch from a cripple if he thought it worth selling. And then there was what he did before that . . .' she leaned forward to whisper across the table – 'he was a buggerone. No, worse than that, he let other men pay to use him, to make him the woman, if you know what I mean.'

Strocchi glanced at Aldo, but he showed no disapproval for her words. 'I've dealt with his kind before,' Aldo said. 'In fact, I arrested Freccia for that crime several times.'

'You should have locked him in Le Stinche and left him to rot,' Vanni sneered. 'Men like Freccia disgust me. They are an insult to everyone. I've never understood why Fiora stayed with him. A good woman deserves better than that bastardo.'

'Why did you consider him a bastardo?' Strocchi asked. 'Was there another reason?'

Vanni stuck her chin down into her chest, mumbling and muttering.

'Sorry, but I can't hear what you're saying.'

'He laughed at me!' She banged a heavy fist on the table. 'Freccia laughed at me. A few days ago, I told him what had happened to my brother. How Negri vowed an exorcism would be a cure but all it gave Cecco was false hope, and that soon killed him. Freccia said Cecco was lucky to have lived as long as he did, even suggested his death was God being merciful. As if taking my only famiglia was some kind of mercy!' Vanni's vehemence made spittle fly from her mouth. 'That's why I call Freccia a bastardo – because he was!'

Chapter Twenty-two

Strocchi exchanged a glance with Aldo while Vanni seethed. Her motivation to kill Freccia was clear: he had mocked her brother and how Cecco had died. That enraged Vanni, and the wound was still raw inside her, the anger close to her thoughts.

'Forgive us for asking, signora,' Aldo said. 'We did not realize . . .'

She shook her head. 'It does not matter.'

'My colleague told me of your conversation earlier today,' Aldo continued, 'how you believe that another man betrayed you. This must have been troubling.'

'It was,' Vanni agreed. 'Signor Zamora seemed to be an ally against Negri, but when I said we should act to stop the exorcist hurting anyone else—' She shook her head. 'Zamora was a weak man. He lacked the strength to do what must be done. He left me no choice.'

'No choice?' Strocchi asked.

'None.'

It was not a confession, Strocchi knew. But Vanni seemed close to admitting her guilt for at least one murder, if not both. 'And what did you do about that?'

She frowned at him. 'Does it matter? I have made my denunzia. May I go?'

Aldo came closer, moving to stand beside Strocchi. 'We have two more things to ask you, signora. Two more ways you can be helpful to us, if you don't mind?'

Vanni hesitated, as if she was about to leave. But eventually she nodded. 'Make your questions swift. Fiora will be waiting at my home by now.'

'Of course, of course,' Aldo replied, his voice full of reassurance. 'Carlo?'

Strocchi cleared his throat. 'Signora Vanni, before Fiora came to stay with you, were you living alone?'

'Yes,' she said. 'My husband Guido was taken by plague years ago, may he rest in peace. I've been alone since Cecco died.'

'And you were at home alone during curfew three nights ago?' The question seemed to bemuse her. 'Of course.'

'Yesterday morning, you were late arriving at the tannery.' 'Yes.'

'May I ask why?' Strocchi persisted.

'Does it matter?'

'Yes,' Aldo replied.

She hesitated, looking away to one side. 'I can't remember.'

'Why not? It was only yesterday.'

'I said I don't remember.'

'Yes, but—'

'Enough!' Vanni rose from the chair, her haste almost knocking it over. 'Enough questions, enough talking. You have my denunzia. Now do something about Father Negri. That priest should not be allowed to exorcize anyone, especially not those like my Cecco. Nothing else matters.' She pulled the door open and stalked from the room.

Aldo waited until Vanni's stamping feet could no longer be heard before closing the door. 'For a moment I thought she was about to confess.'

'I know,' Strocchi agreed. 'Her anger towards Freccia was— What do you think she meant about Zamora leaving her no choice?'

'A good question. If Vanni repeated that in front of the magistrates, they could well conclude she was explaining her motive to murder. But it isn't enough to arrest her. Not yet.'

'Bindi will say we should have made her confess.'

Aldo nodded. It was within the power of the court to torture a suspect or a witness to extract answers. That was why the Otto was the most feared criminal court in Florence. Those summoned to the Podestà knew they could be kept there for hours, made to suffer until they talked. But in Aldo's experience the use of torture served only one purpose: to make a suspect confess, whether they were guilty or not. Hurt someone long enough and they would say anything to stop the pain. That might satisfy the segretario and the law, but it wasn't justice. Far from it. 'You can't let what Bindi might say lead your investigation, Carlo. Have faith in your own judgement.'

'Easy for you to suggest, but I'm the one who has to report to him now.' Strocchi rose from his chair, shoulders slumped. 'We've made no progress, he'll say – and he's right.'

'I disagree. We have narrowed our gaze to two leading suspects, Vanni and Negri. Tomorrow we will prove which of them killed Zamora and Freccia.'

'How? We're not even allowed to talk to Negri, let alone interrogate him.'

Aldo smiled. 'There is always a way around such obstacles. Trust me.' Strocchi's sour expression showed what he thought of that. Aldo opened the door. 'Besides, I'm coming with you to see the segretario. We have someone the court can convict for Grossolano's murder.' Aldo pulled the sealed document from inside his tunic. 'Let's not keep Bindi waiting. You know how

impatient the segretario gets.' Aldo accompanied Strocchi up
the wide stone steps to the administrative level of the Podestà,
before knocking at the door to Bindi's ufficio.

'Who is it?'

Strocchi answered for them both. The segretario used his
habitual strategia of making them wait outside before eventually
calling for both to enter. Aldo followed Strocchi in.

'Well?' Bindi demanded once they stood before him.

Strocchi gave a brisk summary of their findings from that
morning. As he moved on to the investigation into Grossolano's
murder, Bindi held up a flabby hand. 'Stop. Stop.'

'Segretario?'

'If I understand correctly, you have spent three days on this
matter and achieved nothing more than sending three corpses to
the nuns of Santa Maria Nuova, yes?'

Strocchi was struggling to find a suitable reply, so Aldo inter-
vened first. No good would come of rising to the segretario's lure.
Agreeing was an admission of failure, while contradicting him
would be taken as insolence or deemed an insult to Bindi's stature.
'Events have moved on quite some distance in the past few hours,'
Aldo replied.

'I prefer talking to an officer,' Bindi said, 'not wasting my time
with a constable.'

'Naturally,' Aldo agreed. 'But there are certain matters involving
Duke Cosimo and his interest in this investigation of which you
may be unaware.'

The segretario stiffened. 'The duke?'

'Indeed.' If Bindi wanted to hear more, he would have to ask
for it. Aldo arranged his face into a benign smile, knowing how
that infuriated the segretario. Bindi resisted as long as he could
before eventually blurting out a question.

'Well? What does His Grace have to do with these cases?'

'The duke engaged my assistance with a private investigation on his behalf. Alas, I have been forbidden from sharing the details with you, as it is a matter of considerable urgency and importance to the city and His Grace. But I have brought this letter from the duke.' Aldo placed the document on the table in front of Bindi. 'That will explain, at least in part, what has been occupying Strocchi and myself.'

The segretario squinted at six palle pressed into the wax seal, the mark of the city's Medici ruler. 'Will it excuse your lack of progress?' he sneered.

'To know that, you must read the letter,' Aldo replied.

Bindi snatched at the document, breaking its seal with a pudgy finger. He unrolled the letter as if expecting a poisonous creature to emerge from within. The segretario's eyes slid across the words that Aldo had watched Cosimo write. A grimace settled on Bindi's face. 'This states that I must read the remainder of the letter out loud to both of you.'

'Does it?' Aldo said. He arched an eyebrow at Strocchi. 'How unexpected.' It was nothing of the sort, of course. Aldo had asked the duke to write that at the top of the page.

Bindi cleared his throat. 'The magistrates of the Otto are hereby directed to convict Gonzalo Zilio of Venice for the unlawful killing of Signor Tito Grossolano, a gentleman lately of Bologna, who arrived in Florence yesterday. It is understood that the murderer Zilio has already fled the city via Porta San Gallo, most likely returning to Venice. Therefore, a warrant is to be issued by the court for the capture and arrest of Zilio should he ever dare return to Florence. Once these directives have been complied with, the Otto shall consider all matters involving the murder of Signor Grossolano to be concluded.'

The segretario looked up from the page to peer at Aldo, who beamed back at Bindi. 'Is that all? Or did the duke perhaps place a postscript of some manner at the end of his esteemed correspondence?'

Bindi's face curdled even more before he continued reading. 'Lastly, the segretario of the Otto is to offer his congratulations to officer Carlo Strocchi and constable Cesare Aldo for the swift way they have successfully brought this case to a close. Bearing that in mind, both men are to be granted further time to complete their investigations into the other two murders currently before the court. All of this is a direct order by His Grace, Cosimo de' Medici, Duke of Florence, and its dominion.'

Aldo smiled at Strocchi. 'Did you hear that, Carlo? The duke himself has said we should be granted whatever time we require.' Strocchi appeared amazed, his mouth moving but no sound coming out of it. 'I couldn't have put it better myself.'

Bindi folded the letter in half again and again until it was a tiny square of paper clenched between his fingers. 'Well,' he said through gritted teeth. 'Congratulations.'

'Grazie,' Aldo replied, patting Strocchi on the shoulder.

'G-grazie,' the young officer agreed. 'Grazie mille.'

'You shall have more time to conclude this investigation,' Bindi added.

'That's very kind of you,' Aldo said, 'but we expect to conclude it by All Souls' Day at the latest – perhaps sooner. Don't you agree, Carlo?'

'All Souls' Day? But that's Sunday.' Strocchi twisted his head to stare at Aldo. 'The day after next. Are you sure?'

'Yes. Quite sure.'

'In that case,' Bindi said, his habitual smirk of superiority restored, 'I hereby grant two additional days to conclude this investigation.' He settled back in his chair, gesturing towards the ufficio door. 'You may both leave.'

Strocchi stumbled away from the segretario, Aldo following. Inevitably Bindi called to them as Strocchi reached for the door. 'One last thing. If you should fail to resolve these two murders by Sunday, there will be consequences. For both of you.'

Strocchi waited until he and Aldo were in the Podestà courtyard before demanding answers. 'Why did you say we would finish our investigation in the next two days?'

Aldo seemed utterly unconcerned. 'It was necessary.'

'Necessary? The duke had won us – had won me – a reprieve from Bindi's impossible demands. The segretario gives us more time, but you decide we only need two days to find the killer!' Strocchi shook his head, still struggling to grasp what had happened.

'Carlo, it's going to be fine.'

'How? How is it going to be fine, tell me that.'

'Bindi needs to believe the Podestà is his domain. That he is in control of everything which happens within these walls. He could not have tolerated the duke's order for long. Even if he did, Bindi would have begrudged us our freedom and found another way to punish both of us. I've already been demoted, so there's not much more he can do to me.'

'I thought you wanted to be an officer again?'

'I do. I want Bindi to have no choice but to offer me my old position back. You are in far more danger from his moods than me. You're an officer of the court with a wife, a bambina and another on the way. This makes Bindi believe he has control of us. It matters.'

Strocchi could grasp the sense of what Aldo was saying, but still . . . 'You could have talked to me about this first,' he grumbled.

'I'm sorry about that. But I needed your response to be truthful for the segretario. I wanted him to believe I was tripping over my own arrogance.'

To Strocchi that seemed an accurate description of what Aldo had just done. 'Why two days? How do we find the killer by Sunday?'

'We won't need to, they'll find us. I'm certain of it.'

Aldo was making no sense, that much seemed certain. 'How?'

'Until now they have been leading us from one corpse to the next, as if we have been dancing to their commands. We are going to change that, make them dance for us instead.'

'You have a plan,' Strocchi realized. 'That means you know who the killer is.'

'I believe it's either Signora Vanni or Father Negri. Tomorrow, we find out which.'

'But Negri refuses to answer our questions, and the segretario will never seek permission from the diocese to compel the exorcist into talking.'

'Have a little faith,' Aldo replied, smiling at him. 'Negri will talk to us. I've never been more certain of something in my life.'

Chapter Twenty-three

Saturday, November 1st 1539

Aldo hammered at the rear door of San Felice as bells across Oltrarno announced the end of curfew. Low clouds over the city gave the chimes an ominous, hollow tone. It had rained during the night leaving puddles on the streets, while a heavy dew had made the short journey from Saul's home slippery underfoot. Aldo beat a fist at the door again.

He knew Negri lived in two small rooms at the rear of the church, whereas Zati shared a residence for priests north of the Arno. But there was no reply at San Felice, despite the light of a lantern showing through shutters near the back door. Negri must be the soundest of sleepers not to hear the hammering. That suggested he was ignoring Aldo or was elsewhere in the city. Priests could claim an exemption from curfew in exceptional circumstances, such as a visit to a dying parishioner who needed the last rites. But from all that Aldo had learned, Negri did not worry much about his parishioners. The exorcist cared about performing his sacrament and little else. Defending it was all that mattered to Father Camillo Negri, and it seemed he would stop at nothing to do so.

Satisfied there would be no answer, Aldo left San Felice to stride north towards Ponte Vecchio. He made quick time as the road to the bridge remained empty this early. Soon stallholders would arrive to open for the day, followed by those eager to find a bargain. For now, Aldo was able to climb the steep curve unhindered, even if his boots did slip on its stones.

He had been confident the previous evening of proving who'd killed Zamora and Freccia. In the cold chill of morning that seemed foolhardy, born of arrogance rather than facts. He had enjoyed tormenting Bindi with the duke's letter too much, and the moment had gone to his head. The seeds of a plan for persuading Negri to talk were growing, but that would have to wait until later. At least he had been honest with Strocchi.

So far, their investigation had been responding to the killer, rather than seizing control of events. That was understandable with a new body each day, forcing them to find a name for the victim before seeking reasons for the murder. Aldo slowed his pace as he entered Piazza della Signoria, the square where he and Benedetto had stumbled on the first corpse. Zamora was found early on Wednesday, as curfew was close to an end, and Freccia was found on Thursday morning. Yet the killer had not claimed another victim on Friday – why? Had something or someone prevented them?

For now the answers to those questions would have to wait.

After crossing the piazza, Aldo turned north, the brooding silhouette of the Podestà looming ahead. He could see Strocchi outside its entrance, talking with Manuffi and someone unfamiliar – a messenger, perhaps? Whatever was being said seemed to weigh heavy on Strocchi. That could mean only one thing: there had been another murder.

Aldo quickened his stride as the other person hurried away. 'Carlo, what is it?'

'Another attack,' Strocchi replied. 'A priest this time.'

'Who?'

'Father Visconti, at the Church of Santa Maria Magdalena.'

* * *

Strocchi had risen before the bells chimed for the end of curfew, hoping to make a brisk start – and to avoid more teasing from three generations of women. Tomasia and Mama had become fast friends in his absence, learning to appreciate each other. The previous night, he had arrived home to the two of them sharing embarrassing stories about him. Tomasia was whispering things to Mama that made her roar with laughter, while Mama kept pinching his cheeks and telling tales of his childhood in Ponte a Signa. Bianca did not understand most of what was being said but still joined in, pointing at him and giggling. It had been a long night.

He loved his mama, but the sooner she went home, the better.

A young man of no more than fifteen had been waiting outside the Podestà with Manuffi when Strocchi arrived. The messenger brought news of an attack on a priest at Santa Maria Magdalena, but few other details. A parishioner had sent the youth, that was all he knew. Strocchi was still questioning the messenger when Aldo arrived. After hearing what had happened, Aldo suggested Manuffi remain at the Podestà to notify Bindi. While Strocchi was paying the messenger, Aldo took Manuffi aside and whispered something in his ear. Strocchi asked what Aldo had said as the two of them strode north.

'It's not important,' Aldo replied. 'We have more significant questions to answer. Zamora and Freccia lived south of the Arno. We know they had both clashed with Negri, and that Vanni bore a grudge against each man. What connects Visconti to them?'

'We don't know this is the same killer,' Strocchi insisted as they passed the cathedral, low cloud shrouding the top of the Duomo. 'Not yet. The attack on Visconti could be linked to the murder of Grossolano. His body was left across the road from Visconti's church.'

'Have you met him? Father Visconti?'

'He came to the alley yesterday to give Grossolano the last rites while I was there.' Strocchi's pace slowed, a new fear settling inside him. 'Do you think that's why Visconti was attacked? The killer was watching, and saw him tending to the victim?'

'I doubt it. We know Grossolano was killed by someone acting on behalf of the Contessa Coltello. She has no reason to send her men against an ordinary parish priest. It may be the attack on Visconti so close to where that corpse was found is happenstance.'

'I thought you didn't believe in such things?'

'No, but that doesn't stop it being true. Sometimes.'

Strocchi increased his stride again, wanting to believe Aldo was correct. 'Perhaps this has nothing to do with the killings of Zamora and Freccia. It might simply be a thief trying to rob the church and the priest interrupted him.'

'Perhaps,' Aldo said, but he didn't sound convinced.

A handful of gossiping citizens were clustered outside the main entrance to Santa Maria Magdalena. Strocchi ignored them and went into the church, Aldo close behind. The lingering aroma of incense mixed with another scent that reminded Strocchi of warm copper. Visconti was sprawled face-up on the stone floor, a folded blanket stained with blood beneath his head. A sour-faced woman in shapeless clothes and a widow's headscarf knelt by the priest, holding his right hand.

'That's Signora Gonzaga,' Aldo whispered. 'I met her a few years ago, she lives close by. Gonzaga may be the parishioner who sent the messenger.'

A man of perhaps twenty was pacing back and forth near the church altar, wringing his hands. He had dark hair, and there was something familiar about his face, but Strocchi did not recall meeting him. 'What about the nervous one by the altar?'

Aldo shook his head. 'Never seen him before.'

Strocchi approached Gonzaga and the priest. Visconti's eyes were closed. He had an angry red line round his neck, but his chest was still rising and falling. Whoever attacked him must have been interrupted, unable to finish their work. Yet they had taken time to write a word on his forehead with ashes: '*Filii*', the Latin for 'of the Son'. In this respect the attack on Visconti looked as if it had been by the same hand that had killed Zamora and Freccia.

Aldo greeted Gonzaga, introducing himself and Strocchi.

'I remember you.' She scowled. 'You came into my home, asking questions about the nuns that used to have a convent behind this church.'

As ever, Aldo had made a lasting impression. Strocchi crouched on one knee by the priest, positioning himself opposite Gonzaga. 'Do you know what happened here?'

She shook her head. 'I didn't see who hurt poor Father Visconti. I came in early to clean the church for All Saints' Day, and he was already here on the floor.' She pointed at the pacing man. 'Talk to him, he was the one who drove off the attacker.'

'How is Visconti?' Aldo asked.

'Alive, but not much more.' Gonzaga pointed to the blood on the blanket beneath his head. 'Someone hit him, and he hasn't spoken since. He is fortunate the Lord did not take him.' She made the sign of the cross, her dry lips whispering a prayer.

'Grazie, signora,' Strocchi said. He leaned closer to Visconti. 'We will find whoever did this,' he murmured. 'I promise.' After studying the angry red marks around the priest's neck, Strocchi got back to his feet. He and Aldo approached the man pacing by the altar. As they got closer, Strocchi could see the man was younger than he appeared at a distance, a few wisps of hair on his chin and above his mouth. He wore a simple tunic and hose, the clothes of a worker. His skin had been darkened by the sun, evidence of spending most days outside. Yet the face, there was something familiar about that face . . .

Strocchi introduced himself and Aldo. 'Can you tell us your name?'

'Yes, it's—' The man hesitated. 'My name is Marsilio Juvara.'

Santo Spirito! That was why this stranger seemed so familiar. He was Signora Tullia's son, the nephew of Niccolò Zamora. This was the youth believed to have taken his own life after being exorcized by Father Negri. Yet it appeared Marsilio was very much alive. Strocchi exchanged a glance with Aldo. He seemed to have made the same connection. But questions about where Marsilio had been for the past year must wait.

'What happened here?'

'I came seeking counsel from Father Visconti,' Marsilio replied. 'I'd been told he does not judge as harshly as other priests. I entered the church not long after curfew ended, hoping to talk with him before any parishioners arrived for All Saints' Day. That's when I saw . . .' He fell silent; Marsilio's gaze fixed on the sprawled priest.

'What was it?' Aldo asked, his voice a gentle murmur.

'Someone was strangling Father Visconti. Their back was to me, but I could see they had a thick cord in their hands, strung with heavy beads. Like a rosary, but bigger, sturdier. They had it pulled taut round Father Visconti's neck, from behind.' Marsilio clenched his hands together. 'They can't have heard me come in, otherwise . . . I shouted at them to stop. They cursed and ran – that way.' He pointed to a side door beyond the altar. 'I didn't know what to do, so I stayed to look after Father Visconti. He had blood on the back on his head, and something written above his eyes in ash.'

'*Filii*,' Strocchi said.

The young man nodded.

'Can I see the palms of your hands?' Aldo asked.

'Of course.' Marsilio opened his fists. The palms had no marks, no sign of having used a garrotte in recent days. 'Wait, you can't think that I—'

'No,' Strocchi cut in. 'Your hands show you didn't do this.'

'Did Visconti say anything?' Aldo gestured towards the priest. 'After his attacker left, or while you were tending to him?'

'No, not a word.'

Aldo took Strocchi to one side. 'It sounds as if the attacker hit Visconti first to silence him, make it easier to garrotte him.'

'They didn't want Visconti defending himself as Freccia did,' Strocchi agreed.

Marsilio stared at them, his face aghast. 'How can you talk like that? A priest is attacked, left for dead – he would probably be dead if I hadn't come in! Yet you speak about what happened to him as if . . . as if it was nothing.'

'This is our job,' Aldo replied. 'We cannot weep for all those who suffer at the hands of violent thieves or those with murder in their minds. If we did, our tears would never stop.'

Marsilio stepped back as if slapped. Strocchi held up his hands in apology. 'My colleague is simply eager to find whoever did this. Can you describe them for us?'

'Tall, strong.' Marsilio shrugged. 'They wore a cloak, and its hood hid their face.'

'A man or a woman?' Aldo asked.

'A man, I think. But I can't be sure.'

'Anything else?' Aldo said, impatience in his voice.

'I'm sorry, it all happened so fast.'

'Yes, we know that.'

Strocchi glared at his colleague. Marsilio was doing his best, snapping at him was not going to make this any easier. 'Aldo, why don't you go and see how Father Visconti is?'

Aldo stalked away, muttering to himself. Once he was gone, Strocchi guided Marsilio to a wooden bench at the side of the church. 'Please forgive him. He's frustrated.'

Marsilio wasn't listening, instead rubbing a hand to his neck. 'What if the person who attacked Father Visconti had not fled? What if they had come for me next?'

'May I ask you a question,' Strocchi said, 'one that probably has little to do with what happened here?' Marsilio nodded. 'Your name is Juvara?'

'Yes.'

'Does your famiglia live at Palazzo Zamora?'

Another nod.

'Were you outside the palazzo yesterday in Piazza Santo Spirito?'

'I was,' Marsilio replied. 'I wanted to go in, to be with my famiglia. But they believe I'm dead, and the shock of my return . . . I feared it would be too much for them. So I left.'

Strocchi recounted what Querini had shared about Marsilio's exorcism, how the young man had taken his own life by fire in the Tuscan countryside. 'Querini only recognized your body from what was left of your clothes, and a ring you had inherited.'

'They were my clothes, and it was my father's ring,' Marsilio said. 'I gave them to a friend. We left the city after my exorcism. Father Negri had convinced me he could change me, make me want to marry and have a famiglia. But I was too much like my uncle Niccolò.'

'I understand,' Strocchi said.

'I could not stay here in Florence, so my friend and I left together. Both of us were exorcized by Negri. I was fortunate, it did not harm me. But my friend . . . Giorgio was never the same afterwards, it broke something inside him. I took him to the villa my famiglia owns up in the hills near Friesole, hoping he would recover. Nobody stays there in autumn, so I knew it would be empty. But what Negri did still tormented Giorgio. He could not forget what the exorcist had said, his accusations . . .' Marsilio's voice faltered.

'You don't have to tell me any more.'

'No, I must.' Marsilio wiped his nose. 'One night, when I was away from the villa, Giorgio took oil and kindling and a flint and he—'

'Set fire to himself.'

'Yes.' Marsilio slumped back against the church wall. 'In a way, Giorgio set me free by doing that. I realized my famiglia would think his body was mine. I could make a new life for myself, be the person I wanted to be. Not what the Church or Negri said I should be.'

Strocchi nodded. It must have been tempting; a new start, a new life free from the troubles of his past. 'When did you come back to Florence?'

'Yesterday, after I heard of my uncle's murder. I've stayed in touch with another friend here in the city. She sent news about what happened. I had to come back. But when I did, I was too afraid to go into the palazzo. Mama believes I'm dead, as do my siblings. How can I tell them that was all a lie? I needed counsel, so I came here . . .' he stared at Aldo and Gonzaga as they tended the priest – 'and this is what happens.'

'You saved his life. Father Visconti would be dead if not for you. Take comfort in that,' Strocchi said. Aldo was beckoning to him. 'I've one final question. Tell me, who suggested you come to Santa Maria Magdalena for counsel?'

'Father Zati. I approached him yesterday, away from San Felice, after I returned to the city. Gathering the courage to speak with him was not easy.'

'Father Zati? But isn't he . . . ?'

'Yes, he was there when Negri exorcized me. But Father Zati was the only priest to ever show me compassion. He tried to stop the sacrament, told Negri I wasn't possessed. But Negri wouldn't listen.' Marsilio's face crumpled.

'Tell me, if you trust Zati so much, why not ask him for counsel?'

'I did. He was startled when I introduced myself. Once he got over the shock of seeing me, Father Zati suggested I come here and seek advice from Father Visconti. Zati said Visconti was a better man, more courageous. He even called him Papa, such was the affection they shared.'

'Grazie for being so honest,' Strocchi said, rising from the bench. 'If it was me, I would go home. Go to the palazzo, be with your famiglia. Your mama is grieving for the brother she has lost. Your return could help heal her broken heart.' Leaving Marsilio to ponder that suggestion, Strocchi joined Aldo in the centre of the church.

Visconti was regaining his senses, eyes fluttering open.

But would the priest be able to name his attacker?

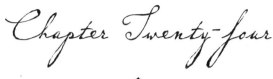

Chapter Twenty-four

Aldo crouched by Visconti, putting a knee down on the cold stone floor. 'Father, can you hear me?' The priest nodded, wincing in pain. 'It's probably best you don't move. You were attacked, hit on the back of the head.' Visconti lifted a hand to his neck, pressing fingers to the angry red line. 'Yes, someone tried to garrotte you. But they were interrupted and fled.'

'W-who?' the priest whispered in a hoarse voice.

'We were hoping you could tell us,' Strocchi said.

'Didn't see . . . their face . . .'

'Did you hear them come in?' Aldo asked.

'Y-yes . . .'

'Did they speak?'

'N-no.'

'Did you notice anything familiar about them? Or something distinctive?'

Visconti's brow furrowed. 'A smell . . .'

'What kind of smell?'

'I . . . I can't remember . . .' His eyes were closing.

Aldo gave Visconti's left hand a squeeze. 'Father, can you recall anything else?' But the priest was gone again, senses giving way to his injuries.

'Is he . . . ?' Gonzaga asked.

Aldo leaned over Visconti, listening. 'Still breathing.' He had seen men at arms suffer similar injuries. Their senses drifted back and forth. Most recovered in time, but others were lost if not allowed to rest. 'He will need constant attention for the next day or two but moving him all the way to an *ospedale* would not be wise.'

'They could care for him in the monastery,' the widow suggested. 'When the convent closed, the diocese gifted the building to a Franciscan order. The monks have an infirmary.'

Aldo glanced up at Strocchi. 'Carlo, can you go and ask the monks for help? They are more likely to agree if the request comes from an officer of the Otto.'

While Strocchi was seeking assistance, Aldo went outside the church to question the parishioners still waiting by the doors. None admitted being present when Visconti was attacked, nor had any of them seen a person fleeing Santa Maria Magdalena. Aldo studied their responses, searching for hesitancy or a familiar face, but found neither.

Strocchi returned with two monks and a large blanket in which to carry Visconti. The priest remained lost to his injuries, denying them the chance to question him further. Once Visconti was in the monks' safekeeping, Strocchi suggested he and Aldo return to the Podestà. Best to keep Bindi informed for his report to the duke. After searching the church for any further evidence without success, Aldo and Strocchi strolled south on via San Gallo.

'What did you make of the message left on Visconti's forehead?' Aldo asked.

'*Filii*? It could explain why *Patris* was written on Freccia's forehead. The killer seems to be using their victims to send a message: *Patris et Filii* – of the Father and of the Son.'

Aldo had reached the same conclusion. The words were familiar from when he still went to Mass, part of the Latin phrase *In nomine Patris et Filii et Spiritus Sancti.* 'I keep thinking about the ash on Zamora's forehead. That might have been the word *Nomine*, but the rain washed most of it away. If so, it suggests the killer has a further target in mind.'

'*Spiritus Sancti*,' Strocchi said, nodding his agreement, 'of the Holy Spirit. If we understood why the killer wrote these particular words on each victim, we might be able to predict who will be attacked next.'

'Indeed.' Aldo had been grappling with that but the answer was still escaping him. Usually, he was able to understand what a killer was thinking with little difficulty, to grasp their intent and use that to foresee their next step. But not this time. They were dealing with a different kind of criminal, one who refused to follow the usual pathways for a murderer. It was frustrating, but also a challenge.

They were approaching the cathedral, earlier mist rising to reveal the terracotta tiles encasing its magnificent Duomo. 'Since we do not have the key to unlock that puzzle,' Aldo said, 'we should return to simpler questions. Why would the killer attack Father Visconti? He has no obvious link to San Felice or the exorcisms.'

'There is someone that links Visconti to the exorcisms,' Strocchi said. 'Marsilio told me it was Zati who sent him to Santa Maria Magdalena for counsel. Zati described Visconti as a courageous man, and even called him Papa.'

'So, if Visconti treated Zati like a son . . .'

'It could explain why the killer would write *Filii* on Visconti's forehead,' Strocchi said. 'They want the man Visconti treats like a son – Zati – to suffer the loss of someone he loves. Zati was Negri's assistant when Cecco Vanni was exorcized. If Signora Vanni is the killer, that would make Zati as much a target for her as Negri.' Strocchi stopped, putting a hand over his mouth, eyes widening. 'Santo Spirito, I should have arrested her when I had the chance! That would have stopped her from attacking Visconti. She could be anywhere now.'

Aldo shook his head. 'Carlo, no. You're being like me, jumping from one stone to another in haste. We have no proof that Vanni is the killer. Besides, I asked Manuffi to keep a watch on her once he'd informed Bindi of the attack on Visconti.'

'That's what you whispered to him outside the Podestà . . .'

'It seemed a wise course of action until we can be certain who the killer is. What if Negri is the one responsible for these murders, and for the attack on Visconti?'

'Well, why would Negri write *Nomine* on Zamora's forehead?' Strocchi asked. 'What does that signify to him?'

'I don't know.'

'And what reason does Negri have for wanting to kill Visconti?'

'I don't know,' Aldo repeated. 'Perhaps he wants Zati to suffer, or there's some other reason. We know too little about Negri to be certain of anything. But I intend to change that.'

'How? We're not permitted to question him.'

'Since when has that mattered to me?'

Strocchi stepped back from Aldo. 'What are you planning to do?'

'Better you don't know. Should this go awry, you can honestly tell Bindi you had no knowledge of what I intended. The cost will be on my head, not yours.'

'He'll still find a way to blame me.'

'Not if you are busy elsewhere.'

'Doing what?'

'Zati can't be present when I talk with Negri.'

'Because Zati knows you,' Strocchi said. 'You need him to be outside San Felice.'

Aldo nodded. 'I'm certain Zati wants to tell us what he knows about Negri, but it will only happen if we get him away from that church. The attack on Visconti could help us, especially if Zati thinks of him like a father.'

Strocchi nodded. 'If we send a messenger to San Felice with news of the attack . . .'

'It will bring Zati to Santa Maria Magdalena. You meet him at the church, take Zati to see Visconti at the monastery. If that doesn't make him talk, nothing will.'

'Meanwhile, you visit Negri at San Felice,' Strocchi concluded.

'I told you, better that you don't know.'

Father Zati was by the main door of San Felice, thanking the few faithful who had come to the early service for All Saints' Day, when a young man sprinted towards the church. 'Are you Father Zati?' he asked between gasps.

'I am.'

'One of the parishioners – at Santa Maria Magdalena – sent me.'

'Why not Father Visconti? Unless . . .'

'He was attacked.'

'*Deus in caelo*,' Zati whispered, making the sign of the cross. 'When? This morning?'

The boy nodded.

'Was he hurt?'

'Yes.'

'Is he . . . still alive?'

The boy shrugged. 'He asked for you.'

'Wait here,' Zati told the messenger. 'I'll fetch coin for your trouble.' He hurried through San Felice to the sacristy at the back of the church, removing the outer robes he had worn to say Mass, his cassock still underneath for warmth. Grabbing a cloak in case of rain, Zati knocked at Negri's private ufficio. 'Excuse me, Father, but I must leave. A fellow priest I greatly respect has been attacked.'

Negri opened the door, a scowl twisting his face. 'What do you plan to do for him?'

'I . . .' Zati hesitated. 'I will offer him comfort and prayers.'

'Can you not pray for him here?' The exorcist gestured at the building around them. 'Is this not a House of God? Or do you think Our Lord will not be able to hear your prayers if they are said within these walls?'

'No, Father, of course not, but—'

'Spare me your excuses, I have no interest in them.'

'Please, Father Visconti has been asking for me. He may not survive the day—'

'If he's as great a priest as you seem to believe, surely he will be taken into the care of Our Lord and find his place at the right hand of God, yes?'

Zati's head dropped. 'I wish to be with Father Visconti, to offer the last rites if they are needed. You must understand that?'

'The last rites? Is that what you would offer him?' Negri stepped closer, peering into the younger priest's eyes. 'I understand you all too well, Father Zati. I see what you are.'

'I have done all that you asked. I already said the early Mass, and will be back for the late Mass. Please, I must go now.' He turned away but Negri grabbed his arm.

'I know all about your friend Visconti,' Negri hissed. 'I know you've been running to him for counsel. I know he's been asking about me at the diocesan ufficio, seeking out those who are fool enough to believe your lies and complaints. I know it all.'

'Let go of me, or else—'

'Or else what? I'm not scared of you, Zati.'

The younger priest shook his head. 'Please,' he whimpered. 'Let me go.'

Eventually the exorcist released him. 'Go, if you must. Run to Visconti, for all the good it will do either of you. Go.'

Aldo watched Zati hurry away from the church, pulling on a cloak as he headed north. The messenger had done their job well, more than earning the handful of small coin. Wanting to be certain Zati was unlikely to return, Aldo waited a while before crossing to San Felice. It was a dismal day, watery sunshine struggling to get through the blanket of cloud over the city. But that was still far lighter than the church's murky interior. Aldo stepped inside, letting his eyes adjust before going any further.

San Felice was a minor church, without the ornate marble and gold decorations found in many others. The aroma of incense still hung in the air from Mass, cloying and heavy. The only decoration of note was the large crucifix suspended over the altar: a painting of Christ on the cross, his arms spread out sideways, legs crossed below the ankles.

Aldo had seen that same pose too often in the past few days. But for Marsilio stumbling into Santa Maria Magdalena, Visconti could well have been left in that same position, ash on his forehead, his tongue cut in two and his life stolen away.

'Father Negri?' Aldo called. 'Father Negri, I need to speak with you.'

There was no immediate response so Aldo waited before repeating his words, louder this time. He heard the impatient scuff of a wooden chair on stone and a door swinging open with a swift creak. A broad-shouldered figure stalked towards Aldo, dressed in the plain black cassock of a priest. His scalp was clean-shaven and his face stern, a distinctive cleft in the chin. Seeing the exorcist for the first time, the resemblance between him and Freccia was clear despite their differences in build and attitude. Negri was a powerful presence, carrying more than enough strength to garrotte a man.

'I am Negri,' the priest announced, stopping short of Aldo. 'What do you want?'

'I come on behalf of a dear friend of mine,' Aldo lied. 'Her brother died a few days ago and she wishes him to be buried in their famiglia crypt beneath this church. She is quite overcome by grief, so her maggiordomo asked me to intercede on her behalf.'

'Both the brother and sister attended Mass here?'

'I believe so.'

'Very well. Come to my ufficio.' Negri stalked back the way he'd come, gesturing for Aldo to follow. They passed the altar on their way through the church, that painted crucifix even more brooding and tortured when seen closer. Negri opened a heavy wooden door, stepping aside for Aldo to enter first. Once they were both inside, the priest closed the door. His ufficio was a plain stone cell, open shutters high on one wall offering a little light while the rest came from candles burning on the simple wooden table. The air was thick with the sharp, bitter tang of Negri's body odour. The exorcist must spend most of his day here. Papers were piled high atop the table alongside ink and ledgers. Negri sat on the far side, resting his right hand on a weighty edition of the Bible. Aldo took the chair opposite.

'When does this woman wish her brother to be buried?'

'As soon as can be done,' Aldo replied. 'His mortal body has been in the care of the nuns at Santa Maria Nuova since his death, but they cannot look after him much longer. Nature will take its course. I'm sure you understand?'

Negri gave a dismissive gesture with his left hand. 'He's beginning to smell, yes?'

'Well . . . yes. If burial in the famiglia crypt cannot be arranged as a matter of urgency, the nuns have said it will become necessary to put him into a communal grave.'

'Unfortunately, you have chosen one of the worst possible days to make this request. It is All Saints' Day, and tomorrow is All Souls' Day. Myself and my colleague, Father Zati, are overwhelmed by services and the needs of our parishioners – those still alive.'

'I see.' Aldo lowered his eyes as if crestfallen. 'Forgive me, I had not thought. The famiglia has been too busy grieving to consider. Forgive me.'

Negri did not reply, muttering something under his breath. Eventually he gave an exasperated sigh, opening one of the ledgers and reaching for a pot of ink. 'Perhaps Zati might be able to help. What is the name of this poor soul?'

'You mean . . . you will be able to do this?' Aldo lifted his gaze again, joy flooding his face. 'Grazie, Father. Grazie mille! Tullia will be so happy to hear that.'

'Tullia?'

'Yes, Tullia Juvara – Signora Juvara, to be precise.'

Negri stopped what he was doing, his eyes narrowing. 'And the dead man's name?'

'Signor Niccolò Zamora.' Aldo smiled, abandoning his pretence. 'You know him, Father. I understand the two of you became acquainted last year when you exorcized his nephew, Marsilio Juvara. It was you who performed the sacrament, yes?' Aldo glimpsed angry red lines across Negri's palms before both hands clenched into fists.

'Signora Juvara didn't send you here, did she?'

'No. After you refused to bury her son, I'm surprised she still attends Mass here.'

'Taking one's own life is a mortal sin,' Negri replied. 'So was everything else about that boy. What he did with others like him was against the laws of God. Sinners like him have no place in this church – in any church.'

'Is that what you told his uncle?'

'His uncle was just as much a sinner. He took other men to his bed.' Negri slammed a fist down on the bible. 'Our Lord is quite explicit about the punishment required for those who go against his laws, against the laws of nature. Men like Zamora and his nephew are the work of the diavolo, luring other men to damnation. They deserved nothing but my disdain and my dismissal.'

'Is that what you did to his famiglia: dismissed them? Or were you punishing them for challenging you? Using what you knew to shame them into silence?'

'You know nothing about this—'

'Niccolò Zamora wouldn't stay silent, though, would he?' Aldo persisted. 'He kept writing to the diocesan ufficio, asking for Archbishop Buondelmonti to make you see sense or remove you from this parish. You couldn't tolerate that any longer, could you?'

Negri pushed the bible to one side. 'Who are you? What are you doing here?'

Aldo had known plenty like Negri, men short of temper who believed themselves beyond reproach. Men convinced their word and their beliefs mattered above all else. To get the truth from the exorcist required making Negri angry. Angry men became careless, fury and indignation getting the better of them. 'My name is Cesare Aldo. I'm with the Otto di Guardia e Balia, and I want to know what you did.'

'You are to leave this place. Now.' The exorcist rose from his chair. 'You have no jurisdiction inside this church, and your court has no power over me or what I do.'

'Then it doesn't matter what you tell me, does it? If you truly are beyond the Otto's reach – if you believe that you have done nothing wrong – then you have nothing to fear from my questions.' Aldo stood up. 'How do you explain those red lines across the palms of your hands? They look like the marks that would be caused by pulling a thick, beaded rope taut around a man's neck. Is that where you got them, Father?'

Negri glared down at his hands. 'These marks are from the scourge I use to mortify my flesh each day. It slips in my grasp sometimes, and marks the skin of my hands.'

That was a credible explanation, but Aldo would expect a cunning killer to have such an answer ready. 'Tell me, Father, do you believe you've done nothing wrong?'

'Leave,' Negri commanded, pointing at the door. 'Get out of this church and don't come back here again. I shall be writing to the archbishop the moment that you leave, demanding he has you dismissed from the Otto.'

'Buondelmonti has no jurisdiction over the court, and no power over me,' Aldo replied, turning Negri's words against him.

'I said get out,' the exorcist snarled.

'Not yet.' Aldo smiled, knowing it would enrage Negri further. 'Not until you tell me the truth.'

Chapter Twenty-five

Strocchi waited outside Santa Maria Magdalena, trying not to worry about what Aldo was doing. The former officer possessed more cunning and guile than anyone Strocchi had ever known. But Aldo also had a reckless streak, especially when dealing with those he did not respect. Announcing he and Strocchi would bring the killer before the Otto by the end of All Souls' Day was the latest example. Aldo seemed determined to provoke Bindi simply to enjoy the segretario's response, not caring about the consequences. How Aldo had been an officer for so long before his demotion was a mystery even he might struggle to solve.

Yet Strocchi could understand what drove him to challenge Bindi. The segretario's dismissive attitude and his impossible demands were too much, even for those with the patience of a saint. More than once Strocchi had considered leaving the Otto. Was it worth withstanding such a bastardo for the coin that being an officer brought? At some point did self-respect not demand dissent? While justice was being done, Strocchi was willing to tolerate the segretario. But more and more it seemed the gap between justice and the law was widening, especially when those standing accused had enough wealth to buy their freedom.

Perhaps Aldo's attitude was correct after all? Better to seek the truth by whatever means necessary and worry about the cost of that pursuit later . . .

Strocchi saw Zati scurrying towards the church, shoulders hunched forward, concern etched into his face. Strocchi approached the priest, hands raised in reassurance. 'Before you ask, yes, Father Visconti is alive.'

'Praise be!' Zati replied, making the sign of the cross. 'Where is he? Can I see him?'

'He's been taken to the monastery behind the church. The monks are caring for him in their infirmary. Follow me.' Strocchi took Zati along the dirt road leading to the main door of the monastery. As they waited to be let in, Strocchi described what had happened. Zati appeared horrified by how close the killer had come to ending Visconti's life.

'I fear this is all my fault,' he said.

'How so?'

'I have been visiting Father Visconti for counsel. I was troubled by the behaviour of Father Negri,' Zati said. 'I still am – more so now, in fact. I needed the wisdom to know what I should do. Father Visconti offered to approach those he knows within the diocesan ufficio.'

'And you think that put him in danger?'

Zati nodded. 'After my last visit here, Father Negri demanded to know where I had been. I did not tell him much, but I fear it still set him hunting for answers. And now this . . .'

That suggested Zati believed Negri was responsible for the attack on Visconti, either directly or by other means. But before Strocchi could ask more, the monastery door was opened by a monk. Strocchi introduced Zati and asked that they be allowed to visit Father Visconti. The monk agreed, but said Zati must come in alone. 'Having too many voices close by will not help Father Visconti. He needs rest and peace to recover.'

Strocchi agreed but took Zati aside for a moment. 'I will wait out here for you so we can talk further. If it is any comfort, your actions helped save Father Visconti today. Marsilio Juvara was the person who stopped the attacker finishing their handiwork, and he only came to the church because you suggested it. Father Visconti owes his life to you.'

Zati shook his head. 'I wish I could believe that.'

Aldo stood his ground, even when Negri stalked to the ufficio door and pulled it open. 'Why will you not defend yourself, Father? Is it because you fear the truth emerging about what you have done? Or is it because you know you're as much a sinner as those you exorcize?'

'I know I'm a sinner,' Negri snarled. 'All of us are sinners. Every day I flagellate my skin, hoping to drive out the diavolo from inside me. Every soul I save in this church, every demon I purge from their bodies – all of it is part of God's great plan!'

'What about Freccia? Was your son part of that great plan?'

The exorcist stepped back a pace. 'My son?'

'He was a thief who sucked cazzi for coin. And he was your child, the fruit of your loins. Tell me, Father, did you create him before or after you took your vows?'

'I don't know what you're talking about,' Negri insisted.

'We both know that's a lie. Is Freccia one of the reasons you scourge yourself? How angry did it make you when he came demanding coin for silence?'

'Leave this church immediately.'

'Freccia even stole from you, or so you told one of my colleagues. Was that true, or merely another lie to escape suspicion?'

Rage twisted Negri's face. 'Get out. Now.'

'You say you're doing God's work—'

'I know I am—'

'Is it God's work to torment those who find love with others like themselves? Is it God's work to damn those still searching for themselves?'

'Yes! Yes, it is!'

'And is it God's work to throttle the life from another man?'

Negri stared at Aldo, his face crimson, spittle at the corners of his mouth – but he did not answer the accusation. He strode from the ufficio instead, his feet stamping on the stone floor. Aldo went after him, refusing to be ignored.

'Well, Father? Have you no answer for me, no Bible verse to offer as a justification for what you have done? Are you willing to tell the truth and face the consequences? Or are you going to hide behind Archbishop Buondelmonti and the diocese?'

'You know nothing of the truth, nor of the burden I carry every day.' Negri stopped at the main entrance of San Felice, pointing through the doorway. 'Go.'

Aldo paused in front of Negri, standing so near their noses were almost touching. This close he could see the uncertainty in the exorcist's eyes, doubt masked by all that righteous fury. Negri believed what he was doing was correct but still it tormented him.

'There shall be a reckoning for this,' the exorcist said.

'Good,' Aldo replied. 'It's time others saw you for what you are.'

Strocchi paced the dirt road outside the monastery, waiting for Zati. When the priest did emerge, he was wiping tears from his face. Strocchi let Zati compose himself before asking about Visconti. 'He was resting most of the time,' Zati replied. 'He murmured a few words, but nothing I could understand.'

'Do the monks know when he might recover? We need to ask him about the attack.'

'If he survives into tomorrow there is hope, but otherwise . . .' Zati's face crumpled. 'I'm sorry, it's . . . I know you have questions.'

'They can wait a while,' Strocchi said. 'Let us walk together, and you can tell me what you must once you are ready.'

'Grazie.'

Strocchi led the priest back to via San Gallo, turning left towards the city's northern gate. The two of them strolled side by side, Zati nodding to those who acknowledged him. 'Do you know all these people?' Strocchi asked.

'Some of them. I have said Mass in several different churches. Parishioners who share their pain and sins with you often believe you will remember them by name. But after a while the faces become one face, always seeking hope or comfort . . . or redemption.'

That made sense to Strocchi. He had only served the Otto three years and already the names of those he'd first arrested were slipping from his recollection. A parish priest must meet hundreds of the faithful and hear many more confessions. All that guilt and suffering and pleading for forgiveness would weigh heavy after a while.

The closer they got to Porta San Gallo, the fewer people there were on the streets. Three-level palazzi gave way to more modest two-level homes, and finally to stables and sheds. The city was slowly expanded towards its outer wall. One day it might even be so large the wall could no longer contain all those wishing to live in Florence. For now, there were still farms within its boundary though autumn had left their fields bare.

Strocchi nodded to the men standing sentry at the north gate, two of whom he knew from when they'd worked at the Podestà.

'Shall we turn back?' he asked. Zati paused, staring out through the gate to the road beyond that wound its way north.

'These last few days I have considered leaving Florence,' he said. 'Leaving my position at San Felice, going somewhere else – anywhere else – and starting a new life.'

'You would still remain a priest, of course.' Strocchi had heard tell of priests who abandoned their calling to the Church, but had never encountered one himself.

'If you had asked me before, I would have said yes in a moment. But now . . .' Zati's chin wobbled, and Strocchi could see tears brimming in his eyes. 'I do not know.'

'You can leave the city once this is settled if you wish. I would certainly understand that. But walking away from what troubles you will not solve the problem. At least, that's what my parish priest told me when I considered running away as a boy.'

'What was his name?'

'Father Colucci. He's a good man, and he cares deeply for his parishioners.'

'I wish I was like him,' Zati whispered.

'You still can be. Perhaps you already are, and do not realize it.'

'No. It is kind of you to say so, but I know the truth about myself.' Zati turned to face the city. 'I have distant famiglia in Venice, but Florence is where I belong. This is my home.' The priest gave a hesitant nod. 'Ask me your questions. I will answer what I can.'

'Grazie.' Strocchi led him south along via San Gallo, back towards Santa Maria Magdalena and the rest of the city. 'Tell me about Niccolò Zamora and Father Negri.'

Zati gave his version of the clash between the two men, confirming much of what Strocchi had already heard. The description of Negri exorcizing Marsilio sounded more like torture than a holy sacrament. 'It was . . .' Zati struggled to find the words. 'Negri's hatred for Marsilio went far beyond anything I had ever witnessed.' No wonder Zamora had sought to have Negri removed by the diocese.

'What about Signora Vanni?' Strocchi asked.

Again, Zati confirmed much of what the investigation had learned, how the failed exorcism of Vanni's brother had led to his death and why Vanni blamed Negri for that. 'She begged him for an apology,' Zati said, 'but Father Negri believes too much in his calling to admit any mistake. He will do whatever he must to remain an exorcist, even if it costs lives.'

'Freccia. What happened between Father Negri and his son?'

Zati's head snapped round to stare at Strocchi. 'You know about that?'

'We know more than you or Negri realize.'

'I didn't, not until a few days ago . . .'

Aldo cursed himself as he stalked the streets of Oltrarno, trying to make sense of what had happened at San Felice. Anger had got the better of him, as it had Negri. Were the two of them alike in some way? Their beliefs might be in opposition, and yet . . . Aldo shook his head, not wanting to accept that. Negri was unable to consider there might be truth or hope in anything beyond his own narrow views. But Aldo believed he could still be persuaded to change his mind, to see things through the eyes of others. When that ceased, the mind became a closed casket, so bound with locks and keys it could never open up. He hoped that was not who he was.

And yet . . .

Stopping to look around himself, Aldo realized he was at the north end of via dei Giudei where it neared the Arno. The Jewish woman he had met the previous day, Tamar, was emerging from Saul's front door. She saw Aldo and smiled. 'Doctor Orvieto's free,' Tamar called, 'if you need to talk. I was the last patient waiting to see him.'

Aldo thanked her as he strolled along the narrow dirt street, a pungent aroma of boiling brassica billowing from one of the houses. He stopped outside Saul's home. The front door stood open as it always did during daylight, always welcoming. Aldo went in.

Saul was in the back room with Rebecca, assessing their stock of remedies. She was making careful notes in a ledger while Saul opened each jar and pot, peering inside to judge the quantity that remained. 'Cloves, we need more cloves,' he announced. 'Get some for me next time you're at the mercato.'

'Of course,' Rebecca replied, adding that to a list beside the ledger.

'May I come in?' Aldo asked.

'As long as you don't have another corpse for us to examine,' Saul replied.

'Not today. Or not yet, at least.'

'I heard somebody else was attacked,' Rebecca said, 'north of the river.'

Aldo nodded. It was no surprise word of that had reached her. Rumours and gossip crossed the city as fast as any messenger. 'A priest, Father Visconti, in his own church. But the killer was interrupted before they could finish their task.'

'Attacking a priest,' Saul said, shaking his head. 'What is this city coming to?'

'That's what I need to discuss.' Aldo smiled at Rebecca. 'Would you mind . . . ?'

'Of course not.' She rose from her chair, taking the list. 'I'll go to the mercato, see if I can find some of these.' Rebecca nodded to Saul on her way out, the soft shuffle of her steps disappearing along the corridor until they were no longer audible.

Saul gestured for Aldo to sit at the table. 'What do you want to talk about?'

Aldo sank into the chair and poured out what had happened at San Felice. How his strategia to goad the truth out of Negri had failed. Why the exorcist's responses had pushed Aldo into accusing him of the murders. 'I was so certain making him angry would force Negri to defend himself. I thought he was so proud of what he had done, he would welcome the chance to throw it in my face. But there were doubts inside him, I saw them.'

'Every man has doubts,' Saul said, taking the seat closest to Aldo. 'Even the most certain of us cannot be sure of everything. I believe in my faith and yet . . .'

'It does not believe in you?'

'Let's say the scriptures would not approve of all my choices.' Saul rested a hand on Aldo's hand. 'But I have learned to live with that. To do what I can to help others and let that be my legacy. I will never have children or be a father, but I enable others to do so. For me this must be enough. What is it you are trying to do, Cesare? What is it you need?'

'I want Bindi to admit he was wrong and make me an officer again. Proving who is responsible for these murders and bringing them before the Otto will achieve that.'

'You're telling me what you want, what you hope might undo past mistakes. I asked, what is it that you need? What will make you happy, or more complete, or less . . .'

'Broken?'

Saul smiled. 'We are all a little broken.'

'Perhaps.'

'So, what do you need?'

Aldo pondered a while before answering.

When he did, it made Saul smile.

Having already passed Santa Maria Magdalena, Strocchi led Zati to Piazza San Marco. There was a stone bench outside the monastery where they could sit. Once the priest was settled, Strocchi asked him again about the exorcist and his illegitimate son, Freccia.

'I did not know Negri was the thief's father,' Zati said, 'not for many months. But I wondered why Freccia came to San Felice at the same time each Friday, and why Negri was always so angry after they met in his private ufficio. A few weeks ago, I stayed outside the door to listen. That's why I learned Freccia was extorting coin, and why Negri paid him.'

This confirmed Aldo's suspicions, but Strocchi needed other answers. 'When I came to San Felice, Negri claimed his handbook had been stolen, probably by Freccia.'

'That was a lie. Negri used it during our last exorcism on Tuesday, and Freccia has not been to the church for a week. He sent a messenger a few days ago, demanding Negri come to via dei Giudei. Negri was hearing confessions, so I accepted the message for him. When I told Negri, his anger was . . .' Zati shook his head. 'I'd never seen him so enraged, not even during the worst of our exorcisms. His face was crimson.'

Strocchi knew the thief needed extra coin with a baby coming. Perhaps Freccia believed that would be easier away from San Felice? But demanding more from Negri had been a mistake. It could well be what had driven the exorcist to murder his illicit son.

'Negri lives in San Felice?'

'Yes,' Zati replied. 'He has a cot in a small room by his ufficio.

When I first joined Negri at San Felice, he told me he did not believe an exorcist should have their own residence. Such comforts were for those less committed to the word of God. Father Negri rarely leaves the church. I have seldom seen him outside its walls.'

That meant Negri could come and go as he wished during curfew, so long as he was careful to avoid the Otto's night patrols. 'But you live elsewhere?'

'Yes, in a shared residence with two other priests who don't have their own parish.'

'What time do you arrive at San Felice each day?'

'Negri expects me there within an hour of curfew's end. But Signora Vanni often waits for me outside the church, demanding to know if the diocese has changed its mind yet.'

'What time did you arrive three days ago?'

'On Wednesday?' Zati frowned. 'I was late. I sought counsel from Father Visconti before going to San Felice. When I arrived, Signora Vanni was outside. Negri scolded me.'

'And two days ago?'

'I was there not long after curfew. Negri was flagellating himself when I arrived. He said the punishment of skin and flesh was necessary to atone for his sins.'

Strocchi nodded. If the exorcist was the killer, his guilt must be overwhelming. 'And when did you arrive at San Felice this morning?'

Zati hesitated. 'Not long after curfew, I think. I said the first All Saints' Day Mass.'

Strocchi rose from the stone bench, rubbing the back of his hose to get some warmth back into his legs. 'Is there anything else you wanted or needed to say?'

Zati stared at the ground in front of him. 'No, there's nothing.'

'If that changes, leave a message for me at the Podestà and I will find you.'

The priest nodded but could not meet Strocchi's gaze. Zati was holding back, unable to share something – but what? It seemed his fear of Negri was so great Zati could not speak the full truth of what was troubling him. If Aldo was here, he would push the priest, using whatever stratagemma was needed. But Strocchi knew this was not his way.

He prayed a gentler approach could still lead them to the truth. To justice.

Aldo was on his way from Saul's home to where Signora Vanni lived when he noticed Marsilio Juvara ahead of him on via Maggio. Aldo had been regretting how harsh he'd been with Juvara; the young man had saved Father Visconti's life at the Church of Santa Maria Magdalena, even if that was down to happenstance rather than heroism. Perhaps this was a chance to make amends? Aldo approached him with a smile and a warm voice.

'Signor Juvara?'

'Yes?' Marsilio swung round, as if startled to hear his own name.

'My name is Cesare Aldo. We met earlier at Father Visconti's church.' Aldo made an apology for his behaviour at the church. Marsilio accepted it without hesitation, but his attention seemed to be elsewhere. 'Is there some way I can help you?' Aldo asked.

'Your colleague . . .'

'Strocchi?'

'Yes, him. He suggested I return to my famiglia, now that I am back in the city.'

Aldo knew Palazzo Zamora was a short distance away, yet the young man had been pacing on via Maggio. 'But you're afraid?'

Marsilio nodded. 'My famiglia buried a body, certain it was mine, but it belonged to a friend. How do I explain that to them? They believe me dead. If I walk into the palazzo now, how will my mama respond? What will that do to her, to my siblings?'

His hesitation was understandable. If Aldo were faced with the same choice, he would struggle too. 'I know this is difficult, even frightening,' he said. 'But I still envy you. I never knew my mama because she died having me. I was born a bastardo yet my papa insisted I be raised alongside his legitimate children. When he died, I was thrown out onto the street. I have been without a famiglia since I was twelve. That is a long time to be alone in the world. You still have a famiglia, people who love you. Yes, your return will be a shock to them. But to have you back . . . it will be worth that.'

Marsilio peered at Aldo. 'You believe so?'

'Yes.'

Marsilio chewed on his bottom lip. 'I'm not sure I can do this alone. Walk with me?'

Aldo nodded. In the circumstances, it was the least he could do.

Chapter Twenty-six

After ushering Marsilio inside Palazzo Zamora, Aldo hurried to the southern end of via Maggio. He found Manuffi in a doorway that gave a clear view of anyone coming or going from Signora Vanni's home. Others would have complained after spending so long there, but the constable was cheerful when Aldo arrived. 'I was beginning to wonder if you'd forgotten me,' Manuffi said, but there was no grievance in his face or voice.

'Never,' Aldo replied as they headed north. 'What have you seen?'

'Very little,' Manuffi admitted. 'Vanni didn't come out while I was there. But she was definitely inside,' he added before Aldo could ask. 'I heard strange noises so I crept over to listen at the door for a while.'

'And?'

'She was weeping, wailing almost. Shouting at herself, and praying too.' Manuffi shook his head as they crossed Ponte Vecchio. 'She doesn't seem a happy person.'

Aldo nodded. If Vanni was this troubled in spirit and faith, was it enough to drive her to kill? Without proof, that was hard to say. He and Manuffi strode side by side across Piazza della Signora. Aldo was surprised to remember it had only been three days since he and Benedetto had found Zamora's body here. Much had happened since.

Aldo had little time for those who swore by luck, but he was relieved to see Strocchi coming towards the Podestà from the north as they approached from the south. It saved sending out messengers to search for him, wasting time they did not possess.

'I was hoping to find you here,' Strocchi said when they met near the front gates.

'I could say the same,' Aldo agreed. 'We have a decision to make.'

'Are we going in?' Manuffi asked, gesturing towards the Podestà.

'No,' Strocchi and Aldo replied in unison.

'We need somewhere else to talk,' Strocchi told Manuffi.

'The private room at Letta's tavern?' Aldo suggested.

Strocchi nodded. 'Manuffi, come with us.'

'I should?'

'This concerns you too,' Aldo said. 'We still need your help.'

Manuffi beamed, standing a little taller at the praise.

'Follow us,' Strocchi said as Aldo led the way north. When they reached the tavern Letta was sweeping the floor, only a handful of drinkers inside.

'Second visit in four days?' she said. 'I'll need to give you your own table.'

'We'd rather have some privacy,' Strocchi replied. 'If that's available?'

'Business isn't exactly booming. Go through, be my guest.' The buxom landlady studied Manuffi as he passed by. 'Who's your friend?' she asked Aldo.

'Manuffi, another constable with the Otto.'

'Tell him he can arrest me any time he wants.'

Aldo ignored the comment, slapping some coin on the bar. 'Bring us wine when you get the chance,' he said, following the others into the private room. Once they were settled, Aldo asked

Manuffi to repeat what he'd seen and heard while keeping watch on Vanni's home. 'She sounded . . . broken,' Manuffi concluded. 'It was sad.'

'But that doesn't mean she's not the killer,' Strocchi said before giving a summary of his meeting with Zati. 'What he told me is not enough to prove Negri's guilt, but it means nobody can vouch for where the exorcist was when the murders took place.'

Aldo sat opposite Strocchi, watching the young officer as he spoke. 'Forget what Zati told you. How did he seem? Was he being truthful?'

'Priests can't lie,' Manuffi said. 'Lying is a sin.'

Aldo patted him on the shoulder. 'You've a good heart, but you still have a lot to learn about the world. Trust me,' he said as Letta bustled in with three cups of wine and the rest of the bottle, 'priests can lie and cheat and kill like anyone else.'

'That's not all they can do,' she agreed. 'One comes in here to drink most afternoons, after he's said Mass. He would be in the tavern now if it wasn't All Saints' Day. As for the others . . .' Letta winked at Manuffi. 'You know what they say about men who go without for too long.'

Aldo glared at the tavern keeper. 'Grazie, Letta. Grazie mille.'

'All right, all right, I'm going.' She left, shutting the door.

'I don't think Zati told me everything,' Strocchi said. 'His fear of Negri is too great.'

'With good reason,' Aldo agreed.

'Perhaps if I had pushed Zati, demanded more answers from him, he might have told me what he knows?'

'You can't be sure of that,' Aldo said. 'When I confronted Negri he stood his ground, refusing to admit any part in these killings.' He recounted his clash with the exorcist at San Felice. Strocchi's shoulders slumped as he listened.

'You've goaded Negri into bringing Archbishop Buondelmonti and the diocesan ufficio down on us. Once Bindi hears what you have done . . .' He shook his head. 'Worse still, all we have are two strong suspects and no proof.' Strocchi drained his wine. 'The last day or two I've been wondering whether I want to remain with the Otto. Now it sounds as if I need not bother resigning. The segretario will dismiss us soon enough.'

'Even me?' Manuffi asked.

'No, not you,' Aldo said. 'But if Bindi does get rid of us, by this time tomorrow you could be an investigating officer.'

'I hope not,' he replied. 'Not if it makes me as unhappy as Carlo.'

'I'm not unhappy,' Strocchi said, though his face suggested otherwise. 'But we have two murders to solve and no way of proving who committed them. The only thing we know is that the killer probably plans to claim another life.'

'They do?' Manuffi asked.

Strocchi explained the pattern in the words written on the victims' foreheads. 'We already had *Patris* – of the Father – and *Filii*, meaning of the Son. That suggests *Spiritus Sancti*, the Holy Spirit, will be written on the next victim. But we don't know who that might be.'

Aldo sipped his wine. 'We can uncover the truth by other means.'

'How?'

'We send two written messages; one to Signora Vanni, the other to San Felice. Each saying much the same thing. We tell our suspects that we know what they did, and invite them to meet us inside Santa Maria Magdalena tonight. If they don't come, we promise to tell the Otto and Archbishop Buondelmonti what we know about them. That carries with it the threat of a trial, imprisonment in Le Stinche – or even excommunication.'

'I don't understand,' Manuffi said. 'Why would they fear a message from us?'

'We don't sign it,' Aldo explained. 'One note will urge them to come to the church as the bells ring for the start of curfew, the other to come when the chimes of midnight are struck. They will not know who sent the messages, only that they are threatened.'

'It could work,' Strocchi conceded.

'It's our best hope of uncovering the truth,' Aldo said. 'I will stay with Visconti for the rest of the day, make sure he remains safe and that the monks tell nobody of his condition. When curfew comes, I'll use the door between the monastery and Santa Maria Magdalena to enter the church and await whoever comes. You two will already be hiding in the church so you can witness what happens, and intervene if the killer attacks me.'

'What if we can't get to you in time?' Strocchi said.

'Make sure you do.' Aldo looked at Manuffi. 'Well?'

The constable rubbed a hand across his throat. 'I'm happy to help but I'm also glad not to be the one putting my neck at risk.'

'And you, Carlo?'

Strocchi shook his head. 'No. This is too foolish, and far too dangerous.'

'Sometimes you must take risks to reap a reward.'

'Some risks are not worth taking. Besides, we can't be sure anyone will come, let alone the killer. This could all be in vain.'

'If nobody comes, we have lost nothing but half a night's sleep – and we will have tried to bring the truth into the light. Otherwise, there is only one other pathway to that.'

'What?' Manuffi asked.

'We arrest Signora Vanni and torture her until she confesses,' Aldo replied.

Strocchi grimaced. 'She could be innocent.'

'True,' Aldo agreed. 'But we can't arrest Negri, he's too protected by the Church. It has to be Vanni. The segretario will have his culprit, and the case is closed.' He arched an eyebrow at Strocchi. 'What is it to be? You can pursue truth and justice, or you can serve the law. Which master do you wish to serve, Carlo?'

Strocchi sank back in his seat. 'Those are the only ways?'

'The only ones I can see.' Aldo waited. He knew what the young officer would decide, but it still had to be his choice. After a long while Strocchi sighed and gave a nod.

'Who's going to write these messages?' he asked.

'Better that I do,' Aldo volunteered. 'Should this go awry, Bindi could put all the blame on me. You two can deny knowing what was in my mind.'

'Very well,' Strocchi said. Manuffi nodded his agreement.

'Grazie. Go home to your famiglia, go see the people you love or get some rest. We've a long night ahead of us.'

The contessa smiled as her maggiordomo finished his report. 'It is as you expected,' Pozzo said. 'Our man on the northern gate confirms that a standing warrant has been issued by the Otto for the arrest of Zilio, should he attempt to re-enter Florence. The court convicted him in absentia for the murder of Grossolano, and the investigation has been closed.'

'That is most satisfactory,' she agreed. But the contessa could not deny a pang of regret. This meant there was less of a reason to expect a visit by Aldo soon, not unless she provoked the duke with another clumsy attempt to recruit one of his courtiers. That had worked well with Dandolo, but she was loath to repeat such a stratagemma. Better to keep a rival guessing by not doing what they expected. 'Is there anything else?'

'No, Contessa,' Pozzo replied.

'Then you may go. I have a letter I must write, and it requires using the Council of Ten's latest set of tiresome ciphers. Come back in an hour with a good wine. I shall have need of that by the time I finish drafting my correspondence to them.'

'Of course.' The maggiordomo bowed on his way out of the salone.

The contessa went to the writing table she kept at one end of the chamber, preparing paper and ink before consulting the new ciphers Zilio had left on his visit. She would miss teasing Zilio, but he had proved an unreliable ally when it came to managing the expectations and directives that emerged from Venice. An intermediary that was no longer able to manage those for whom they worked was of little use to her.

For the attention of the Inquisitorie di Stato, the contessa wrote.

By the time you receive this missive it is likely that your envoy Zilio will have returned to Venice with news about the disappearance of Signor Tito Grossolano, your choice to succeed me as the Venetian representative here in Florence.

It is with the deepest of regrets that I must inform you Signor Grossolano was killed within a day of arriving in this city. He had been staying here at Palazzo Coltello but, after indulging in rather too much wine, Signor Grossolano ignored my warnings and unwisely chose to go out into the city after dark. It seems he was murdered by an individual who has been stalking Florentines of late during the hours of curfew, a killer who had already taken two lives. As such, Signor Grossolano was most unfortunate to fall victim to their deadly ways.

*I hesitate to add further woe to this injury but must also
inform you that the Otto di Guardia e Bali – Florence's powerful
criminal court, as I'm sure you are aware – has chosen to convict
Signor Zilio of this murder. That was done in his absence and
without anyone present to defend him. My informants within
the court of Duke Cosimo de' Medici allege this blatant
miscarriage of justice was carried out on the direct orders of His
Grace. It means that Signor Zilio can never return to Florence,
not while a warrant for his arrest is outstanding.*

*I can only offer my sincerest regrets at these tragic and
unforeseen developments.*

*If I may be so bold, I hereby offer to continue in my current
position as your representative in Florence – at least until a
suitable replacement can be appointed.*

*For now, please pass on my condolences to any famiglia
who will mourn the loss of Signor Grossolano. In the brief
time I knew him he was a lively individual, filled with a rich
and powerful lust for life. I fear that may be what led to his
demise, though I have no evidence to support it. My
informants shall continue to investigate this terrible crime.*

I remain your humblest servant,
Contessa Valentine Coltello

Having composed a draft in plain language, she began the
laborious task of using the ciphers to make the text illegible to
anyone without the necessary key to decrypt it. The sooner Pozzo
returned with that wine, the better. But the letter should suffice
in keeping the Inquisitorie di Stato on the back foot for a while.
It served this new tribunal right for having the temerity to usurp
her without thinking through the consequences of that folly.

A smile played about her lips. Perhaps she would contrive a

reason to bring Aldo back to her. He had been a most amusing diversion, and such talents were all too rare. She could not help wondering what he was doing, and how he would respond to such a summons.

After sending notes by messenger to Signora Vanni and to San Felice, Aldo strode north-west through the city. It was a relief not to be soaked through by rain when he reached the monastery at Santa Maria Magdalena. The monks were reluctant to allow Aldo in at first until he persuaded them.

Once inside, Aldo went directly to the infirmary, surprising the kindly monk who had offered to guide him there. 'I've been here before,' Aldo explained, 'when this was still a convent.' He had nearly died then, but Brother Bonaventure did not need to know that.

Visconti was one of three patients at the infirmary, all lying in cots. The other two were wizened monks, their faces sunken by age and illness. Incense lingered in the air, as if someone had said Mass in the long chamber hours earlier. 'Father Visconti was here before dawn to give one of our brethren the last rites,' Bonaventure whispered. 'Now he's lying in one of the cots himself. But he is making a good recovery, and should be on his feet tomorrow, God willing. However, I doubt he will have the strength to say Mass for All Souls' Day.'

'May I sit with him for a while?' Aldo asked.

'He would be glad of the company, I'm sure, even if he does not wake.'

'Father Visconti hasn't spoken since he was brought here?'

'No, I don't believe so. But I haven't been by his side the whole time.' Bonaventure smiled. 'Let me fetch you a stool. I'll be right back.'

Aldo went to Visconti's cot. The priest appeared at peace, hands folded together on his chest atop the sheet, a serene calm on his face. He was dressed in a plain nightshirt, his clerical robes folded at the foot of the cot. The monks had washed the ash from his forehead, so the angry red line around Visconti's neck was the only sign of how close the killer had come to claiming a third victim.

Bonaventure returned with a simple wooden stool which he gave to Aldo. 'Are you happy to sit alone with Father Visconti? I could have one of the younger monks pray beside you—'

'No, grazie,' Aldo said, smiling at the monk. 'I prefer to pray silently.' He raised his eyes towards the heavens. 'Our words are always heard, even if they are not spoken aloud.'

'Amen,' Bonaventure agreed. 'In that case, I shall leave you in silent contemplation.'

Aldo thanked him again, and sat on the stool by the cot, close to Visconti. If the priest did murmur something, Aldo wanted to hear it. His vigil was soon rewarded. Visconti shifted in his cot, eyes fluttering open. 'P-Pagolo? Is that you?'

Aldo leaned closer. 'Father Zati isn't here,' he whispered. 'He was earlier.'

Visconti's head tilted towards Aldo, his gaze sharpening. 'I know you . . .'

'Yes.' Aldo introduced himself, explaining how the priest came to be at the infirmary. 'Do you recall what happened? You were preparing your church for early Mass.'

'Yes . . . I heard someone come in, said I would be with them in a moment.'

Aldo nodded. Finally, a witness who could reveal more about the killer. But Visconti mustn't be rushed. His testimony had more value if it was not guided.

'I had dropped a small candle and was bending over to pick it up,' Visconti went on. 'Something struck me from behind.' His nearest hand reached for his throat. 'The next thing I knew, I was choking . . .' His mouth moved but no sound came out, fear filling his face.

Aldo took hold of Visconti's hand. 'You're safe, Father. They can't hurt you now.'

Visconti shook his head. 'You don't understand,' he rasped. 'I know who it was. I know who tried to kill me.'

Strocchi arrived home to find Mama and Tomasia hugging while little Bianca stood to one side, tears running down her face. 'What's happened? What's wrong?'

'Thank goodness,' Mama replied. 'I was worried you wouldn't be back in time.'

'In time for what?' Strocchi looked at his wife.

'Father Colucci came by earlier,' Tomasia explained. 'He's returning to Ponte a Signa and offered your mama a ride home in his carriage.'

'It'll be much more comfortable than having to walk back,' Mama said, 'and much quicker. My old legs aren't so swift as they once were.'

'But—' Strocchi began.

'Hush, Carlo, it's for the best.' Mama smiled at him. 'Your pretty wife is much better now, and I got to spend lots of time with Bianca, my wonderful nipotina! Besides, everybody knows a guest is like a fish from the Arno. You are pleased to have one at first but nobody wants it staying in your home too long.'

As ever, he couldn't fault what Mama said. 'Well, we're sad to see you go.'

No sooner were the words out of his mouth than there was a knock at the door. 'Come in!' Mama shouted, her voice far too loud for the room. She was used to village life where people called to one another and there were few secrets.

Father Colucci opened the door, taking the black biretta from his head. 'Carlo, it's good to see you again!' A smile split the kind priest's face, genuine warmth evident there. After dealing with the vicious sanctimony of Negri, it made a welcome change.

Strocchi shook Colucci's hand, inviting him inside.

'I wish I could linger,' the priest replied, 'but my carriage driver is impatient to go. We need to be through the city gates before they are locked for curfew.'

There were hugs, kisses and tears while Mama said goodbye to Tomasia and Bianca. Strocchi carried her bag downstairs to the street, accompanied by Colucci. Eventually Mama joined them there, giving Strocchi a crushing hug and kissing both his cheeks.

'You look after that wife of yours,' she insisted. 'You found a good one when you met Tomasia, she has a wise head on her shoulders.'

'Yes, Mama,' he replied.

She waved up at the shutters where Tomasia was leaning out, Bianca balanced on one hip. 'If you have any more trouble with the baby, send for me at once, yes?'

'Of course, Mama.'

Father Colucci cleared his throat. 'I'm sorry but we must go.'

'Of course, of course!' She pinched Strocchi's left cheek between her thumb and forefinger. 'My little bambino, all grown up with a famiglia of his own. Be happy, Carlo. You worry too much. Everything will be as it should.' Mama strode towards the carriage, calling for the priest to keep up. Colucci smiled and shrugged before hurrying after her.

Tomasia was waiting at the door when Strocchi returned upstairs. 'Well?'

'They've gone.'

She looked around at their home. 'It's going to be a lot quieter here now.'

Strocchi put a hand to her swollen belly. 'I'm sure this one will change that.'

'Your mama was right, Carlo – you do worry too much.'

'Only when I have good cause. What Aldo has planned for tonight . . .'

Tomasia closed the door behind him. 'You'd best tell me all about it.'

Chapter Twenty-seven

When the bells chimed for curfew, Aldo used the connecting door from the monastery to the Church of Santa Maria Magdalena to pass between them unseen. The killer could be watching the main entrance; better to give them no reason to suspect a stratagemma. A few candles were burning in small recesses along the church's stone walls. Enough to see a little, but not much more. Strocchi and Manuffi were already inside, whispering to one another in the shadows at one side of the chancel, not far from the altar.

Strocchi approached Aldo, concern on his face. 'Offering yourself as a victim to the killer like this, it's too dangerous.'

'Too dangerous,' Manuffi agreed, joining him.

'Far safer for us to wait outside and arrest whoever comes to the church for breaking curfew. A night in the cells at the Podestà should persuade them to talk.'

'And if it doesn't?' Aldo asked. 'What do you suggest we do then? If Negri comes, how will you explain to Bindi that you've arrested a priest he forbade you to even question?'

'We worry about that in that morning,' Strocchi said, without much conviction.

'We have to worry about it now, Carlo. We need a confession. Without that, we have nothing and the killer is free to continue—'

A sudden noise from the far end of the church silenced them.

Someone was opening the main door, its old metal mechanism protesting.

'Get out of sight,' Aldo hissed, pushing them back towards the shadows. He sank to his knees in front of the altar, eyes fixed on the heavy wooden cross that stood atop it. He was facing away from the church doors, head bowed and hands clasped together as if in prayer.

'Hello?' a voice whispered. 'Are you the person who sent me the note?'

Cautious footsteps approached, stopping short of Aldo but near enough to attack him if they chose. He nodded in response to their question. Paper rustled behind him.

'Your note, it says you know what I did . . .' That was Vanni's voice, but this was no surprise – Aldo had invited her to come to the church as curfew began. 'But how could you?'

Aldo stayed silent, letting his quietness be an inquisitor.

'Cecco and I were the only ones there when it happened,' Vanni said. 'We argued all the time after his exorcism. He believed it had driven the illness away for good. But I could see he was wrong and told him so. Cecco didn't want to hear the truth. He refused to listen when I pleaded with him to be careful . . .'

Aldo could hear the gentle sound of tears falling on the stone floor.

'Go on,' he murmured.

'One day we argued so much Cecco stormed out. I went after him, pleading for him to come back . . . The next thing I remember, we were at the top of a stone staircase, shouting at each other. I grabbed his arm but he pulled away. And then – then he was falling . . .'

Vanni wept, and Aldo let her. This was the anguish that had tormented her for a year. This was the guilt that had driven her to such lengths. Eventually the sobs died away, her grief spent for now. 'I know his death was an accident,' she said, 'but I still feel responsible. If I hadn't gone after him, if we hadn't argued . . . my brother might still be alive.'

'Is that why you came here tonight?' Aldo murmured.

'Yes,' she admitted. 'But there's more.'

Strocchi huddled in the shadows with Manuffi, straining to hear what Vanni was saying. An imposing woman with broad shoulders, she certainly possessed all the strength needed to garrotte a man. Yet the way she stood, the sadness in her face . . . none of that had the appearance of a killer. Vanni was confessing something to Aldo, but Strocchi did not believe she was responsible for the murders. Her tears were proof of guilt and regrets.

'What are they saying?' Manuffi whispered.

'I can't tell,' Strocchi replied, keeping his voice to a hush.

'If she was going to attack Aldo, she would have done it by now.'

'I suspect you're right. You know what that means . . .'

Manuffi shuddered. 'Negri is the killer.'

Vanni stopped speaking, glancing at the shadows where they were. Had she heard them? After a moment Vanni turned back to Aldo who was still kneeling in front of the altar.

'Keep your voice quiet,' Strocchi whispered. 'Or say nothing at all, yes?'

Manuffi opened his mouth to reply, but closed it instead and nodded.

Vanni was speaking to Aldo once more.

Strocchi leaned forward to listen.

'I've blamed myself for Cecco's death,' Vanni said, 'but I blamed others more. Negri, for giving my brother false hope. Father Zati, for letting Negri do what he did to my brother, and not having the courage to speak up. The diocese, for denying Negri had any part in what happened to Cecco. The archbishop, for not giving me an audience, no matter how I begged.'

Aldo nodded his agreement. Ordinary working people were certainly beneath the consideration of those who held power in the diocese. If Vanni had been wealthy, she might have bought the audience she craved. Yet Signor Zamora had also been denied, with even his wealth not enough to secure a hearing from the leader of the Church in Florence.

'After I got your letter today, I paid to have a denunzia written,' Vanni said. 'I left it at the diocesan ufficio on my way here. The archbishop and his clerics would not listen to my voice, but perhaps they will read the words and do something about them.'

Aldo got up, turning to face her. 'You paid to have a denunzia written?'

'Yes.'

'You cannot write?'

'No. I've been working since I was a child. I never learned to read or write.'

'When you got my message earlier, how did you . . . ?'

'I had someone read it to me.'

Aldo cursed himself for not realizing sooner. Vanni was a peasant who worked in a tannery; of course she could not read or write. That meant she did not know Latin, and she could not have written in ash on the victims' foreheads . . .

Signora Vanni was not the killer.

'What does this denunzia you took to the diocesan ufficio say?' Aldo asked.

'Terrible things,' she replied. 'I accused Negri of . . . I can't say the words out loud. Not here, not in a church. But the diocese will have to act now. They have no choice.'

'Is that what you want?'

'I . . . I thought it was. I used to believe making Father Zati's life a misery outside San Felice each morning would make mine better. But it didn't. And I'm still so angry.' Her face was full of sadness and bewilderment. 'What should I do?'

Aldo looked around at the church they were standing in. 'Tomorrow is All Souls' Day. When you pray for your brother, also pray for God's forgiveness,' he suggested.

'I will,' she said. 'But what if that isn't enough?'

Aldo considered the heavy wooden cross atop the altar, remembering the good sisters of the convent that had once occupied the buildings behind the church. The nuns had believed in helping others. Perhaps they could do that for Vanni?

'When you are ready,' he said, 'go to a convent and ask if you may assist the nuns. I'm told there is solace in simple acts of kindness and tasks done with no thought of reward.'

'Yes,' Vanni replied. 'I will do that. Grazie. Grazie di cuore.' She shuffled away, still thanking him. Aldo waited until he heard the church door close before putting a hand on the altar for support. Sweat had soaked through his tunic, and both his hands were trembling.

Strocchi and Manuffi stepped from the shadows, their faces anxious. 'What did she say?' Manuffi asked. 'We couldn't hear much of it.'

Aldo told them what Vanni had confessed, how her lack of learning proved she was not the killer.

'That means it was the exorcist who killed Zamora and Freccia,' Strocchi said. 'But will he risk coming here?'

'We'll know in a few hours,' Aldo said.

Strocchi suggested taking turns on watch outside, giving each other a chance to rest. Negri was not due for hours but better to be ready if he came early. Knowing they could be at the church much of the night, Strocchi had brought a small basket of cheese, bread and wine. He shared some of it with Aldo, leaving the rest for Manuffi who was taking first watch.

'Do you think Negri will come?' Strocchi asked between mouthfuls.

'I'm not sure. The exorcist is a proud man who believes what he says and does should be beyond question. The message might goad him into coming.' Aldo shrugged. 'How is Tomasia? I've heard she hasn't been well.'

Strocchi told him about the unhappy pregnancy, and the visit by Mama. It was good to talk about something other than murder or the investigation. But a question that had been itching at Strocchi for the past few days needed to be asked.

'Why do you think Negri writes on his victims' foreheads with ash? Most killings are angry and full of hatred, or about greed or lust. This . . . this is something else.'

Aldo rubbed a hand across his greying stubble. 'The killings themselves are not that strange. A blade or a garrotte, the result is the same. But the way the murderer arranges the bodies, putting ash on the foreheads, cutting tongues in two and pages torn from the exorcism handbook inside his victim's clothes – that's the work of someone who has dwelled with the urge to kill a long time. You're right, this is something else.'

Strocchi smiled. 'You didn't answer my question.'

'A careful man keeps his own counsel.'

'Perhaps, but what's your answer?'

Aldo frowned before replying. 'I suspect this killer believes they have a holy duty. Anyone who stands against that is a threat. They must be stopped in the name of God.'

'*In nomine Patris et Filii et Spiritus Sancti.*'

'Exactly. The killer sees his murders as . . . a sacrament.'

That a man like Negri could live within the Church, could even prosper, troubled Strocchi. Yet when he said this, Aldo laughed.

'You're a good investigator, Carlo, but sometimes I forget how young you still are. This is Florence, not a friendly Tuscan village. Power always preserves power here. Worse still, the more certainty you have that what you are doing is right, the more others are eager to believe in you. Strength of will earns respect, no matter how wrong that will might be.'

Aldo was right, but Strocchi still wanted to believe the best of people and especially of priests. They were servants of God, after all, not of their own ambition. He kept that hope to himself; saying it out loud would only bring another bitter laugh from Aldo.

Strocchi was taking his turn on watch outside when he saw a figure approach Santa Maria Magdalena from the south. The bells had not yet chimed for midnight and it was too dark to make out much more than a shape, but their urgent stride was still evident. Strocchi hurried into the church, giving a low whistle to announce someone was coming. Aldo knelt before the altar, while Strocchi pushed the yawning Manuffi into the shadows of the chancel.

They did not have long to wait.

The main door creaked open, and someone slipped inside. The new arrival did not call out as Vanni had done. Instead, they crept towards Aldo, keeping the sounds of their approach quiet. They were wearing a long cloak, its hood up over their head.

'Who is it?' Manuffi whispered.

Strocchi struggled to see in the dim light. The intruder was not as imposing as Strocchi had expected. But there was something familiar about them . . .

Aldo rose to his feet but continued facing the altar.

'You sent a letter to San Felice saying you knew what I had done,' the intruder replied. 'Was that meant for me or the other priest there?'

Santo Spirito! Strocchi knew that voice, but it couldn't be . . . could it?

Aldo swung round. 'And yet you still came, Father Zati.'

'Zati?' Manuffi murmured. 'But we were waiting for Negri, the exorcist.'

Strocchi put a finger to his lips, urging the constable to silence.

Zati pushed back his hood, revealing an ashen face.

'How did you know I would come?'

'I was at the monastery watching over Father Visconti,' Aldo replied. 'He recovered enough to tell me who attacked him. He could not believe it was you, but he saw your face.'

'Santo Spirito,' Strocchi whispered. Why hadn't Aldo told him this earlier? No, that was a question that must wait until later.

'I feared Father Visconti had seen me,' Zati admitted to Aldo.

Strocchi stepped from the shadows, Manuffi close behind. 'Father Visconti was your friend, you told me he was counselling you. Why try to kill him? Had you told him about your other victims? Did you fear he was going to reveal what you'd done?'

'Other victims?' Zati shook his head. 'I've killed no one. I could never . . . Never.'

'Stop lying, Father,' Manuffi urged. 'Don't add that to your sins.'

'My sins?' Zati turned to Aldo. 'What is he talking about?'

Aldo studied Zati. The priest was pale, the bitter tang of his body odour overwhelming the church's stale incense. He bore the look of a man who had not known sleep in days. Zati's distress was evident, but would it be enough to bring out the truth at last?

'Confession is good for the soul,' Aldo said, 'isn't that what men like you always preach? Admit your guilt and perhaps we can help. It's the only hope for redemption. You should know that better than any of us.'

Zati's legs gave way and he sank to the floor. 'God in heaven, forgive me.'

Strocchi and Manuffi moved to help but Aldo waved them back. He advanced on Zati until he was standing over the priest. 'God may absolve you, but the Otto di Guardia e Balia is far less forgiving. Tell us what you did.'

Zati stared, his eyes wide. 'It was Negri. It was all Father Negri.'

The answer gave Aldo no satisfaction, despite confirming his suspicions. 'Manuffi, go outside and keep watch. We may have another visitor soon.' As Manuffi departed, Aldo gestured Strocchi closer. 'Carlo, help me get this one up.' Together they pulled Zati to his feet, guiding him to a wooden bench beneath a stained-glass window.

'I should've spoken up sooner,' Zati whispered. 'If I had, perhaps those poor souls . . .'

'Why didn't you?' Strocchi asked. 'I gave you the chance, so did Aldo.'

'I wanted to, and yet—'

'You were afraid,' Aldo said.

Zati nodded. 'Negri threatened me. He promised to tell others all the lustful desires I had admitted to him during confession. At first, I did not believe he would breach that holy trust. But when I heard what happened to Signor Zamora . . .'

'You knew it was Negri.' Strocchi scowled. 'You've known all this time, and said nothing?'

'I couldn't be certain,' Zati insisted, 'not at first. I considered sharing my fears with Monsignor Testardo.' Zati looked at Aldo. 'You know him, he led the visitation to the Convent of Santa Maria Magdalena with which we were both involved. But the monsignor had always blamed me for what happened to poor Signor Cortese inside the convent . . .'

Aldo could see confusion on Strocchi's face. 'Cortese was a lay member of the visitation. He burst in on one of the nuns and she wounded him with a knife. Monsignor Testardo was away from the convent when it happened.'

'It was the monsignor who had me moved to San Felice after Signor Cortese died,' Zati continued, 'as punishment. Monsignor Testardo was the one who made me Father Negri's assistant; I couldn't be sure he would believe me. So, I came here instead to share my fears with Father Visconti, but still the words would not come.' He put a hand to his throat. 'It was as if the truth was caught inside me, and I could not speak it aloud.'

'Tell that to the men Negri garrotted,' Strocchi muttered.

Aldo caught Strocchi's eye, mouthing the word 'no'. There would be time for anger later. Getting the truth from Zati mattered more now.

'I know,' Zati said, close to tears. 'Believe me, I know. I prayed so long for guidance but none came. And then I heard of a second murder . . .'

'Did you confront Negri with your suspicions?' Aldo asked.

A shake of the head. 'I was too much of a coward. But last night he stopped me as I was leaving San Felice. Said if I did something for him, he would keep my secret.'

'He told you to attack Father Visconti.'

'Yes.'

'Why?'

'Father Visconti approached clerics within the diocesan ufficio, asking questions and suggesting Negri be moved to another role. Negri wanted me to punish him for that.'

'How? What did he tell you to do?' Aldo asked. They needed details Negri could not refute to have any hope of making the exorcist face justice.

'He gave me a page from his handbook to put inside Father Visconti's cassock, and a small pouch of ash to write a word on his forehead.'

'*Filii*,' Strocchi said.

Zati nodded.

'Why that word?' Aldo asked.

'I'd told him Father Visconti reminded me of my papa, rest his soul. Negri said that made me Visconti's son, so I should write *Filii* on his forehead as penance for my weakness.'

'What else?' Aldo urged.

'He gave me his beaded belt, told me to pull it tight round Father Visconti's neck.'

'What does this belt look like?'

'It's a thick cord strung with wooden beads as a rosary. Negri wears it during every exorcism. He says it keeps him close to God, helps to purge the diavolo.'

That matched the markings the killer's garrotte had left around the necks of Zamora and Freccia. If the pouch of ash and the belt could be secured . . .

'Do you still have them?' Strocchi asked before Aldo could.

Zati shook his head. 'I couldn't do what Negri wanted. That's why I told Marsilio to come here early, knowing he would interrupt me. When he did, I fled to San Felice and told Negri what had happened. He took back his belt, the ash and the page from his handbook before banishing me from his sight. I returned to San Felice later and found the letter you sent—'

Manuffi burst in through the church's main door. 'Someone's coming!' the constable hissed. Bells chimed in the distance; midnight was upon them.

Aldo resisted the urge to curse. 'Manuffi, get Father Zati out of here. Escort him to the Podestà. We'll meet you there later.'

'I can't take him out of the main door. We'll be seen leaving.'

'We can go through the sacristy,' Zati said. 'That's where I went this morning.'

'Go to the Podestà with Manuffi,' Strocchi told the priest. 'You need to make a denunzia about what Negri made you do. That will help us build a case against him.'

'But he will deny it—' Zati began.

'Carlo's right,' Aldo cut in. 'Your denunzia alone is not enough to convict him, but it gives us a way to bring the truth into the light. Now, go. Go!'

Strocchi returned to the shadows at the side of the chancel, watching Aldo kneel in front of the altar. Negri would arrive soon, yet the waiting seemed unending. Strocchi dreaded these moments, the intake of breath before a blow. No matter what happened, there would be pain.

A few days ago, he would never have believed a priest could be a killer. The Church was a place of refuge and solace, a comfort to those suffering and a joy to those held in its embrace. Yes, in Florence it was different to what he'd known in Ponte a Signa. Here the diocese favoured displays of wealth, houses of God full of marble and gold. Yet the Church remained at the heart of most citizens' lives even if trade and banking was in their blood.

But the actions of Negri had broken that belief. He had taken two lives in ways that defied sense. Why arrange their bodies to resemble Christ on the cross, why cut their tongues in two and write on them with ash? Perhaps Aldo was right and Negri believed the murders were a sacrament. All Strocchi could see were the tortured faces of Zamora and Freccia, the torment left for those who cared about them. That could never be forgotten, nor forgiven.

The church's main door opened and Negri stalked into Santa Maria Magdalena. The exorcist had a satchel, its strap slung across his chest. There was none of the fear or hesitancy Vanni or Zati had brought with them. Negri wore no cloak, made no attempt to hide his face.

Strocchi braced himself for what was to come.

The exorcist had arrived.

Chapter Twenty-eight

*A*ldo stood in front of the altar, facing away from Negri. Would the exorcist attack him, or seek answers? Aldo pressed both hands together in front of his throat, as if praying. That should stop Negri easily applying the garrotte and give Strocchi time to intervene.

Hopefully.

'What is the meaning of this note?' the exorcist demanded.

Aldo breathed out; Negri wanted answers. That didn't mean he wouldn't attack, but it offered a chance to get some of the truth from him first.

'It says you know what I did,' Negri went on. 'What do you claim I've done?' He waited but Aldo gave no reply. 'If you want payment, I have nothing to give.'

'I have no interest in your coin,' Aldo said, turning to face Negri. 'But the fact you came here tonight proves you have something to hide.'

Hatred twisted Negri's face. 'You.'

Aldo bowed a little. 'At your service, Father.'

Negri twisted on his heels and strode away, back towards the church door.

'Don't you want the answers to your questions?' Aldo called.

The exorcist stopped. 'You have no answers, and no proof. Only accusations.'

'Wrong. I have a witness, someone who knows the truth about you.'

Negri glared over his shoulder at Aldo. 'Who?'

Revealing that was a risky stratagemma, but Negri's assistant was safely on his way to the Podestà. 'Zati told us how you made him come here to silence Father Visconti.'

'I did no such thing,' Negri hissed.

'Zati couldn't go through with it, so he made sure he was interrupted—'

'Lies, all of this. Lies.'

'We know your beaded belt was used to garrotte Zamora and Freccia,' Aldo continued, strolling towards the exorcist. 'Pages from your handbook were hidden in each man's clothes.'

Negri shook his head. 'I told the officer who came to San Felice, those were stolen from me, from my possession. I had nothing to do with how they were used.'

'You only told Strocchi about the handbook's theft, not the beaded belt. Why omit that, Father? Were you ashamed of its loss? Or were you trying to hide your crimes?'

'You don't understand what you're talking about.'

'Help me understand. Tell me why you did this.'

'No.' The exorcist clenched both fists at his sides.

'Tell me why you wrote Latin words on your victims' foreheads with ash.'

'No.' A vein was throbbing in Negri's forehead.

'Tell me why you cut their tongues in two.'

'No,' Negri snapped, his face crimson.

'Tell me why, Father,' Aldo sneered.

'No!'

'Tell me!'

Negri lunged forward, his hands raised, clutching and grasping.

Aldo stumbled back, trying not to lose his footing.

Negri kept coming, snarling and roaring.

'Strocchi!' Aldo called out. 'Help—'

Then Negri was on top of him and they were tumbling over.

Aldo's back slammed into the cold stone floor, forcing the air from him.

Negri clamped his powerful hands round Aldo's neck, squeezing, clenching.

A shadow burst from the chancel, rushing towards them.

The exorcist flung out a leg, kicking at Strocchi.

Aldo twisted his head to one side.

Strocchi was staggering back, gasping.

Negri tightened his grip on Aldo's neck.

'I warned you to stay away,' the exorcist spat at him.

Aldo flailed at Negri, but to no effect.

'I warned you to leave me in peace!'

Aldo shoved a thumb into Negri's face, finding an eye.

He pushed.

Hard.

Negri screamed, rearing backwards.

A shadow passed over Aldo.

A dull thud filled the air.

Negri cried out, falling sideways.

His hands slipped from Aldo's throat.

The exorcist slumped across the stone floor.

Aldo gasped in air, coughing and choking.

He pulled himself out from beneath Negri's legs.

The exorcist lay prone, not moving.

Strocchi was standing close by, the wooden cross from atop the altar in his grasp.

'Is he . . . ?' Strocchi asked, staring at Negri's body.

The exorcist did not move.

He did not move.

At last, Negri gave a groan of pain.

Strocchi slumped back against the altar.

'Grazie,' Aldo croaked, his voice a harsh rasp.

'Prego,' Strocchi replied.

Aldo managed a weak smile. 'What took you so long?'

Aldo found the beaded belt inside the satchel and used it to bind Negri's wrists behind his back. It needed both Strocchi and Aldo to move the exorcist. They sat Negri with his back against the altar. When his senses returned, Negri demanded they release him.

'You tried to strangle me,' Aldo said, rubbing a hand across his neck where Negri's powerful hands had been. The skin would have a livid bruise by morning, and his voice was a husky rasp. 'You would have killed me but for Strocchi intervening.'

'I lost control,' Negri said, shaking his head. 'But I would have stopped. What I did was a warning, nothing more.'

'Did you mean to stop with Zamora?' Strocchi asked. 'With your son, Freccia?'

'I admit nothing. You are not my confessor.'

'What about the beaded belt I found in your satchel? That's what was used to murder them. You said before it was stolen. If you didn't kill those men, why do you have that belt?'

'I found it at Father Zati's lodgings on my way here,' the exorcist replied. 'I went to confront him, but he wasn't there.'

Aldo's hollow laugh became a coughing fit. He nodded at Strocchi to question Negri.

'You're claiming Zati is the person responsible for the murders?'

'Yes. When we were alone together, he often talked about the murders. He never confessed to committing them, not out loud, but he was obsessed with them. He kept wanting to tell me the details, things he could not have known unless . . .'

'Unless he was the killer?'

Negri nodded. 'It was as if Father Zati was a different person.'

'Why didn't you tell anyone?' Strocchi asked. 'You had plenty of chances, and doing so might have saved Freccia's life.'

Negri shook his head. 'I should have, but I couldn't be certain it was the truth. Only when you came to San Felice and said the killer was putting pages from my handbook inside their victim's clothes did I know for certain that Zati was responsible.'

'But you tried to make me believe your son had stolen the handbook.'

'I needed to protect San Felice from what Zati had done. I urged him to go to the diocese and make his confession to the archbishop. I could do no more, not without risking everything I have spent years building.'

'Until tonight,' Aldo said.

Anger darkened Negri's face. 'You will find the handbook Zati stole from me under his mattress at his lodgings. That will prove I am telling the truth.'

'You could have put it there,' Strocchi said, 'to incriminate him.'

'You fool,' Negri snapped. 'Can't you see the truth? Zati is the killer. I'm guilty of nothing more than trying to save him from himself. If what he had done became known, the diocese would be forced to shut the doors of San Felice. All my good work—'

'Enough!' Aldo snapped, swallowing hard to keep from coughing. 'Enough. We've heard enough of your lies and justifications. You can spend what's left of the night in a cell at the Podestà. Tomorrow is All Souls' Day, the feast to remember those who have died. Maybe then you'll be willing to speak the truth.'

'I am telling you the truth—'

'He said enough,' Strocchi insisted. He pulled the exorcist up. Aldo gathered the satchel before leading Negri to the main door.

'I'm innocent,' he insisted. 'Why would I murder Zamora? Yes, he was a stone in my shoe after we exorcized his nephew, but Zati told me Marsilio is alive.'

'Keep walking,' Aldo said.

'Freccia was my son, why would I kill my own son?' Negri asked.

'Because he was extorting coin from you,' Strocchi replied.

'I was giving him that freely—'

'Quiet,' Aldo hissed as Strocchi opened the door. 'Good people live along these streets and they're trying to sleep.'

Negri did as he was told until they were approaching the Podestà. The exorcist began protesting his innocence again, demanding an immediate meeting with the segretario.

'Signor Bindi will not get out of bed during curfew,' Aldo replied, pushing Negri in the back to keep him moving. 'Dragging him here now would not do you any good – quite the opposite, in fact. You can ask again in the morning.'

Manuffi and Father Zati were waiting in the courtyard as Aldo and Strocchi brought Negri in. 'What's he doing here?' the exorcist demanded.

'He's admitted attacking Father Visconti,' Strocchi replied, 'on your orders.'

'He's lying,' Negri insisted.

Aldo opened a door to one of the dark stone cells at the edge of the courtyard. The stench of stale piss and merda billowed outwards, catching in his throat and making him cough. 'Why isn't Zati in a cell?'

'Should he be?' Manuffi asked.

'Yes,' Strocchi replied. 'He admitted attacking Father Visconti.

That's a serious crime, even if there was no intention to kill. Put him in the cell next to Negri.'

Aldo untied the beaded cord from the exorcist's wrists before pushing him into the cell. 'Please, no, you mustn't do this,' Negri protested. Aldo pulled the door shut, ramming home the bolt to secure it. Negri kept begging to be heard, but his words became a whimper, as if he was close to tears. 'If you don't believe me, ask the mother of my boy. She will tell you why I can't have killed Freccia or Zamora!'

'Who is she?' Aldo asked.

Negri whispered a name.

Aldo stepped back. No, that couldn't be true . . .

Strocchi and Manuffi led Zati into the next cell, promising he would be let out in the morning to account for his actions. The younger priest went in willingly, praying as he did.

Once his cell was bolted shut, Strocchi told Aldo and Manuffi to go home. 'It'll be morning soon enough. We all need rest before facing the segretario.' Manuffi ambled away, leaving Strocchi and Aldo in the courtyard. 'What was Negri saying after you shut the door on him?' Strocchi asked.

'More wild claims and accusations,' Aldo replied. 'We can talk about it tomorrow.'

Strocchi nodded. He strolled out of the Podestà alongside Aldo. 'Why didn't you tell me Father Visconti had said Zati was the one who attacked him?'

'Didn't I?'

Strocchi shook his head.

'I meant to,' Aldo said. 'But when I came into the church from the monastery you and Manuffi wanted to abandon the plan. Then Signora Vanni arrived and . . . I forgot. Sorry.'

They stopped outside the main gates. Strocchi had a rueful

smile on his face. 'When you told Bindi we could bring him the killer so soon, I never thought it would work.'

'Sorry, Carlo. I should never have put you in that position.'

'Well, don't do it again.'

'I won't. I promise.'

'Someone once told me never to make a promise you can't keep,' Strocchi said.

'They sound a wise person. You should take their advice.' Aldo clapped a hand on Strocchi's shoulder. 'Buona notte, Carlo.'

'Buona notte.' Strocchi headed north and Aldo turned south. It was far too late to wake Saul, better to go back to the bordello. The investigation was done, but now they had to confront the consequences of what had been uncovered.

Knowing Bindi and the archbishop, someone would suffer for that.

Chapter Twenty-nine

Sunday, November 2nd 1539

*A*ldo woke early, despite having slumped into his bed at the bordello long after midnight. A little light was seeping through the shutters, the inky blackness of night gradually giving way to the first hints of blue. Aldo got up and emptied his bladder, taking care not to make too much noise. Signora Robustelli and her women were always busiest on feast days which brought sinners flocking to the humble building on Piazza della Passera. Having All Saints' Day followed immediately by All Souls' Day meant the bordello would know little rest.

He considered going back to bed, but fresh thoughts were jousting for his attention. The *stratagemma* of the previous day had been a success. Aldo had hoped one person might come to Santa Maria Magdalena, two at the most. Having Vanni, Zati and Negri respond was more than he'd expected. The truth had finally been forced into the light.

Or so it had seemed last night . . .

Now Aldo wasn't so certain.

Vanni's testimony had been honest, he was sure of that. She spoke from the heart, admitting her guilt about the death of her brother. Vanni's presence in the investigation had been a stone thrown into a stream so they could not see the truth clearly. But she could now be set aside, her part in things a distraction that no longer needed any attention.

Zati's words had seemed equally credible when he'd spoken them in the church. His fear of the exorcist was all too believable, explaining why he had attempted to kill Father Visconti. There could be no denying it after the bewildered Visconti had named his attacker. The claim that Zati had acted on orders from Negri matched Aldo's suspicions that the exorcist was a man of absolute belief who would stop at nothing to get his way. It was confirmed by Negri's subsequent arrival, the brutality with which he had attacked Aldo, the snarling hatred in his face. Aldo rubbed a hand across his neck, wincing at how tender it was. There were probably bruises, too.

So, Negri was the killer.

And yet . . .

His denials had been as absolute as his belief in the power of exorcism. Negri was convinced of his own innocence, despite what he had tried to do in the church, and despite having the beaded belt used to kill Zamora and Freccia. Nonetheless, Negri was vehement in his utter repudiation of being the one who'd killed Zamora and Freccia.

Could he be telling the truth?

Aldo did not want to believe it.

He despised Negri. The exorcist represented all the worst aspects of the Church. The way Negri treated those who were different, those who did not meet his vision of what a good follower of Christ should be. The way Negri used position and authority to impose his will, his morality on others. The way he refused to listen to reason or argument, the fact that nothing anybody else said could alter his obdurate mind.

Men like Negri were the reason Aldo had not sought the solace of a church or the mercy of God's forgiveness in twenty years. He could not recall the last time he had confessed his sins, or taken Holy Communion. He could not remember the last time he still believed as Strocchi did. Aldo had seen too much to have faith in anything but caution, a blade and the few people he trusted.

Negri made it impossible to accept his claims of innocence.

And yet . . .

Aldo glanced at the shutters above his bed. The sky was the colour of a mottled bruise, reclaiming what night had stolen away. Florence was stirring from its slumber to face All Souls' Day, when the faithful prayed for those they had lost to death.

Archbishop Buondelmonti would want this matter settled at once. No scandal could be left to sully the feast day, no whispers of murderous priests and unholy practices should be allowed to fester among the faithful. When word of Zati and Negri being held at the Podestà reached the diocesan ufficio, there would be a swift and merciless response. Their release would be demanded, and Bindi would cravenly give in, as he always did.

Once the diocese intervened there was no chance of either man standing trial, not that there had ever been much hope of it. But uncovering the truth mattered, even if the law could not bring the priests to justice. Aldo needed to know.

He needed to be certain.

Strocchi had arrived at the Podestà as bells chimed to announce the end of curfew. He'd wanted – no, he needed – to be there when the segretario waddled into the courtyard, demanding a report on the number of suspects in the cells. Those convicted by the Otto were moved to Le Stinche to commence their imprisonment the same day as sentence was determined. This meant Bindi always knew how many suspects were within the walls of

the Podestà. If that number changed, it indicated an arrest had
been made during the night.

The presence of two priests would not go unnoticed.

The fact that one of them was a man Bindi had forbidden
Strocchi and Aldo from even approaching . . . that was grounds
for an immediate dismissal.

Unless Strocchi could convince the segretario otherwise.

A quick check of the cells confirmed each suspect was still
inside and still alive. Desperate men had taken their own lives at
the Podestà before, unable to face what was to come. Fortunately,
Zati and Negri were as Strocchi had left them. The younger priest
simply stared when asked a question, while the exorcist demanded
his immediate release. How he could maintain his innocence when
the evidence was so overwhelming defied sense.

Nearby guards snapped upright, their lethargy banished.

Bindi was coming.

Strocchi strode to the courtyard entrance to meet the segretario
as he arrived. Bindi's face was as sour as spoiled milk when Strocchi
greeted him. 'Yes? What do you want?'

'There are two new suspects in the cells.'

'Brought in by the night patrols? Good, good. Reassuring to
know Benedetto and the others are still capable of doing their
jobs without Aldo's presence.' The segretario pushed past Strocchi,
stamping towards the wide stone staircase leading up to the administrative level.

'No, segretario. It was Aldo and I who arrested these suspects,'
Strocchi volunteered.

'Indeed? Does that mean you have fulfilled Aldo's boast and
brought the killer in to stand trial? Or should I say killers? You
mentioned two suspects, did you not?'

'Yes.'

Bindi glared at him.

'Yes, sir.'

The segretario gave a satisfied nod. 'Very well. Come up and give me a full report on them. I must present my briefing to the duke soon, and he shall want to know everything.'

'Very good, sir.' Strocchi glanced over his shoulder. He had expected Aldo to be here for Bindi's arrival, knowing how the segretario would respond to hearing the names of those they had arrested. Aldo would not leave him to face Bindi alone . . . would he?

Aldo strode into the salone at Palazzo Zamora, ignoring the protests of the maggiordomo. A woman sat in the weak autumn light seeping between two shutters, embroidering leaves on a circle of cloth. Aldo had not met her before, but she matched the description Strocchi gave for Signora Tullia Juvara: kind-faced, close to forty, with dark hair worn in a plait atop her head. The widow looked up from her needlework, surprised by his presence.

'Buon giorno,' she said. 'I did not realize we were expecting visitors.'

'This constable pushed his way in—' Querini began.

'Forgive my unannounced arrival, signora,' Aldo said before introducing himself.

'Your name is Cesare Aldo?' Juvara asked.

'Yes, signora.'

'I must thank you for helping to restore my son Marsilio to this famiglia, to his home. He came here yesterday at your urging, I understand.'

'Prego,' Aldo replied. 'It was my colleague with the Otto who urged Marsilio to return to you, but I helped in my own way.'

'Then you both have my gratitude,' she said.

'I have an urgent question I must ask. The lives of two men depend on your answer.'

Juvara frowned. 'You may ask your question, though I do not know how I can assist the court.' She looked past Aldo. 'Querini, you may go. I will call if you are required.'

The maggiordomo withdrew, scowling as he closed the doors on his way out. Aldo had little doubt Querini would be lurking outside the salone, straining to hear what was said.

Juvara set down her embroidery. 'Well, how is it that I can help?'

Aldo expressed his sympathies for the loss of her brother. 'You may be aware that another man was killed the day after Signor Zamora, the body left in Piazza Santo Spirito.'

'Querini made some mention of that, I believe. All my thoughts have been with poor Niccolò, and caring for my children. We have lost so much already . . .'

'The dead man was about twenty-two. His name was Freccia. Does that mean anything to you?'

Juvara shook her head, no sign of deception in her face. 'I'm sorry, should it?'

'I believe you know the dead man's papa.' Aldo lowered his voice so Querini would not hear. 'His name is Father Negri.'

Juvara flinched. 'Father Negri? The exorcist?'

'One and the same. It seems he sired a son some years ago. The mama was unable to keep the bambino and he was taken to an orphanage. But the boy had a difficult life, never finding a famiglia to care for him. He took to crime and other vices to survive, adopting the name Freccia. It's not clear how, but in recent months he was reunited with his papa. Father Negri gave him coin, either from guilt or to keep their secret safe.'

Juvara stiffened. 'Why are you telling me this? You said there was a question I might be able to answer. Ask your question and go, or else I shall have to call Querini.'

'Last night Father Negri was arrested for the murders of your brother and Freccia, but he is protesting his innocence. When I asked for proof, he told me to ask Freccia's mother. Negri said she would bear witness that he couldn't have killed Freccia.'

'You should leave now,' Juvara said, her face tightening.

Aldo picked up a chair and carried it to the salone door. He pressed the chair against the door and sat on it. 'Father Negri told me you were Freccia's mama. Is that true?'

'What are you doing?' Juvara asked before calling out, 'Querini, I have need of you.'

No sooner had the words left her mouth than the door behind Aldo pushed inwards. He leaned back against it, using the chair and his weight to stop anyone entering. 'Tell me, Signora Juvara – are you Freccia's mama?'

'Querini! This intruder has blocked the door. You'll have to force your way in!'

'Negri was telling the truth, wasn't he? You wouldn't respond this way if it wasn't so.' A heavy weight slammed against the door, but Aldo kept his place. 'I'm guessing it was before you were married. Having a bambino out of wedlock would have been quite the scandal, so you gave the child away. Was Negri already a priest? Was that how you met?'

'Querini!' she called. The maggiordomo shouted back, vowing to get inside.

'What happened that long ago doesn't matter to me, but it did to someone else. Negri came to you, didn't he? Told you that Freccia had found him, was asking questions.'

Juvara shook her head, but tears were brimming in her eyes.

'He did, didn't he?' Aldo demanded, bracing his back against the door as more voices joined Querini outside. They would be through in moments. 'Tell me!'

'Yes!' she shouted back, rising to her feet. 'Yes, he did . . .' She sank back down on the chair, shaking her head. 'My little bambino . . . my first-born . . .'

'What did you do, Signora Juvara?'

She stared at Aldo.

Strocchi delayed going to the segretario's ufficio for as long as he dared, lurking out of sight in the courtyard while waiting for Aldo. Eventually Bindi lost patience and sent one of his assistants to fetch Strocchi. He followed them up the stone steps, trying and failing to devise some stratagemma that would soothe the segretario's inevitable anger. But there was nothing to be done, and nothing that could be said to stop the coming fury.

For once, Bindi chose not to make Strocchi wait for permission to enter; that did not inspire confidence. Nor did the scowl on his face, resembling a dog trying to chew wasps. 'Well?' Bindi snapped as Strocchi came in. 'What do you have to say for yourself?'

'Apologies, segretario. I was waiting for Aldo to—'

'I've no need of him to hear your report.'

'No, sir, but I—'

'Enough excuses. Tell me about the two priests in my cells.'

Ahh. So, Bindi already knew about them. That made sense, Podestà guards were often eager to share gossip with their administrators in the hope of securing a reward.

'What are their names?' the segretario asked, sifting papers atop his table.

'Father Pagolo Zati,' Strocchi replied. He was finding it difficult to swallow.

'And?'

'Father Camillo Negri.'

'Negri?' Bindi abandoned his papers. 'You have arrested the exorcist and brought him here after I expressly ordered you to stay away from him and the Church of San Felice?'

'Yes, sir.'

'This other priest, what was his name?'

'Zati.'

'And is he also from San Felice?'

Strocchi nodded. 'He is Father Negri's assistant.'

'Have you lost your senses?' Bindi demanded. Strocchi didn't know how to reply but it didn't matter. The segretario had more than enough words for both of them.

Having got what he needed at Palazzo Zamora, Aldo hurried north across the river. He should have been at the Podestà to help Strocchi explain why there were two priests in the cells. No doubt Bindi was humiliating Strocchi, hurling scorn at the officer for daring to go against one of his edicts. But there was one more person Aldo had to see before presenting his evidence.

Fortune was smiling on Aldo this morning. As he neared the diocesan ufficio, he saw Monsignor Testardo approaching the entrance from the north. Testardo remained as severe as Aldo recalled from the brief time they'd both spent at the Convent of Santa Maria Magdalena. The cleric still had a sharpness to his gaze, but the hair slicked back beneath his zucchetto was now silver rather than grey.

'Monsignor!' Aldo called, quickening his pace to catch Testardo.

The cleric paused, peering at him. 'Aldo, isn't it? From the Otto.'
Testardo's eyes narrowed. 'What do you want?'

'I need to talk with you about the priests at San Felice.'

Testardo scowled. 'Then you'd best come inside.'

'What we must discuss can be said on our way, if you'll come with me.'

As Aldo ushered Monsignor Testardo up the wide stone stairs inside the Podestà he could hear Bindi's ranting from the administrative level above. 'Do you know what the archbishop will do when he hears of this? And how am I supposed to explain your foolish stupidity to the duke? He and Buondelmonti have been arguing with each other for months!'

'Both priests admitted to committing a crime,' Strocchi replied in a much quieter voice. 'Father Negri attempted to strangle Aldo—'

'We've all wanted to do that,' Bindi said as Aldo led Testardo to the segretario's ufficio. The door was ajar, the voice of Bindi booming out from within.

'Nonetheless,' Strocchi persisted, 'we have reason to believe—'

'It does not matter what you believe,' Bindi snapped.

'It only matters what you can prove,' Aldo agreed as he strolled into the ufficio. 'So you will be delighted, sir, that I have brought proof of whom was responsible for the murders of Niccolò Zamora and the thief Freccia.'

'How dare you come into my ufficio unannounced,' Bindi snarled. 'You know you must always knock before—' But his blustering words died as Testardo followed Aldo in. 'Welcome, monsignor,' Bindi managed to say, rising a little to bow to Testardo.

'What took you so long?' Strocchi whispered out of the side of his mouth.

'Let's just say I've been busy,' Aldo replied.

Bindi sank back into his chair. 'Am I to understand that this constable has had the temerity to summon you to the Podestà?'

'That is correct,' Testardo said. 'I've dealt with Aldo before. He is an irksome, self-satisfied creature, but he also has a talent for finding truth that others prefer to ignore.'

Aldo suppressed a smile. That qualified as praise from Testardo. The monsignor was an officious, dismissive man but also unflinchingly honest, something that could not always be said of those close to the archbishop. Having Testardo present should ensure the truth came out. The killer would never admit what he had done without a church authority present.

'Grazie,' Aldo said to Testardo. 'Segretario, may I make a suggestion?'

Normally such a request would be dismissed, but the monsignor's presence obliged Bindi to be more accommodating. 'You may,' the segretario replied through thin lips.

'To bring the truth out, it might be wise to have Fathers Negri and Zati brought up from the cells.' That got Testardo's attention.

'You've arrested them?' The monsignor glared at Bindi. 'Was this your idea?'

'Far from it,' the segretario replied. 'I ordered my men to stay away from San Felice.'

'We did not go to San Felice,' Strocchi said. 'Both men came to us.'

'And you are?' Testardo asked.

'His name is Carlo Strocchi,' Bindi said, 'and he is the court's youngest officer. Far too easily led for his own good. I doubt he will retain his rank much longer.'

'Be that as it may, this ufficio is too small . . .' The monsignor's face curdled as he inhaled the ripe body odour given off by Bindi –

'and too confined for our task. Do you have a larger chamber where we might go?'

'The great hall, across the loggia on this level,' Bindi said. 'That's where the magistrates of the Otto hear evidence and pass judgement on those accused.'

'It sounds an appropriate place,' Testardo agreed. 'Let us go there. Now.'

Aldo waited until the monsignor had swept from the ufficio, Bindi waddling after him, before giving a sealed document he had obtained from Signora Juvara to Strocchi. 'Take this. Manuffi is waiting in the courtyard. He and I will bring the priests up.'

Strocchi grabbed Aldo's arm. 'What are you doing?'

'Have I ever led you astray before?'

'Frequently.'

'Then you should be used to it by now,' Aldo said with a smile.

'This isn't funny.'

'Trust me, Carlo.'

When Aldo and Manuffi marched the two shackled priests into the great hall, Bindi and Testardo were already seated behind the long table used by the Otto's magistrates. After Aldo's time in the Tuscan countryside and many months spent on night patrols, it was nearly three years since he had last been in the huge chamber. The tall stone walls and high vaulted ceiling were as impressive as ever, but this was no time to appreciate them.

Zati had remained silent while they brought him from the cells, but Negri complained bitterly about pain from where Strocchi had struck him the previous night. The exorcist demanded to be freed from the shackles round his wrists. Negri's protests finally stopped when he saw the monsignor. 'Praise God you're here,' Negri said, approaching Testardo.

Aldo pulled him back. 'Stand still. You have questions to answer.'

'But I—'

'Do as he says,' Testardo commanded before nodding for Bindi to proceed.

'Neither of the prisoners is permitted to speak until given permission by this hearing,' Bindi announced. 'Strocchi, please tell the monsignor about your investigation. But make the report brief. We are both busy men and do not have all day.'

The young officer gave a brisk summary of the two murders; how Zamora and Freccia were garrotted and their bodies posed

343

like Christ on the cross, their tongues cut in two, with ash on their foreheads and a page from the exorcist's handbook inside their clothes. He noted the distinctive red line round their necks made by the killer using a thick beaded cord as a garrotte, and spoke of the links between both victims and the priests of San Felice.

'Was there not another murder?' Testardo asked. 'I heard talk of a body being found close to the Church of Santa Maria Magdalena.'

'Correct, monsignor,' Strocchi said. 'A Venetian called Tito Grossolano. His attacker made it seem as if the same killer was responsible, but there were many differences between Grossolano's corpse and those of the earlier victims. Our investigation into that matter led to another Venetian called . . .' He trailed off, glancing at Aldo.

'Gonzalo Zilio,' Aldo said. 'He had already fled the city when his involvement was uncovered. Zilio was convicted by the Otto for killing Grossolano.'

'The court has issued a warrant for Zilio's immediate arrest,' Bindi added, 'should he be foolish enough to return to Florence.'

Testardo gestured at Strocchi to continue. Aldo noted that the monsignor had been following the investigations. That was not a surprise; over the years, the monsignor had intervened with the Otto in matters concerning the diocese. It was part of his duties to ensure the Church maintained its jurisdiction over criminal matters that involved priests, nuns and properties owned by the diocese. But Testardo's stern face gave no hint of how he might respond when the truth was revealed.

Strocchi described the failed attack on Father Visconti the previous morning, and how their suspects had been lured to Santa Maria Magdalena after curfew. 'The first to come was Signora Vanni. She was questioned but dismissed as the killer, so we—'

'Why?' This time the interruption came from Bindi. 'Why was she a suspect and, more to the point, why did you dismiss her from suspicion?'

'Vanni's brother Cecco died soon after being exorcized at San Felice,' Aldo replied. 'She blamed Negri and Zati for that, and has hounded them – Father Zati especially – ever since. Vanni has the strength of a killer, but not the will. She is neither able to read nor write, whereas the killer wrote Latin words on his victims' foreheads – something that is quite beyond her. We were convinced of her innocence.'

Testardo leaned forward in his chair. 'A letter was delivered to the diocesan ufficio yesterday from a Signora Vanni, accusing both these priests of immoral behaviour and worse. That was one of the reasons I agreed to come, to determine if her claims had any truth.'

'Vanni had those letters written for her,' Strocchi said. 'She has since recanted her accusations. The signora is seeking forgiveness from the Church for bearing false witness.'

'Very good,' the monsignor said.

Strocchi continued his report: how Zati had come to Santa Maria Magdalena long after curfew; that he had admitted attacking Father Visconti, but said this was on orders from Negri. Strocchi described how Negri had entered the church soon after and attacked Aldo when accused of the killings. The exorcist had brought with him the same thick beaded cord that had been used to garrotte Zamora and Freccia. 'Negri claimed Zati was responsible for both murders and the attack on Father Visconti,' Strocchi said, 'but offered no evidence to support this.'

Aldo saw Negri bristling during Strocchi's report, but that final statement was too much for the exorcist. 'I should not need to provide evidence,' he snarled. 'I have spoken only the truth in all my dealings with the court's representatives. Monsignor Testardo knows better than anyone all the things I have done for the Church. It was Father Zati who stole my handbook, and Father Zati who used my rosary belt to kill those men – not I.'

'Enough!' Bindi thundered. 'You were warned at the start of these proceedings to stay silent unless permitted to speak. Obey that instruction or you shall be taken back to the cells and your fate decided in your absence. Is that clear?'

Negri's face soured, but he gave a curt nod.

Bindi jabbed a finger at Zati. 'That warning applies to you too.'

The younger priest remained silent, his face pale.

'Is there anything further to report?' Testardo asked.

Strocchi shook his head.

Aldo cleared his throat, making Strocchi look round. Aldo pointed at the sealed document, still clutched in Strocchi's hand. 'There is one more thing—'

'No, we've heard quite enough,' Bindi interjected. 'Monsignor Testardo, I suggest we withdraw to discuss this unfortunate matter. Better it be resolved quickly and quietly, yes?'

Aldo watched Bindi lead Testardo to the far end of the great hall. This was typical of the segretario. Far easier to reach a private agreement without others present or any written record of what was said. That way there was no evidence to be used against him if problems arose, and silencing a scandal for the Church made an ally of Testardo.

Aldo pulled Strocchi aside while Manuffi kept watch on the two priests. 'Why didn't you show them Signora Tullia's testimony?'

'I don't know what it says. Only a fool presents evidence he hasn't read.'

It was a fair point. After ensuring Bindi and Testardo were still busy and too distant to hear, Aldo told Strocchi what was in the document. 'Now you know why it must be read out.'

Bindi and Testardo were returning to their chairs. 'We have considered all the evidence before us,' Bindi announced, 'and—'

'Forgive me for this interruption, segretario,' Strocchi said, 'but—'

'Silence!' Bindi snarled, slapping a hand down on the table. 'We have listened long enough. You shall show the monsignor and myself the respect we deserve.'

'I . . .' Strocchi hesitated. Aldo willed him to keep going, to challenge their authority. But Strocchi wilted before the segretario's glare. 'Yes, sir.'

Bindi cleared his throat before continuing. 'As I was saying, we've heard the evidence brought before us and considered its significance. Zati admits attacking Father Visconti, but denies involvement in the two killings and accuses Negri of committing them. Negri attacked Aldo, but denies any involvement in the murders and accuses Zati of those crimes. Both the accused are men of God, and yet both cannot be telling the truth. This being the case, Monsignor Testardo and I have agreed—'

Aldo stepped forward, cutting Bindi short. 'No.'

'How dare you interrupt me,' the segretario hissed.

Aldo ignored him, addressing Testardo instead. 'Forgive me, monsignor, but you have not heard all the evidence. Strocchi holds a sealed statement from a witness that will prove one of these priests is innocent of murdering Signor Zamora and the thief Freccia.'

'Is this true?' Testardo asked Strocchi.

'Yes, monsignor,' he replied.

'Then we should hear what this witness had to say,' Testardo announced. 'It would only be just and proper.' He turned to Bindi. 'Unless you disagree with that, segretario?'

'No, monsignor,' Bindi said, his face crimson with fury. 'Whatever you wish.'

Strocchi broke the document's seal, hands trembling as he unrolled it and read aloud.

My name is Signora Tullia Juvara. I live at the palazzo of my dear departed brother, Signor Niccolò Zamora, overlooking Piazza Santo Spirito. More than twenty years ago, before I was married, I fell in love with a young priest. I became pregnant by him and was sent away to our famiglia estate in the hills outside the city to have the child, a boy. He was taken from me and given to an orphanage. When I returned to Florence, the young priest had been moved to another parish and I was persuaded that it was best not to search for him.

In time I married and had a famiglia of my own. When my beloved husband died, Niccolò invited us to live with him at Palazzo Zamora. After my son Marsilio became troubled, I was advised to seek help at San Felice. But when I visited the church, I recognized the exorcist, Father Camillo Negri – he was the priest with whom I first fell in love.

This chance meeting was both kind and cruel. I realized I was still in love with Father Negri, yet he was steadfast in his vows and for many months refused to meet with me alone. I have no wish to relive the events involving my son Marsilio, nor speak of my brother's anger when he discovered Father Negri was the priest who had once been my lover. Niccolò forbade me from meeting Camillo and from ever setting foot in San Felice again.

I fear Niccolò would still be alive if I had listened to him.

Over time I wore Camillo down and he agreed to meet with me alone, though I know it troubled him deeply. I saw

fresh wounds on his flesh where Camillo had scourged himself
as penance for breaking his vows, yet we could not resist each
other. We were together the night my brother was murdered, so
I know Camillo can have had no hand in that.

The day after Niccolò's body was found, I went to San
Felice as curfew ended for the night. Camillo spoke to me at
the door but refused to let me in. He said God was punishing
us for our sins and forbade me from ever approaching him
again. I understand that this means Father Negri cannot have
committed the second murder.

I swear on the souls of my children that all of this is true.

A long silence lingered in the great hall when Strocchi finished.

Bindi and Testardo exchanged a glance before the monsignor fixed his gaze on the exorcist. 'Is this correct? Were you with this widow the night her brother was murdered?'

'Yes,' Negri replied. 'May God forgive me for the weakness of my flesh.'

Beside the exorcist, Zati shook his head, but said nothing. Aldo studied the younger priest's face. For a moment he seemed amused, but that was gone in the blink of an eye.

Aldo cleared his throat before addressing Testardo. 'May I ask Negri a question?' The monsignor gestured at Aldo to proceed. 'I took that statement from Signora Juvara this morning. She seemed unaware that the second victim, Freccia, was her son. Is that correct?'

Negri nodded. 'I could not tell Tullia about our son, what he had become. It would have broken her heart. That was why I paid Freccia for his silence – to protect her from his poison.'

'Did anyone observe you meeting with Freccia, or giving him coin?'

'His busybody landlord might have heard us arguing, but I was careful to keep my face hidden when I went to Freccia's rented room.'

'Anyone else?' Aldo asked.

'Is there some point to these questions?' Bindi demanded.

Aldo ignored him. 'Anyone else, Father Negri?'

'Nobody. Well, except Father Zati, of course . . .'

'Of course.' Aldo turned to the monsignor. How would he respond to this?

Testardo pressed his fingers together in a steeple before his face. 'Father Negri, it is clear you have broken the laws of this city by attacking a constable of the Otto, whatever your motives for that crime. It is also clear you have broken your vows as a priest in meeting alone with this widow. But you have given the diocese and this city great service in a difficult role, and done your best with an added responsibility that was placed upon you. Nonetheless, you must stand before the archbishop to face whatever penance he deems fit for your sins. You will no longer be permitted to perform the sacrament of exorcism. Instead, you shall remain here at the Podestà until a diocesan escort can take you to San Felice to gather your things before being brought before the archbishop for his judgement.'

'But I only did what you asked of me—' Negri protested.

'Silence!' Testardo demanded. 'You will do as you are told. Is that clear?'

Negri bowed his head, still scowling. 'Yes, monsignor.'

Strocchi removed the exorcist's shackles before Manuffi led Negri away. Once the doors had closed behind them, Aldo gave Strocchi a nudge, urging him forward.

'It is clear that Father Negri could not have killed Signor Zamora or the thief Freccia,' Strocchi said. 'He is many things, but not a murderer.'

'Agreed,' Testardo said.

'Agreed,' Bindi echoed.

'That leaves us with one suspect.' Strocchi faced Zati. 'What do you have to say?'

The priest clasped his shackled hands together as if praying to God, his eyes closed. '*In nomine Patris et Filii et Spiritus Sancti*—'

'Answer the question!' Testardo snapped.

Zati opened his eyes, dropping both hands. Aldo watched as Zati straightened his back, becoming taller, more upright. His usual expression changed, his face hardening. It took a moment for Aldo to realize what this reminded him of: a snake shedding its skin.

'Very well,' Zati said. 'What do you wish to know?'

'Did you kill Signor Zamora?' Strocchi asked.

The priest nodded.

'Out loud,' the monsignor commanded. 'Let there be no doubt.'

Zati glowered a moment before calm returned to his face. 'I killed Niccolò Zamora.'

'And the thief, Freccia?' Strocchi asked.

Zati sighed, as if bored by the question. 'Yes, yes – him too.'

Aldo studied the priest. Most killers showed guilt when confronted with their crimes, or at least regret for being caught. A few boasted about what they had done, but such men – and it was always men who boasted about murder – were fools awaiting the end of a rope, eager to convince others or themselves of their importance.

Pagolo Zati was different.

Aside from a hint of anger when told to speak up, Zati betrayed little. The way he stood, the flatness of his voice . . . It was all absence, as if there was an emptiness where others carried their hopes and fears. Had the face Zati usually presented to the world been no more than a mask he wore all this time? With that now gone it revealed the absence that had lingered behind. What remained was chilling.

Aldo had known Zati before this investigation, when they had accompanied Testardo to Santa Maria Magdalena to seek a killer. If the hollow priest standing accused in the great hall was the true Zati, there had been no hint of that in his past behaviour. Had Zati always been like this and adept at hiding it, or had something brought out the killer lurking inside him?

'How?' Testardo asked. 'How did you kill them?'

Zati rolled his eyes at the question. 'You've already heard how. I stole the thick beaded rosary cord that Negri used as a belt, along with his handbook. I took ash from the jar he kept on a shelf high in his ufficio, certain he would not notice its absence before Lent. I went to Zamora, knowing his anger towards Negri, with a promise of evidence that would force the archbishop to remove Negri from San Felice. The other priests at my lodgings were busy elsewhere, and Zamora came willingly to my room. I gave him too much wine and, once he was beyond help, pulled the beaded cord taut around his neck. That was quite simple. Getting him to Palazzo della Signoria during curfew was more of a challenge, but a good handcart proved a most helpful assistant for that task.'

'What about Freccia?' Strocchi asked. 'He fought against his killer. Against you.'

'Yes.' Zati's mouth turned down at the corners. 'I watched him for days after I heard the thief arguing with Negri at San Felice. From a distance Freccia looked as if there was nothing to him, yet he was far more of a challenge than Zamora. The true surprise was how little attention his neighbours paid when I was moving the body to the piazza in front of Santo Spirito. Cover something with a blanket and people are happy to ignore it.'

'And Father Visconti?'

Zati shrugged. 'I was using him to create suspicion against Negri, but Visconti became too curious, was asking too many questions. Silencing him became necessary.'

Aldo watched Strocchi step back from the priest, staring at Zati with disbelieving eyes, while Testardo shook his head, clearly dismayed. Even Bindi said nothing, his anger and frustration forgotten in the presence of such a cold, calculating individual.

Aldo turned back to Zati. The difference in him was as stark as lighting a lantern in a room at night. No, it was more as if someone had snuffed out a lantern in a room at night, leaving only darkness. That was where this Zati belonged – in darkness.

But there were still questions to be answered.

'Why?' Aldo asked. 'Why did you select Zamora and Freccia as your victims? Why arrange them to look like Christ on the cross? Why write Latin words on their foreheads with ash, and why cut their tongues in two? Tell us that.'

Zati made a dismissive gesture at Aldo as if he was a tiresome insetti. 'No.'

'No?'

'You heard me.'

'Don't you want us to understand?' Aldo asked.

'Why should I care?' the priest replied.

'Or are you afraid?'

Zati laughed. 'Afraid? Of what?'

Aldo stepped closer, holding Zati's gaze. 'Afraid that if you had to explain yourself, we would see who you truly are: an empty shell, a creature who kills without reason or pity.'

A flicker of anger showed in Zati's face. 'Are you describing me, or yourself?'

Aldo shook his head. 'Unlike you, I take no pleasure from killing.'

The anger turned to hatred in Zati's black, staring eyes.

'I can know love and longing,' Aldo said, 'feelings that are quite beyond you.'

The priest's hands clenched into fists at his side.

'All you are is what we can see here today: an emptiness, a nothing.'

Zati hurled himself at Aldo, shackled hands clawing at the air, but Aldo stepped aside, leaving a leg in Zati's way.

The priest tripped and fell forwards, his face smacking hard into the polished stone floor of the great hall. A crack of bone echoed around the high walls. When Strocchi helped Aldo get Zati back to his feet, blood was pouring from the priest's nose and dripping down his chin. But that cold, calculating clarity still shone from his eyes. Zati spat a mouthful of blood on the floor, his mouth twisting into a sneer.

'Congratulazioni,' he told Aldo and Strocchi. 'You have solved your little case. But I am protected by the diocese. Archbishop Buondelmonti will do whatever he must to spare the Church the embarrassment of admitting one of its own priests is a killer.'

Chapter Thirty-one

*A*ldo knew Zati was right. The Church could not allow his crimes to become known – that would be devastating for the faithful of Florence. But Aldo nodded to Strocchi anyway. It was time to finish this. The young officer cleared his throat before speaking.

'Pagolo Zati, you are hereby charged with the murders of Signor Niccolò Zamora and the thief Freccia, and the attempted murder of—'

'No, he isn't.'

Aldo had expected Testardo to intervene. But it was Bindi who spoke.

'Whatever Zati's crimes,' the segretario said, 'he is beyond the jurisdiction of this court, its investigators or its magistrates. Any decision about his punishment is therefore a matter for Archbishop Buondelmonti, not the Otto di Guardia e Balia.'

'The segretario is correct,' Testardo agreed. 'I shall arrange for Zati to be taken before the archbishop. There he shall face judgement by the proper authorities.'

'But monsignor—' Strocchi protested, approaching Testardo.

'Carlo, don't,' Aldo said, but it did no good.

Strocchi stopped in front of the long table, imploring Testardo and Bindi to listen while pointing back at Zati. 'That man is a killer. He admitted it in front of all of us, even boasted about what he had done. How can it be just for him to escape the judgement of this court? He should stand before all eight members of the Otto and answer for his crimes.'

Testardo said nothing, while Bindi merely shook his head.

Aldo went to Strocchi, placing a hand on his shoulder. 'Carlo, step back.'

Strocchi eventually did as Aldo urged, retreating from the long table to stand by Zati.

'Forgive him,' Aldo said to Testardo. 'These have been difficult days, and to discover a man of God could also be a murderer . . . That troubles my colleague.'

'Understandably so,' the monsignor conceded.

'Grazie.' Aldo returned to guarding Zati with Strocchi.

Testardo stood. 'I must praise the way both of you conducted this investigation. The behaviour of Father Zati has troubled the Church for some time, but we had no grasp of his true nature. It is doubtful that others would have uncovered what he has done. This should be commended.' He gestured at Bindi beside him. 'Don't you agree, segretario?'

'Yes,' Bindi said through a scowl.

'The archbishop would be most dismayed if he heard that either of these men had been disciplined for contradicting your orders during their efforts to uncover the truth.'

'I . . .'

'And the archbishop's dismay can be quite ruinous to a man's reputation.'

Bindi gave a curt nod.

Testardo smiled. 'Indeed, you should consider rewarding Strocchi and Aldo. Solving two – no, three – murders in a few days is worthy of commendation, is it not?'

'Yes, monsignor,' the segretario agreed.

'Very well. Then this matter is settled. I shall return to the diocesan ufficio and inform the archbishop of what has happened here.' Testardo smoothed out the creases in his cassock while addressing Aldo and Strocchi. 'I suggest you return Zati to the cells until the diocese sends men to collect him. Buon giorno.' The monsignor strode from the great hall, gently humming under his breath. Only when Testardo had gone did Bindi speak.

'Well, what are you two waiting for?' he snapped. 'Take Zati to the cells. Now!'

Aldo caught up with Testardo as he strode north from the Podestà. 'Monsignor, a word?' Testardo kept going, his pace quickening a little.

'Every time we meet, you cause me nothing but difficulty,' the monsignor said. 'I have had quite enough of your company. Whatever you wish to know can wait.'

'I shall be brisk,' Aldo replied, falling into step alongside him.

Testardo muttered under his breath before replying. 'What is it?'

'You said Zati's behaviour had troubled the Church for some time.'

'Indeed.'

'How? How was his behaviour troubling?'

The monsignor stopped, looking around before beckoning Aldo into an alley between palazzi. 'If you mention this to anyone, I will have you excommunicated,' Testardo warned.

'I swear it will go no further,' Aldo said, making the sign of the cross. The gesture meant little to him, but seemed to satisfy the monsignor.

'Pagolo Zati was considered a good priest, a man of some

promise. That changed after he was part of the visitation to the Convent of Santa Maria Magdalena.'

'How?'

Testardo hesitated before replying. 'Disquieting rumours started to emerge from his parish. It was said Zati became eager to attend the elderly among his flock, those who were believed close to death. He would be there to offer the last rites, day or night.'

'As would all good priests,' Aldo said.

'This was something else. The number of his parishioners dying was unusually high. Some were expected, but others seemed to die before their time – and Zati was with all of them at the end. He insisted on it. Not only that, but he sent each famiglia out of the room before he would say the last rites. When they were allowed back, the parishioner was dead.'

'Zati was killing them?'

'That was impossible to prove. But he became known as Father Death because so many people died in his presence.' Testardo shivered, his disquiet obvious. 'Soon older parishioners were refusing to have Zati attend when they became unwell. The diocese realized it had to find Zati other duties.'

'And that was when he went to San Felice?'

'Not quite. Zati was given to me to watch over. May God forgive me, but I did not take the stories about him seriously. The two of us went to visit Signor Cortese, the visitation member grievously wounded when we went to Santa Maria Magdalena.'

Aldo remembered it well. Cortese had forced his way into the private cell of a troubled nun called Suor Violante, wrongly believing her responsible for a killing. Violante lashed out with a blade, slicing deep into Cortese's face, chest and one hand. Zati was close by when it happened, blood from the wounds spattering the young priest's face and cassock.

'Cortese had been lucky to survive,' Testardo continued. 'He suffered for months but was slowly recovering, and asked to meet with me. When I arrived, Cortese seemed much better. I left him alone with Father Zati for a few minutes, and when I returned . . .'

'Cortese was dead.'

The monsignor nodded. 'I could prove nothing. But I saw the excitement in Zati's eyes when I came into the room. He denied any involvement, of course.'

'But you knew,' Aldo said. 'You knew he was a killer.'

'I believed it was . . . a possibility.'

'And you told nobody.' Aldo shook his head. Zati could have been stopped if the diocese had listened to those who depended on it for their salvation. Niccolò Zamora and Freccia would still be alive, and perhaps many more.

'I told Negri,' Testardo said. 'He needed to know why Zati was being made his assistant. I told him to keep Zati away from those who might become his victims.'

That made sense of Negri's guilt and denials when he was confronted at San Felice. 'You made the exorcist a jailor of sorts. That's why Zati did all he could to make us believe Negri was responsible for the murders of Zamora and Freccia. It was revenge.'

'So it seems,' Testardo agreed, staring at the dirt beneath his feet.

Aldo fought the urge to berate the monsignor; it would do no good now. 'What will happen to Zati? You can't let him near a parish again.'

'No, never. I will recommend to the archbishop that Zati be banished from the city. The Church cannot have a murderer as one of its priests. I believe Zati has distant famiglia in Venice, perhaps he will go there.'

'Why solve a problem when you can send it somewhere else,' Aldo said.

Testardo glared at him. 'What would you have me do instead?'

Strocchi slammed the bolt into place, securing Zati in his cell. The priest had uttered not a word when led to the cell, but his satisfied smirk spoke for him. Strocchi could not grasp how he had been so blind to Zati's true nature. He had been convinced Zati was a good but weak man, cowering before the righteous anger of Negri.

Yet it was Zati who had carried murder in his heart.

Strocchi stumbled towards Manuffi, who was keeping Father Negri company in the courtyard. It had been a long night and a worse morning, exhausting in body and spirit. The exorcist was hunched forward on a stone bench, head in his hands. Manuffi met Strocchi halfway across the courtyard. 'Is it true that Zati was the killer? What will happen to him?'

Strocchi explained how the Church had exerted its jurisdiction over the Otto.

Manuffi shook his head. 'But . . . Zati killed two men and nearly did the same to Father Visconti. Shouldn't he stand trial before the Otto?'

'He should.' Strocchi glanced up and saw Bindi glaring at them from the loggia. 'But it seems justice and the law are two different things here.'

Aldo appeared with a gleam in his eye. That meant trouble.

'Zati is in his cell,' Strocchi said.

'Good,' Aldo replied. 'Testardo believes Zati will be banished from the city.'

'Is that all?'

'Being banished is still a punishment,' Manuffi said.

'Not compared to the sentence Signora Vanni would have received from the Otto if we had proved she was the killer,' Strocchi replied. 'Zamora's famiglia are left to mourn and Freccia's widow will give birth to a bambina or bambino without a papa. But Zati faces no more punishment than a thief cast out of the city. All so the diocese can keep its secrets.'

'No, it isn't justice,' Aldo agreed. 'But you serve the Otto di Guardia e Balia.' He looked up at the cold stone building that surrounded the courtyard. 'If you want justice, you cannot expect to find it here. Not while Massimo Bindi is segretario.'

'Then I must have been a fool for thinking otherwise,' Strocchi said, stalking away.

'Where are you going?' Manuffi asked.

'Anywhere but here.'

Aldo caught up with Strocchi as he left the Podestà. 'Testardo has given me permission to question Zati until the diocese takes him away.'

'I've no interest in hearing what that man has to say,' Strocchi replied.

Aldo pulled back the bolt, opening the door to Zati's cell. The priest was leaning against the opposite wall, arms folded. 'Am I leaving already?' he said. 'Normally the diocese takes days to act on a decision, no matter how urgent it might be.'

'The archbishop's men will come for you soon enough,' Aldo replied. 'But you don't have to wait in there if you don't want to.' He beckoned Zati out into the courtyard. The priest gave a shrug before strolling from the dark, dank stone cell.

'If this is an attempt to get more answers, it will do you no good,' Zati said. 'Ask your questions but don't expect any replies. Not unless I deem you worthy of them.'

'Of course,' Aldo said. 'I simply thought you'd be more comfortable elsewhere.' He led Zati to the room where Signora Vanni had made her denunzia the previous day. Two plain chairs remained on either side of a simple wooden table. 'Have a seat.'

The priest gave a mocking nod of his head before taking the chair furthest from the door, which also gave the best view of those entering. It was the one Aldo would have taken if he was a prisoner or a suspect. Always keep a way out in view, and always choose the chair that gives the most time to prepare for any oncoming threat.

Aldo took the chair opposite Zati, studying him anew. There was none of the warmth or anguish he had displayed before, no trace of the kind young priest Aldo had known when they were visitors at the convent several years before. Had it all been a performance from their first meeting? Or had something in Zati changed to make him the indifferent creature on the other side of the table? Asking such questions directly would bring no answers. Better to let the prisoner believe himself in charge.

'*In nomine Patris et Filii et Spiritus Sancti,*' Aldo said.

'What of it?' Zati asked, his voice a sneer of disdain.

'You wrote parts of that on the forehead of each victim.'

'And?'

'I was wondering who would have had *Spiritus Sancti* written on them. Negri, I suppose.'

'Does it matter?'

'No. Monsignor Testardo tells me he will recommend to the archbishop that you are banished from the city. Better to cast you out than have the whole of Florence hear what you did. I cannot change that decision. What happens to you now is quite beyond the hands of a constable in the service of the Otto. So, tell me, don't tell me – it makes no difference.'

Zati's head tilted to one side while he stared at Aldo. 'But you're still interested.'

'Consider it . . . a professional courtesy. You kill people, while I hunt those who kill. I'd like to know if I was following the right path. That's all.' Aldo sat back in his chair, hands resting together in his lap. Zati could not be compelled to talk without using torture and, even then, whatever come from his mouth would not be reliable. But he might be persuaded.

'And what makes you believe you deserve to know?' the priest asked, brushing a speck of dust from his cassock sleeve.

Aldo suppressed a smile. For all his apparent indifference, Zati could not resist the urge to preen or demonstrate his superiority. If it were otherwise, he would simply have ignored this gentle prompting. Zati wanted to talk, but only on his terms.

'It's not that I deserve to know,' Aldo replied. 'But I have never encountered a killer like you before. I wish to know more in case I meet someone similar again. It would help to see them for who they are, not what they want the world to see. You are a master of that particular skill, standing in plain sight the whole time yet I did not realize.'

'You seem to believe that a few words of praise will be enough to part my lips,' Zati said, 'much the same way as flattery parts the thighs of those willing to be taken.'

'Whether you speak or not is your choice.' Aldo leaned forward, fixing Zati in his gaze. 'But if you look into my eyes, you'll see I know what it takes to end a life. I know the right place to thrust a blade, and the strength needed to throttle a target. I've seen the moment when life leaves the body long before its time because of me, because of my intervention.'

The priest stared back at Aldo, eyes narrowing. 'Indeed.'

'Then answer my questions, if you wish. We have time.'

A smile played across Zati's lips. 'As a professional courtesy?'

Aldo nodded.

'Very well. One killer to another. What do you wish to know?'

When Strocchi was ushered into the salone at Palazzo Zamora, he found Signora Juvara far happier than the last time they had met. Then he had brought word of her brother Niccolò's murder, which had proved too much for her to bear. Many things had happened since – another murder, shocking revelations and unwelcome interventions. But it seemed the return of her son Marsilio had brought some joy back to this famiglia, at least.

Juvara perched on a chair, Marsilio standing beside her. She rose to greet Strocchi as the maggiordomo Querini brought him in, before returning to her seat. 'I'm glad you are here,' she said. 'I wished to thank you for persuading my eldest son to come home. It was a shock, but one that has brought us great joy. I still worry that I shall wake and discover his return was just a fantasia.' Juvara clasped Marsilio's hand, smiling up at him. 'But he is here, and we have you to thank for that. Grazie mille.'

'Prego,' Strocchi replied, bowing his head a little. 'I wanted you to know that the man responsible for Signor Zamora's death has been discovered, and he faces banishment for his crimes. He shall never bother your famiglia again.'

'Banishment?' Juvara frowned. 'Is that all the punishment he gets?'

'I share your unhappiness,' Strocchi agreed. 'But I have no say in such matters.'

'I see,' she replied, though it was clear his words had been no comfort.

'There was another reason for visiting you,' Strocchi said. 'During the investigation we made certain discoveries about those involved, including yourself and Father Negri.' He stopped, uncertain whether to continue in front of Marsilio.

'You may speak,' Juvara said. 'When my son returned home, we made a vow never to keep secrets from one another again. I know why he left after his exorcism, and he knows what I did before I married his papa.'

Strocchi nodded. 'Then I shall tell you both. The baby you gave up for adoption grew into a young man called Freccia. He had a difficult life and was known to the Otto. I'm sorry to tell you that his body was the one found out on the piazza a few days ago.'

'Oh.' Juvara shook her head. 'I don't know what to say. I had always hoped that baby would find a good home, a famiglia that could care for it after I couldn't . . .'

Marsilio crouched by his mama. 'Are you unwell? Can I fetch you anything?'

She waved his concern away. 'No, it's . . . I should feel something for this poor soul. He was my child, but I never knew him. Now he's dead and . . . I never will know him.'

'I appreciate this is difficult,' Strocchi said, 'but I thought you should be told.'

'Of course,' she replied.

'Your son Freccia was married,' Strocchi went on, 'and his wife is heavy with child. If it survives to full term, you will have a grandchild.'

Juvara stared at Strocchi. 'A grandchild?'

He nodded.

'This woman, what is her name?'

'Fiora.'

'And where can we find her?' Marsilio asked.

'She is waiting in the palazzo courtyard,' Strocchi replied. 'I brought her here in case you wished to meet her, but I have not told Fiora why. She works in a tannery but will have to stop soon for the baby's sake. There is nobody to care for her now Freccia is dead. She has no famiglia and will have no home once she stops working.'

'Then she must live here,' Juvara said. 'If she wishes, of course; I would not force her. But she is welcome to stay and have her baby here.' Marsilio nodded his agreement.

'I could go to the courtyard and bring her up,' Strocchi offered.

'Grazie,' Juvara said. 'Grazie mille.'

Strocchi bowed before withdrawing. This had been the right thing to do. Some good did come from working for the Otto . . . sometimes. But was it enough to be worth staying?

Chapter Thirty-two

Aldo had no wish to waste this opportunity to discover the truth about Zati. Better to take his time and find the right question than rush into an uninteresting alleyway. 'Looking back, it is clear why you choose Zamora and Freccia. Both had grievances with Negri that should not take long for those investigating to find. Positioning the bodies like Christ on the cross, the Latin words written in ash on their foreheads . . . it all pointed to a killer obsessed with faith. You even put pages from Negri's exorcism handbook inside each victim's clothing.'

'Yes, that was a little pointed,' Zati agreed. 'But Negri was becoming increasingly suspicious of me. I needed to make your task simple, otherwise I would never have got away from San Felice. I certainly had no intention of spending any more time there, not with Negri watching my every move. He really is the most tiresome of men.'

'You couldn't know a downpour would wash most of the ash from Zamora's forehead and all but destroy the torn page you had put inside his tunic,' Aldo said.

'Ahh, that's why it took so long for someone from the Otto to come to San Felice.' Zati smiled. 'You almost caught me that first night. I had just positioned Zamora's body by the statue of David when someone came running into Piazza della Signoria. I hid in the shadows but you and that other constable were too distracted to notice me. Such a pity.'

'Indeed,' Aldo agreed. He cursed himself for not scouring nearby streets and alleys for the killer that night. If he had . . . But there was no value in such regrets.

'You still haven't asked me a question,' Zati observed.

'All that you did with the victims was designed to lead us towards Negri. It was unlucky that Signora Vanni's presence distracted us for so long—'

'That woman,' Zati sneered, his face curdling with distaste. 'Every morning she seemed to be waiting for me outside San Felice, determined to make my life a misery. Vanni should consider herself fortunate she did not become one of my victims.'

'Why didn't she?'

'I have no interest in women,' the priest said, 'either as victims or as lovers. But if I was ever to change my mind, Vanni would have been first on my list.'

'She was not intended to have *Spiritus Sancti* written on her forehead,' Aldo said.

'Of course not. That would have been Negri's honour, but only if he had succeeded in stopping the investigation by the Otto. Then I would have killed him and left the city before his body could be found. Another day and he would have succeeded. That's why I attacked the old fool Visconti, but ensured Marsilio Juvara would interrupt me. I wanted to be caught so I could make my accusation against Negri. I knew that would push you and Strocchi to intervene, freeing me from him.'

Aldo nodded, his suspicions confirmed. 'There is one thing I do not understand about those victims – Zamora and Freccia. Why cut their tongues in two? That was never going to lead us towards Negri . . .'

'Consider it a jest of my own devising,' Zati said. 'Both were liars. I cut their tongues in two so each resembled a serpent, like the creature that tempted Eve in the Garden of Eden.'

'That was you, leaving your own mark on them.'

The priest laughed. 'I could hardly sign their corpses, could I?'

There was shouting in the Podestà courtyard, someone demanding to know where the accused priest was. Aldo had asked Manuffi to delay the diocesan clerics, but that would not keep them busy for long. That meant he had time for one more question, two at most.

'Monsignor Testardo told me why you were assigned to assist Negri at San Felice. How the Church realized parishioners were dying with you alone by their side.'

Zati waved a dismissive hand. 'Those were the work of a novice still learning his craft. I do not consider them worthy of note.'

'Naturally,' Aldo agreed, though it was chilling to hear the priest dismiss his past killings as no more than practice. What of each famiglia that had lost loved ones? What of the lives Zati had claimed to become better at murder? Aldo pushed those questions aside. The voices in the courtyard were getting closer. 'Testardo seems to suspect you only started all of this after witnessing what happened to Signor Cortese at the convent. But you and I both know that the urge to kill, the qualities needed to take a life – those are already inside us long before we choose to act upon them, yes?'

'Naturally,' Zati said, echoing Aldo's previous response. 'I have always known I was different from those around me, better than them. They were so concerned with what others thought, didn't understand that is weakness. To become who you truly are, you must trust in your own judgement above everything else.'

'Have you always known that?'

'Not always. For a long time, I was made to fear my differences, my superiority. I was persuaded to join the priesthood, told that would help me find the answers I sought. But that fool Testardo is right about one thing: it was seeing Suor Violante use a blade against Cortese that showed me I need not fear what was within me any longer. There was beauty to be found there, purity in what I must do.'

The door to the room swung open, and two clerics in black cassocks stalked in. 'Father Zati, you're to come with us,' one of them announced.

'Of course,' he replied, a genial smile on his lips.

The clerics marched Zati out. As he was led away Zati looked back over his shoulder.

'Perhaps we shall meet again one day? I do hope so.'

If that ever happened, Aldo wanted to have a stiletto in his hand.

Strocchi paced in front of the building where his famiglia lived. It was becoming a habit, but not one he enjoyed. He wanted to go in, to hug Tomasia and kiss her belly, to play with Bianca and forget about Zati, Bindi and the Otto. Neighbours passed by, nodding to him, but none dared ask how he was. What must he look like?

'Carlo?' Tomasia said from the stairs that led up to their home.

He held up a hand, not ready to talk yet.

She sat on the stairs, one hand behind her and the other braced on the wall to ease herself down. Once settled, she let out a sigh. 'That was a mistake,' she said. 'How am I ever going to get up from here now?'

Strocchi kept pacing, going over and over what had happened at the Podestà. Was Aldo correct? Was it wrong to expect the Otto to administer justice, and not just enforce the laws of Florence?

'Carlo, talk to me,' Tomasia said. 'What's wrong?'

He took a breath . . . and told her what had happened. All of it. He did not care if anyone else heard about Negri fathering a child, about who had murdered Zamora and Freccia, or about the Church intervening to protect itself. Tomasia waited a while before replying.

'It seems to me your problem is not with the Otto, or even with Bindi. He is a bully but, for once, he had no hand in most of this, Carlo. The Church is who you should blame.'

'The Church?'

'Yes. Or it might be fairer to say the diocese of Florence is to blame. It is the diocese that has ensured Zati will not stand trial. These lies and killings . . . They were all by priests.'

Strocchi stopped his pacing. As ever, Tomasia was right.

'You are angry,' she went on, 'but most of all you are disappointed. You've believed in the Church and its teachings all your life, just as I have. But this faith blinds you to the fact that priests and other clerics are no more or less than any other man. They deceive and sin, break their word and their vows. You want every man of God to be a saint, but they are all sinners, like you or I. None of us are perfect. Putting on a cassock doesn't alter that.'

'But what can I do?' he asked. 'I have to do something . . .'

'Do you still believe in God?'

'Of course.'

'Then you have your answer, Carlo. Faith matters more than what Zati did.'

Strocchi nodded. 'And what about the Otto? I used to believe my work for the court was more than enforcing laws, it was about seeing justice done. What should I do now?'

Tomasia smiled, reaching out a hand. 'Come, help me up.' Strocchi did as she asked, pulling Tomasia back to her feet. She embraced him, leaning over her belly to wrap both arms around his shoulders. 'You don't have to work for the Otto if you don't want to. We will get by without your officer's pay, if needs be.'

'Are you sure?' he asked.

She gave him a kiss.

The contessa had not been expecting a visitor, and certainly not this one. After the upheaval of recent days, she would have wagered a good handful of coin on the duke and his courtiers leaving her be a while. The contessa had no illusions that Cosimo was unaware of who was truly responsible for the killing of Grossolano, despite her supplying Zilio as a credible suspect. It was an obvious stratagemma, but one the duke seemed happy to accept for now.

Getting Zilio exiled from Florence ensured she would remain as Venice's spymaster here for now. She might tire of that role one day but, if so, any change would be on her terms. The Council of Ten's new tribunal would think twice before sending another replacement.

When Pozzo came to the salone and announced who was asking for an audience, the contessa could not keep the delight from her face. 'Have him come up,' she told the maggiordomo, 'but let him wait a while first. I wouldn't want our visitor thinking he can simply call on me whenever the mood takes him.'

Pozzo nodded his agreement before withdrawing. It was quite a while indeed before he returned, a mark of how much the visitor had irritated the maggiordomo. Finally, he ushered the guest into the salone, announcing the name with a sneer.

'Cesare Aldo to see you, Contessa.'

'That will be all, Pozzo,' she replied, waving him away with a flutter of her fingers. Once the maggiordomo had retreated and closed the doors after himself, the contessa patted the chair beside her. 'Come, sit beside me. We have much to discuss.'

Aldo was just as she remembered, despite the dark smudges of sleeplessness beneath both eyes. A playful smirk teased at the corners of his mouth. He sat close to her, seeming as eager to share what he knew as she was to hear it. 'Grazie for seeing me, Contessa, especially without prior arrangement or notice of my arrival.'

She put a finger to his lips for a moment. 'Do not waste words on polite nothings, Aldo. We two can speak as we wish when others are not present to overhear us, yes?'

That hint of a smirk became a broad smile. 'Of course. Shall I tell you what has been happening within the Otto, and the ufficio of the archbishop today?'

The contessa rested a hand on his thigh, enjoying the tremble that caused. Her sources seemed certain Aldo had no interest in women, despite living in a bordello; nor had he taken a female lover that anyone could name. Nonetheless, it was a matter of pride that she could still unsettle him. 'How delicious! Please, tell me everything.'

The tale that followed would have been beyond belief if spoken by another man, but she sensed Aldo was being truthful in his account of the exorcist and the killer. There was no hesitation in his voice, no looking to one side or evading her gaze. When he finished, Aldo sat back in his chair. 'It seems likely the archbishop will banish Zati from the city as a way to protect the Church from what he did. And if word of his crimes does become widely known, the diocese can always claim it is not responsible for the acts of one sinful priest.'

'A fascinating story,' the contessa said, 'and I must commend you for bringing it to my attention. I wasn't sure whether we would encounter one another so soon.'

'The duke did not ask me to come,' Aldo replied, 'if that is what you wish to know.'

'It wasn't, but I appreciate the candour.' That smirk teased his mouth once more, and she could not help wondering what it would be like to have Aldo in her bedchamber. If reports of his preferences were accurate, she imagined he had talents that most men lacked. Anyone who resisted the chance to learn more about the ways of the body was a fool or a prude – or both. 'So, tell me, why did you come today if not at the behest of Duke Cosimo?'

'I wanted to let you know how dangerous Zati is, since he may go to Venice next. He has famiglia there. You might wish to pass word of him to your . . . friends – in Venice.'

'My friends, as you so coyly describe them, are perhaps less enthusiastic at present about any intelligence I might send. A consequence of proving my worth is they will now view my reports with some suspicion. That will pass, in time, but until then . . .'

Aldo nodded his understanding. 'These things happen.'

'Quite.' The contessa considered saying farewell to him but another path suggested itself. 'However, I might be able to see that other measures are taken. Something to ensure this Zati is met with a suitable response should he go to Venice.'

'Indeed?'

She smiled. 'Accidents happen there, I'm told. Unwary visitors fall into one of the many canals, and not all are able to swim. Not in Venetian waters.'

'That would be . . . unfortunate,' Aldo said, returning her smile.

'Of course, if such a thing were to befall this priest, it would come at a cost.'

'The city of Florence would be most indebted to you. As would I.'

'Then we have an understanding.' The contessa reached out a hand, which Aldo accepted. She stroked one of her fingers along the inside of his palm, savouring the small gasp that escaped his lips. Yes, perhaps she would invite him to her bedchamber one day.

But not yet.

'Very well, then,' she said, rising to her feet. 'Pozzo?' The maggiordomo swept into the salone, his disapproval of Aldo still obvious. 'Please show my guest out. Our business is concluded . . . for now.'

Once Aldo was gone, she went to the shutters to study the piazza below. He soon appeared on the street, pausing to glance back up at her. A small nod of the head and he was gone. She did appreciate a man who knew when to take his leave, and when to stay silent.

Having Aldo as a weapon or a plaything?

Either would be her pleasure.

Aldo waited more than an hour in the courtyard of Palazzo Medici before being shown to the duke's private ufficio. Campana had warned him Cosimo was busy with other matters; Aldo spent the time watching visitors come and go: bankers and merchants, clerics and courtiers, men and a few women.

Most notable was how many of them dressed in fine doublets and gowns, the fabric and style from far beyond Florence. There had been much gossip about Eleonora de Toledo, the duke's new wife. She was three years his junior but brought with her wealth and a large staff, all Spanish. It was said she refused to speak in the Tuscan tongue, that guards and servants accompanied her everywhere, that she was distant and aloof. Yet she had provided

Cosimo with prestige and status that benefitted all of Florence. Better still, the pair had been married a matter of months and Eleonora was already carrying an heir.

Eventually Campana reappeared, beckoning Aldo upstairs. 'His Grace has but a few moments,' the duke's private segretario said. 'Maria Pimentel, mother of Eleonora, has died and Cosimo is drafting his condolences.'

Aldo was soon standing before the simple table where Cosimo worked, its surface covered with scraps of discarded paper. The drafting process was not going well, it seemed. 'Forgive my intrusion, Your Grace. I will be as brief as I can.'

Cosimo did not look up, a murmur of assent his only response.

Aldo gave a brisk summary of events involving Zati, Negri and Testardo. 'It's likely the archbishop will have this killer banished to spare the Church embarrassment. Zati has famiglia in Venice, so he may well go there.'

'Then he shall be somebody else's problem,' the duke said. 'I will hear most of this from Bindi in his next report. Was there something else you wished to share?'

'Yes, Your Grace.' Aldo revealed the details of his deal with the Contessa Coltello, how she was willing to have Zati meet a suitable end should he seek refuge in Venice.

'A suitable end?' Cosimo asked.

'She mentioned how unwary visitors sometimes drown in the canals. If that happens, I would be in her debt.'

The duke looked up from his papers. 'You're telling me you have arranged with the spymaster of a rival city to have a Florentine priest murdered in Venice? And you did this without seeking my approval or permission?'

Aldo glanced at Campana but the private segretario would not meet his eye. 'I saw it as an opportunity to place myself in the contessa's debt, ensuring she now believes I am an asset to be used as she sees fit. That is what you asked me to do.'

Cosimo studied him a moment before a smile split the duke's face. 'It is pleasing to find someone who takes the initiative and is willing to risk their life in my service. Grazie!'

'Prego,' Aldo replied, bowing. 'Now I shall withdraw so Your Grace may return to more urgent matters.'

But before Aldo could leave, the duke had another matter to discuss . . .

Chapter Thirty-three

'Y̲ou're leaving the Otto?' Bindi spluttered, chins wobbling beneath his pink, flustered face. 'But where will you go? What will you do?'

This was a moment the man standing opposite the segretario had often pictured. He savoured watching Bindi's mouth flap uselessly. Perhaps it was not quite so delicious as the anticipation which had come first, but few things could have matched that. Nonetheless, there was much pleasure to be had here . . .

. . . and Cesare Aldo was enjoying every morsel of it.

'I just offered you a promotion to officer,' Bindi protested, 'with the promise of no more night patrols. And this is how you repay me?'

Aldo could not keep the delight from his face. 'I owe you no thanks and certainly no repayment,' he said. 'I have served this court well, even when you have shown nothing but disdain for that service. More than once I have saved you from the folly of your vanity and the inconsistency of your whims. And how have you rewarded that? By demoting me to constable, banishing me from the city. Even when I worked my rightful way back to Florence, you put me on night patrols for close to a year and a half.'

'But . . . But . . .'

'I will leave it to you to devise a suitable explanation for

Monsignor Testardo as to why you failed to follow his guidance in this matter. I would advise you to treat Strocchi and the other diligent servants of this court with more respect and dignity – but I doubt you will act on that. Instead, I shall leave you with a final thought . . .'

Bindi hesitated before speaking. 'Yes?'

'You are one of the most ineffective and ineffectual individuals I have ever had the misfortune to serve. You are bloated by your own self-importance, lurking here in your ufficio like a spider who believes it is spinning a beautiful web made of wit and silk. But, in truth, you have all the charm of week-old piss, and you smell worse.' Aldo marched to the door before bowing to Bindi, not bothering to conceal his disdain. 'Buon giorno . . . sir.'

'You will never work for another court in this city, do you hear?' the segretario bellowed as Aldo departed. 'No merchant will pay you to guard his latrina, let alone reward the supposed skills you seem to value so highly!'

Aldo smiled as he strolled down the wide stone steps one last time. He would not miss the biting cold of the Podestà, nor the surly faces of the guards in its courtyard. Reaching the courtyard, he paused for a final look around. No, he would not miss this place at all.

'Going somewhere?' Strocchi had come into the Podestà, clutching a folded piece of paper in one hand. This was a good opportunity to tell him the truth in person, rather than Strocchi hearing it via whatever lies Bindi would concoct to conceal being wrongfooted.

'What makes you say that?' Aldo asked.

'You seem . . . happy. As if you've had some wonderful news.'

'More that I have made my own. I told the segretario I am leaving the Otto.'

'Leaving?' Strocchi glanced down at the paper in his grasp. 'But . . . when?'

'Today. Now. Immediately.' Aldo gestured through the stone corridor that led to the street, the city and the rest of his life. 'Once I walk out, I shall not be returning.'

'Not unless you've been arrested.'

Aldo laughed. 'Let's hope that doesn't happen.' Bindi was still shouting in his ufficio, but the words were indistinct, the distant rage of an impotent man. 'Good luck with the segretario. He's not taken my leaving very well.'

Strocchi grimaced. 'So I can hear.'

Aldo looked down at the piece of paper. 'What's that? Fresh evidence?'

'Nothing for you to worry about . . . not anymore.'

'True.' He offered a hand to Strocchi. 'Grazie, Carlo. For everything.'

The young officer clasped Aldo's hand in his own. 'Grazie, Cesare. I would not be an officer now if I had not been able to learn from your example . . .'

'And from my mistakes?'

Strocchi smiled, releasing Aldo's hand. 'Those too.'

'Remember that when you despair of Bindi or the Otto. There is always another way.'

'So . . . what shall you do now you no longer work here?'

'I have a new employer. Duke Cosimo has asked me to be his agent in certain matters, when the need arises. As for the rest of the time . . . I'm sure something will keep me busy. I was going to say keep me out of trouble—'

'But we both know that is unlikely.'

Aldo nodded. He strode past Strocchi to the street outside. A carriage rolled by, heading north towards the Duomo, while a messenger boy ran past going south, towards the Arno. Aldo breathed in, filling his chest with crisp autumn air.

He grinned while deciding which way to go from here. Onwards!

Historical Note

Divine Fury is a work of fiction, but the story is based in part on real incidents and people. The character of Father Negri is inspired by texts about exorcisms from around the sixteenth century, in particular *The Rhetoric of Exorcism* by Hilaire Kallendorf and *The Devil's Scourge: Exorcism During the Italian Renaissance* by Girolamo Menghi. The Church of San Felice still stands in Florence today, although its interior has been much remodelled across the centuries. A tour guide once claimed that exorcisms are still held inside San Felice on Wednesdays, though I have yet to test this for myself.

Much of the information about Duke Cosimo de' Medici and his new wife Eleonora de Toledo comes from the Medici Archive Project: http://bia.medici.org. This online resource holds transcriptions and translations of documents from the period, including letters written to, from, and about the duke. The recently married Cosimo was indeed awaiting the birth of his first child with Eleonora in late 1539 while he recovered from a bout of smallpox.

The Contessa Valentine Coltello is my own creation, but Venice's Council of Ten to whom she reports was a real organization. It was responsible for creating one of world's earliest state intelligence organizations. The Council employed a complex system of ciphers to protect covert communications between it and agents serving the interests of Venice far beyond the Serene Republic. The Council formed its Inquisitorie di Stato in 1539, with the three-man tribunal tasked to run special counterintelligence operations in rival territories. For more on the Council of Ten I suggest *The Secret Service of Renaissance Venice: Intelligence Organisation in the Sixteenth Century* by Dr Ioanna Iordanou.

The contessa's home in Florence is based on a real building, Palazzo Bartolini Salimbeni, which is considered a masterpiece of Renaissance architecture. Built in the 1520s by Baccio d'Agnolo, the palazzo was controversial at the time, which prompted the architect to have the Latin phrase *Carpere promptius quam imitari* – criticizing is easier than imitating – carved above the entrance. Standing a block north of the Salvatore Ferragamo store, the palazzo overlooks the triangular Piazza Santa Trinita. These days it contains the Collezione Roberto Casamonti, a stunning collection of modern and contemporary artworks.

Venture across the Arno and you can explore Piazza Santa Spirito, where one of the victims is found in *A Divine Fury*. At the south-east corner of the square stands Palazzo Guadagni, renamed Palazzo Zamora in the novel. It was built for a silk merchant and stands a level taller than the surrounding buildings. Palazzo Guadagni is now a hotel, but visitors can sip cocktails on the same loggia overlooking the piazza where Strocchi questions Querini.

Acknowledgements

$\mathscr{I}$ am indebted as ever to everyone at Pan Macmillan for their faith in my Cesare Aldo novels. Without the team at the Smithson *A Divine Fury* would not read so well, nor look so splendid. Special thanks are due to my editor Alex Saunders, cover designer Neil Lang, publicity director Pips McEwan, senior desk editor Rebecca Needes, marketing manager Natasha Tulett, rights manager Mairead Loftus, and everyone else at Pan Macmillan for believing in this series of historical thrillers.

I owe a debt of gratitude to booksellers and librarians for helping spread the word about Cesare Aldo. Special shout-out to my local independent Atkinson-Pryce Books and many others for supporting the series, including (deep breath!) The Edinburgh Bookshop, Far From the Madding Crowd in Linlithgow, the Wallingford Bookshop, Night Owl Books in East Linton, the Portobello Bookshop, the Shetland Times Bookshop, Cogito Books in Hexham, The Bookhouse in Broughty Ferry, and Imagined Things Bookshop in Harrogate. Ngā mihi to Wardini Books, Unity Books, Page & Blackmore Booksellers and Time Out Bookstore in Aotearoa for pressing my tomes into the hands of readers across New Zealand.

A doff of my digital cap to the many bloggers and wonderful book cheerleaders on Instagram and other social media for raising me up; there are too many to name everyone, but I appreciate each of you. Grazie mille to the podcasters and YouTubers who kindly invited me talk about Cesare Aldo, including *Crime Time FM*, *Publishing Rodeo*, *Words From the Bubble*, *Writer's Routine*, *The Luke Deckard Show* and *The Writing Community Chat Show*. A shout-out also to wonderful websites like Imagined History, Writing Desk and Historia for showcasing my words and stories.

Thank you to all the literary festivals that have welcomed me since I last wrote acknowledgements – Theakston's Old Peculier Crime Fiction Festival in Harrogate, Bloody Scotland in Stirling, the Wigtown Book Festival, Shetland Noir, Granite Noir, the Portobello Book Festival, the Bookmark Festival in Blairgowrie, Newcastle Noir and Bay Tales in the north-east.

I'm grateful to my Creative Writing colleagues past and present at Edinburgh Napier University – Sam, El, Dan, Noelle, Ally, Elizabeth and Nick – for their support and patience.

Praise be to Father Dennis O'Neill for naming Brother Bonaventure in chapter twenty-six.

I remain blessed to be represented by the wonderful literary agent Jenny Brown, who lifts so many writers up with her empathy and boundless enthusiasm.

Lastly, thank you to my better half who listens and nods when I talk or grumble about how the next book is going. I owe you another gelato in Oltrarno, yes?

If you missed where the story began,
then here's an extract from

City of Vengeance

BY D. V. BISHOP

Chapter One

Sunday, December 31st 1536

Cesare Aldo took no pleasure from killing, but sometimes it was necessary.

There was no honour in ending another man's life, no wisdom found in the moment when that last breath left his body. Most killings were bruising and brutal, the violence of steel and blood. Then the stench as a corpse lost control, voiding itself of dignity. Poets never mentioned that when they wrote about the nobility of the battlefield.

There was something else poets never wrote of: a tightening in the palle when death felt close. The blood quickened, yes, and so did the breathing, becoming fast and shallow as instinct demanded a choice: stand and fight, or flee the threat. In that moment every part of the body clenched – especially the palle.

Aldo felt his body tensing as the road ahead narrowed between two steep stone slopes. The birdsong that had accompanied them from Scarperia was gone, an unnerving quiet in its place. This early in the day, the road south from Bologna was more shadow than sunlight, giving potential attackers plenty of shelter. With Florence still twenty miles off, and not a castello or farmhouse in sight, this was the perfect place for an ambush.

Aldo twisted in the saddle to glance back at the man he was

guarding. Samuele Levi was past his prime, thick of waist and weak of chin. Doubtful he'd ever held a blade, except to open letters. If an attack came, Aldo would have to fight for both of them. He slid a hand to the stiletto tucked in his left boot. Better to be—

Something hissed through the air, and Aldo's horse flinched as if stung. A bolt was buried in the beast's neck, a mortal wound. He gripped tighter as the horse's front legs kicked at the sky. As he tumbled from the horse, another bolt cut the air where Aldo had been. His left knee hit the ground first, pain lancing through him from the sudden impact.

Levi's horse panicked, unseating its rider. The moneylender tumbled towards the stones and scrub that lined the side of the road, still clutching the two leather satchels he always carried. Levi's cry cut off abruptly as he hit the ground head first. Knocked senseless, if he was lucky. Levi's hired horse raced forwards, hooves thundering past Aldo. It sprinted away and his mount followed, hastening death with every stride.

Aldo rolled over, feigning moans of pain as loud as possible to mask slipping the stiletto from his boot. Whoever had fired those bolts would be closing in for the kill. Boots approached from the south, more than one set – two, maybe three. The last did not come close; probably the one with the crossbow, a weapon more effective at a distance. Aldo moaned again, sounding as weak and vulnerable as possible. 'Please . . . please, somebody help us.' He gave a pathetic, feeble cough as a bandit loomed over him.

'Too easy.' Not Florentine, judging by the voice.

'Please,' Aldo whimpered in an effeminate tone. 'My friend, I fear he's hurt.'

'Shut up.' The bandit spat rancid phlegm at Aldo's face. It took every ounce of willpower not to strike back. Shoving a knee into

Aldo's chest, the bandit pinned him to the ground. Rough hands scoured Aldo's prone body. He offered no resistance, keeping the stiletto hidden up one sleeve, a hand closed round the hilt. 'Nothing,' the bandit announced.

'Find the other one,' a stern voice called from further away – probably the man with the crossbow. He sounded authoritative, used to giving orders.

'Over here,' a third voice called from where Levi had fallen. Aldo watched a heavyset thug with a musket examining the limp body. 'He's dead.'

'Make sure he is,' the ringleader said. 'We need to be certain.'

Aldo's attacker turned to look – and Aldo plunged his stiletto into the man's boot, stabbing through leather and flesh. The bandit screamed in pain, doubling over. Aldo twisted his blade to widen the wound before pulling it free. A swift thrust drove the stiletto up behind his attacker's chin, piercing the tongue. The bandit collapsed, fingers clawing at the blade.

The ringleader shouted a warning to the man standing over Levi. The bandit whirled round, firing in haste. A musket ball fizzed past Aldo's head, missing by a finger's width. He rolled closer to the fallen bandit, using him as a shield. While the bandit with the musket reloaded, Aldo found a blade still in its sheath on his crumpled assailant. 'A wise man draws his weapon before confronting an enemy.' The fallen bandit was too busy bleeding to reply.

Aldo pulled the dagger free, balancing it in one hand to test the weight. The bandit with the musket was still reloading, but any attempt to flee meant risking the crossbow. There was only one way to improve the odds. Aldo rose for a moment, pulling back the dagger. Palle, the musket-bearer was shouldering his weapon. A fresh bolt pierced Aldo's sleeve, brushing skin. He hurled the dagger, the blade flying end over end as it cut the air. A misfire born of haste spat hot gunpowder across the musket-bearer's fingers as the dagger buried itself in his throat. He stumbled over Levi and fell, one blackened hand twitching.

Aldo dropped back close beside the bandit he'd stabbed, counting himself lucky.

The ringleader cursed his men from the shadows. Cover for sliding another bolt into that crossbow, no doubt. Would he retreat, or close in to finish the job? Most bandits melted away when facing determined opposition. But the sound of approaching boots proved this was no ordinary robbery. The ringleader wanted his prize.

'You fight well. Most guards would've run for their lives.'

'I'm no guard.' Aldo searched for another weapon. Any weapon.

'A condottiere, then? Didn't know Florence still had any.' The ringleader was circling round, using the conversation to distract from his quest for a clearer shot.

'A condottiere leads men at arms. As you can see, I'm on my own.' Aldo stared at his stiletto, its blade still wedged through the fallen bandit's lower jaw and tongue. 'I'm an officer of the Otto di Guardia e Balia.'

'Ahh, a law enforcer – a professional. That explains a lot.'

Aldo rolled the bandit on his side, wrapping an arm round the man's shoulders, his other hand grasping the hilt of the stiletto. 'When I get up,' Aldo hissed, 'you do too. Understand?' The bandit shook his sweat-soaked face, the stink of shit thick in the air. This one hadn't waited for death to empty his bowels. Aldo twisted the stiletto. 'Understand?' This time, a nod.

The ringleader edged closer. 'I thought your jurisdiction ended at the city walls?'

Aldo rose, pulling the bandit up in front of him. 'You thought wrong.'

The ringleader stopped, crossbow ready to fire. He was shorter than Aldo expected, with a grizzled face sun-browned even in December, making the pale pink scar on one cheek all the more vivid. Beneath greying hair, flint-blue eyes narrowed. 'So I can see.'

'Back off,' Aldo warned, 'or I kill both your men today.'

'Let me save you the trouble.' The crossbow fired straight and true, its bolt puncturing the wounded bandit in Aldo's arms. 'Don't come this way again,' the ringleader warned as he backed away into the shadows. 'Next time you might not be so fortunate.'

Aldo waited till the ringleader was long gone before dropping the punctured bandit. He limped across to where Levi had fallen, cursing the moneylender as each step brought a fresh stab of pain from the injured knee. The task had been simple: escort Levi from Bologna back to Florence, safe and unharmed. So much for simplicity. Now he would have to take back a body instead, and get it to the city without any horses to help.

But as Aldo approached, Levi opened one eye to peer around. 'Is it safe?' His face was streaked with blood from a deep cut to the forehead, but he looked otherwise unhurt.

'For now,' Aldo replied, shaking his head. 'You make a good corpse.'

Levi sat up, wincing. 'My kind know how to stay alive, even if it means playing dead.' He rose to one knee but sank back down again.

'Don't try moving yet.'

Levi nodded, touching two fingertips to his bloodied face.

Aldo checked the bandit who had fired the musket – he was dead. But the man who had first attacked Aldo was still alive, faint gasps audible in the narrow hillside pass. The stiletto wedged behind his jawline was trembling, as was the bolt embedded in his chest. Aldo limped back towards the dying bandit. 'Why did you attack us?'

The bandit coughed, unable to reply with a blade still pinning his tongue. Aldo pulled the stiletto free, and blood poured from the wound. 'Your capo murdered you. Tell me his name so I can make him pay.' The bandit gurgled, crimson bubbling from his lips. Aldo leaned over the bandit's mouth and got blood spat in his face, along with two final words.

'Get fucked.'

For most Florentines, attending church on Sunday was a chance to pray and give worship to God. For courtesans, church was a chance to be noticed. Mass offered a rare opportunity for unmarried women to meet and mingle with men of means. Whether those men were single made little difference to the courtesans, though married men were less likely to be possessive, or occupy too much of an independent woman's time. So common was the practice that some churches used a curtain of coarse cloth to divide the sexes, keeping those women without families on the left-hand side – the sinister side, in Latin. But a mere curtain was no match for the courtesans, women of cunning and guile.

The imposing Church of Santa Croce so dominated its surroundings that the eastern quarter of Florence was named after it. Outside the church sprawled a huge, open piazza – one of the largest in the city. The piazza remained cold all morning in winter due to the long shadow cast by Santa Croce. But inside the vast church courtesans were doing their best to raise the temperatures of any man watching. They spent the precious minutes before Mass competing for the pew that offered the best chance to see and be seen. Overt displays of flesh were not possible, but a sly smile and a gown that accentuated a woman's natural assets were enough to turn the head of many a wealthy merchant. If this also turned his wife's face to vinegar, well, that was simply proof of success. A sour wife usually meant her husband was liable – even eager – to reward those who offered more willing, more imaginative company.

Among the courtesans at Santa Croce, two were acknowledged as the queens of the curtain. Venus Cavalcante was a slender woman with a hawkish face whose artistry inside the bedchamber was as celebrated as the sharpness of her tongue outside it. Time's cruel passage meant she no longer drew the gaze of younger men, but Venus argued for the virtues of her mature clients. They were unlikely to rise to the occasion more than once, and their conversation afterwards was often as valuable as any payment they might leave behind.

Her chief rival was Bella Testa, a younger and more voluptuous woman with greater enthusiasm than skill, if the rumours were true. The twinkle in her eyes and the generous swell of her bosom made Bella the courtesan of choice for quite a few clients, especially the sons of wealthy families. Young Florentine men of means were happy to spend their seed in anyone willing to accept it. Make the recipient a beautiful woman – readily available, at a suitable price – and the lure was often overwhelming.

Each Sunday Venus and Bella did battle for the most prized seat in the vast church, one that provided the best position from which to be seen by men on the other side of the curtain. To achieve that, the winner had to be last into the desired pew, forcing those already seated to move along. From a distance, the courtesans' polite gestures and smiling faces were the image of courteous civility. Step closer and their hissed insults told another story.

'My dearest Venus, I wouldn't dream of making you stand a

moment longer. A woman of your many, many years shouldn't be expected to remain on her feet.'

'You're too kind, my darling Bella, but I must insist you sit first. Someone in your condition shouldn't put such a strain on herself.'

'My condition?'

'You are with child, are you not? How else to explain the spreading of your waist?'

A sharp intake of breath from those nearby brought a smile to the face of Venus. Her barb had struck a nerve with the other courtesans. But when she turned to savour their expressions, Venus found her rivals staring elsewhere.

A newcomer was approaching them, narrow of hip and dressed in a sumptuous gown. A coy face hid behind a veil, but what could be seen was exquisite – and devilishly young. The new arrival paused by Bella and Venus. 'I believe Mass is beginning. Shall we sit?'

The warring women found themselves ushered into the front pew, accepting less favourable seats while the fresh face stole their prized position. Venus glanced at the newcomer during Mass. This usurper was unfamiliar. The voice had been sweet and definitely Florentine, yet the features remained unrecognizable. Most galling of all, the new arrival was attracting the gaze of every likely prospect in church. Venus had been hoping to lure one man in particular, Biagio Seta, the middle-aged middle son of a family of prominent silk merchants. His childless elder brother was ill, unlikely to see another summer, putting Biagio in line for the business and all its wealth. But he had not a glance for Venus this Sunday, only for the newcomer beside her.

When Mass was concluded, most families hastened home to eat together. But a few men remained in the cloister beside the church or the piazza in front of it, claiming an urgent need to discuss business. The courtesans also lingered, gossiping with their maids about who was wearing what. Once the families were gone, men with a need for company could send a message to the maid of their preferred courtesan.

Most Sundays, Venus and Bella had their pick of the offers. But today the messages were going to another courtesan. The upstart did not even have a maid, instead accepting the invitations personally. Venus watched Biagio make his approach, a coy look passing between him and the one he desired. Biagio blushed – he actually blushed! – when the narrow-hipped vixen nodded at him. The couple departed the piazza in different directions, but Venus had little doubt they would be together soon, in all the most intimate ways.

'Must be losing our touch,' Bella observed.

Venus sniffed her disdain. 'Men. They always want first taste. But the novelty soon wears off. Did you hear a name for our new friend?'

'Dolce Gallo, according to my maid.'

Venus couldn't help laughing. 'I wonder what her real name is?'

With no horses to ride, Aldo and Levi had to continue their journey south towards Florence on foot. But hours of marching did Aldo's bruised, swollen left knee no good. It had already been unreliable before the bandit attack, weakened by an old injury from years spent as a soldier for hire, riding alongside one of the great condottieri. A bad fall had ruptured the joint, forcing Aldo to abandon life as a mercenary and sending him back to Florence. Falling from his horse as the bandits attacked hadn't been as bad, but the pain was all too familiar.

Levi seemed to be suffering even more, his body and spirit ill prepared for marching of any kind, so progress was slow and painful. When they stopped for the third time, Aldo pressed Levi for answers. 'You never told me why you wanted a guard for this journey.'

The moneylender dabbed a cloth to the wound on his forehead 'Isn't what happened proof your protection was necessary?'

'Yes, but it doesn't answer my question. What made you think you were in danger?'

Levi waved a dismissive hand. 'It was a sensible precaution. Bandits are common on this road – too common, from what I've heard.'

'And I've heard you make this trip three times a year, but never before have you asked the Otto for a guard. In summer, I'd understand it. But robbing people in winter is treacherous, with few rewards.' No answer. Levi might be little use against a blade, but he was a master at avoiding sharp questions. 'I'd go so far as to say today's attack was no happenstance. Those bandits were waiting for us. For you.'

That got a reaction, though Levi masked it in moments. 'They attacked you first.'

'If a target can protect himself, he doesn't need a guard. I was obviously guarding you, so it made sense to deal with me first. To eliminate the more significant threat.'

Levi shrugged. 'Speculation proves nothing.'

'Having taken me down, our attackers didn't finish me when they had the chance. "Find the other one," the ringleader said. "We need to be certain." They wanted to be sure who you were before killing us both.'

Levi avoided Aldo's gaze. 'You've a strong memory.'

'Being that close to death sharpens the mind. The ringleader was calm, he didn't panic when the first attack faltered. And he didn't hesitate to kill his own man on hearing I'm with the Otto. Few robbers are that ruthless.'

'You want to meet ruthless men, try being a moneylender.'

'Had the ringleader employed better men,' Aldo snapped, 'we'd both be dead by now. Think on that.' He peered at the sky. 'We won't reach Florence before dusk at this pace, and the horses bolted with all our provisions. We need to find shelter, and soon.'

Levi got to his feet with difficulty. 'Where do you suggest?'

'I rode with a condottiere who kept a home near Trebbio. We might find a welcome there. It's a few miles south. Can you get that far before sunset?'

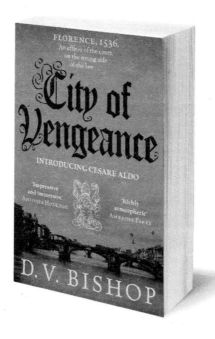

'An impressive and immersive debut set in a beautifully
realized sixteenth-century Florence'
Antonia Hodgson

'A first-class historical thriller . . . Bishop's spirited and
richly detailed story is a tour de force'
David Baldacci

'Richly atmospheric . . . transports you to
another time and place'
Ambrose Parry, author of
The Way of All Flesh

**Discover the explosive first novel in the Cesare Aldo series
today - available in paperback, ebook and audiobook**

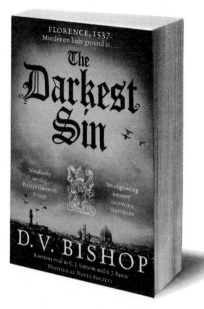

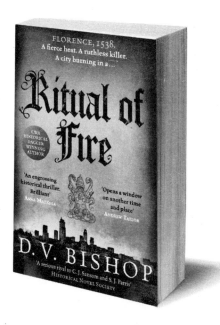

'It's hard to think of a better guide than D. V. Bishop to the brutality and glamour of Renaissance Florence. Religion and lust? Money and politics? It's all here, combined into a murderous brew'
Andrew Taylor

'A deft and engrossing historical thriller set in Renaissance Florence drawing on the fascinating and troubling legacy of Girolamo Savonarola. I thoroughly enjoyed the latest – and I think best – in D. V. Bishop's brilliant series'
Anna Mazzola

'In *Ritual of Fire*, the third scintillating Cesare Aldo novel, D. V. Bishop once again immerses us in sixteenth-century Florence and the heady intrigues of Renaissance Italy. Aldo is a magnificent creation'
Vaseem Khan

Discover the third novel in the Cesare Aldo series today - available in paperback, ebook and audiobook

About the author

D. V. Bishop is the pseudonym of award-winning writer David Bishop. His love for the city of Florence and the Renaissance period meant there could be only one setting for his historical thrillers. The first Cesare Aldo novel, *City of Vengeance*, won the Pitch Perfect competition at the Bloody Scotland crime writing festival and the NZ Booklovers Award for Best Adult Fiction Book. Book two in the series, *The Darkest Sin*, won the prestigious Crime Writers' Association Historical Dagger. He teaches creative writing at Edinburgh Napier University.